Praise for *Game 7: Dead Ball*

"If you like baseball and thrillers, *Game 7: Dead Ball* is a must read. Even those who are only so-so on the national pastime but enjoy complicated plots with well-drawn characters will find this book most satisfying."
—Great Books Under $5

"Remaining my favorite genre to watch or read to this day, mysteries give my mind something to satisfy its continuous curiosity; mulling over plots and characters long after I've put the book down. Allen Schatz served me well with *Game 7: Dead Ball*."
—Big Al's Books and Pals

"Wow! This one kept me guessing and reading—great characters and an even better storyline!"
—Erik Gustafson (*Fall Leaves and the Black Dragon*)

"I think what I loved most about this book is how Schatz artistically weaved details into every scene. Everything, down to the smallest fragment, popped off the screen."
—Suzie Carr (*The Fiche Room*)

GAME 7: DEAD BALL

Also by Allen Schatz

7th Inning Death*

Rally Killer**

*eBook available now; coming to print Fall 2011

**eBook coming August 2011, print version 2012

GAME 7: DEAD BALL

Allen Schatz

ISBN 13: 978-1-463-53092-1
ISBN-10: 1-463-53092-7

For Sandy, Michael, and Samantha

"The great thing about baseball is that there's a crisis every day."
Gabe Paul, 1910-1998, baseball executive

PROLOGUE

June 20, 1997
Bluefield, West Virginia

Opening day for the minor league Bluefield Orioles baseball team was one of the few bright spots in this otherwise dismal and decaying town long removed from its former glory days. The same was true for Tammy Rogers. Her luck had been mostly bad for a long time and prospects of something better were fading faster than the worn-out shingles on the building where she lived. She needed out in a bad way.

On this night, she would get her wish.

The journey started, as it usually did, at a place called Wild Aces. At best, the bar was nothing more than a dive where the legal drinking age meant little, making it a must-stop for most of the ballplayers after every game. That many of these young men were barely out of high school never deterred Tammy because she was very good at ferreting out those old enough to play *her* game.

Her first pitch came shortly after ten P.M., when she paused just inside the bar's entrance to size up the crowd—and let it return the favor. At twenty-six, she had a natural look and all the right curves in all the right places. Her uniform this night was a knee-length, spaghetti-strapped, pale yellow sundress. She had her long blonde hair loosely tied into a messy updo, and a light application of make-up finished the look.

Satisfied she'd delivered strike one, she sauntered to the far side of Aces' long bar and worked herself onto her usual stool. She was greeted there by Billy Dubbs, the tavern's proprietor and a man with whom she'd once shared a night. It never went beyond that, outside of being the reason for the always open and waiting stool after every Orioles home game.

"Hello, Tammy," Billy said as he placed two drinks in front of her, a shot of Jack and a Miller Lite. "I'll start your tab. Try not to forget to settle up this time."

"Oh, Billy, it was only that *one* time," Tammy said, applying her cutest smile. "And I made up for it, didn't I?"

"You did," Billy said, his head shaking but a smile giving him away.

A man standing near the bar at Tammy's right was watching the exchange with great interest, and when she quickly downed the whiskey, he perked up even further. Tammy noticed the stare and adjusted her position on the stool to get a better look. The light around her, somewhere between an old flashlight and a handful of candles, was enough to allow for a decent view.

Liking what she saw, she fired her next pitch, a mouthed "Hi" in the man's direction. He responded with a smile and moved toward her. The closer he got, the better he looked, and it was Tammy's turn to perk up. As he reached her stool, he extended his hand and she took it. The touch sent a shiver down her back and she shuddered.

"Tammy," she said after recovering.

"Nice to meet you, Tammy," the man said before motioning to the empty stool next to her. "May I join you?"

That he failed to introduce himself never registered.

"Please," Tammy said with a small nod.

Her heart was racing as the man sat, and she silently chided herself for being so flustered. It was usually the other way around, especially with the baseball boys, and as the man settled onto the stool, she took a swig of Miller and tried to regroup.

"You're not from Bluefield, are you?" she said after swallowing.

"Nope, first time," the man said as he motioned to Billy for a new drink.

"Oooh, a traveler," Tammy said in her best pick-up voice.

The man offered up a nonchalant shrug.

"I get around."

"I'll bet you do," Tammy said through a sly grin.

Billy interrupted the dance when he arrived with the man's refill. Tammy used the break to take another sip of beer, accidentally-on-purpose dribbling some down her chin in the process. As the liquid made its way to the space between her breasts, she pinched a napkin off the bar and made an elaborate show of dabbing at the moisture.

"You missed some," the man said before using the side of his finger to wipe a drop from her chin.

The touch produced new shivers and Tammy's nipples got rock hard under the thin fabric of her dress. The man's eyes took notice of her excitement.

Strike two.

"All fixed," the man said.

Tammy pushed some air through her lips.

"*Yes, it is,*" she said under her breath.

The man smiled and sampled his beverage. Tammy waited for him to finish.

"So, what brings you to town?" she said. "Are you a ballplayer?"

"I've been known to play a game or two," he said as his finger came back to her body.

He used it to draw an imaginary line across her shoulder and down her arm. Goosebumps sprouted and Tammy closed her eyes to absorb the sensations. What had started as her game had become his. She was wet from the simple touches and more than ready to go. All the man had to do was ask. An hour later he did.

Strike three.

It was the last time Tammy was seen alive.

Chapter 1

Present Day
Thursday, October 30, 2008
Citizens Bank Park
Philadelphia, Pennsylvania
Game 7 of the World Series

Swing and a miss, struck him out! Second strike-out for O'Hara and the Rays are retired in order in the top of the first...

I didn't need to hear the radio broadcast booming through the stadium concourse to know what was happening. I was in the middle of it. And I wanted it to end. Whatever thrill I'd felt from being tapped to work the World Series had faded under the avalanche of shit that had come with it during the past two weeks.

It had been a nightmare.

It still was.

"Connors," a voice said from behind me.

I turned to find Nikolai—Nik (pronounced Neek)—Sanchez, catcher for the Tampa Bay Rays, walking toward me. Nik was like me, one of few in the ballpark who knew of the events happening outside of the game. Also, like me, he was thought to be but another victim.

That was about to change.

"Hey, Nik," I said as he neared me. "Looks like we made it, huh?"

"It ain't over yet," he said in an odd tone as he presented his right hand.

It wasn't so much the tone, but the look in his eyes that gave me a stop. I'd seen something similar from him years ago, during an on-field argument, but it didn't fit now and I hesitated before accepting his hand, distracted by the memory. That distraction gave way to something else after we shook.

When his hand pulled away, a small piece of paper remained in mine. I did my best not to react, but it wasn't easy. People didn't usually pass me notes on the field. OK, it had *never* happened, but I didn't have time to dwell on whether or not it was appropriate. I was having too much trouble trying to comprehend the content.

GIVE ME THE MONEY OR SHE DIES

I looked up at Nik, but I couldn't see him, blinded by the memories of everything that had brought me to this spot. I should have been elsewhere, on vacation, sitting in the sun on a beach, recovering and regrouping from a long season, my biggest concern being not to forget the sunblock. But now... now I was faced with danger far more serious than too much sun.

People had already died. More were going to if I didn't do something.

Too bad I had no idea what that might be.

Chapter 2

Michael O'Hara was in trouble.

In baseball terms, it was time for a call to the bullpen. Michael had experience with that, having played in the major leagues for thirteen seasons during the '70s and '80s, first as a starting pitcher, then as a closer. It had been a relatively successful, but well-traveled career, mostly because of Michael's bad temper. He had stints with Cleveland, Texas, New York (the Mets), and Philadelphia, before each club tired of the tantrums and moved him along.

The fiery makeup had served him well on the mound, but not so much in his current passion, poker. He could mostly control the anger, but had never quite mastered the art of quitting while ahead— *or behind*. That failure left him staring at a $1.5 million line drive of debt, $850,000 of which had come off the bat of the handsomely dressed, bald-headed, and very large dark-skinned man sitting opposite Michael at a small conference table.

The man's name was Dikembe Dukabi and he was not happy.

"Mr. O'Hara, I don't believe you understand the gravity of your situation," Dukabi said.

It was just after two A.M. Michael was probably tired, but didn't have time to think about it. The room's lighting gave Dukabi's face a menacing appearance. Michael didn't spook easily, but the situation was unnerving.

"I, uh—"

He was cut off when a slight movement from Dukabi's hand drew two bodies out of the shadows. Had Michael not been so scared, he might have recognized something in the man on Dukabi's right. He had a stubbled face, unkempt dark hair, and was dressed in black from head-to-toe, but it was the slight limp in his stride that should have been Michael's clue. The second man was a polar opposite, short and stubby with a bulbous head covered by obviously fake black hair, and an outfit consisting of a slew of colors and patterns that were an affront to the eyes.

Michael eyed both for a second before finding his best sneer.

"Oh, so now you're gonna threaten me?" he said. "Nice try."

Dukabi scoffed and Michael flinched at the loud noise, bluff called and raised.

"Mr. O'Hara, there is no need for us to *try* anything."

Michael knew Dukabi was right. He had been in some tough situations before, but this had gone south of tough long ago. He had only himself to blame. The income earned on the field should have been more than enough to repay the debts, but like a few too many things in his life, hanging onto money was something of a challenge. Not all of it was gone, but it wasn't necessarily still in his possession. It was going to be difficult to change that.

"OK, OK, my bad," Michael said. "I can see I've touched a nerve—"

Again, he was cut off, this time when Dukabi stood. The black leather chair in which he'd been sitting hissed a sigh of relief. A similar noise escaped Michael.

"You have done much more than that," Dukabi said as he began to pace the room. "You have insulted me."

Michael followed, his eyes catching some of the background in the process. There was African art on the walls and unfamiliar titles on several bookcases, but the most notable feature—besides Dukabi—was a huge mahogany desk in the middle of the room. It dwarfed the two armchairs in front, leaving absolutely no doubt as to which side held the power. Michael started to wonder why Dukabi had picked the conference table instead, but the thought disappeared when the big man stopped next to him and leaned in.

"I am *most* disappointed, Mr. O'Hara," Dukabi said.

Up close, his face had an even more ominous appearance. Someone of lesser fortitude might have needed fresh underwear, but Michael managed to remain dry and stain-free. If nothing else, he had balls, despite the fact he often misused them.

"I, uh, I can see that," he said.

"And I can see you are lying," Dukabi said, his eyes narrowing. "I expected payment, but now you tell me you are unable to comply. What am I to make of this?"

Michael tried to swallow, but came up empty. A small hack of a cough escaped his mouth.

"I, uh, I just need a little more time," he said after recovering.

"Go on," Dukabi said as he straightened up and took a step back.

His slightly-clipped English accent carried a distinct tone of higher education, but he was a complete mystery to Michael, as he was to most everyone. Such was on purpose. It provided a distinct advantage in situations such as this. It left his opponents confused. Michael was no exception.

"*Mr. O'Hara?*" Dukabi said when Michael hesitated.

Michael flinched again at the boom.

"Um, yeah, well, a few people owe me," he said after remembering how to breathe. "I, uh, I need a couple more days to get the money. Then I'll be able to give it to you."

The fib was a dangerous play. Michael had no idea how much Dukabi might already know about his background, and he held his breath again as he waited for the reply. The first response was a glance back at the guards, as if Dukabi were looking for confirmation—or something else—but neither man reacted. Dukabi began to nod and Michael stole a fresh breath.

"Very well, Mr. O'Hara, I shall play along. I have learned business done in haste is bad business, something your situation proves most elegantly. You may have more time."

Michael stood.

"OK, then, I'll, uh, be in touch—"

A raised hand from Dukabi stopped him.

"Do *not* test me, Mr. O'Hara," he said as he looked directly into Michael's eyes. "You *will* repay… one way or another."

He flicked the hand as if brushing at a gnat. Michael didn't wait for the next swat. He pushed out a smile, turned, and made a beeline for the door, not stopping until he was safely inside the elevator outside Dukabi's penthouse. After jabbing at the button for the lobby, he fell back against the mirrored interior of the car. The reflection staring back seemed annoyed.

"Nice save, asshole," Michael said to it. "But *now* what are you going to do?"

The reflection didn't reply.

Chapter 3

Each year, approximately 300 students in total attended the three main professional umpire schools in operation. The five-week courses, all in Florida—Jim Evans' *Academy of Professional Umpiring* in Kissimmee, Harry Wendelstedt's *School for Umpires* in Ormond Beach, and Buck Walters' *Umpiring 101* in St. Petersburg—were the umpiring world's equivalent of the bar exam, but with far fewer participants.

The number of students was close to the volume of umpires currently working in the major and minor leagues combined. With a low turnover rate, most of those in attendance at the schools would never get to see a professional field other than from the stands. At best, they would take the lessons and memories home, satisfied with knowing they'd at least given it a try.

Buck had conducted his school, run in the fall, for the past sixteen years. His qualifications included thirty-five years of major league experience, during which he was considered one of the best umpires ever. He was now sixty-nine and no longer actively umpiring, but the school and a few other chores for Major League Baseball kept him close to the game.

On this day, as usual, Buck was first to arrive at the facility, the ballfields of St. Petersburg College. It was the penultimate day of the course. Buck had pushed the students hard and everyone, including him, was tired. Despite being the oldest in the group, he showed it the least. No one should have been surprised by that. Buck was strong in many ways.

After parking his car, he began unloading gear from the trunk. It was mostly quiet around him and the early-morning sun was warm on his back.

"Hey, old man," a squeal of a voice said from behind. "You need some help."

Buck turned and raised a hand to shield his eyes from the sun. A short, squirrely man was in front of him, but Buck couldn't find the face in his memory. It was not a student, something confirmed by the man's ridiculous outfit. Someone without Buck's manners might have laughed. He was able to keep it to a friendly smile instead.

"That's OK," he said in a thick Southern accent as he turned back to his car. "I'm fine."

"I don't think you understand," the little man said, stepping forward. "It wasn't a question. *You need some help.*"

Buck turned again.

"Pardon me, son?" he said, his tone less hospitable. "What's this about?"

Despite the sternness and a distinct size disadvantage, the little man held his ground. Buck was a touch over six feet tall, weighed 230 pounds, virtually unchanged from his active umpiring days, and had a linebacker's body. The man in front of him looked like a penguin—think Danny DeVito's version from *Batman Returns*.

"It's pretty simple, really," the penguin said. "The World Series umpire crew has an opening. You need to make sure that opening gets filled by Marshall Connors. Oh, and Connors needs to be chief."

Buck tilted his head as he tried to process the words.

"What are you talking about, son," he said. "There's no ope—"

He was cut off when the penguin revealed a gun beneath his loud jacket.

"That's what I thought," the little man said.

Two cars pulled into the far side of the lot. Buck realized he needed to end things before someone noticed the confrontation. He couldn't risk anyone else's safety.

"OK," he said. "Say I was to believe you. What makes you think I could do what you ask?"

"You'll figure something out," the penguin said.

The cars parked and two of the umpire students stepped out. Buck knew he was out of time.

"And if I don't?" he said.

The little man made a honking noise that may have been a laugh as his hand went to the gun.

"You and your boy get dead."

Paperville, Tennessee

William "Wil" Clemmons was on his knees next to a planting bed bordering the front porch of his Victorian-era house. Pots of colorful mums sat nearby, awaiting their turn to be set in the freshly tilled soil. The afternoon sky was a perfect blue, and a light breeze was providing a nice offset to the sun's warmth. The scene left Wil dreading the thought of leaving home, even if it was to serve as umpire crew chief in the World Series. He loved the game, but days such as these left him looking forward to the off-season.

"Very nice," a voice said from behind his back.

Wil turned to find a smiling but unfamiliar face on the sidewalk. The stranger made a small motion with his hand, a wave of sorts. Wil returned the gesture and used the interruption as an excuse to stand.

"They sure are pretty this time of year," he said. "Do you plant?"

"Afraid not," the stranger said with a frown. "My thumbs aren't very green."

"Don't tell anyone, but neither are mine," Wil said through a smile as he pulled off his gloves and extended his right hand. "The name's Wil Clemmons, nice to meet you."

The stranger came forward, a slight limp in his stride, and gripped Wil's hand.

"Nice to meet you, Mr. Clemmons," he said in a pleasant tone.

Wil caught the omission of a name, but didn't have a chance to pursue it, interrupted when the stranger yanked hard and pulled him close. He was shocked by the move, but more so by the sight of a syringe in the stranger's left hand.

"What—"

"Don't fight it old man, you'll be fine," the stranger said, cutting him off.

He jabbed the needle into Wil's neck. The cocktail of Succinylcholine and Versed worked quickly and Wil slumped in the stranger's arms, the shrill sound of an approaching siren the last thing he heard as the stranger lowered him to the ground.

Seconds later an ambulance roared around the corner and screeched to a halt at the curb in front of the house. Two EMTs hopped out.

"Thank God you're here," the stranger said. "I think he had a heart attack or something. We were talking and he just fell down. I was gonna start CPR, but—"

"That's OK, we'll handle it," one of the technicians said, cutting him off.

After kneeling next to Wil, the EMT looked up at the stranger.

"Are you related to this man?" he said.

"No. I was just walking by. Goddamn, is he gonna be OK?"

Chapter 4

"Enjoy your stay, Mr. Connors."

"That isn't going to be hard," I said. "Thanks."

And with that, I was officially on vacation. I stepped away from the counter to take in the view. The lobby of the Don Cesar Beach Resort was as beautiful and luxurious as the rest of the hotel, meaning expensive. I didn't mind. The MLB umpire pay scale was $120K to $350K, depending on years of service. I was closer to the former, but was an admitted penny-pincher who'd been saving for this trip. Add in a partial reimbursement, part of my time here was for work, and I was easily able to swing it.

In truth, even without the kick-back from the league I'd have made the same decision. My parents had asked me to join them on their annual European trek. Hey, I loved them, but the thought of spending three weeks cooped up in hotel rooms and tour buses was more than I could handle. The baseball season might have been a grind, but *that* would have worse.

Like I said, this was *my* vacation and I wanted to enjoy it. The work part, if you could call it work, was to help Buck Walters at his school. That the sessions were being held a mere three blocks from the Gulf of Mexico, close enough to smell the salt spray, only further solidified my choice. I think my folks understood, although I was fairly certain I'd hear about it from my mother when they got back—and probably every time I saw her for the rest of my life.

After a quick stop to check out my room, I took in some breakfast at the hotel, an awesome Eggs Benedict and large glass of orange juice, before heading out. I arrived at the school a minute before nine A.M. The mid-October sunshine felt great on my face and I let it soak in for a few seconds before turning my attention to the field. I spotted Buck right away. He was wearing a powder-blue umpire shirt under a light-weight black warm-up suit. His bald head was covered by the standard black MLB umpire cap.

The sight of the students around him took me back to when I'd been one of the hopefuls here. These schools were all about getting noticed. You had to be good, but you also had to be lucky. It also helped having someone in your corner. For a few guys, that was a father who was a former major league umpire. For me, it turned out to be Buck. He took me under his wing from day one. You'd have to ask him why, but I was grateful for it.

After the school, I spent six years in the minors traveling to pretty much every small town in the eastern United States. That's a shorter span than for most. It took seven to ten years to get to the bigs on average. There were a handful of people who thought I hadn't earned it, but I liked to tell them that's why it was called an average.

My home during that time was a well-used twenty-eight-foot Rockwood Bayport RV. The years were something I'd always remember, but wouldn't have survived without Buck's help. There were times I wanted to quit, but with his urgings and support, I stuck with it and first appeared in the majors as a vacation replacement in 2003 before being permanently assigned the following year.

I was never really sure how much influence Buck had, but helping out at his school every year since was my way of saying thanks. It was normally for the entire session, but the playoffs got in the way this year. Still, the way I figured it, two days was better than none and I was pretty sure he would take it.

When he spotted me, I waved. He returned the gesture and headed in my direction. Right away I saw something off in his stride. I doubt anyone else would have noticed, but it made me wonder. As he drew closer, it got worse and I began to worry. There was a forced smile on his face and, when he spoke, an obvious strain on his normally jolly twang.

"Hey, son," he said. "Let's go sit. There's something I need to tell you."

Every student was "son" to Buck, but I'd always taken it to mean more. That was probably selfish, but whatever. He was like a second father to me, especially during those years when I was on the road. If there *was* a problem, I wasn't going to push it. He gestured with his head and led me to the bleachers along the third-base side of the field where we sat in the first row. His eyes went to the field, and for a few seconds neither of us said anything.

"Buck, what's going on?" I said, breaking the silence.

"It's a pretty decent batch this year," he said. "A few remind me of you."

He was deflecting. I stopped not pushing.

"Nice try, old man," I said. "Now let's hear the truth. What's up?"

His head came around. I didn't like what I saw. He'd seemed to have aged a lot since we'd last been together, close to a year earlier. The lines on his face were a lot deeper than I'd remembered. More than that, there was anger or pain in the creases. I couldn't tell which.

"Buck?"

"You're working the Series. You're gonna be chief."

I thought the sun and salty air must have damaged my brain because it sounded like he said I was working the World Series *as crew chief*, but that couldn't be right. I'd had a good season, but I'd already worked an earlier round of the playoffs. We weren't supposed to get more than one "special" event like that each year.

"Nice try," I said again.

He glanced at me. There was nothing there to suggest he was kidding, but I still wasn't convinced. He was known to be a bit of a jokester at times.

"C'mon, Buck, you're shittin' me, right?" I said.

"Nope," he said as he shook his head. "Ole Wil Clemmons had a heart attack two nights ago. He'll be OK, but he's done for the year. You're gettin' the gig."

I hadn't seen or heard anything about Wil. I'd been busy with my trip prep and purposely avoiding the news. I would feel bad about his misfortune, if true, but there were at least five or six guys I could think of more likely to get tapped to replace him before me.

"All right, enough," I said, shaking my head. "This isn't funny."

Buck turned to face me and gave me the kind of look he used on the field to end arguments with coaches and players.

"No, son, it's not."

Chapter 5

St. Petersburg

The shock of Buck's disclosure gradually wore off as the day progressed. Working with the students provided the eraser. It reminded me of how I'd gotten here. I had just graduated college, was single with no attachments, same as now, and there was nothing holding me back. I came down to Buck's school with no grand expectations. If I hadn't made it as an umpire, I would have traveled around in the RV for a while and eventually moved on to whatever.

"I appreciate the help," Buck said as we were cleaning up. "I know it wasn't easy for you."

That much was true. My head was still swimming a bit, but being on a ballfield was always the perfect antidote.

"Hey, don't worry about it," I said. "It was my pleasure. I look forward to this every year."

He scrunched up his face at me.

"What's there to look forward to? It's a damn school for wannabes."

"True, very true," I said after chuckling. "Don't get me wrong. It's not like I would trade working the Series for it, but the scenery does soothe the soul."

Around us, the faint sound of the Gulf in the distance and a whisper of wind in the trees were playing a delicate symphony to accompany the setting sun. A handful of puffy clouds painted with spots of orange and yellow dotted the pale blue evening sky. I started thinking that if there *was* a heaven, I bet it looked like this. Buck let out a deep sigh and patted me on the shoulder.

"That it does, son," he said. "It's the only place to be."

He was right. For me, there was nothing like the game of baseball. The perfection of the dimensions, the subtle skills involved, the sounds, the smells, all of it. If I had to be stuck somewhere for the rest of my life, this was what I'd pick. It'd be all I would ever need.

"Well, young man," Buck said, breaking up my daydream. "I think it's time we get going. As pretty as this is, you've got a World Series to handle. I think that trumps things a bit."

The solemn tone told me something was still weighing heavily on him, but I let it go. He was right, I had a lot of work to do and it wasn't the time for bad thoughts to be getting in the way. We nodded at each other and headed for the parking lot.

"So, old man, any last words of advice?" I said as we reached his car.

"Same thing I've always told ya, son," he said. "It ain't rocket science. Just see the ball and make the call."

"And this 'How did I get here' feeling I've had all day? What about that?"

A little darkness came to his face.

"That don't matter none. Just go do the damned job."

The "something's off" sensation from earlier in the day came back, but I pushed it away. I'd known Buck since I was twenty-three. He would never do anything to hurt me. I was probably just being paranoid.

"OK, then," I said. "Thanks, Buck... *for everything*."

He shook his head as he slid into his car. After he buckled in, he looked up at me. The darkness was gone, but there was still something in his eyes.

"No, son, *thank you*," he said before driving away.

ed by the conflict of emotions, I didn't check my
until I got back to the hotel. I'd gotten a call from the
of umpires giving me the official word on the assignment,
and another from Mark Rosenbaum, MLB commissioner, offering
congratulations. Both brought back the reality of what was
happening.

I was going to work the World Series.

The thought started my head spinning again, but I did my best
not to get caught up in it. It wasn't easy. I was excited, scared, and
confused, not to mention still a little worried about Buck, and it all
got worse when I got a third call. This one came from Thomas
Madison Hillsborough, my best friend. That he was calling wasn't
bad. It was what he said that freaked me out.

"It seems congratulations are in order."

"Um, I'm not sure if I'm relieved or worried that you already
know," I said. "Then again, it's been one of those days, so I'm not
even going to ask."

Thomas once worked for—and maybe *still* did—the CIA. It
wasn't something we talked about a lot, if at all, but I was pretty sure
he'd spent seven years there and gathered a wealth of experience the
likes of which I could never hope to match. There might have been a
gunshot wound or two in the mix, but I tried not to ask about that
part. All I knew for sure was that he was always several steps ahead
of everyone else, especially me, so hearing he already knew about
my promotion wasn't a complete shock.

In the scheme of things, it fit.

"I understand," he said. "My apologies if I have added to your
discomfort."

Something about his flat tone, one of his trademarks of sorts,
almost always made things better, and after a few more minutes of
light conversation, I was relatively stable again. The fact was, I was
lucky to have Thomas in my life. He might tell you it was more the
other way around, but I'm going to stick to my version.

We met during my sophomore year at Temple University in
Philadelphia. I saved him from a fire in our dorm building. I'm sure
anyone else would have done the same thing in that situation, but he
vowed to repay me. I was never going to hold him to that, but I'd
given up telling him not to worry about it. He tended to be
persistent. I could do worse.

"So I'm due back in Philly tomorrow around four," I said as we neared the end of the call. "Any chance you can pick me up at the airport? We'll go celebrate."

"That sounds delightful," he said. "Call when you land."

I was about to say something else, but he was gone. I closed the phone and fell back on my bed and stared up at the ceiling. The quiet was nice and I started to relax again. I thought about Buck and Thomas and how happy I was to have two such highly-skilled friends, each with unique talents. One had guided me to the zenith of my profession. The other thought he owed me something commensurate with saving his life.

Like I said, I could do *a lot* worse.

Chapter 6

I woke at six-thirty, got in a quick workout and shower, and headed down to check out. The gal at Don Cesar's front desk seemed genuinely disappointed I was already leaving, but I knew she'd get over it about three seconds after I walked away. I was a bit disappointed, too. The weather outside was absolutely perfect and it wasn't going to be as nice in Philly.

Then again, I would be working the Series and quickly concluded it was a fair trade.

After leaving the hotel, I grabbed some breakfast at one of the many diners along Gulf Boulevard. The scrambled eggs and Belgian waffle added to my great mood, and the weird feelings from the day before had all but faded by the time I got to the airport. There was a slight blip getting through security. An older gentleman in front of me wasn't familiar with the various post-9/11 requirements; TSA agents made him toss out several non-sanctioned containers after a lengthy argument. I didn't let it bother me.

At my departure gate, I found a seat near the top of the Jetway. Per my usual anal tendencies, I was more than two hours early but had prepared by bringing along three newspapers from the hotel. With a hot coffee at my side, I filled the time flipping through the pages. I didn't find anything about Wil or me, which probably wasn't unusual. It wasn't like umpires got a lot of press except when we fucked up; then we couldn't get away from it.

No, "unusual" didn't come until about thirty minutes later when Thomas called again. I caught something in his tone as soon as he said hello and some of my good mood faded.

"Is your flight still on time?" he said.

I knew there was no way he didn't already know the answer, but I played along.

"Yep," I said. "Why, is there a problem?"

The slight hesitation that followed chipped a few more pieces from my mood.

"Too soon to tell," he said. "I should know more by the time you arrive."

One of the gate attendants announced pre-boarding, but I didn't move. No one else seemed to know about my assignment, but I began to wonder. Thomas' words were freaking me out again because he *never* overreacted. Something was definitely up.

"OK… *I guess…* although you kinda just ruined my morning."

"Safe travels, Marshall."

The use of my first name was normally done as a form of reassurance. I didn't bite this time.

"Yeah, whatever, you're a dick. Just be ready to explain when I get there."

I closed the phone and looked around. Everything had been normal except now none of it was. I hated when that happened. It was going to make for a long trip home.

New York City

"Damn it."

The shout came from Mark Rosenbaum's office and reached his assistant, Suze Keebler, a split-second before another more disturbing noise. She grabbed a pad and pen and waited for the inevitable follow-up. It didn't take long.

"Suze, I need you."

She found him mostly hidden from view behind a leather sofa to the right of his desk. He was on his knees picking up what appeared to be pieces of his desk phone. Suze helped and a minute later the newly-found items were added to another pile of wreckage already on Mark's desk.

"Shit," he said. "Can you ask the boys to bring me a new phone? This one's dead."

Suze made a note on her pad as Mark swept the remains into a wastebasket.

"Ooh, very smooth," she said.

"I try."

Suze caught the slight smile on Mark's face. She wasn't surprised. His spurts of anger were usually short.

"OK, enough of that," he said. "Is Gabi around?"

"He won't be able to fix the phone," Suze said.

"Good one," Mark said. "But ask him to come up anyway... *please.*"

He added a lot of emphasis to the last word. Suze smiled.

"OK, since you said 'please' I guess I can do that," she said.

"That would be nice of you."

She stood and moved for the door, seemingly gliding across the floor. Talk about smooth, Mark thought, as he watched, amazed as always by her grace. It wasn't the reason she'd been hired, but it was a nice added benefit. After she was gone, Mark busied himself with paperwork until Gabi Loeb arrived. His gait was less graceful than Suze's, but appreciated just as much. He was MLB's Director of Security, a job he'd performed quite capably for the past eight years.

"Gabi, come, sit," Mark said. "We have a problem."

"Another?" Gabi said as he landed in one of the chairs in front of Mark's desk.

Mark had told him about Wil Clemmons' heart attack and that Marshall had been selected to fill in, but not about the conversation with Buck and the true nature of the situation. Mark had debated that decision, but concluded it was the best course of action, at least for now.

"I just got off the phone with Director Harris said.

The mention of the FBI tightened Gabi's features

"It seems a relative of one of the players is in t casinos."

"I'm guessing a key player?" Gabi said.

"Terry O'Hara," Mark said. "His father, Michael, is up to his eyeballs in outstanding markers. There's no indication of anything illegal, but given that Terry is about to throw the first pitch in the World Series, Director Harris thought we should know."

"I should have already known," Gabi said under his breath before recovering. "First Wil Clemmons, now this. Helluva weekend, huh?"

Mark nodded.

"I need you to have a talk with the O'Haras," he said. "I do *not* want another Pete Rose situation."

"I'll take care of it."

The next few minutes were spent discussing other Series security arrangements. When Gabi was finished with the report, he left the office. A second after he disappeared through the door, Mark instinctively reached to his left without looking.

"Suze," he said in a shout when his hand came up empty. "What's the word on my phone?"

A few seconds later Suze's head appeared in the doorway.

"Um, it's been like nine minutes since you broke the old one," she said. "*And it's Sunday.*"

Mark's brow knitted up.

"OK," he said.

It came out like a question. Suze rolled her eyes.

"Just use your damn cell phone," she said.

"Oh, shit, yeah, duh," Mark said.

Suze could see he was clearly distracted. She offered up a tender smile.

"It's OK, sir, I understand," she said.

When her head disappeared, Mark turned toward the windows behind his desk. The call from Buck rushed back into his thoughts.

"Yeah, well, that makes one of us."

Chapter 7

Tampa

An upgrade to First Class was a welcome surprise after the call from Thomas. I'd been dreading the endless noise and discomfort awaiting me in Coach. Sitting next to a chatty-Kathy or a screaming baby would not have been good. My mind was racing and I needed to sort through all the conflicts of the past day. I was on vacation, but then I wasn't. Buck gave me great news, but was holding something back. Thomas found out without me telling him, but then he got concerned. It was all a bit much.

As the plane took off, I sat back and closed my eyes, trying to find something else to occupy my mind. What I came up with was another conflict, one I hadn't thought about in a long time.

Terry O'Hara had once been my best friend. He was now a professional ballplayer and just happened to be one of the starting pitchers for Game 1 of the Series. That I was now going to be behind the plate for it should have made me happy, but the relationship had died long ago and I really had no idea why.

The friendship started after my parents and I moved to d, Pennsylvania, in the summer before my junior year in high school. Terry, a ninth-grade freshman at the time, and his mother, Samantha, lived around the corner and their backyard touched a corner of ours. There was a batting cage and pitching mound set up there and it quickly became my favorite place. I later found out the equipment was courtesy of Terry's father, ex-big leaguer Michael O'Hara. For a baseball freak like me it was totally cool.

The shared love of the game became the basis for our friendship. It never mattered that on the field we were complete opposites. I was a rarely-used utility player, but Terry was a star who went on to put up some seriously gaudy pitching statistics during high school: 37-4 record, 603 strikeouts, 1.28 ERA, and two State championships. I was happy to have witnessed most of it firsthand.

What I wasn't so happy witnessing was the relationship between Terry and his parents. Samantha was a control freak and had her fingers on every major decision. Terry couldn't do much of anything without her say-so. I don't know if it was out of protection or because of Michael. Per Terry, their divorce had been bitter, and the endless bickering left him feeling stuck in the middle. It was something we talked about often and it came to a head just before MLB draft day in June of '93.

There was little doubt Terry would be a high draft pick, but he also had several college scholarship offers. He and Michael got in a big fight about which direction to take and it didn't end well. Terry ended up choosing USC, I think because it was so far from home, and he and Michael became estranged. My friendship with him was forever damaged as well.

Whether it was the fight with Michael or something else, the sense of innocence I once felt in him was gone. We did stay in touch during his first year at school, but his anger was never far from the surface and things quickly deteriorated. He never really explained it to me and after a while I just quit asking. Eventually we quit talking all together and became as distant as he and his father. It was something I regretted.

Terry seemed to fill the hole quickly, the biggest plug being Nik Sanchez, one of his teammates. Nik's love of baseball developed in a different manner than mine and Terry's. His mother, a Russian-born immigrant, and his father, a Cuban-refugee, defected to the U.S. in the late 70's and never had much money. That hardship drove Nik to

L.A.'s gang life at an early age, but when his father was killed in a drive-by shooting, Nik's mother moved them out of the city. Devastated by the death, Nik turned to baseball as an escape.

He worked hard and became a decent catcher and earned a scholarship to USC. He and Terry had a great on-field rapport and the friendship grew out of that. Eventually, they moved into an off-campus apartment together. Things were going great until Terry got injured in a freak accident there, shattering several bones in his right arm. The damage was so severe I didn't think he'd ever be able to pick up a ball again, let alone pitch.

I was devastated by the news, but when I wanted to visit, Terry refused to allow it. I always had a feeling there was more to the story, but I never pursued it. I chalked it up to the fact he'd moved on and so had I. Stuff like that happened. Sure, it would have been nice to have shared his long, hard journey back to the majors. It was a great story, but I guess that's the way life worked sometimes. I just wished I understood it better.

I could have said the same thing about the past twenty-four hours.

Some turbulence somewhere over the Carolinas rattled the plane and I opened my eyes. I think maybe Karma had something to do with it because when I looked out the window I saw we were directly above a ballfield complex. Even from thirty-thousand feet it was beautiful and reminded me where I was headed.

A smile filled my face as I stared down at the diamonds. Sure, it was a business and a job, but it was still just a game. I started thinking maybe my surprise assignment was a blessing in disguise and Terry and I could get reacquainted. The game had brought us together once before. Maybe it would again.

I could deal with that.

Chapter 8

St. Pete Beach

Buck grabbed a beer and made his way to the wicker rocker on the screened-in back porch of his home. Like most days, he would be alone there. Barbara, his wife of forty-two years, had died months earlier after suffering a stroke. The couple had no children, Barbara was unable to conceive, and no pets, and while there had been discussions over the years about adopting some of each, their careers had kept it to nothing more than talk.

Despite the shock of Barbara's death, Buck declined Mark Rosenbaum's repeated urgings to let someone else handle the school. Baseball was his first love after Barbara and would help him get through the pain of losing her. The rest of his pain was something he needed to get through on his own.

A few minutes after he sat, the phone rang, shattering the quiet. Buck glanced at it, then back at the still water of Boca Ciega Bay. Of the two, the water was the more pleasing option, but he managed to break loose from the lure and grab the receiver after the fifth ring.

"This is Buck," he said, his voice thick from Budweiser and fatigue.

"Hey, Buck," a familiar New York accent said into his ear. "Glad I caught you."

"Ain't no place else I need to be, now is there?" Buck said.

"Are you on your porch?" Mark said.

"I am."

"Well, then I'd have to agree."

Buck coughed or laughed. Either way, it didn't sound pleasant and Mark cringed a little on his end of the line.

"You OK?" he said after the noise stopped.

"About what I'd expect," Buck said.

Outside the porch, a pelican landed on a small boat platform at the end of the yard. There was no longer a vessel there, but Buck still cast a line into the Bay from time to time. He hadn't today and the big bird was going to be disappointed by the lack of free eats.

"I didn't expect to hear from you again tonight," Buck said. "Is there a new problem?"

"Not at all," Mark said. "I was actually calling to thank you for returning the evaluations so soon. I appreciate that."

Buck's last official duty had been the course evaluations, completed in the hour before he'd made his way to the porch. Three participants were going to be recommended for advancement. The rest would go back to whatever they'd been doing before, but at least with a little more knowledge of the game. Despite the inherent disappointment in that, Buck drew some comfort knowing that a part of him, his experiences and knowledge, would survive after he was gone.

It was a small victory at this point in his life.

"No point having that hanging over our heads, too," he said.

The words reminded Mark of the shared predicament they were facing.

"Are we doing the right thing here?" he said.

"No use fretting," Buck said. "Not a damn thing we can do about it now but wait and see."

Mark agreed. The urgency of the situation hadn't allowed for a lot of analysis. He'd done what he thought was right. Only time would tell.

"Listen, Mark, it's done," Buck said. "Just make sure you look out for the boy. None of this shit is his fault. He can't get hurt."

Again, Mark agreed. Involving Marshall had been the biggest hurdle to overcome.

"I'll do everything I can to protect him, you have my word," he said; then after a pause. "Besides, no one will even think twice about it. Yes, it breaks a rule, but I'm the commissioner, I get to do that. Marshall is probably our best umpire right now. He more than deserves to be on the crew."

"*No one* deserves what we did."

Mark let the comment go when Buck coughed again. He knew the source of the hack, one of a few with such knowledge. Buck was dying, victim of a rapidly spreading cancer. Doctors had given him less than six months to live, but that had been more than a year ago. The fact he was beating it was another testament to his character and strength.

In truth, he was in serious pain, but wasn't going to complain. He was fairly certain no one at the school had seen any hints of the illness, including Marshall. Buck knew he needed to tell the young man soon, not just about the cancer, but about everything.

After a few more minutes of baseball chatter, the call ended. Buck finished off what was left of his now-warm beer and walked down to the dock. The pelican didn't move. It was long used to the presence of humans, especially this one. Buck nodded at the bird before looking west. Dusk had brought with it a light mist from the ocean that had painted everything grey. It was both beautiful and sad, much like his feelings in general.

After about five minutes of staring into the quiet, time in which Buck's thoughts went back to Marshall, the pelican clomped out a loud complaint when it must have realized that dinner wasn't coming.

Buck turned.

"Sorry, friend," he said. "I'm afraid you're on our own tonight."

The bird clomped again and took off.

"Maybe tomorrow," Buck said as he watched the creature disappear into the low clouds.

The message was as much for Marshall as it was for the bird.

Philadelphia

My plane landed in Philly on time and I hurried off as soon as the door opened. Less than five minutes later I was on the curb in front of Philadelphia International's Terminal B baggage claim. Exactly two minutes after that, a sparkling pearl-blue Acura TL pulled to the curb. Thomas had an affinity for cars, but never owned more than one at a time. He compensated by often rotating the stock, but this particular gem had survived eight months.

"Wow, still the TL," I said as I slid into the passenger seat.

"Yes, she may be a keeper," he said.

That he would feel that way might have been a surprise to some. Thomas had money. OK, that's an understatement. He was filthy rich. His family had done very well since coming to America in the 1700's. Banking, railroads, and oil provided the basis for the wealth. Thomas was one of two remaining heirs who inherited most of it.

To him the money wasn't important. He had always felt it isolated him and his sister from real life. Their experiences were based on societal status, staid events that left no place for genuine feelings. Thomas felt suffocated by it all and eventually grew to resent it. It was my guess, but never confirmed, that those feelings had driven him to a less-than-Ivy League school like Temple and then into the CIA.

Whatever the case, I liked his choices, including those made on cars.

"Sweet," I said in reference to the TL.

"Indeed," Thomas said with a nod.

That word was another trademark. It almost always fit.

"Onward," I said.

He pulled the car away from the curb without asking for a destination. My apartment was in Radnor, not far from his, but he knew I would be taking advantage of MLB's official accommodations at the Four Seasons in Philadelphia. Of course, that wasn't the only reason behind his not asking. We had other things to discuss. It's not like I'd forgotten, but it wasn't like I wanted to dive in either.

"OK," I said after a minute or so. "What's going on? And please use small words because I already have a headache."

The hotel was about fifteen minutes from the airport, well, fifteen for most drivers. It would only take Thomas about ten, but that still left plenty of time for his efficient debriefing. When he finished, I used the next two minutes to process. I wasn't as efficient as he was.

"So, uh, how do Michael O'Hara and his gambling problems affect me?"

Thomas glanced at me, but showed no emotion, as usual.

"The private poker game is run by a former acquaintance of mine by the name of Dikembe Dukabi. No, you may not ask. Your employer is aware of Mr. O'Hara's casino problems, but not his Dukabi problem. The latter is far worse. Dukabi can be *aggressive* when it comes to debt collection. Terry is playing in the World Series. You are umpiring in the World Series."

If life were a cartoon, a light bulb would have popped up over my head.

"Oh wow, now I get it," I said. "Sorry, jet lag."

We were about a minute from the hotel. I processed for half of that before talking again.

"So how do *you*... never mind, I don't want to know," I said before regrouping. "Just tell me if you think this Dukabi character is going to come after me or Terry."

I looked for an answer in his face, but there was nothing there. Or maybe there was, I didn't know. I'd become relatively decently skilled at reading him over the years, but there were still a lot of times I couldn't. That failure was often frustrating.

"Thomas?" I said.

The hotel was in front of us. He turned the Acura off Eighteenth Street and guided it to a stop near the front doors. A bellhop appeared out of nowhere and opened my door. Thomas waved off a second one from his.

"Dude, seriously, what's up?" I said.

"I don't yet know, but you need to exercise care."

I turned away.

"I'm guessing the fact you're just sitting there means we're not going to be doing any celebrating, right?" I said.

The question was met with a nod.

"I apologize, Marshall," he said. "I'll be in touch tomorrow. For now, go have fun."

"Should I have stayed in Florida?" I said.

"No, this is where you need to be."

I chewed on my lip for a second.

"Yeah, right," I said. "Thanks for the ride. And you're still a dick."

"Goodnight, Marshall."

Chapter 9

Dukabi and his assistants were in his office. He was on the business side of the mahogany desk. The helpers were in the visitor chairs. Each was wearing a version of the same outfit they'd worn the night before. They'd just finished confirming that their latest chores had been successfully completed. Dukabi's head seemed to be glowing from the reflection of the room's lights as he processed that information, but his onyx-colored face showed no emotion. After a blast furnace sounding deep breath, he turned to the penguin first.

"What more have you learned of Mr. O'Hara?"

The little man's name was Elliot Stevens. He'd been with Dukabi for nine years. Despite severe character flaws, Elliot had his moments, namely when it came to research.

"A' 'ight, here's what we already knew," he said as he pulled out a small notepad. "O'Hara's fifty-eight, divorced, and lives in a condo off JFK Boulevard. The ex lives in the suburbs, been there ince the split. Their only kid is the son pitching in the World Series."

"And his finances," Dukabi said. "What more do we know?"

Elliot flipped a page.

"Yeah, it's pretty much what we thought. He's got some equity, but it ain't very liquid. He's gonna have a hard time coming up with what he owes you without help, especially when you add in the casino chits. This guy *really* likes to lose, even when the games aren't fixed. As to getting help, he and the boy don't get along, so best guess is he'll have to make a play on the ex. She's executor of a divorce trust. The trust was the only way she could make sure he didn't screw her. Oh, ha, *screw her*, get it?"

Elliot chuckled, but the other two were unmoved by the accidental play on words. After a second, he cleared his throat and resumed his report.

"Yeah, so, anyway, the settlement was one-sided. The Mrs. had leverage from O'Hara's wanderings and was fully prepared to use it. It looks like he signed without protest."

"What is the size of this trust?" Dukabi said.

"I'm still tryin' to get a balance, but it started with sixty-five percent of their savings, just over a million bucks. After that it got funded from O'Hara's playing salary. It was a savvy move because it protected the Mrs. big time. O'Hara definitely lacks any financial sense, but we already knew that, didn't we?"

Dukabi nodded as he silently appraised the information. After a few seconds, he turned to the other man. His name was Peter Arcadia. It was a phony moniker, but served its purpose as neither Dukabi nor Stevens needed to know who he really was. All they needed to know was that he did his job. Story over.

"Do you concur?" Dukabi said.

"Yeah," Arcadia said. "We can use it."

Dukabi leaned forward in his chair. The glow on his head became more threatening.

"I am fascinated by the value you Americans place on sporting endeavors. In this case, however, I agree. It is very much to our benefit. Carry on with your plan, Mr. Arcadia."

A confused look filled Elliot's face.

"Is someone gonna fill me in on this plan at some point?" he said.

Neither Arcadia nor Dukabi answered. The latter's only reaction was to sit back and glance down at the Rolex on his wrist. After seeing *6:49 P.M.* he began to nod.

"You may go," he said with a wave of his hand.

"Boss, I—"

Elliot got cut off when the back of Arcadia's hand whacked him hard across the arm. A stern head-shake followed and Elliot realized the conversation was over. He and Arcadia stood and made their way out of the office without another word.

"So, c'mon, what's this plan?" Elliot said when they reached the elevator doors. "I don't mind helpin' out, but it'd be nice to know some details."

Arcadia kept his eyes on the doors.

"It doesn't matter," he said.

Elliot shrugged and decided to drop it for now. He'd eventually get his answers.

The usually elegant contemporary classic furnishings of the Four Seasons lobby were drowning in a sea of baseball paraphernalia. I doubted any of the hotel's regular guests liked the garish displays, but I thought they were great, especially the pep band playing near the front desk. The music helped me forget about Thomas and find my smile again.

After listening to a couple of tunes, I made my way to the front desk and was greeted there by a clerk wearing a Phillies jersey. A small tag on her chest told me her name was Jennifer.

"Good evening, sir, welcome to the Four Seasons Philadelphia," she said.

"Good evening to you, Jennifer. I love the outfits."

To her left another clerk was adorned with a Tampa jersey.

"We drew straws," Jennifer said with a smile. "I got the better end of the deal."

"I'd agree, but it would get me fired," I said in a whisper after leaning towards her.

She chuckled as I straightened up.

"Checking in, please," I said in a normal voice. "Marshall Connors, I'm part of the MLB party. Hopefully, you'll find me on the list anyway."

Jennifer took a peek at my ID and tapped out a few letters on a keyboard in front of her. Seconds later a printer next to the computer spit out several sheets of paper. In one fluid motion she grabbed them, spun them around, and placed the small stack neatly in front of me.

"Oooh, well done," I said. "That must have taken years of training."

"An entire semester at hotel school," she said.

A grin played on her face and I immediately liked the hotel even more.

"And how many room keys will you need?" she said after walking me through the itinerary.

What I thought: *"Two and you keep one."* What I said was a little less forward. OK, it was *a lot* less forward. My flirting skills were a little rusty. It had been awhile.

"One is fine, I'm on my own."

"Aw, too bad, it's a beautiful room. You should find someone to share it with."

Her smile grew and she tilted her head. Damn, I should have said two.

"Well, you never know, maybe I will," I said.

I bounced my eyebrows for effect.

"Oh, well, good luck with that," she said. "Now, if you need *anything else*, just call. I'd be happy to assist."

Her expression was, well, it was sultry. Maybe my flirting *had* worked.

"Jennifer, you are too kind."

"Thank you, Mr. Connors, you are as well. Enjoy your stay."

She gave me one last knockout look and I almost forgot my name. Enjoy my stay, huh?

With Jennifer around, I began to think I just might.

Chapter 10

Michael O'Hara met Samantha Alyson Johnson while he was playing for Cleveland. She was an intern with the team, working for the traveling secretary, a job she held while pursuing a business degree at Case Western Reserve University. Her responsibilities saw her spending a lot of time around the locker room. She was twenty-one and attractive and the players didn't mind. They were spoiled and immature professional athletes. It was inevitable they'd like her, but she did her best not to get involved with any.

Michael broke through that wall. He had an outgoing personality and confidence. Some said it was arrogance, but Samantha never saw that. They started dating and eventually moved in together. Michael was not immune to the questionable activities in which players tended to get involved, but Samantha was able to look past it, for a while anyway. They were extremely passionate in bed, which seemed to compensate.

They were married shortly after Samantha graduated from college. It was the first and only for both. Terry was born in March of 1975 and would be their only child. They stayed together until 1980, Michael's third season with Texas. Fed up with his cheating, Samantha filed for divorce and sole custody of Terry. She easily prevailed.

After the split, she moved back to the Philadelphia area to be near family. Having a decent-paying job meant she could forsake alimony, instead allowing all scheduled payments to be reinvested back into the trust. She was primary beneficiary, but rarely withdrew anything. She wanted it to be available *just in case*. Her son had dreams and she wanted to make sure money never stopped them from coming to fruition. She couldn't stop other happenstances from doing so, but using her business acumen, she skillfully guided the investments and the balance grew rapidly over the years, reaching its current level of just over $5.4 million.

Michael sat in his darkened living room and contemplated the money. His mind had drifted toward it and Samantha during a morning-long internal debate that lasted through his five-mile run, a long shower, and a light breakfast. No matter how he dissected it, it was, as Elliot Stevens had suggested, his best option.

Michael had never made it to the playoffs, let alone the World Series, but he knew how important it was, especially to a fierce competitor like his son. There was no way he could bring himself to be a distraction to Terry's preparation, not after the long battle to get there. That left Samantha and the trust.

It also left the chore of asking her, something that wouldn't be easy. Not by a long shot.

It was a few minutes past ten in the morning before he finally worked out the right words to say, and the nerve, to make the call. After dialing on his cell, he held his breath and tried to picture her reaction, but couldn't find her face. The only thing he could see was Dukabi's from nights before and how much worse it might get if this attempt failed.

The nasty scowl was close to what arose on Samantha when she saw Michael's name appear on her phone's caller ID. She couldn't remember the last time they'd spoken, but was sure it had ended badly. Most conversations with the man did. Her first instinct was to let it ring and then delete any message he might leave. After several deep sighs, however, she finally gave in and snatched the receiver off the wall.

"What do *you* want?" she said in an icy tone.

On his end, Michael cringed, but quickly recovered.

"Come on, Sam, don't be like that," he said tentatively before remembering some of his script. "Can't I call the mother of my child and say hello?"

The recovery had left him sounding cute, but Samantha didn't bite.

"No, you can't," she said, the ice still thick.

Michael resisted an urge to give up and shifted to something more adult-sounding.

"Ooh, nice, I see you've still got it bad for me, huh, babe?"

There was a pause. Michael got scared.

"And now I'm hanging up," Samantha said after the break.

Michael couldn't see it, but she started to do so. He shouted into his cell.

"Whoa, whoa, whoa, hold on," he said. "Don't hang up."

Luckily, or maybe not, Samantha heard him and brought the phone back to her face.

"*What?*" she said.

The ice was approaching berg status. Michael was going to need a series of serious course corrections to avoid a collision. He scrapped the script and went with something approaching honesty.

"Please, I'm sorry," he said in the sincerest tone he could find. "I *really* need your help."

He held his breath again through another pause.

"Jesus, Michael, what have you done now?"

The ice was still there, but so was something else. Michael began chipping to get at it.

"Let me come over and I'll explain," he said. "I don't want to do this on the phone."

There was a loud sigh in his ear followed by Samantha's voice.

"Fine," she said. "Be here in an hour… *or I won't be.*"

Springfield, Pennsylvania

Samantha was sure whatever Michael was up to revolved around money. It always did. In a panic, she logged onto the trust account website to check the balance, thinking he'd somehow gotten access. She was relieved to find all of the money still in place and made her way to the kitchen to wait for his arrival.

The late-morning sun was shining through the bay window over the kitchen sink, but it failed to move her. The call from Michael had already ruined the day. She doubted it would get any better once he arrived. In fact, some part of her was hoping he wouldn't show up, that maybe he'd change his mind.

The sound of the doorbell squashed the thought.

"Oh, well, this should be good," she said aloud as she made her way to the front door.

With a deep breath, she pulled it open. The face staring back was not Michael's.

"Uh, may I help you?" she said.

The man, much younger than Michael and even her, extended his hand.

"Afternoon, Mrs. O'Hara," he said. "My name is Gabi Loeb. I'm the Director of Security for Major League Baseball. I apologize for the unannounced visit, but I was hoping you might be able to help me locate your husband."

Small world, Samantha thought, as she eyed Gabi closely. When it became obvious she wasn't going to take his hand, he withdrew it. Samantha punctuated the shunning when she crossed her arms in front of her chest.

"I'm not married," she said in a combative tone.

"Yes, ma'am, sorry," Gabi said. "I meant your ex-husband, of course."

Samantha wasn't moved by the apology. In her mind, the MLB's director of security showing up on the same day Michael called for help couldn't be a coincidence. It meant trouble. She suspected very deep trouble.

"Of course," she said. "Do you have ID?"

Gabi quickly produced a wallet. Samantha feigned studying the credentials for a moment. Mostly she was stalling. It worked. Over Gabi's shoulder she noticed another car pull to the curb. When Michael stepped out, a smile filled her face. She returned the wallet to Gabi and relaxed her stance a few degrees.

"Thank you," she said. "Now what was it you said you wanted to chat about?"

Gabi's eyes narrowed at the sudden change before relaxing.

"I was hoping you could help me locate Michael. We can't get him to return any calls."

Samantha nodded.

"He can be like that, yes, but I think I can help."

She made a twirling motion with her hand. Gabi figured it out and spun to look behind.

"Hello, Michael," Samantha said over Gabi's shoulder. "This nice young man was just asking about you."

Michael and Gabi did not shake hands as Samantha led the way into the foyer.

"To your right, Mr. Loeb," she said as she pointed. "We'll sit in the living room."

As Gabi went around the corner, Michael closed in from behind and stepped into Samantha's personal space. His proximity made her cringe and she took a step back to restore a buffer.

"What the fuck, Sam? You called league security?"

"I wish," Samantha said. "He showed up on his own."

"No way," Michael said.

Samantha started to respond, but he angrily pushed past and went down the hall. She watched in silence until he reached the kitchen. She took a second to regroup before heading into the living room. Gabi was at a baby grand piano surveying a collection of photos on top. Most were of Terry. When Samantha reached the piano, she picked up one of the photos and ran her fingers over the image.

"You recognize my son, of course?" she said.

"I do. We're not supposed to cheer for anyone, but I admire your son. His is a great story."

"Thank you," Samantha said as she lightly touched Gabi's arm. "That's very kind of you."

"He's gone through a lot," Gabi said just as Michael reappeared behind them.

"No shit I've been through a lot," he said.

His face was twisted into a sneer, but it drew nothing more than a chuckle from Samantha.

"Michael, please, like most conversations in this house, this one did not concern you."

Samantha was enjoying the fact Michael was visibly shaken by Gabi's presence, but she began to feel something else as well. It wasn't dread, but close.

"Yeah, whatever," Michael said as he moved into the living room.

Samantha's eyes lingered on him for a moment. She could see his face had added a few lines over the years, but all seemed to be in the right place, giving him a rugged handsomeness. He had aged gracefully and she reluctantly admitted he still looked good.

The same could be said of her. At fifty-five years old she looked much younger. The Pilates and yoga classes did their jobs nicely, thank you very much. Her blonde hair was shoulder length, the same as it had been most of her adult life, and the dark pink sweater and black slacks she wore accentuated her curves, something Gabi's eyes had confirmed several times.

Samantha turned to him again.

"Mr. Loeb, should I leave the room?" she said.

This situation was a fortunate turn of events, but Samantha was never intended to be part of it. Gabi nodded.

"That might be best, ma'am," he said.

"I understand. I'll be in the kitchen if you boys need anything."

As soon as she moved out of the room, Michael stepped toward Gabi.

"OK, cut the *Mr. Polite* bullshit, Loeb. What the fuck are you doing here?"

Gabi held his ground.

"I was about to ask you the very same thing."

Chapter 11

Springfield

A sound in the foyer made Samantha look up from her tea. Gabi was standing in the hallway just outside the living room. She couldn't see Michael, but guessed he was just inside the doorway out of view. She stood and headed in their direction.

"Nobody said you had to like it—"

Gabi cut himself off when he saw Samantha.

"All finished?" she said in an innocent tone.

Gabi pushed out a smile.

"Uh, yes, ma'am," he said. "Thank you very much for your time."

"You're quite welcome. Come, let me walk you out."

She hooked his elbow and guided him toward the front door. A glance into the living room as she moved past revealed Michael at the fireplace, his head lowered as if staring into a fire that wasn't there. Samantha shrugged it off and turned her attention back to Gabi.

"If you're ever in town again, stop by. I'd love to show you more of Terry's things."

"I would like that," Gabi said; then after a pause. "Again, I'm sorry for the intrusion."

"Oh, it was no problem," Samantha said. "Glad I could help."

She shook his hand and waited on the porch until he reached his car. After a wave, she turned back into the house. Michael was standing in the foyer.

"We need to talk," he said.

There was too much attitude in his tone.

"Michael, you came into *my* home and said you needed *my* help, so I would appreciate a little respect. Otherwise, you can leave now and good luck with your problem."

Michael backed off a couple of steps, his face filled with concern, but not necessarily for her.

"You're right, I'm sorry," he said as he raised his hands in surrender. "Loeb caught me off guard. I didn't mean to take it out on you."

Samantha eyed him suspiciously, her face taut with anger.

"Whatever, Michael," she said. "Just tell me what's going on."

Michael took a deep breath and considered her for a moment. Gorgeous but tough, nothing like the countless bimbos he'd fucked over the years—and he truly did nothing more than fuck them. Each was a release from whatever anger he was feeling at the moment, whether a bad night on the field or at the tables. All of it was stupid, like a lot of things he'd done.

"Your friend told me I was persona non grata at the games."

"He's not my friend," Samantha said.

Something flashed across Michael's face, but he recovered quickly.

"Right, I know that," he said.

Samantha's eyes narrowed. She'd tired of the stalling.

"What kind of trouble are you in?" she said.

Michael's jaw muscles flexed a few times as he looked away from her for a second. As he turned back, he tried to swallow. The effort appeared to be difficult.

"I, uh, I owe some people some money," he said. "The league doesn't want me hanging around the players. They're uptight about the whole gambling thing, especially for the Series. They thought—"

"They don't want you hanging around *Terry*, right?" Samantha said, cutting him off.

Michael slowly nodded.

"Right," he said in a defeated tone.

Samantha's head began to shake.

"How much do you owe?"

Her eyes were fixed on his. It was a stare he'd never seen. It felt like she was digging into his soul, one handful at a time, and a sharp pain rose up in the back of his head. He wanted to look away but couldn't. No matter how cool and strong he thought he was he knew he was no match for her.

"*How much do you owe, Michael?*" she said again.

Michael's head began to throb. What he was about to do was known in baseball as a set-up pitch. It was where the pitcher purposely threw one pitch in anticipation of the next, something to get the batter off-balance. It was part of the strategy of the game.

"In total… *two million*," he said.

He was sure the shock of the amount would bring about a counter offer, but that was the set-up. He would then settle for what he really needed, namely, enough to get the casinos off his back. It was a calculated risk. He couldn't swing both debts, but if he got some money from Samantha, it would buy him time with Dukabi. The only hole in the strategy was that he forgot the batter didn't always fall for the set up.

No counter came.

Samantha simply said no and told him to get out.

Philadelphia

After leaving Samantha's house, Gabi drove to South Philadelphia and Citizens Bank Park. His first stop there was at the executive offices to let folks know he was around. Unannounced visits from MLB Security tended to spook some people. He'd been lucky to catch Michael; he didn't want to push that luck with Terry. Inside the doors of the offices he found a pretty face behind the counter belonging to a young woman named Marie. When she looked up from her work, an expression of recognition filled her face.

"Oh, wow, Mr. Loeb," she said with genuine excitement as she stood. "What are you doing here? I didn't know you were coming today."

She started rechecking the appointment calendar on her desk.

"I'm not on anyone's schedule," Gabi said. "I was in the area and thought I'd stop by."

"Oh, OK," Marie said with a shrug. "You want me to tell Mr. Sakowski?"

Jordan Sakowski was head of ballpark security and Gabi's usual contact.

"Please," Gabi said. "Tell him I'll be on the field. I have my cell."

Twelve minutes later, Gabi was standing in front of the Phillies dugout, along the first-base side of the field. Terry was with him, his back to the infield. He was wearing uniform pants and game shoes, but a short-sleeved workout jacket had taken the place of his game jersey. There was a towel in his right hand.

"Sorry for interrupting your workout," Gabi said.

"No problem, I'm done," Terry said as he draped the towel over his shoulder. "What's up?"

"It's about your father. He's in a bit of a jam."

Terry's reaction was to wipe at some sweat and switch the towel to the other shoulder. Gabi saw several emotions in the movements, but couldn't tell if it was anger or surprise or both.

"What'd he do now?" Terry said in a low voice.

"He owes a lot of money to some Atlantic City casinos and is no longer welcome there. We need to make sure it doesn't filter down to you. We'd hate to think what might happen if the wrong people decide peddling influence over you might be a viable repayment opt—"

He was cut off when Terry closed the gap between the two, leaving their faces mere inches apart. If nothing else, Gabi had his confirmation. Anger had won the battle.

"Let me get this straight," Terry said through a tight jaw. "Are you suggesting my dad is in enough trouble that someone would try to get me to throw a game?"

"Not at all," Gabi said in a calm voice. "But it's my job to make sure that doesn't happen. Part of that is to make you aware so you can be mindful of anything odd in the coming days."

"Anything odd, huh… *Like this?*" Terry said.

Gabi ignored the dig.

"I realize you might be upset, but the timing couldn't be helped," he said. "It's a lot better you hear this from me than to be surprised by someone approaching you. I can protect you better this way."

A smirk came to Terry's face.

"Forgive me if that doesn't give me goosebumps."

He wiped at another batch of sweat as he backed off a few steps and began to look around. Jordan Sakowski had quietly approached and was standing nearby, watching. He acknowledged Terry with a nod. Terry returned the gesture.

"Does he know?" Terry said to Gabi with a tilt of the head.

"Not yet," Gabi said. "I'll brief him shortly, but your father and I have already chatted. I ran into him at your mother's—"

"Wait, you involved *my mother* in this?" Terry said, cutting him off. "Goddamn it."

Gabi put up a hand.

"I only went there to see if she could help me find Michael. I had no idea he would show up at the same time."

Terry's face took on a confused look.

"Why was my dad *there?*" he said, more to himself than to Gabi. "Ah, shit."

Gabi detected a realization in the last words and hesitated before responding. He could see Terry was working through it.

"This is fucked up," Terry said a few seconds later. "I better find out what's going on."

Gabi handed him a business card.

"If you do and there's something I need to know, call me anytime," he said.

"Huh? Oh, yeah, sure," Terry said.

He took the card and slipped it into the back pocket of his pants.

"Like I said, Terry, I'm sorry," Gabi said.

He extended his hand.

"It's not your fault," Terry said. "You're just doin' your job, right?"

He took Gabi's hand and held the grip a few seconds longer than necessary. Gabi got a feel for the strength in the surgically-repaired arm. It was impressive, but not what caught his attention most. A sly smile had slowly filled Terry's face and stayed there as he released the grip. Gabi wasn't sure he liked it.

It was the exact same look Michael had given him an hour earlier.

Chapter 12

Philadelphia

Elliot had spent the day doing what he did best: research. The discussion about Michael and its aftermath had inspired him to finally get around to looking into Arcadia's background. Because of the short notice it had taken a few more dollars than normal to inspire some of his usual sources to help, but it was worth it. He still didn't know what "the plan" was all about, but he now had a pretty good idea of the reason behind it.

That left him staring out the windows of his office in Dukabi's complex, wondering what to do next. There was a beautiful sunset under way, but Elliot barely noticed. His mind was stuck on the calculations brought on by the information acquired. He could see a profit, but could also see danger. Either way, he knew too much to simply do nothing.

"Ah, fuck it," he said aloud.

His greed had won out, as it usually did. He turned from the window and reached for his cell phone. After dialing, he sat back and began playing with his tie as he waited for the signal to reach its

There was a new stain on the silk, but he didn't dwell. If ed, he could buy some new neckwear.

lis?" a gruff voice said into his ear after a couple of rings.

"It's Stevens," he said. "I need to speak to Mario."

There was a pause.

"Wait," the voice said.

Mario was Mario Pastelli, a specialist of sorts in Atlantic City, one who dealt in buying and selling bits of data related to betting activities at the casinos and elsewhere. The data was extremely valuable and extremely difficult to obtain. There was a lot of risk involved because Mario often played both sides of the same equation, a practice he knew would get him dead if ever found out. It was a lot like what Elliot was about to do.

That's why he'd picked Mario to ask for help.

"What the fuck, Elliot?" Mario said coming on the line. "I told you to never call me at work. This fuckin' better be good."

"Oh, it's good all right."

The Philadelphia FBI field office was at the corner of 6th and Arch Streets, across the road from the National Constitution Center at the northern end of Independence Mall. Several hundred dedicated government workers called the building home, including Special Agent Sandy Hood, a determined young woman who had worked her way up from analyst to special agent in just over five years.

Sandy's current assignment was serving as liaison to Major League Baseball. In this position she was responsible for coordinating background checks for World Series access. The MLB security office would send over lists of names and she would process each through a search program. If anything of interest turned up, Sandy or another agent would investigate. If not, an "all clear" would be issued.

The results of the latest request, a follow-up on the first search on Terry O'Hara's father, were displayed on a computer screen in front of Sandy. The initial findings were behind the call to Mark Rosenbaum. Gabi Loeb made the follow-up request. All of it had

Sandy off balance. Terry was her favorite player and his father being in trouble was unsettling.

"And what are you still doing here?" a voice said from above Sandy's head.

Sandy looked up. Alex Harris, the director of the office, was peeking over her cubicle wall.

"I'm trying to make sense of this O'Hara stuff," she said. "But it's starting to get to me."

Alex gave an understanding nod.

"Hey, worse things could happen," he said. "Why don't you go home and reboot. The MLB crew knows we're working on it. It can wait for morning."

Sandy's head bobbed from side to side for a couple of seconds, a movement she often made when thinking.

"I suppose," she said. "But—"

"No 'buts'," Alex said. "That's an order."

He was smiling. Sandy returned the expression and added a small salute.

"Aye, aye, Captain," she said. "Consider me gone."

Alex disappeared and Sandy returned her focus to her desk. She saved and closed the report before navigating to her e-mail. Despite Alex's command, she hated leaving anything undone. It took her about five minutes to get through the contents of the Inbox; there was nothing of substance in any of the messages. As the machine began to shut down, Sandy stood and stretched. Her muscles complained about the movements—or the lack thereof in the several preceding hours—and a groan escaped her lips. She quickly concluded a workout was in order as soon as she got home.

She arrived there twenty minutes later, a one-bedroom unit on the third floor of The Chatham at Rittenhouse Square. It was a nice place in a beautiful location. Across the street, Rittenhouse Square Park was a little oasis in the city and Sandy's current favorite hangout outside of the office. She ran there almost every day and couldn't wait to get back on the paths to work out some of her frustrations about Terry's situation.

She quickly changed clothes and got in three miles before returning to the apartment and throwing herself into a forty-five minute yoga session. The twisting, turning, and mental cleansing worked nicely. Her muscles stopped complaining and she forgot all about Michael O'Hara and whatever mess he'd gotten himself into.

After a shower she made her way to her kitchen. A yogurt and a bottle of water came back with her as she wandered over to a small desk in the corner of her living room. She sat and tapped the touchpad on her laptop. The screen came to life. A double-tap on a small FBI logo started a security loop. Two minutes and several spoonfuls of yogurt later, Sandy's personal workspace appeared.

Despite being emptied two hours earlier, her Inbox now had fourteen messages. Sandy frowned at the list and skimmed through it until stopping on a new email from Alex.

> I need you to go deeper on Michael O'Hara. Add his ex-wife. And include Terry's history, too. Use your "special" program. Yes, I know about it. No, you're not in trouble - as long as you find me something good.

Sandy stared at the words. The "go deeper" part confirmed some of the suspicions she'd started to get at the office, but it was the part about her "special program" that was more troubling. A familiar pain began to boil up insider her. She sat back and closed her eyes, hoping to fight it off, but it didn't work.

The memories came rushing back.

On a beautiful day in July 2002, Sandy's sister, Amy, and a friend named Lauren Bishop took the short trip to Reading to watch a minor league baseball game. Just before nine P.M. that same evening, each girl called home to check in and let family members know they were going to be late getting back. They were headed to a restaurant near the field where the players hung out. Obligatory "Be careful" rejoinders were delivered and the girls said good-bye.

It was the last time either was ever heard from.

At a few minutes before noon the next day, Sandy answered a call from Lauren's mother. No, Sandy told the frantic woman, Amy wasn't home, but she would check with her mom to see where she might be. In minutes, all three were frantic. Amy, like Lauren, had not returned. Husbands and brothers were thrown into the mix, but after several hours of searching, no sign of the girls was found.

Resigned to the worst, Sandy's father called police. Detectives determined the restaurant in question was a place called Penn Street

Pub. It was more bar than restaurant, and based on interviews, it was unanimous that all in attendance had a great time, but none remembered anything specific about the two girls. As weeks became months and months became years, it was obvious they were gone forever.

Crying and alone in her room two years after the disappearance, Sandy made a promise to Amy's memory and to herself. She would do everything in her power to make sure no other family went through what theirs had. That led her to create the "special" program, a complicated and powerful search algorithm. Using all her spare time she hunted for clues and for hope, not just for Amy, but for all the missing.

It was the driving force that led her to the FBI and drove her up the ranks. The job afforded her a unique ability to pursue her promise. That Alex somehow knew about it gave her pause. She didn't want to disappoint him. She didn't want to disappoint anyone. There'd been too much of that in her life.

She opened her eyes again and sniffed away the thoughts as she refocused on her computer. A few keystrokes later the program's input form appeared. She entered various keywords related to the O'Haras and clicked *Execute*.

"OK, Alex, I'll find you something good," Sandy said to the screen. "I promise."

When Arcadia stepped into the lobby of Dukabi's building, the doorman buzzed him past the gate without a word. That was just as well. Like Elliot, Arcadia was busy contemplating the recent events surrounding Michael O'Hara. In his case, it was because they had given him renewed hope his years of patience and planning were about to pay off.

The thoughts left a smile on his face as he stepped off the elevator in front of Dukabi's suite. He tapped an entry code into the pad by the door and stepped into a foyer with three additional doors. His chose the middle and it put him in a hallway outside Dukabi's office. As he approached, the room's large faux-wood steel door was slightly ajar. Arcadia picked up the sound of a voice coming through the opening. It was Elliot's.

"... like I said, I don't trust him."

A thought he was speaking to Dukabi was erased when the big man's booming voice sounded from behind. Arcadia turned.

"Ah, Mr. Arcadia, good, you have returned. Come, let us rejoin Mr. Stevens, he awaits inside."

Dukabi was first through the opening. His sudden appearance startled Elliot and he snapped his phone shut mid-sentence. There was a slight twitch on Dukabi's face in response, and Arcadia joined his boss in eyeing Elliot with suspicion as everyone assumed their usual spots around the mahogany desk.

"What more do we know?" Dukabi said.

Elliot went first. Admittedly, the research was thorough, but Arcadia had more intimate knowledge Elliot would never find and caught the lies and omissions in the man's details about Terry. It left him convinced the little shit was up to something. When it was his turn, he ran through the information he was prepared to share about Samantha, knowing full well neither Elliot nor Dukabi would find any holes.

When he finished, Dukabi immediately changed the subject. There was no further mention of Michael or his debts. Such would come in a few hours, but Arcadia didn't mind.

What were another few hours on top of so many years?

Chapter 13

Philadelphia

Terry's annoyance from the conversation with Gabi was still with him several hours later. He'd tried to let it go during his post-workout stretching, but while the session helped his arm relax, it did little for his head. He was still struggling with it as he took a seat in front of his locker after a long shower.

Game 1 of the Series was his first priority, but he couldn't get past the need to know what his father had done. Like Gabi had said, the last thing he needed was for the problem to somehow end up in *his* lap, more so than it already had. He had worked too long and too hard to get back to the majors. The World Series was the payoff and he was not about to let Michael ruin that.

"What the hell, Dad?" he said aloud as he began to dress.

In the quiet that followed, an idea emerged.

Thomas did not frighten easily, if at all. The fire, shootings, and countless other close calls had given him a thick skin to go with his calm nature, and Marshall's situation had barely registered. Still, "barely" was enough to raise an annoying prick at the back of Thomas' head, a feeling he got when he didn't have enough information. The puzzle was definitely short a few pieces, but as fate would have it, the person on the other end of the ringing of his phone was about to help fill in some of the holes.

"This is Thomas," he said after eyeing the ID.

On the other end of the line, Terry took a deep breath and smiled. The voice was as calm as he remembered. Calling had been the right decision.

"Hello, Thomas," he said. "It's been a while."

"Mr. O'Hara, forgive me if I say I am not surprised to hear from you," Thomas said.

Terry hesitated, but quickly recovered.

"I wouldn't expect someone like you is ever surprised," he said.

"I try my best," Thomas said.

"I know. That's why I called. You're good at this stuff and I need your help."

Taking Thomas' advice, I spent most of the afternoon walking the streets of Philadelphia. Hey, in my head, it was fun. The city was full of vibrant fall colors—with an extra splash of red—and had a certain sparkle to it. I think the Phillies being in the Series had a lot to do with that. This was a great sports town, the fans here some of the best anywhere, and they were starved for a championship. It had been twenty-five years since the last one, a few more than that for the baseball team. They had a right to be excited.

In my case, I was happy because I got to air out. It felt good. I was able to refocus on doing my job, satisfied knowing Thomas was around doing his, whatever that might be. I figured he might tell me at dinner, but if not, I had convinced myself not to worry about it. The only thing I could do was umpire.

All in all, I was in a really upbeat mood as I waited in the hotel lobby for his arrival. Then it got to be seven P.M., the previously agreed to pick up time, and he had yet to do so. Twenty minutes later, he called.

"Hey, you're late," I said. "You're just stuck in traffic somewhere, right?"

"My apologies—"

I cut him off.

"Aw, man, seriously?" I said. "You're gonna stiff me *again*?"

"Unfortunately, yes," he said.

I knew him well enough to know it was pointless to protest so I just said OK and closed my phone. I trusted him more than I trusted Buck, so whatever it was that interrupted our plans must have been important. At some point, he'd tell me or not. I was used to the mystery.

I let out a heavy sigh and looked around the lobby, contemplating my next move. There was an MLB function taking place in the ballroom. I could go get some food, mingle, and act happy, or I could head up to my room and pout. When I saw Mark Rosenbaum and Suze Keebler walking past, I made my decision. Fuck pouting.

"Yo, Mark, wait up," I said as I headed toward them. "Are you guys going to the dinner?"

"We are," Mark said. "Come, join us. You remember Suze, right?"

She smiled and added a cute little wave. I put out my hand. We shook. I'd forgotten how much of a knockout she was and held her hand too long. She didn't seem to mind.

"I do," I said. "It's nice to see you again, Suze."

"Same here," she said.

Thomas' rejection faded under the glow of her smile.

Yeah, this was going to be *a lot* better than pouting.

Radnor, Pennsylvania

Thomas was travelling south on I-476. Around his car, traffic was its usual rush-hour mess. Distracted by the details of the conversation with Terry, he didn't notice he had a tail until the SUV's blue-white headlights flashed in his eyes through the TL's rearview mirror.

"What have we here?" he said aloud to the reflection.

The lights flashed again and then remained on high.

"OK, I'll play."

He did a slow count to ten then punched the gas pedal. The TL screamed in delight as it raced forward, leaving the SUV flatfooted in its wake. Thomas deftly maneuvered through the other cars around him, but the SUV's lights returned moments later as the final exit before I-95 was approaching on Thomas' right. He decided to find out more about his pursuer and pushed the TL up the ramp. This was clearly not an angry commuter.

A traffic light on the left side of the exit's fork turned green. Thomas took that option and made a hard left onto MacDade Boulevard. The SUV followed suit, but didn't reach the light before it went red. The driver ignored the signal and barreled across the intersection, eliciting a cascade of horns and screeching tires.

"All right, enough of this," Thomas said aloud.

He made a hard right into the parking lot of a shopping center, followed by a quick left toward a CVS pharmacy and another left against a *Do Not Enter* sign, leaving the TL in a spot facing MacDade. The SUV pulled into a spot in a perpendicular row, maybe fifteen feet away. The big black vehicle screamed Government Issue, but there was only one head inside, unusual for a G-car. The headlights went out and the driver-side door opened. The emerging man's body language was casual. Thomas matched it when he stepped out of the TL.

"Mr. Hillsborough," a firm voice said. "Nice driving."

For the second time in the past two hours, Thomas recognized the voice, and like the first, it had been a long time since he'd last heard this one.

"You did pretty well, too, Agent Hastings. That big thing can't be too easy to handle."

"It has its moments."

"I imagine so," Thomas said.

Special Agent Damien Hastings stepped forward and held out his hand.

"Care to explain?" Thomas said as they shook.

"Director Harris would like to speak with you."

Thomas lifted an eyebrow. Like his tone, it was something of a trademark.

"And what, his phones are out of order?"

A half of a smile settled on Damien's face.

"Nah, I was in the neighborhood and didn't have anything better to do."

"I'm sure that's it," Thomas said. "Try again."

Damien looked down for a second before bringing his eyes back to Thomas'.

"Alex thinks you might be able to help on a case."

"I'm not surprised," Thomas said.

"Yeah, that's what I told him. You never are."

Michael was glad he was alone. The person on the other end of his phone was pissed.

"I'm sorry, Michael, it sounded like you just said you *don't* have the money?"

Michael did his best to steady his breathing before replying. He might not have been calm, but he needed to at least sound it.

"Listen, I told you I'd get it and I'll get it," he said. "It's just taking longer than I thought."

The unexpected call had come several hours after he'd left Samantha's, interrupting his effort to find a solution to her rejection. Part of that effort was a bottle of Jack Daniel's, but making Arcadia go away would take a lot more than that.

"You know what? Don't bother, Michael," Arcadia said. "You had your chance, now it's my turn. I'll fix it for you. But then that's how you like it anyway, right? Find someone else to do your dirty work."

Something in the words triggered a memory. As Michael processed it, he shivered, and when he tried to talk, his throat wouldn't work.

"Did you hear me, Michael?" Arcadia said.

Michael coughed and pushed out a few words in a broken rasp of a voice.

"You don't need to do anything. I'll pay."

"Yes, Michael, you will."

Chapter 14

Redington Beach, Florida

Nik Sanchez entered his apartment for the first time in more than a week. Like most of the Tampa Bay Rays traveling party, he was in desperate need of fresh clothes and a few hours of sleep in a familiar bed. He had expected that second event would come after sex with his girlfriend, Olivia, but she was noticeably absent.

After depositing his bags in his bedroom, he made his way to the kitchen. Still no Olivia, but he did find a single red rose on the counter near a stack of mail, a hand-written note beneath it.

> Nik—I'm bored so I'm leaving. When you want me to start
> playing with your balls again, come find me. XOXO, Oli.

Nik looked around. The neatness he saw confirmed she was, in fact, gone. He muttered something nasty in Russian before dropping the note into the trash can. The rose went with it.

"Like I need this shit," he said aloud in English as he moved to the living room.

His answering machine was on a long, thin table backing the sofa. He expected to find a number far greater than the red "1" blinking at him.

"Fucking bitch," he said aloud as he pushed *Play*. "If you deleted any—"

He stopped when he heard a familiar voice. That it wasn't Oli's only made things worse.

Philadelphia

The MLB-sponsored dinner was a "Tastes of Philly" spread with hoagies, cheese steaks, and myriad other goodies. I ate too much and probably flirted with Suze too much, but it felt good and sure beat worrying about Thomas. The time passed too quickly, however, and when Mark and Suze said goodnight at a few minutes before eleven, I realized I still had an urge to call him. Call me a glutton for punishment.

"OK, partner, enough putzin' around, I'm dyin' here," I said after he answered. "Are you ready to share with me yet?"

"No."

The single word stopped me in my tracks. I closed my eyes and pinched the bridge of my nose. Me and my damn urges, I'd never learn.

"OK," I said, drawing out the letters. "That was worse than when you said nothing. What's going on?"

"I'm not at liberty to discuss that at the moment."

I scratched at my head. I'm not sure why; it didn't itch.

"Well, yeah, I kinda got that from the 'no' two seconds ago."

"You are observant," he said.

I started to respond, but it died as a simple hiss of air. After a fresh breath, I tried again.

"I get it. You're with someone and I don't want to know, right?"

"Not at all," he said. "I'll be happy to share as soon as I finish educating my friends at the FBI on how to solve a crime."

The FBI was Alex Harris' second career. His first was in the Marine Corps where he served eight years and reached a final rank of Major. His last assignment was with MARSOC, the Marines special ops unit, where he liaised with the CIA on sundry projects. It was high pressure stuff. Alex burned out after a couple of years, but not before developing an extensive network of special friends. Thomas' name was near the top of that list.

"You didn't think it might just be a case of an old friend keeping in touch?" Alex said.

He was at his desk. Thomas was on the other side. Damien Hastings was there as well.

"It seemed a little too subversive," Thomas said.

A slight chuckle escaped Alex.

"Ah, yes, that," he said. "We needed to put some miles on a new asset. Agent Hastings volunteered for the duty."

Damien made a slight bowing motion with his head.

"He did a fine job," Thomas said. "It did leave me wondering why he was following me, however."

A ripple ran across Alex's features.

"I'm sure it did," he said before pausing. "Truth is your name came up in a search. It took me a couple extra phone calls to remove it. Turns out it got us to the same place in the end."

"Which is?" Thomas said.

Alex motioned with his hands, a "here" signal.

"We could use some help," he said.

"Get in line."

Alex's brow knitted up a few stitches.

"Really, someone else needs your help?"

"You first, Mr. Director," Thomas said.

"Fair enough," Alex said.

Thomas listened for the next thirty minutes as Alex explained the work his teams had been doing on local gambling operations and the World Series and the striking coincidences that were piling up around both. Only some of it was new to Thomas and when Alex stopped, he failed to show a reaction. Alex knew he rarely did, but on this occasion found it troubling.

"Hmm, I don't like that you're just sitting there," he said. "I get the feeling there's something going on with you that I should know about."

"Eventually," Thomas said in his best flat tone.

The two men had a long history and deep mutual respect for each other, but they were no longer bound by the same rules. As Alex studied his friend and thought about that, his hand came up and he began rubbing at the stubble on his cheeks.

"Does that mean you're not interested in helping?" he said.

"That depends on your willingness to be flexible."

Alex let out some air. It wasn't a full sigh, but close.

"I can be *very* flexible," he said. "I have a consulting budget."

"Then I'm interested," Thomas said.

"I thought you didn't care about money."

"I don't," Thomas said. "But I'm going to bill you anyway."

Chapter 15

Nine years earlier
Charleston, South Carolina

Waterfront Park, bordering Charleston Harbor, was one of many picturesque vistas in the city. Encompassing more than 1,000 feet along the water, the park provided spectacular views and was an ideal location to spend a lazy afternoon or relax after work. Jonathan Darby was one of many who visited the park on a regular basis, in his case to use its paths for his daily run.

Jon was not what you would call a warrior, but did just enough to keep the middle-age bulges at bay. On this particular morning, he arrived at his usual time of six-thirty A.M. It was already hot and he decided four loops, about two miles, would be sufficient. Halfway into his third loop, on a stretch of path not more than ten feet from the water, he noticed something. He stopped and stared, trying to make out the object bobbing near the small rocks along the shore.

"Aw, man, no way," he said aloud.

He turned away and retched into the tall grass near the water's edge. He remained bent at the waist for a long time as he tried to find his breath again. After a few minutes, he took another peek at the

object and retched again. It was another five minutes before he f̶
enough strength to stand upright. This time his body didn't revolt
and he sprinted for the pay-phones in the parking lot.

"Nine-one-one?" he said in a shout after dropping a quarter into
the nearest one. "Yeah, there's a body in the harbor. Send someone
quick."

Violent crimes were not unusual in Charleston. The city ran
above the national average in most categories, including murder.
Police quickly compiled a description of the body Jon found and
circulated it to the media: Caucasian female, mid-to-late twenties,
medium-length blonde hair, wearing white sneakers, cut-off denim
shorts, and a Charleston RiverDogs baseball jersey.

The RiverDogs were Charleston's latest minor league baseball
team and had played a game the night before the discovery. Police
hoped someone at the game might know something and two days
later the body was identified: Maureen Sullivan, age twenty-six,
formerly of Heathwood, a suburb north of downtown, now living in
an apartment near the park.

Maureen had been at the game with two girlfriends. All three
traveled together to a bar afterward, but Maureen stayed longer than
the other two. Her apartment wasn't far and she told the girlfriends
she'd walk home. A half-hour after the friends left, a handsome man
began chatting with Maureen. When they left together twenty
minutes later, no one noticed the man's slight limp. In fact, no one
noticed anything at all.

Soon after, Maureen was dead.

Chapter 16

The first thing on the agenda was a group breakfast in the hotel ballroom. I wasn't big on forced social gatherings, but being hungry I attended without complaint. When I arrived I found Art Mahaffey (no, not the old Philadelphia Phillies ballplayer, but a distant cousin), Jimmy Banks, and Kirk Unger at a table near the front of the room. They greeted me with back pats and hand shakes and a few minutes of playful abuse.

"We seem to be short a few bodies," I said after settling into an empty chair. "Where are the other guys?"

"Bartolo is in the john and we haven't seen Chris yet," Jimmy said.

Bartolo was Bartolo Casaba, and Chris was Chris Pike, the final members of our six-man crew. With Wil Clemmons gone, Chris was senior man and most likely to be pissed about not being chief. I was about to ask if anyone knew what kind of mood he might be in when a large hand gripped my shoulder.

"Marshall Connors, cómo está, Amigo?"

It was Bartolo, Bart to most. His face was consumed by a huge smile as per usual and I stood to greet him. He planted a kiss on each cheek before engulfing me in a massive hug.

"I'm fine, big man, and you?" I said after he released me.

"I'm great," he said in Spanish.

I first met Bart in the minors and we'd worked on the same crew the past two seasons, rooming together on the road. In that time I don't think I'd ever seen him anything but happy. His accent and frequent use of Spanish only added to his overall joyful outlook on life. In short, he was fun to be around.

"You two should get a room," another voice said from behind us.

It was Chris Pike. I had my answer as to his mood, but Bart tried to intercept it.

"Hola, Chris," he said looking past me. "How are you, my friend?"

"I'm OK, Senõr," Pike said in a cold tone.

He nodded at the other guys as he moved to an empty seat on the far side of the table.

"Hey, Chris," I said after he sat. "Good to see you again."

I leaned across and offered my hand. He took it, but applied extra pressure.

"Connors," he said with a blank expression.

An awkward silence descended over the table, but it didn't last long thanks to a thumping noise coming from the room's sound system. Mark Rosenbaum had taken up station at a podium at the front of the room. He took the next few minutes to give a short speech in which he thanked everyone for their hard work during the season and wished all good luck during the Series.

As soon as he was finished, the air quickly filled with noise as the individual conversations resumed. You could almost feel the positive energy ramping up. Mark had a way of doing that, but at my table, a different kind of energy was building.

"So, Connors," Pike said, his tone still prickly. "I'm surprised you didn't run up there and kiss his ass, seeing as how he's breaking the rules for you."

I didn't have to respond. The other guys jumped all over him.

"Yo, man, don't be such a jerk," Kirk said. "Everyone else is OK with this."

"Yeah," Jimmie said. "You're fuckin' with my good mood, so knock it off."

I was happy for the interventions, but Pike's expression didn't change. After about twenty minutes, the guys started to head out, eventually leaving him and me as the last two at the table.

"Listen up," he said under his breath. "I don't know how you pulled it off, but if you think I'm going to be happy about this shit, you're wrong. I should be chief, *not you*. You shouldn't even be working these games. I'll do my job, but you need to stay the fuck outta my way."

When he stormed off, Mark noticed and joined me at the table.

"OK, what was *that*?" he said.

"Nothing," I said.

He gave me a skeptical eye.

"Sure looked like something."

"Yeah, well, just ignore him, that's what I'm going to do."

Springfield

Samantha's heart nearly exploded when she heard her son's voice on the phone. It had been too long since they'd last spoken. She couldn't remember why, but it suddenly didn't matter.

"Oh, Terry, honey," she said as tears filled her eyes. "I'm so glad you called."

"Mom, *are you crying?*" Terry said with phony disgust. "You know there's no crying in baseball. What the heck?"

Samantha chuckled.

"Oh, that's right, Coach Dugan, I forgot. No crying in baseball."

A League of Their Own had always been a shared favorite movie.

"Just don't let it happen again," Terry said in a bad imitation of Tom Hanks' character.

They both laughed before an awkward silence set in. It was as if someone had thrown a blanket over the conversation, momentarily suffocating it. Terry was first to kick the cover loose.

"I'm sorry I haven't called," he said, his tone solemn.

"Oh, stop," Samantha said. "You've been busy with your job. I understand."

She didn't, not really, but it was the kind of thing a mother said.

"No excuse, Mom, I'm an ass."

"Now that's enough of that," Samantha said. "No one's an ass. Well, your father is—"

She cut herself off.

"Yeah, he is," Terry said. "Gabi Loeb came to see me. What's going on?"

It was subtle, but Samantha caught an increased anger in his voice. She pushed past it and told him about the conversation with Michael. When she was finished, Terry's anger was no longer faint.

"What do you mean you're *not* going to give him any money?"

Samantha had wanted to stay above the anger riptide, but it caught hold of her, too.

"Why would I?" she said, the edge sharp. "I want no part of whatever he's gotten into. I don't want you involved either."

"It's too late for that," Terry said. "I know about it now. I *am* involved."

"But—"

"No, Mom, don't you see?" Terry said, cutting her off. "He's going to be desperate and Michael O'Hara and desperate *do not mix*. Shit, who knows what he might do now."

Samantha let the words sink in. Her son was right. She hadn't thought through the refusal, it had been a reflex inspired by hatred.

"Oh, my, Terry, I'm so sorry," she said as she began to cry again.

The sharp hiss of a sigh hit her ear.

"Listen, Mom, just forget about it, OK?" Terry said. "I'm gonna take care of it."

It took a few seconds before the words registered. Samantha sniffed loudly, momentarily halting the flow of tears.

"What do you mean *you're* going to take care of it? No, Terry, I don't want—"

"*I'm dealing with it, OK.* Just drop it."

The sharp rebuke regenerated the tears. Samantha just let them run their course. It was close to thirty seconds before Terry's voice came back to her ears.

"I'm sorry, I'm not mad at you," he said. "I'm the one who screwed everything up."

"Stop that," Samantha said. "That was a long time ago. It wasn't your fault. Your father and I are the ones to blame."

Terry agreed with that, but let it go. He knew now was not the time, it would only make matters worse, and he took a couple of deep breaths to regroup. The anger receded.

"OK, Mom, I gotta go. Stay out of it and I'll see you soon. I love you."

"I love you—"

A click cut her off and opened the flood gates to a flow that lasted close to an hour. When it finally ended, an idea had worked its way through the pain. Samantha picked up the phone again and punched in a number. A pleasant voice hit her ear.

"Four Seasons Hotel, how may I direct your call?"

Chapter 17

Philadelphia

Crushed under the weight of Arcadia's threat, Michael had been unable to sleep. A bad hangover from the whiskey only added to his discomfort. He couldn't shake the frightening feeling that had started during the call, that there was more to Arcadia, but he still couldn't figure it out, and the more he thought about it, the deeper the muck seemed to get. Before he got completely submerged, he was interrupted when his phone began to blare out its ringtone for unknown callers, a Van Halen tune, circa David Lee Roth.

"Who the fuck is this?" he said after punching the speaker button.

"I am a friend of your son," a calm voice said.

The mention of Terry served only to increase Michael's annoyance and anger. He picked up the phone.

"What the fuck is that supposed to mean?" he said. "Is this some kinda game?"

The aggressiveness rolled off of Thomas without leaving a mark.

"I can assure you, Mr. O'Hara, this is no game," he said. "Terry thought I might be able to help with your problems."

Considering Michael's "problems" weren't public knowledge, the mention of it from this stranger further exacerbated his fragile state.

"How do you know about my business? *Who is this?*"

The aggressiveness had given way to fear.

"My name is Thomas Hillsborough. As I said, your son has asked me to help. To do that, I'm going to need to know exactly what you've done."

Michael sat back and stared at the phone as the questions raced through his head. Who is Thomas Hillsborough and how does he know Terry? And how does he know about my debt? Is this another of Dukabi's goons? *What the fuck is going on?* No answers came and when he spoke again his voice had a thick layer of confusion on top of the fear.

"Why would… why should I tell you?" he said. "Why should I *trust* you?"

"Fair questions," Thomas said. "The answer is that you have no reason *not* to do so. I assure you, I am no threat, but if you don't start being honest with me that will not last."

I was determined not to let Pike get to me as I headed to the lobby to wait for the shuttle to the ballpark. I got some help doing that when Suze intercepted me on the sidewalk just as the van pulled in. Some of last night's flirtations jumped into my head as she handed me a large envelope.

"Hi, Marshall, here's your itinerary," she said through a big smile. "My cell number is in there. Call me right away if I missed anything."

I gave her a confused look.

"I thought we had an intern for this stuff?" I said.

"We do," she said. "But Mark said it would be OK if I did it instead."

I wasn't quite sure what to make of that, but I decided not to argue. It would appear I wasn't so rusty in the courting process after all.

"Works for me," I said. "Thanks, Suze. I'll, uh, I'll be sure to call."

"I'd like that very much."

She gave me a quick peck on the cheek and moved away. I stood there, lost, trying to figure out if I'd just asked her out—and if she'd just said yes. When I remembered how to walk, I bounded up the van steps. Bart was in the first row and I slid in next to him.

"Cute girl," he said.

"Huh? Oh, yeah, definitely," I said.

"You ever gonna ask her out?"

I looked out the window then back to Bart.

"I think I just did."

The Four Seasons operator recorded the information from Samantha's call and put the slip of paper into a small white envelope. The envelope was slid into a time punch and *9:47 A.M.* appeared at the upper left-hand corner along with the date. The operator typed the room number into a form on her computer screen and dropped the envelope into a metal basket on the counter behind her. Within seconds the hotel's automated phone system placed a call to Marshall's room to notify him he had a message.

It would be a few hours before he'd find it.

The wait had frayed what was left of Michael's nerves. When the doorbell sounded, he simply opened the door and nodded.

"Hillsborough?" he said in a low voice.

Michael's normal modus operandi in such a situation would be to size up his opponent as soon as possible. In this case, it took all of about three seconds for him to realize he was seriously overmatched and he didn't even bother with any false bravado. He just moved aside and let Thomas in.

"You want a drink or somethin'?" he said in a dead voice.

"It would appear you've had plenty for both of us," Thomas said.

Michael shrugged and poured himself another shot anyway.

"So, whataya wanna know?" he said after downing it.

When he finished fifteen minutes later, Thomas' face was not quite empty. That Michael's story had produced a slight frown spoke volumes.

"Your son was correct," he said. "You have a very serious problem."

Thomas did as well. A lot of holes had been filled in, but a gaping new one existed. He did not trust Michael. Something about the story or the story-telling did not match what he'd learned on his own several days prior. He tucked the concern away before speaking again.

"It will be best if you stay out of sight."

Michael reacted with an expression of pain mixed with confusion.

"Whataya mean? I can't just sit here," he said. "These guys might go after my son."

"He's not the one you should be worried about."

Chapter 18

Atlantic City, New Jersey

There was a heavy knock on the door and one of Mario Pastelli's "assistants" poked his big head through the opening. Mario held up a finger for the man to wait.

"Hang on a sec," he said into his cell phone; then to the man at the door. "What?"

"Stevens is here."

"Let him in," Mario said.

The other man disappeared and Mario returned his attention to the phone.

"I'll let you know what he says," he said into the mouthpiece. "I'm sure it'll be good."

He disconnected and seconds later Elliot waddled into the office. As usual, he was dressed in an array of colors and patterns, none of which matched. Mario simply shook his head at the sight, having long since given up trying to figure out Elliot's wardrobe.

"You're early," he said. "I'm still printing Dukabi's lists."

The lists were filled with data compiled over the weekend for various people of interest for Dukabi, card players who would soon be invited to one of the man's private games. Elliot made the trek to A.C. every week to collect the data. It was *never* delivered other than by hand.

"That's OK," he said. "I thought maybe we could talk more about my idea."

Mario shook his head again. He had already figured as much.

"You sure you wanna go through with this?" he said. "I mean, if some of that shit you turned up is true, I'm not thinking you're gonna wanna fuck with this guy."

Elliot scoffed at the warning.

"What? Why?" he said. "When I tell him what I know there's no way he won't play ball."

Mario's head was still shaking and a corner of his lips curled into a sort-of-half-smile.

"Is that what you think?" he said.

"Yeah, that's what I think," Elliot said. "Besides, I ain't afraid a him."

Mario's head stopped moving and the grin disappeared.

"You should be."

Philadelphia

The only light in Dukabi's office was from an antique table lamp resting on the corner of the mahogany desk. He was alone, having sent his boys out for their weekly duties. It had been another successful weekend of play and Dukabi was making notes in a journal. Along with the data from Mario, the notes regarding game-play tendencies and habits allowed Dukabi to literally stack the deck against his guests and manipulate the games in a manner best suited in his favor.

After a final notation, he closed the journal and replaced the cap on the Montblanc Meisterstück solitaire pen he'd been using, a gift from one of his regulars, a German banker, and placed both in the top drawer of the desk. He locked the drawer and reached over and pulled the chain on the lamp, instantly painting the room black.

He took a deep breath and reclined. The chair hissed out an approval as he closed his eyes and began to stretch the large muscles in his neck. Several dull pops drifted up into the silence as the vertebrae reacted to the movements. Relaxed, he let his thoughts drift to Elliot and the odd reaction from the little man prior to last night's meeting. It had accentuated a long-brewing suspicion that he was up to something.

Before Dukabi could get too far into the analysis, a soft chirping noise interrupted. He slowly opened his eyes and sat forward to pick up his cell phone. Few had access to the line, and until that moment, the name appearing on the caller ID was not thought to be one of them. Based on experience, however, Dukabi was not entirely surprised that was no longer the case. Something that might have been fear settled onto his features, and it was another two rings before he answered.

"You and I need to talk," a familiarly calm voice said into his ear.

Several beads of sweat erupted on Dukabi's temple.

"Yes, I imagine so."

The first order of business at the ballpark was a walk-through of the ground rules. Unlike what we would face in Tampa, the layout at Citizens Bank Park was fairly straight-forward and we finished quickly. Next up was a lightly attended press session designed to give out background info on the crew. It was going fine, meaning quickly and uneventfully, until a reporter, Collin George from the Philadelphia *Daily News*, tossed a bottle of gasoline onto the smoldering embers otherwise known as Chris Pike.

"Oh, hey, Chris, one last question," Collin said. "With Clemmons out, why aren't you crew chief? Aren't you senior man now?"

Pike's expression went back to the glower he'd shown me at breakfast, but I wasn't the only one to notice this time. The other reporters all perked up like dogs at treat time. There's nothing like a good controversy to inspire the journalistic sharks. A few began eyeing me, but I refrained from tossing any chum into the water. I was determined to stick to my promise of not getting sucked into Pike's nastiness. Not that it stopped him, of course.

"I *am* senior man," he said. "I have no idea what happened. Connors isn't even supposed to be working this series. Maybe you should ask Rosenbaum why he decided to break the rules. I'd love to hear the reason."

Admittedly, I'd had a similar thought when Buck first told me I was working the Series, but I'd assumed Mark had consulted with our union guys or whoever and everyone was OK with it. It was a non-issue as far as I was concerned—well, it had been. Thankfully, the MLB press liaison stepped in and applied a deft spin to it.

"Seniority doesn't necessarily equate to specific assignments, and this one was complicated by the extenuating circumstances of Mr. Clemmons' sudden illness," he said. "There's certainly nothing nefarious taking place. Anyway, that's all the time we have. Bios for the crew are available on the table on your way out."

There were grumbles from some of the writers, but they all began to slowly filter out of the room. Pike looked like he wanted to say something else, but the sight of Buck moving toward us stopped him. I hadn't even noticed Buck's presence until then, but he quickly made up for it. As soon as the room was free of outsiders, he eyed each of us closely. He ended up focused on Pike.

"Y'all are supposed to be a team," he said in a stern tone. "That includes you, Chris. If you have a problem workin' with these boys, I'm sure we can find someone to fill the hole."

Pike's face worked through a series of ticks and twitches before he responded.

"I'm sure you can," he said in a sharp tone before stalking out.

A few awkward seconds and accompanying shrugs later, the other guys started to wander out as well. When I stood to leave, Buck motioned for me to hold back.

"Son, I need to apologize," he said after we were alone. "I was afraid something like this would happen when I told Mark you had to be chief."

A popcorn-kernel of a headache that had been lingering at the back of my head since breakfast exploded like it was in a microwave. I started to get the feeling some of the stuff going on around me wasn't so unrelated. I flashed on Thomas before refocusing on Buck.

"Uh, Buck," I said. "What are you talking about? What do you mean you *told* Mark I had to be chief? Why would you have to tell him something like that?"

He winced, as if he was in pain, and the memory of his laboring stride in Florida ran across my mind. Something was very wrong here.

"Buck, are you OK?" I said with concern, but no longer only for my assignment.

He took a few deep breaths and seemed to recover.

"It's not what you think," he said. "Mark asked for my opinion and I gave it. That's all."

I studied him closely for a few seconds. That *wasn't* all, but I decided to stop pushing. Whatever was going on was bigger than Buck. It was time to take my concerns to a higher authority.

"OK, old man, if you say so," I said after a loud sigh.

He nodded as a forced smile filled his face.

"I say so," he said. "You're the chief and no one needs to know any more than that."

Chapter 19

Philadelphia

Thomas was moving east along Market Street, walking quickly through the early-afternoon crowds, but taking note of every face around him. Experience had taught him to never underestimate anyone. He was probably being overly cautious, but despite the genuine fear Michael O'Hara had displayed, Thomas believed him to be something other than a victim.

As he crossed 11th Street, he pulled out his phone. Alex answered on the second ring.

"We need to talk," Thomas said. "This thing has a few more tentacles than first thought."

"Why do I get the feeling I'm not going to like that?" Alex said.

"That's not for me to say."

"OK, what do you want to say and when?" Alex said.

"I have an errand to run first," Thomas said. "I'll check in later."

He ended the call without waiting for Alex's reply and switched his Blackberry to its data function. A couple of taps on the screen opened a layout of Dukabi's penthouse. An apartment took up three-quarters of the space. The rest was filled by several offices and the poker room. The security system wasn't complex, but Thomas wouldn't be breaking in, so he didn't spend any time on it. After mentally recording the schematic he stowed the phone.

One minute and thirty seconds later, he was standing in front of Dukabi's building. His face didn't reveal it, but he was dealing with a range of emotions as he stared up at the structure. Like Dukabi's penthouse, anger was at the top.

It was time to remind the big man of the reason for the beads of sweat.

I didn't know about the rest of the guys, but I was glad when Pike didn't sit with us at lunch. My conversation with Buck had been troubling enough. I didn't need Pike's shit adding to it. That small victory continued when he also skipped our next chore, something I called the mud bath. Baseballs out of the box had a slippery shine to them. We applied a mud, Blackburne's Baseball Rubbing Mud, a canned muck from a mostly-secret place in New Jersey, to get rid of it. The rule-mandated process can be messy and tedious, but we filled the time with storytelling. Without Pike, the edge was gone and it was nice to smile for a little while.

After finishing the rubdown, but before we headed back to the hotel, Thomas called me. The conversation was short and mostly one-sided. I was getting used to that from him.

"I still owe you a recap, but I thought you'd like to know your description of Mr. O'Hara was very accurate," he said. "Some of the stories you've shared make a lot more sense."

He was talking about Michael and stories I'd shared back in college, about my time around the O'Hara family. I wasn't surprised he still remembered. He had an amazing attention to and retention of details. Nothing ever seemed to get past him. The CIA must have loved him for it. I know it made me feel pretty lucky to have him on my side. If nothing else, it tempered some of the disappointment of being totally in the dark about whatever the hell he was working on.

Eventually I knew I'd get my answers.

At just after five P.M., Dukabi summoned Arcadia and Elliot to his apartment, a rare request. He was sitting on a large sofa in the living room and motioned the two men into matching armchairs in front. Arcadia recognized the implications of the setting. Elliot did not. The same held true for the verbal message that followed.

"Gentlemen, games have been cancelled indefinitely," Dukabi said.

Arcadia didn't react, but Elliot made a face and couldn't stop himself from talking.

"Yo, boss, you never cancel," he said leaning forward in his chair. "What's going on?"

Dukabi's eyes narrowed.

"Mr. Stevens, the reasons are of no concern to you," he said in a booming voice.

Arcadia was sure he heard several of the china pieces on the shelves behind the sofa rattle. Elliot either didn't notice or was too stupid to understand what it meant.

"Geez, sorry I asked," he said in a smart-assed tone.

In a flash, faster than Arcadia would have imagined, Dukabi shot from the sofa and took hold of Elliot's neck. A split-second later, the massive hand wrenched Elliot out of the chair.

"Never question me again," Dukabi said in a low growl as Elliot's feet left the ground.

Elliot's face began to turn red. Three, four, five seconds passed until, with the flick of a wrist, Dukabi sent him sprawling across the freshly polished hardwood toward the room's antique double doors. Elliot coughed several times before rolling over and pushing himself to his feet.

"Go now, before I lose my temper," Dukabi said.

Arcadia thought *"before?"* but kept it to himself as Elliot fumbled with the doorknob for several seconds before making his escape. When he was out of sight, Dukabi turned.

"Mr. Arcadia, I am no longer interested in pursuing collections against Mr. O'Hara. You are to terminate all such activities immediately."

Arcadia's brow knitted up, but he quickly erased the frown. He would not make the same mistake as Elliot and chose his next words very carefully.

"Is there something I should know?" he said in an even tone.

"There is not," Dukabi said with a severe glance.

He moved back to the sofa and sat before taking a few seconds to rearrange several pillows on either side of the cushion on which he'd landed. Arcadia used the time to contemplate the sudden change. While unexpected, it was more interesting because of the added complications it created, but his search for a response was interrupted when Dukabi looked up. The expression was one Arcadia had never seen.

"Now, before you go, there is another matter," he said before pausing to wipe at his slacks.

Arcadia waited patiently.

"I would like you to eliminate Mr. Stevens. He has become *tiresome.*"

Arcadia had to work hard not to react. This command was a pleasant and useful surprise.

"I'll take care of it."

"Marshall Connors, please," Samantha said into her phone.

"May I have the room number?" a pleasant-sounding voice said in reply.

A look of frustration quickly filled Samantha's face.

"I don't have the room number," she said; then after a pause. "My name is Samantha O'Hara. I left a message this morning. Do you know if it was delivered?"

"I'll check, ma'am, hold please."

The line filled with music, Bach or Beethoven, Samantha could never tell the difference, and it was a long minute before the hotel operator's voice returned.

"Yes, ma'am, your earlier message was delivered. Would you care to leave another?"

~*~*~*~*~*~*~

Determined to start getting some answers, I hustled off the shuttle as soon as it pulled to a stop in front of the hotel. Inside, I found Jennifer working the front desk again. The Phillies jersey had been replaced by a regular-looking hotel uniform. She still looked pretty good.

"Hello, Mr. Connors," she said when I reached her. "May I help you with something?"

Some of the flirt was still in her tone.

"Hello to you, Ms. Jennifer," I said. "What happened, you get traded?"

I motioned to her outfit.

She faked a frown.

"I spilled some coffee on it," she said. "I'm a klutz."

"Not that I remember," I said. "But I understand."

"Thank you," she said with her smile back in place. "Now, what can I do for you?"

"I need to page someone," I said.

I gave her Mark's information before pointing to the lounge.

"I'll be right there," I said.

She nodded and I started to move away, but she called out to stop me.

"Oh, Mr. Connors, hold on a second, you have a message," she said. "Wait, sorry, you have *three*. It seems you are Mr. Popular."

She handed me several small envelopes held together with a rubberband.

"I try," I said.

"I'll bet you do."

OK, she was definitely flirting again, but I managed to break free from it. A few seconds later I landed in a chair at the hotel's lobby bar. I had no idea how long it might take for Mark to respond to the page. I didn't even know if he was in the hotel, but I was determined to wait it out. I had no plans for the evening other than getting some answers.

I let my eyes fall to the stack of messages. Each envelope had my name, room number, and a time printed on the front. One was from the morning, just after I'd left for the field, and the other two were more recent. A waitress came by and I asked for a glass of water as I pulled out the first message. It was from Samantha O'Hara. I couldn't remember the last time I'd spoken to her, but for some reason, wasn't surprised to see she'd called, maybe because it seemed to fit with everything else going on the past few days.

I shrugged it off and moved on to the second. It was also fro Samantha, called in a couple of minutes after five. OK, two calls from her in the same day *didn't* fit, unless maybe she was calling about Terry. I sat back and looked around the lobby. Still no Mark, but a new headache had started to work in from the edges of my brain as I debated calling Samantha back.

The waitress came by to pour a refill of my water. I asked if she had any Advil. Surprisingly, she did, and I downed the pills as I moved on to the third note. The nasty paper cut I got as I opened the envelope should have been a warning to stop, but I blew past it and pulled out the slip of paper. All thoughts of Samantha—and Mark—immediately disappeared.

"What the fuck?" I said aloud as I jumped out of my chair.

My leg banged into the table and the glass of water went flying. An old dude sitting next to me took a direct hit, but I ignored his angry shouts as I ran for the front desk. Jennifer was assisting another oldster, a female, but I interrupted them mid-sentence.

"Hey, is this some kinda joke?" I said.

Jennifer's face scrunched into a frown as the old woman made a "Harrumph" noise.

"I'm sorry, Mr. Connors," Jennifer said. "Just let me finish—"

"Fuck that," I said, shaking the note at her. "I need to know where this came from."

The elderly gal made a tut-tut sound and her face morphed into an expression usually reserved for use when stepping in dog shit, but I stayed focused on Jennifer as she read the note.

"Oh, my God," she said.

"Yeah, that's what I was thinking. Go get your manager, *now*."

Chapter 20

Philadelphia

Mark, Gabi, and I were in a small conference room down the hall from the front desk. The looks on their faces were close to mine. Mark's might have been a touch or two darker, but neither had said much of anything after reading the note. At this point, we seemed to be in a shared state of confusion.

"You got any ideas?" Mark said to Gabi.

"Not yet," Gabi said.

He was about to say something else when we were interrupted by a knock on the door. Two men and a woman entered. The older of the men was dressed in a black Brooks Brothers suit. I'm not sure why, but I instantly disliked him; maybe because he remained standing near the window as the others joined us at the table.

"My name is Gordon Drucker," he said in a horribly phony English accent. "I am the manager on duty this evening."

"Mr. Drucker," Mark said as he stood. "Mark Rosenbaum, MLB commissioner."

They shook hands. Drucker then motioned to the table, a flimsy limp-arm kind of movement. I think I may have rolled my eyes.

"This young man is Yong Lee, my security chief, and this is Karen Hall, one of our phone operators. Ms. Hall took the message."

Mark introduced Gabi and me. His gestures as he said our names were a lot firmer than Drucker's had been. We exchanged quick handshakes with Lee and Karen, but ignored Drucker.

"Yes, well, the authorities will be here presently," he said. "Now if you will excuse me, I have *guests* to attend to."

Apparently he'd forgotten that Mark, Gabi, and I *were* guests, but we ignored the insult. He was leaving. It was a fair trade. A few seconds later, another man and woman came through the door. Their blue jackets gave us their basic identities, FBI. The man filled in the details.

"Good evening, everyone," he said in a strong tone. "I am Special Agent Hastings. This is Special Agent Hood. I apologize for our delay getting here."

I hadn't realized there'd been a delay, but I took Hastings' word for it. He seemed to be the leader of the two and looked like he knew what he was doing. Given the circumstances, that was good enough for me.

"So, tell us about this message," he said as he sat at the head of the table.

I handed him the note.

> Time: 6:02 PM
> From: Peter Arcadia, no return number
> Message: Her death will be on your hands.

Hastings' posture noticeably changed. Welcome to my world, I thought, as we waited for his response. It came in a question to Karen.

"And you took the call?" he said.

"Yes," she said in a meek voice.

She looked seriously upset, but Lee came to her rescue.

"I can provide you with the call records," he said. "Our system records all incoming calls. As best as I can tell, the caller used a masked source. Caller ID revealed nothing."

"You've reviewed the recording?" Hastings said.

"Yes, I felt it prudent to do so," Lee said.

Hastings nodded and made a note in a small pad he was holding.

"OK," he said. "We'll want the originals when we're done here."

Lee nodded as Hastings turned to Karen again.

"Ms. Hall, we'd like to ask you a few questions."

"OK," she said.

"Was the caller a man or woman?"

The question came from Agent Hood. Her tone was direct but not heavy.

"A man," Karen said.

"Outside of the message, what else did he say?"

Karen raised herself more upright in the chair and when she spoke again her voice was much more audible. Apparently she'd found some strength from Hood's attitude.

"At first he asked for Mr. Connors, but I said I needed a room number. That's our policy. You can't just call in and randomly ask for someone. He said I should take the message. We try not to do that, too many chances for mistakes, so I said he should leave a voice message, but he insisted I take it."

"After the man gave you the message, what did you think?" Hood said.

"I thought it was a joke. I mean, who leaves that kind of message? And he seemed calm, almost too calm really, if you know what I mean."

She paused as Hood made some notes in her pad. The rest of us stayed quiet.

"Go on, Karen, what else happened?" Hastings said.

The two agents had a very smooth methodology. The way they played off of each other told me they'd done this a few times before. The furtive glances I'd noticed passing between them also led me to think they might be more than just working partners, but I didn't dwell on that.

"I asked him to repeat the message and he did," Karen said. "I didn't totally believe he was for real and I said 'Are you serious?' and he said 'Oh, yes, very.' It was *scary*."

She bobbled her next breath and as she recovered, folded her arms across her chest. It was obvious she was finished. Everyone stayed quiet after that, as if trying to process what we'd just heard. I didn't get very far. It still didn't make any sense.

"Mr. Lee, Ms. Hall, can you accompany Agent Hood to retrieve the recording?" Hastings said after a few seconds. "Anything you can tell her about the phone system will be helpful."

Hood stood and led Lee and Karen out of the room. Hastings stayed long enough to ask me a few questions before heading out to get statements from the rest of the hotel staff on duty. His mannerisms reminded me a lot of Thomas and I began to wonder if they knew each other, but again, I didn't dwell on the thought. I was trying to figure out how to bring up the original reason I'd been looking for Mark.

"So, uh, not that this isn't fucked up enough," I said. "But there's something else I need to ask you guys... well, maybe just Mark."

Both turned to me.

"Why did Buck tell you to make me crew chief?"

Mark's face got darker than it had been after first reading the note. Gabi's was more, well, *blank* for lack of a better word. I took it to mean he had no idea what I was talking about. I wasn't sure if that was good or bad, but I was leaning toward the latter, especially after Mark finally answered.

"Don't worry about it," he said in an edgy tone. "Just do your job."

Thomas arrived exactly twelve minutes later. He must have been close by because the hotel was at least thirty-five minutes from his home at his driving speed, but I didn't ask. I was just glad to see him. We were sitting on facing sofas in the lobby. I hadn't eaten in a while and my headache was about a hundred times worse than earlier.

"Do you have the note," he said.

I handed him a copy. Hastings had taken the original.

"Odd," he said before looking up. "And this name?"

I slowly shook my head.

"No idea," I said.

He nodded slightly.

"I can't imagine the threat is on your mother. Do you have a significant other you haven't told me about?"

I flashed on Suze and Jennifer and a few others I'd flirted with in the past month, but none would be close to such a classification.

"Dude, you know more about me than I do. What do you think?"

"Yes, true," he said with a raised eyebrow; then after a pause. "I need to visit with Agent Hastings."

The way he said it told me I'd been right earlier, that they knew each other. Score one for me.

"You do that," I said. "I'm going to go find some food and then lie down somewhere. After that I may just sneak off to someplace warm because to be honest with you I kinda wish I was still on vacation."

"I understand," Thomas said as we stood. "This does change things a bit."

"Ya think?"

Chapter 21

Wednesday, October 22, 2008
The day of Game 1 of the World Series
Philadelphia

It was close to one A.M. by the time Thomas and I had finally retreated to my suite. In the thirty or so minutes after that, I ended up slouched down on a sofa and he landed in an armchair across from me. His eyes were closed, but he wasn't sleeping.

"Can I ask you something?" I said.

"You may," he said without opening his eyes.

"Hastings didn't seem surprised by anything I told him. Is that what you've been doing the past few days, you know, when you said you were educating them? Did he already know?"

"It's an active case, Marshall. I can't discuss specifics with you."

I sat up. He still hadn't moved.

"OK, that's... there's... what the fuck, Thomas? What's going on?"

His eyes slowly opened and he pushed himself into a more upright position.

"The FBI has retained my services to assist with a situation that now includes your note."

"Wait, *now* includes it?"

His eyebrow shrugged.

"What?" I said. "You're the one that got all freaked out when I got this gig. And now I get this crazy-assed threat or whatever the hell it is. I have no idea what any of it means and no one is telling me shit. Forgive me if I'm a little out of whack here."

His face returned to its normal nothingness. I did my best not to scream at him.

"Very well," he said in the familiar flat tone. "We believe the threat is related to your assignment. How so or how much so, we don't yet know."

"And what is all that related to?" I said. "You *will* tell me when you figure it out, right?"

"I will," he said.

When he closed his eyes and let his head fall back in the chair again, I knew that was all I was going to get out of him. I stood.

"I'm guessing you'll, uh, be slipping out unnoticed in the morning?" I said as I headed for my bedroom.

"Yes," he said without moving.

I sighed and turned away.

"You're still a dick, ya know?" I said over my shoulder.

"Goodnight, Marshall."

Terry arrived at the ballpark just before six A.M. The night watchman was shocked to see one of the players so early, especially this one.

"Shouldn't you be resting?" the guard said after Terry's black Porsche stopped at the gate.

"Hey, how am I supposed to sleep?" Terry said. "It's the World Series."

The guard nodded as he pushed a button to open the gate.

"That it is," he said through a smile. "Good luck, Terry."

Terry returned the smile and pulled through into the empty lot. After parking in a spot in the front row he killed the engine and stepped out. The sunrise hadn't yet erased the darkness of the night, but Terry didn't mind. He'd spent a lot of his adult life in the dark especially during the long journey back to the majors. He was comfortable there.

"Long time, Amigo," a voice said from somewhere over his shoulder.

He turned as a man stepped out of the shadows at the far side of the Porsche. Recognition came quickly.

"It has been," Terry said. "You lost or somethin'?"

"Most of the time, yes," Nik Sanchez said as he extended his hand.

Terry took it. After the shake, he stepped back to size up his old friend.

"You OK?" he said. "You look like shit."

Nik looked away from Terry's gaze for a second. When he turned back, there was something in his eyes.

"I got a call last night," he said. "It was from AJ."

Terry's eyes got wider and he backed off a few steps.

"Tell me you're kidding," he said.

"I wish I was."

~*~*~*~*~*~*~

As expected, Thomas was gone by the time I rolled out of bed a little after seven. He had been kind enough to set the coffeemaker in the kitchenette and a fresh pot awaited me. I silently thanked him for the java as I took a seat at the counter and poured a cup. Score an A-plus for the hotel because it was the best coffee I think I'd ever tasted. How much of that was because I was still distracted was uncertain, but I savored every drop anyway.

I was happy for another small victory. As I flipped through the morning paper, I built on that and made a promise to myself to keep finding such. Today was the first day of the World Series. I was the lead umpire. There was nothing I could do about all the crap off the field. I needed to stay—no, *get* and then stay focused on my job and my job alone. Thomas and the FBI could deal with the other stuff.

I was pretty sure I was safe. I had a good feeling Thomas would keep it that way.

That's all I could ask.

~*~*~*~*~*~*~

at the FBI building by seven-fifteen. It was earlier
~~~~ ~~~~~~, out he wasn't alone. He was seated at the head of a
table in a large conference room down the hall from his office. There
were eight others with him, including Damien and Sandy. There was
a lot of work to be done. The threat against Marshall had
complicated things, how much so remained to be seen.

"Good morning, people," Alex said. "Thanks for coming in
early. I've read Agent Hastings' recap of last night's events. What
I'd like now are some opinions on what we should do about it. Who
wants to start?"

Sandy Hood was first to respond.

"I did a quick search, but nothing came up in any police records
for this Peter Arcadia. I'm expanding the search, but I've been
getting a feeling the name might be bogus. None of the MLB people
recognized it, including Connors."

Alex nodded and turned to Damien.

"And what about you, Agent Hastings, you got anything new for
me?"

"Nothing that wasn't in my report," he said. "Connors is very
single at the moment. On the outside chance this threat is on his
mother, we set up a casual watch. She's in Europe, vacationing, but I
seriously doubt she is the female in question."

"Does Mr. Hillsborough concur?" Alex said.

"He does."

Alex let out some air and looked around for a couple of seconds.

"All right, anyone else got anything?"

"Yes, sir," an agent at the far end of the table said.

The agent's name was Rudy Marquez. He was not one of Alex's
favorites. He was a politician, always posturing and maneuvering in
an attempt to get ahead instead of producing quality work. The man
was known to take shortcuts and as far as Alex was concerned, was
mostly useless. Whatever he was about to say, Alex didn't expect it
to be very useful.

He was right, but for the wrong reasons.

"About an hour ago, the switchboard got a call," Marquez said.
"No one else was around so they forwarded it to my desk. The caller
wouldn't give his name, but he suggested the O'Hara family was

going to manipulate the World Series with help from Connors. I just now realized the connection."

Alex should have known about such a call already. The fact he didn't meant Marquez had squashed it in an attempt to score points. Alex gave him a big fat zero.

"Are you kidding me?" he said. "You *just now* realized it?"

Marquez missed or ignored the scathing bite in the words and delivered the rest of his theory.

"We know Connors has a past connection to the O'Haras," he said. "It's not a stretch to think they might try to fix games, especially with what we know about Michael O'Hara's problems. The huge debts are the motive. I believe the threat at the hotel was meant to throw us off."

Alex closed his eyes tightly and pushed his thumbs into his temples for a few seconds. He was seriously annoyed at the delay in being notified of the call, but the fact the theory held water was worse. He let out a loud sigh as he opened his eyes to look around the room again.

"Anyone care to comment?"

"Yes," Sandy said. "That theory is ridiculous."

Chapter 22

Philadelphia

Following through on the self-promise to stick to as much of my game-day routine as possible, I headed down to the hotel exercise room for my morning workout. Bart and Kirk were already hard at it by the time I got there a minute or so after seven-thirty. Kirk was running on a treadmill and Bart was working hard on an elliptical machine nearby.

"Gentlemen," I said as I stepped up on a treadmill next to Kirk.

Both nodded, but said nothing. Twenty quiet minutes and three miles later, I ended my run and headed for a Cybex machine in the center of the room. A few minutes after that Kirk quit running as well.

"I'm gonna hit the sauna," he said. "You guys interested?"

"I still got a while here," I said through a leg press. "Thanks, anyway."

Bart's legs stopped moving and he looked up at Kirk.

"Maybe in a bit," he said. "I need to talk to Marshall first."

"Fair enough," Kirk said. "Catch you boys later."

He disappeared out a door as Bart came to sit across from me. I had switched around to do leg extensions. That left me looking at him upside-down, something that made the expression on his face look odd. When he spoke, the tone in his voice made it worse.

"How are you?" he said.

I stopped working and spun up to a seated position.

"OK, Bart, qué pasa?" I said.

"You have the worst accent, my friend," he said.

The deflection reminded me of Buck's from Florida. I shook my head.

"You're one to talk," I said. "But let's not dwell on that. What's up?"

"Hey, Mark, wait up, I need a minute," I said entirely too loudly.

He was near the front desk, already in suit and tie. I was still in my exercise clothes and dripping sweat on the lobby's beautiful Italian marble tile floor.

"Good workout?" he said as I neared him.

I shook my head. Some sweat flew off.

"I don't know, I never finished," I said. "I got interrupted. Seems maybe there's something you need to tell me."

I didn't know if it was my tone or the words, but Mark's face darkened again. It was somewhere between the two versions from the night before.

"Not here," he said. "Come with me."

He motioned me toward the elevators and led the way. We found a car waiting and stepped on. As soon as the doors closed he turned to me.

"Now, what's this all about?" he said.

I used the sleeve on my t-shirt to wipe at some sweat.

"Bart was wondering why I was still here," I said. "Said he heard I'd been replaced after last night's fun. Something about an executive committee meeting, some of the members don't like what's going on. The threat got to them. So did Pike."

Mark's eyes narrowed for a split-second before relaxing.

"Goddamn rumors," he said. "The truth is *I* called the meeting to tell everyone I'm *not* making any changes. I said the same thing to Mr. Pike a few minutes ago. If anyone gets replaced it'll be him after that display at the press conference."

I studied him for a moment.

"I don't like this," I said.

It wasn't an accusation, more like frustration. Mark nodded.

"Easy, kid," he said. "I'm on your side."

The elevator stopped. Mark stepped out, but held the door open with his arm.

"I understand how you feel," he said. "Trust me, I'm not replacing you. Pike won't be giving you any more trouble. As for the executive committee, they know where I stand. You'll hear nothing more about them. The FBI and Gabi will handle the note. Everything will be fine."

I wiped at some more sweat as I mulled his words. *"Trust me. It will be fine."* It was the same stuff Buck had tried to peddle to me, Thomas, too. I guessed maybe I needed to actually start believing everyone.

"It's just… eh, never mind," I said. "I'm thinking too much."

Mark smiled.

"Yes, you are," he said. "Now stop and get outta here. I've got work to do and so do you."

He moved his arm and the door swooshed shut. I sighed and tapped my floor number. A minute or so later I was back in my room. The little red light on the phone was blinking, but I decided to ignore it. Whoever it was would just have to wait. I needed a shower and a fresh start before I'd be ready to deal with anyone else.

Twenty-five minutes later, refreshed and more in control, I made my way to the kitchenette and poured a cup of coffee. Mark, Buck, Thomas, they were all right. I just needed to trust the experts to do their jobs while I did mine. OK, easy enough, I thought, as I sipped at the brew. A few drinks in, the little red light caught my eye again.

I pulled the phone closer and touched the *Message* button.

"You have one *new message."*

Turns out it was another call from Samantha. After the threat, I'd forgotten all about her. I wasn't sure if this was a third attempt to reach me or simply a follow-up from the two the day before, but either way, I figured I'd better find out what she wanted.

When I called, her voicemail picked up.

"Samantha? Hi, it's Marshall," I said to the machine. "Sorry I'm just now getting back to you. I, uh, I had some *issues* last night. Anyway, that's not your problem. Try me again if you still need to talk. Oh, and good luck to you and your son, too."

I closed the phone and tossed it to the bed. The thoughts of Samantha went with it. Like Mark said, I'd been thinking too much, and if history was any indicator, the drama that was often the O'Hara family would only make that worse. I had plenty of my own issues to deal with. I didn't need theirs on top of it.

Too bad I had no idea they were all one and the same.

A cab pulled to the curb in front of Dukabi's building. Elliot stepped out at the same time Arcadia emerged from inside the building and the two met on the sidewalk.

"Here's the address," Arcadia said as he handed Elliot a slip of paper. "Don't fuck it up."

Elliot eyed the slip carefully before looking up.

"Does Dukabi know about this?"

"Just go do it," Arcadia said.

Elliot's head began to shake.

"No, no, I don't think so," he said. "I'm not your errand boy. I'm gonna go up to ask—"

He got cut off when Arcadia stepped forward. The stare on his face produced a violent shiver up and down Elliot's spine. Mario's warning came back to his mind.

"What you're gonna do is get it done," Arcadia said with a serious edge.

Elliot took a step back. Sweat had broken out all over his face.

"Uh, yeah, fine," he said. "Whatever."

He stepped back into the cab and it pulled away. Arcadia watched the car for several seconds before surveying the area around the front of the building. He did not spot Thomas, eyeing the exchange from inside a doorway on the opposite side of Chestnut Street, and soon turned and went back inside.

Thomas was there thanks to the information garnered during his conversation with Dukabi the day before. He'd also learned that of the two helpers, Arcadia would be the more difficult with which to deal. After watching the two together, he began to understand. Everything about the man was angry. The source of said anger was unknown, but Thomas was intent on finding it.

And he was very good at solving mysteries.

Chapter 23

Philadelphia

It was four hours before first pitch. Gabi and Mark were standing in front of the Phillies dugout watching the grounds crew apply some finishing touches to the field. Both were confident the game would go off without a hitch, but the same could not be said of the two FBI agents standing with them.

"We'll be watching Connors and O'Hara closely," Rudy Marquez said. "They're our number one suspects right now."

"Really," Mark said. "And what exactly are they suspected of?"

He was eyeing Marquez with a skeptical expression because as far as he and Gabi knew there were no suspects because no one had any idea what the threat meant or where it had come from.

"I can't, um, I can't discuss the specifics," Marquez said. "But we're on top of it."

Mark sighed and shook his head.

"That's great, Agent," he said. "I'm sure we'll be fine. Is there anything else?"

Gabi smiled at the subtle dismissal. He figured Marquez would miss it, but got a pleasant surprise when after a few seconds the agent and his partner turned and retreated into the dugout.

"Do you have any idea what he's talking about?" Mark said.

"There's definitely something they're not telling us," Gabi said.

"What makes you think that?"

The sarcasm was thick. Gabi caught it and smiled. After a quiet minute or so, he turned to Mark again. His expression was a little less upbeat.

"Is there something *you're* not telling me?" he said.

Mark looked hard at his security chief.

"Why do you ask?" he said.

"The way you responded to Marshall's question about Buck," Gabi said. "I've actually been wondering the same thing. Why *is* Marshall working this series?"

"Because I said so," Mark said.

The snap wasn't severe, but it hit home. Gabi considered his boss for a few seconds.

"Understood," he said, despite the fact he really didn't.

"Good," Mark said. "Now, I need to get upstairs. I'll check in with you later."

Gabi nodded as Mark walked away. He had a great relationship with his boss and could see something was definitely not kosher. After a few seconds he pulled out his phone.

"Hey, good, you're here," he said. "I'm coming down. I need to talk to you."

On the other end of the line, the tone caused Marshall's face to take on a look usually reserved for bad food. He had the feeling that whatever Gabi was about to serve, it wasn't going to taste very good.

Terry was face down on a massage table in the trainer's room off the clubhouse, being worked on by Ernie Goff, the team's stretching guru. His legs were being manipulated into unnatural angles, but the movements were not uncomfortable. Ernie had been doing this to a lot of players for a lot of years. He was one of the very best at it.

"All right, young man, flip over and sit up," he said. "Let's work on the arm."

Terry rolled onto his side and pushed into a sitting position. Ernie moved around and took hold of his right arm from behind. For the next five minutes he worked the limb, slowly rotating and twisting it over, behind, and to the side of Terry's body. Terry's eyes stayed shut the entire time and his face was never anything other than the picture of calm.

"What, two-, three-hitter tonight?" Ernie said as he switched positions.

Terry's eyes opened.

"Let's say no more than two or three runs," he said.

Expecting to give up runs might have seemed odd, but Terry was not one to overstate his own abilities. He knew his job was to give the Phillies a chance to win, and with the team's potent offense, allowing only a couple of runs would do that. Considering his uncanny feel for the game, his teammates would agree. They'd long since learned to trust his abilities.

As Ernie continued to work, a cell phone rang. Terry slowly opened his eyes and looked toward a bag on the floor.

"Sounds like mine," he said. "Just let it ring."

Springfield

"Damn it," Samantha said aloud as the call went to voicemail.

She checked her watch and realized she'd waited too long. Terry was no doubt in the middle of his pregame preparation and would never pick up now. She'd missed Marshall again, too, and was beginning to think she was running out of options.

She dropped into a chair at the kitchen table and tried to collect her thoughts. Outside the window above the sink it was overcast, but that wasn't the reason for a sudden shiver. The dread or fear or whatever the feeling she'd gotten during Michael's visit was creeping back in from the edges of her mind.

She turned from the window and her eyes caught sight of an object stuck to the bottom corner of the bulletin board above her head. It was Gabi's business card. She lifted it and stared at it for a long minute.

"OK, maybe you can help."

Philadelphia

Thomas and Damien had reconvened on a park bench across the street from Independence Hall. The volume of pedestrians around them was light, a by-product of the overcast sky and chill in the air. It wasn't exactly a great night to play baseball, but neither the game nor the weather was the topic of discussion.

"We still got nothing on the threat," Damien said. "How'd your day go?"

Thomas handed him a slip of paper.

"What's this?" Damien said.

"Something that might help," Thomas said.

Damien eyed the note. On it was a license plate number. After a few seconds, he looked at Thomas again.

"Alex said I should expect some surprises from you," he said.

"Director Harris is a smart man."

Chapter 24

Philadelphia

Gabi's visit to Marshall was delayed by the call from Samantha. The story itself was simple and to the point. It lasted ten minutes, if that, but the attempt to process the details was taking Gabi much longer.

Samantha wasn't proud of the affair, but didn't regret it either. The young man had been one of Terry's USC teammates, a close friend of his she got to know during her many visits to see her son. She described him as the perfect example of a Californian: handsome, great body, blonde hair, and a perfect tan. She said he was charming and she was flattered by his advances, but at first resisted. The man kept after her and she finally gave in. She was single and lonely and it was a chance to fulfill a fantasy of being with a younger man. But like most fantasies, it didn't last. The man became more and more attached, eventually reaching the point of obsession. Samantha tried to end the affair, but the man was devastated and things got ugly.

She had long since pushed the episode to the far corners of her mind, but a phone call from the man changed that. He said he was coming back to reclaim what was his, all the things that had been stolen away.

"Terry was working too hard on his dreams for me to complicate things," Samantha said to Gabi during the call. "I thought I could make it go away on my own. I guess I was wrong."

"I don't understand," Gabi said. "What was stolen?"

"*Everything*... he thinks I stole everything."

I was alone in the umpires' room when Gabi found me. That was good because he was wearing a thick curtain of concern on his face. I wouldn't have wanted my crewmates to see it.

"You don't look so good," I said. "What's up?"

He sat next to me at my locker stall. He was playing with his phone and looking everywhere but at me. I didn't like that I was getting used to people acting like that around me.

"Gabi, you're, uh, freaking me out," I said. "What is it?"

He turned. His face looked a lot like Buck's had in Florida a couple of days earlier.

"I started out coming down here to tell you about the FBI, but something else just came up."

Wow, two for the price of one, I thought. With that much luck I should buy a lottery ticket.

"Well, I'm listening," I said. "Start with the Feds."

He nodded. Actually, it was more of a shrug, but either way, it was a distracted movement. Again, I was reminded of Buck's demeanor.

"Those two agents assigned to help me are fixated on you and Terry," he said. "I think they think you guys are up to something. I figured you should know about it."

I took a second to process. *I'd* been threatened, why would *I* be up to something? And what the hell did Terry have to do with—oh, shit. Thomas' revelations came back to mind. *The FBI thought I was going to try to fix games.* That had to be it, not that I remotely agreed.

"All right, well that's bullshit," I said in disgust.

Gabi nodded. We both then went quiet for a few seconds.

"Shit, fine, thanks," I finally said. "So tell me about this 'something else.' What happened?"

He turned to me again. His eyes had a pained look.

"The call I got was from Samantha O'Hara," he said.

Samantha *again*, I thought. OK, now that *can't* be a coincidence.

"What about her?" I said.

"She, uh, she just told me a very disturbing story," Gabi said. "Does the name Andrew Singer mean anything to you?"

"Whoa."

I'd known him as AJ, but if that's why she'd been trying to reach me—

"I think maybe this guy threatened her or something," Gabi said before I could finish the thought. "I told her to go to the police, but she said she couldn't."

It took an extra click for that last part to register.

"Huh? Did she say why?" I said.

"She said people would get hurt."

"What people?" I said, although I was thinking I already knew the answer.

"Her and Michael and Terry," he said.

"Whoa," I said again.

He wasn't finished.

"And *you*."

After Gabi left, I did my best to process everything. Things were definitely getting stranger by the minute, but I passed on calling Thomas. The other guys had started to arrive. I wouldn't have time to get into it with him and he would definitely want to get into it. That left me distracted, something Bart noticed not three seconds after landing in the locker stall next to mine.

"Qué pasa, Marshall, are you OK?" he said.

His "you" always came out more like "jew." That quirk from his accent usually made me smile, but not this time.

"Ah, I'm good, big man," I said. "I'm just tryin' to find my game face."

He frowned at me.

"If you say so," he said as he gave my shoulder a squeeze.

He turned away and I watched as he started unpacking his gear. The distraction of the movements helped, and twenty minutes later, as I pulled on the last of my gear and uniform, I was ready to go. Samantha, the FBI, and the note could all kiss my ass. I was there for the game.

That was plenty.

"Mr. O'Hara, I can't let you pass."

The words came from a large security guard blocking Michael's path. The confrontation was taking place at the southeast entrance gate off Pattison Avenue, near the statue of Phillies great Robin Roberts.

"Sure you can," Michael said. "Just get outta my way."

"Mr. O'Hara," the guard said. "It says here you're not—"

He was stopped by the sight of Gabi moving in behind Michael.

"Come with me," Gabi said in a low growl.

He took hold of the ex-pitcher's arm and pushed a thumb into the soft spot inside the elbow. The years of damage there screamed in protest and it was more than enough to convince Michael to comply. As soon as they got to some open space, Gabi turned so they were face-to-face.

"Are you really that stupid?" he said. "Which part of 'don't come' are you not getting?"

"Who are you calling stupid?" Michael said as he moved to within an inch of Gabi.

"You," Gabi said.

The two stared at each other as the big guard moved closer. When Michael noticed, he decided to fold. Bluffing would do no good. Gabi had an unbeatable draw.

"Yeah, well, I'm stubborn," he said; then after a pause. "Can you blame me? I just wanna watch my son play."

Gabi's expression lightened a touch before he turned to the guard. The guard's name was Clarence Riggs.

"Clarence, make sure he doesn't move," he said.

Riggs stepped forward as Gabi stepped away and pulled out a cell phone. In the wait, Michael eyed Riggs and saw something familiar in his face.

"Hey, didn't you use to play for the Eagles?" he said.

"I did," Riggs said without looking at Michael. "And you should shut up."

Michael quickly realized the appropriateness of the fold and simply nodded. It was another few seconds before Gabi came back.

"Please escort Mr. O'Hara to the commissioner's box," he said to Riggs. "And make sure he stays there."

"Done," Riggs said.

"Thanks," Michael said.

Gabi shook his head.

"Don't thank me. If it were up to me I'd leave your ass out here."

I took a deep breath and led the crew up the dugout steps and onto the playing field. The sight was overwhelming. Every seat was taken and there was a hum in the air. The sound seemed to have a life of its own and it reminded me why I was really there. World Fucking Series, I said to myself, as I looked around. I had never been so pumped up in my life and when the National Anthem finished, a tear worked its way out of my eye. It was that intense.

"This is way cool," I said to Bart who was standing next to me.

"Yes it is," he said, although I could barely hear him over the roar of the crowd.

After the field cleared of non-essential personnel, a representative from each team joined us at the plate. I took their line-up cards, but it was mainly for show. We had done the official exchange and ground rules earlier, when it was a lot quieter. As the coaches walked away, each of the guys rapped me on the chest for luck, even Pike, before heading out to their positions.

Pike was in right field on the foul line, Art Mahaffey was in left, Bart was at third, Kirk at second, and Jimmy Banks at first. I watched each for a second or two before turning my attention to the mound. Terry was warming up and I flashed back to all the times I'd watched him do that very thing when we were young.

I missed it, the friendship, but any pang of sentimentality got lost in wondering if any of what Gabi had said was true. Did someone *really* think we might try to fix the games? Was that what all the crap was about? I didn't want to think about it. Not now. It was time to play ball.

As Terry finished, he looked my way and nodded. I returned the gesture and for a brief moment all was right with the world.

If only it could have stayed that way.

Chapter 25

Springfield

After the call to Gabi, Samantha felt a little better. Terry would be disappointed she was not at the game, but would deal with it like always. He was used to it. Samantha got too nervous when he pitched. She'd been that way since he was young and would have been jumpy even without the call from Andrew Singer. With it, there was no chance she could have sat still through the game.

She pulled together a light dinner and ate alone in the quiet of the kitchen, picking at the meal as she flipped through a magazine. Just before game time, she moved to the sink to clean up her dishes. The external houselights prevented the darkness outside the window from being frightening and Samantha found herself smiling at a memory of Terry and his friends working out under the fluorescent glow. Day and night, hot or cold, the boys worked on their craft.

Samantha hated that she'd almost killed that by getting involved with Andrew, but the memory vanished when something more tangible caught her eye.

"That's odd," she said aloud.

The back porch light on the Connors house was flashing on and off. Samantha was sure they were out of town and wasn't sure what to make of it. She watched closely for several seconds until the bulb stayed unlit. She shrugged it off to a flame-out and made a mental note to leave them a message about it later as her attention returned to the dishes.

She was drying the last glass when a powerful jolt of electricity shot through her body and she fell to the floor. Every one of her muscles was going haywire and the only thing she had control of was her eyes. In the confusion, an odd voice worked into her ears through the spasms.

"You look like you need help," the strange voice said.

Seconds later, a frumpy little man came into view. In Samantha's mind, she was recoiling in horror. In reality, she was doing nothing more than twitching.

"Yeah, I get that a lot," the man said.

Seconds later Samantha's world faded to black.

Philadelphia

Just outside the door of the commissioner's suite on the Hall of Fame level, Riggs stopped and pushed Michael firmly against the wall. He pinned him there with his forearm and leaned in until he was less than an inch from Michael's face.

"Behave," he said in an ominous tone.

He stepped back and pulled open the door. Michael took a second to regroup before moving through the opening. Another equally-as-large body was waiting just inside. Michael's eyes bounced from one to the other. He concluded it was a tie. Both were scary.

"Got it," he said. "I'll be good."

Riggs left and Michael moved past the second guard into the room. There were fifteen or so people milling about inside and another group in the seats on the other side of a sliding glass door. Mark Rosenbaum was in one of the seats outside. Michael headed in his direction.

"Mr. Commissioner," he said after reaching Mark. "I'm told I have you to thank."

As was his nature, Michael's tone had enough sarcasm to be noticeable. Mark looked up, but whatever bad thoughts he might have had about it were masked behind a façade of the perfect host. If he was pissed, he wasn't about to let the other guests know.

"Michael," he said looking up. "So glad you could make it. Sit here next to me."

Michael did and Mark leaned in so only he could hear.

"You are on *extremely* thin ice. Stow the attitude and try not to fuck it up."

Michael managed a nod.

"No problem."

Marie, the receptionist in the Phillies executive office, was about to head out to her seat for the game when the main line on the switchboard lit up. She debated letting it go to the call center, meaning the unlucky interns down in the ticket office, but gave in and answered.

"Philadelphia Phillies, this is Marie, how may I help you?" she said with her usual gusto.

"I need to leave a message for the home plate umpire," the caller said.

Marie hesitated. This was a new request. It took a few seconds to find a suitable reply.

"Um, I'm not sure," she said. "It might be best for you to call the MLB offices in New York. They'd know how to handle—"

"No, *you* can do it," the caller said sharply, cutting her off.

The harsh tone gave Marie the chills. What came next made it worse.

"Now just take the fucking message."

Alex was about to leave the office for the day when his cell phone interrupted. He looked at the caller ID and rolled his eyes.

"I was just heading out, Agent Marquez. Can't this wait?"

"No, sir, it can't," the agent said. "There's been another threat to Connors."

Alex reached up and rubbed his face a few times before responding.

"Sit tight, I'll be there in fifteen minutes."

Damien and Thomas were nearby, having decided to stop at McGillin's Ale House on Drury Lane to catch a bit of the game as they waited for word on the plate number. The bar, Philadelphia's oldest continuously operated pub, was packed when they arrived, but neither minded. There were lots of TV screens and plenty of imports on tap. They got lucky to find two open stools at the bar and five minutes later an Amstel was in front of each of them. After a few sips, Damien's cell phone beeped. He took a minute or so to read the incoming text.

"The car is registered to a Mr. Elliot Stevens," he said leaning toward Thomas. "They're running the name now and we put the word out to the locals. Maybe we'll get lucky and someone will see him."

Thomas nodded and moved his eyes to one of the screens above the bar. Marshall was in the shot and a small smile worked onto Thomas' face.

"Hey, there's your boy," Damien said.

"Indeed," Thomas said before a vibration from his cell phone interrupted.

He pressed it to his ear and his features quickly changed.

"Say again," he said in a shout into the phone.

Damien's head turned.

"What's up?" he said as Thomas closed the phone.

"I'll tell you in the car," Thomas said. "We just got lucky, but not in a good way."

I cleaned the plate and took one last look around. I can say without hesitation that I had never been as happy as I was at that moment. Everything bad from the past few days disappeared as I moved into position behind the catcher and the first hitter dug into the batter's box. When he was ready, I pointed to the mound, to

Terry, and shouted the same words umpires had been using for more than a hundred years.

"Play ball!"

Let the real fun begin.

Chapter 26

Philadelphia

In Mark's suite, all eyes were on the field as Terry kicked and delivered the first pitch, but the emotional reactions were varied. For Mark, it was relief. After a great regular season with exciting pennant races and some entertainingly tense games in the early playoff rounds, the last thing he wanted was something off the field to interfere with the Fall Classic. For him, it was nice that the game was finally taking center stage again.

At Mark's right, Michael had his hands clenched tightly in front of his face as he stared out at his son. His chest was bursting with pride and there was a tear on his cheek. Despite all the times he'd watched Terry play and all the games he'd played himself, there was nothing in his life that compared to this moment, not even the day Terry was born. He was happy he'd ignored Gabi's warnings to stay away. This was where he needed to be.

A few seats to Mark's left side, Buck was watching with the same intensity and pride, but his focal point was sixty-five feet closer, to where Marshall stood. The scene was bittersweet for Buck and the conflicting emotions briefly blocked out the pain from the cancer. He felt joy watching his young protégé take charge of the game, but the reality of the danger Marshall was in and the reasons for such weighed heavily.

Below the men and slightly to the left of the commissioner's suite, in section 127, row 6, seat 2, there should have been another massive dose of pride, but instead there was only emptiness. It was not due to any emotional failings. It was because Samantha was not at the ballpark, nor was she watching on TV, and she missed her son's first pitch.

Another group missed the pitch as well. Gabi, Agent Marquez, and Jordan Sakowski were in the Phillies executive office trying to console Marie. The young woman was shaking and sobbing and Gabi's gentle words did little to stem the flow of tears. The cause was the message taken just before the first pitch, a message now on a slip of paper in Gabi's hand.

> This is your second warning, Connors. Her death will be on your hands.

Springfield

In the living room of the home of Sean and Candace Connors, two men stood silently and watched the first pitch on TV. The home's automatic timers had provided sufficient lamp lighting and neither was worried anyone would notice the added colors emitted by the screen.

"She's secure?" the larger of the two said.

"Whadda you think?" the other said a bit too snottily.

There was a blur of movement and the smaller man hit the floor, writhing in pain and moaning softly.

"You need to find a better attitude, Elliot," Arcadia said without looking down.

Philadelphia

In the Tampa Bay dugout, Nik was on the bench with his head hanging toward his shinguard-covered knees for all of the first half-inning. It looked like his usual pregame quiet time, but the game was not in his head. No, his mind was on the message received in Florida, a message that meant a very different battle was coming, one he had expected for a long time.

I'm coming Nik. You can't hide any longer.

Alex, Damien, and Thomas missed the entire first inning as they were in route to the ballpark, Alex alone, and Thomas and Damien together in the agent's cruiser. Alex drove in silence, but the other two filled the time trying to make sense of things.

"Let's go through what we know," Damien said. "Marshall gets threatened by Arcadia. Arcadia works for Dukabi. So does this Stevens character. Michael O'Hara owes Dukabi a lot of money. Marshall used to be close to O'Hara's son, Terry. Both are in the World Series in positions of, um, influence. Some at the office think the fix is in."

"Reasonable," Thomas said.

"Yeah, so is that what this is and does that make it Dukabi's doing?"

He glanced at Thomas.

"No and no," Thomas said as the ballpark lights came into view through the car's windshield.

"You seem sure," Damien said.

"I am."

"Care to explain?" Damien said.

"Not yet," Thomas said. "Too many holes remain."

Damien frowned as he turned the car onto Pattison Avenue. Another second or two went by before he nodded.

"Yeah, like this 'her' thing in the threats," he said. "Who the hell is 'her'?"

Damien turned the cruiser left onto Darien Street and left again into the team parking lot. He stopped the car illegally along the sidewalk near the stadium-side of the crowded space.

"I do not know," Thomas said. "I do know Mr. Dukabi is a businessman and Mr. O'Hara owes the money, not Marshall. That makes the latter's inclusion bothersome."

After Damien shifted the engine into park, he turned to Thomas. He knew the last statement was more about friendship than anything else. Thomas' features were their flattest. Damien had almost forgotten that trait, and that it *didn't* mean the man was without ideas. He pushed for one.

"OK, that all makes sense… in that it *doesn't* make any sense," he said. "So, if not a fix and not Dukabi, then what and who?"

"Someone with another agenda," Thomas said.

"You got anything more concrete than that?"

"Nothing firm," Thomas said. "We have a lot of pieces, but almost as many holes."

"That's what I was afraid of," Damien said as they both stepped from the car.

The briskness in the air was more intense than earlier in the day. Damien found it fitting.

"Well," he said as he eyed the ballpark. "Let's go see if we can't fill some in."

After watching Terry breeze through the top of the second inning, Michael went inside to check out the food. He ended up at a table along the wall with bowls of nachos and various dips. He was filling a plate when Clarence Riggs charged into the room. Michael's stomach dropped, but he quickly recovered when Riggs ignored him and went out through the sliding door to Mark instead. Seconds later, both hustled out of the suite.

"Whatever that is, it can't be good," Michael said aloud as he turned back to the food.

"I beg your pardon?" a woman working the food table said as she gave him a nasty look.

"Oh, sorry, not this," he said. "All of this is great."

There was a skeptical expression on the woman's face. Michael got the message.

"Right, I, uh, I think I'll go get something to drink."

~*~*~*~*~*~*~*~

When Mark and Riggs reached the executive offices, they found the others waiting in a conference room there. After quick hellos, Agent Marquez gave the basics. The room went quiet after that as those hearing things for the first time processed the words. Alex was about to break the lull when a move from Mark's hand interrupted.

"There's, uh, there's something else," he said.

"Mark?" Alex said.

"Would it be possible to speak to you in private?" Mark said to Alex.

Alex's brow knitted up as he considered the request.

"Sure, why not," he said. "Let's clear the room."

Damien and Thomas were not part of the exodus. Mark looked a questioning frown at Alex. The director shook his head.

"They stay," he said. "Whatever you have to say, they need to hear."

Chapter 27

Philadelphia

Some people could paint. Some could write. Some had other talents, like throwing or hitting a baseball. I couldn't do any of those things very well. My gift was the ability to umpire. It was as natural to me as walking. Sure, I practiced, as much as you could practice judgment, and studied the rules and exercised to stay in shape, but mostly I just reacted without thought or effort. On this night, despite the magnitude of the situation and all the potential distractions, things were no different.

Of course, the job was made a lot easier by Terry and the Rays hurler; both were on top of their games and we reached the third inning with neither team yet to have a baserunner.

That changed when Nik came to bat for the first time. The first pitch from Terry, a fastball, drilled him in the center of the big blue twenty-two on the back of his jersey. The thud was loud enough to be heard over the crowd noise and he let out a yelp as the ball dropped to the ground at his feet. I think I winced a little, too, but not because of any pain Nik might be feeling.

Guys got plunked; it was a part of the game. Sometimes it was obvious, but most times it was accidental or done in a way that no one noticed. It was that last variety that was trickiest to deal with—like during the Chicago Black Sox scandal of 1919. Eddie Cicotte's signal to Arnold Rothstein that the fix was in was that he would hit the first Reds batter. With all the crap in the days leading up to the game, that's where my thoughts went right away.

It fit except that it didn't, not after what I saw in Nik's eyes.

The look there caused me to flash on a memory of my first encounter with him. It was in May 2000. I was working a minor league game in Greensboro, North Carolina. Nik was there on a rehab assignment. We had a slight disagreement about a pitch. On the surface it shouldn't have been a big deal, but he reacted with excessive anger and I had to toss him. His behavior that night didn't fit. He'd gone way overboard.

I'd tried to forget about it, but a couple hours later that night something else happened that left me wondering. I was at a bar with Buck and his wife, Barbara. Buck was on his annual trek through the minor leagues to evaluate umpires. Barbara had tagged along like she sometimes did. Among the topics of discussion was Nik's behavior.

"You handled Sanchez pretty well," Buck said. "He looked a mite bit upset, but he's just pissed about being down in the sticks. Don't worry about it, he'll be back up top soon enough."

"I don't know, Buck," I said. "It seemed like a lot more than anger."

"Oh, my," Barbara said.

"You saw it too—"

I stopped when I realized she wasn't talking to us. Her eyes were on a TV over my shoulder where a reporter was speaking into the camera.

"*...Police are combing the banks of Buffalo Lake, but as you can see the spotlights can only do so much. It looks like they'll probably call things off until morning...*"

The reporter was standing near some water. It was dark around him, but the lights from several police and rescue vehicles could be seen off to one side of the shot. Some graphics on the screen said something about a body being found. I wasn't sure why, but the report made me think about what I had seen in Nik on the field. I imagined killing another human being would create some intense emotions and that's what Nik had displayed, something seriously intense. I didn't think him the killer, but it did give me a stop.

I had completely forgotten about the episode until now.

Nik had the same look again.

Springfield

"Interesting," Arcadia said after seeing Nik get hit by the pitch.

"What's interesting?" Elliot said from over his shoulder. "Something finally happen?"

He was standing in the opening to the living room. A can of soda and a bag of chips were in his hands. Arcadia gave him a hard look. Elliot seemed to shrink a little from it.

"What?" he said. "What I do now?"

"You should reconsider that food," Arcadia said turning away. "We're borrowing these accommodations, not stealing them. Nothing can appear to have been changed."

Elliot's face filled with confusion framed by annoyance and anger.

"You're shittin' me, right?" he said.

Arcadia didn't respond. It was as telling as any words.

"Shit," Elliot said turning back for the kitchen. "What the fuck am I supposed to eat?"

Chapter 28

Philadelphia

Alex was trying to process Mark's disclosure. Part of him understood the man's reasoning for keeping the threat quiet, but the rest of him was annoyed because it had been stupid and put a lot of people at risk. Before he could voice that thought, Gabi interrupted.

"There's more," he said.

Alex gave him a hard look.

"Seriously?" he said. "You guys are full of surprises tonight."

Gabi shifted slightly in his chair.

"Samantha O'Hara called me before the game. She said a man from her past threatened her. She told me she couldn't go to the police because the man said he would hurt her and some others if she did."

Alex's eyes got a little wider.

"What man and what others?" he said.

"She said his name is Andrew Singer," Gabi said. "And he threatened Michael, Terry and Marshall."

A few more eyes went wide. Only Thomas' went in the opposite direction.

"When did this call take place?" he said.

"Last couple days," Gabi said. "I didn't get the exact time of it."

Alex turned to Thomas.

"What are you thinking?" he said.

"Yeah, does that fill a hole?" Damien said.

"It would seem so, yes. Based on the commissioner's description, the man who visited Mr. Walters in Florida was Elliot Stevens. That adds him to Arcadia in the threat-making department. And now we have a call to Mrs. O'Hara from a third person."

"Singer," Alex said. "So what are we looking at? Does he work for Dukabi, too?"

"In a way, yes," Thomas said.

"Oh shit," Damien said.

"What 'oh shit'?" Alex said.

Thomas replied.

"Arcadia and Singer are one and the same."

Mark and Gabi were excused with an urging from Alex not to discuss things with anyone else. The only exception was granted for Marshall. Gabi volunteered to bring him up to the conference room as soon as the game was over, but given the contest was still scoreless, Alex wasn't sure how long that might be. To fill the time, he tossed out various scenarios and theories to Thomas and Damien, but there was nothing definitive added to the Arcadia/Singer theory.

"OK, I guess I can work my head around that," Alex said as it neared ten o'clock. "But that brings me back to Michael O'Hara again. How's he fit in all this?"

"I'm not convinced he is a victim," Thomas said.

Alex took a deep breath and slowly exhaled.

"Which means we still have a lot of holes, right?" he said.

"Yep," Damien said. "I think Samantha O'Hara can plug a lot of them. If nothing else, she can confirm if Singer is Arcadia... or if Arcadia is Singer. At least we won't have to wait around until the analysts figure it out."

Alex nodded and Damien made a quick phone call to Jordan Sakowski. Afterward, the three men revisited the details several times until Alex was mostly convinced the theory was solid. That lasted until twenty minutes later when Sakowski stuck his head into the conference room with an expression that screamed bad news.

"Samantha O'Hara is not here."

Terry met a lot of professional pitchers when he was young. The best of them followed one truism: work fast and throw strikes. Once ahead in the count, it was a lot easier to make a batter look silly. Terry was putting those lessons to good use and making the Rays look like fools. They were swinging and missing more than anything else. I was pretty much just along for the ride.

The same was true on the other side of the field. The Rays pitcher was also locked in, and the game reached the bottom of the eighth inning in less than two hours and, more importantly, scoreless. All in all, it was a helluva game, something I mentioned to Nik right before the bottom of the eighth.

"Good stuff, huh?" I said as we waited for the first hitter. "How's your back holdin' up?"

He tensed up and his eyes narrowed.

"Let it go, Connors," he said. "It's none of your fuckin' business."

The sudden change reminded me again of that night in Greensboro, but I didn't get time to pursue it. Seconds later, the game changed just as suddenly when the Rays pitcher made his only mistake of the night. I didn't know if it was because Nik called the wrong pitch because he'd been mad at me or if the pitcher had simply missed his spot, but either way, the damage was significant. When the ball landed 450 feet away for a home run, the crowd erupted.

The score was just 1-0, but with Terry's dominance, the deficit seemed a lot larger.

In the top of the ninth, he came back out. I was a bit surprised to see him. Although his performance was reminiscent of Jack Morris' ten-inning masterpiece for the Minnesota Twins in Game 7 of the 1991 Series, complete games were a dying breed, in the playoffs, even more so. If something were to go wrong now, people were going to have a field day, especially considering the Phillies had arguably the best closer in the league.

Terry put that all to rest by easily retiring the Rays in order to give the Phillies a 1-0 series lead. After such a great game there was no way *not* to feel good when I left the field, despite the odd exchange with Nik, but the upbeat mood lasted less than five minutes. Gabi was waiting for me in front of the umpires' room, his expression a few degrees worse than before the game.

"Nice job," he said, but with no life behind the words. "We, uh, need you down the hall. Get out of your gear as soon as you can and come with me."

"What's going on?" I said.

"I'll let the others explain."

"What others?" I said, trying hard not to get annoyed.

Gabi's jaw flexed a few times. Apparently, he was *already* annoyed.

"Just hustle up, Marshall, please. It's important."

I had just finished being part of one of the greatest World Series games ever, but I found myself feeling like shit. I wasn't sure I wanted to know what else had happened.

"OK, give me a minute," I said when I finally moved again.

I would never stop loving baseball, but this was getting ridiculous, and as I stepped into the locker room, I started thinking the three weeks in Europe with my folks would have been the better choice. I deserved whatever crap they wanted to give me when they got back.

I promised myself to listen next time.

Chapter 29

Philadelphia

Sandy was happy the Phillies had won, but didn't get much time to celebrate.

"Agent Hood," she said after picking up her cell.

"Hey, I know it's late, but we have some new developments," Alex said. "I need you to run a new name."

Sandy hustled to her desk and grabbed a pen and paper.

"OK, go."

"Andrew Singer."

Sandy started writing, but stopped.

"Why do I know that name?" she said, forgetting she was still on the line with Alex.

"I don't know, but figure it out fast," he said. "I need something on my desk by morning."

"I'll get right on it."

Sandy closed her phone and looked down at her notepad again.

Damn it, she thought, I know that name, *but why?*

~*~*~*~*~*~*~*~

The sight of Thomas sitting with Director Harris and Agent Hastings was comforting only until they told me what happened.

"I never met Singer," I said when it was my turn to talk. "I only know about the affair from Terry. We'd already kind of fallen apart at that point. I, uh, can tell you it was bad at the end. Other than that, I couldn't say."

"Do you know any reason Singer might begrudge you?" Hastings said.

"Like I said, I'm pretty sure I never met him. Do you guys think Samantha is the person in the threats?"

"Good question, Mr. Connors," Director Harris said. "With some luck we'll have an answer by morning."

"And if you don't get lucky?" I said.

No one bothered to reply.

Mark and Gabi ended up alone in Mark's suite after the game. The grounds crew was working below them, repairing the field and rolling out the tarp. There was rain in the forecast, but Game 2 did not appear to be in jeopardy, at least not from the weather.

"You should have told me sooner," Gabi said, breaking up the quiet. "I might have been able to do something more."

"I did what I thought was best," Mark said.

Gabi considered him for a moment before nodding.

"Yeah, that's what you always do, so I can't be too mad."

Mark returned the nod and they sat in quiet for another moment.

"So, where does that leave us?" Gabi said.

Mark took a deep breath and blew it out.

"Getting ready for game two," he said. "I think I'll focus on baseball for a while and leave all the heavy lifting to you and the FBI from now on."

"I'll go along with that," Gabi said as both men stood.

He stopped in front of a small fridge on the way to the door.

"Hey, you want a beer?" he said from behind Mark's back.

Mark turned and a small smile formed on his lips.

"Sure, why not? Maybe it will help."

~*~*~*~*~*~*~

It was hard to tell Terry had just won a World Series game almost by himself as he answered the post-game questions. He was as cool as he'd been out on the mound until the last query. It came from Collin George. Terry took a sip from a bottle of water as he listened.

"What's up with you and Sanchez?" the reporter said. "From upstairs it didn't look like that pitch was an accident. Was that some kinda message?"

Terry slammed the water bottle to the table, causing some to splash out. After a deep breath, he leaned into the microphones.

"Shit happens," he said.

With that, he stood and left the room.

A few minutes later, Nik went through a similar process at his locker. He had a towel around his waist and another draped over his shoulder. An Ace bandage held an icebag against his back. Under the bag was a baseball-shaped welt. The impact of the pitch had left a mark from the seam and Nik was in a good deal of discomfort. The adrenaline from the game had long since left his body, and the four Advil he'd taken were no match for the pain, but he didn't bitch, not with the reporters anxiously feeding off every word. He simply gritted his teeth and stuck with the required clichés.

"It was supposed to be a slider away, but we missed the spot. It's a game of inches. You gotta give the batter credit. He still had to hit it. It's only one game. We're still in this thing. We just have to keep plugging away."

When he'd finally had enough, he put an end to it with a big smile.

"Anything else, guys?" he said. "I need to get some rest."

Most of the reporters moved away, but Collin George edged forward, tape recorder in hand.

"It looked like O'Hara was sending a message with that pitch in the third. Any chance you retaliate?" he said, obviously hoping to stir up a little controversy.

Nik stared at the reporter for a few seconds.

"I doubt it," he said. "Shit happens."

Chapter 30

After the press conference and post-game arm treatments, it was close to two A.M. before Terry got some alone time. The locker room was empty as he dressed, the other players long gone. Through the quiet he heard a small beep and realized it was his phone. He had two new messages. One was from Michael, but he sounded drunk and Terry deleted it without listening to the entire recording. The second was from someone in the front office telling him his mother had not picked up her tickets.

"Aw, Mom, what the hell?" he said aloud.

Nik had also received two messages during the game. Like Terry, only one got his full attention. It had come during the third inning. The voice was familiar.

"Ouch, that must have hurt. Looks like Terry is mad at you, I wonder why. Oh, yeah, that's right. You fucked him over, too. Maybe you should be more careful next time."

Nik deleted the message and tossed the phone to a chair near the window. He was back in his hotel room and walked to a full-length mirror on the wall. He twisted his body around so he could see his back. The welt had become an ugly mass of purple, red, and black, and was extremely sore to the touch.

"Yeah, it hurt," he said to the reflection. "But not as much as I'm going to hurt you."

As Terry reached his car, a voice called out from behind.

"Great game," Clarence Riggs said.

Terry and Riggs knew each other well. They'd shared more than a few beers while trading stories about their careers. Riggs' in football was cut short by a nasty knee injury and now he was a security guard. The situation always reminded Terry how lucky he was to have recovered from his arm injuries and still be playing.

"Thanks, Cee," he said. "It was fun."

"Looked like it."

Terry opened the driver-side door and tossed his bag across the seat. When he turned back to Riggs, the big man spoke in a different tone.

"Hey, I know he's your dad and all, but I gotta tell ya, Michael is a real piece of work."

"I know it. He can be an asshole."

"Yeah, well, you said it, not me, but that's what he was tonight," Riggs said. "If you get a chance, tell him I won't be so nice if he carries on like that again."

Terry let out a small laugh and thought back to the deleted message. After a second, he nodded his head at Riggs.

"Hey, man, do what you have to do. I'll understand."

Sandy fell asleep at the small desk in her living room. That turned out to be a good thing, courtesy of a dream. In it, she was with her sister, standing on a pitcher's mound. Amy was in a long white gown that belonged to the girls' mother, but was wearing a Phillies cap instead of a veil. She wasn't talking, but kept pointing to a scoreboard above the outfield fence. A line-up was there, but as Sandy struggled to read the names, they started flashing on and off until everything suddenly evaporated.

Sandy's eyes shot open. She was staring sideways at a three-inch stack of papers on the corner of her desk. A single sheet had fallen off and was facing her. As she tried to focus on it, she lifted her head too quickly. The movement caused a severe cramp in her neck. She used one hand to rub at the pain as the other reached for the paper. The kink was slowly replaced by a realization of what she was seeing. It was the list from the Michael O'Hara background check. About halfway down in the "known associates" column Sandy found the treasure.

Andrew James (AJ) Singer

"Son-of-a-bitch, I knew it," she said aloud. "Thanks, Amy."

Springfield

The sleek form of Terry's car raced south along I-95 and then north along I-476. It was almost three A.M., and there was little traffic to impede his progress. The driver-side window was down, but Terry didn't mind the cold air whipping through the car's interior. It felt good to be airing out.

Ten minutes after leaving the parking lot at Citizens Bank Park, he reached the Springfield exit. A minute or so later he was at Rolling Road and the intersection with Thornridge Avenue. He stopped there and looked through the darkness to his childhood home. He could see the outline of his mother's car in the garage. Her absence from the game was eating at him, and for a fleeting moment he thought of going in, to confront her about it.

Yes, she got nervous, and yes, they'd had a fight, but that was no excuse, not now.

"Christ, it's the fucking World Series," he said aloud.

After a pause, he shifted the blame.

"Goddamn it, Dad, why are you always fucking things up?"

With a heavy sigh, he turned away and began inching the car further along Rolling Road, past Marshall's old house on the left. The RV was still in the driveway and a small chuckle escaped Terry's lips. The Rockwood had hosted a lot of parties—and more— and the memories made him realize how much he missed Marshall. Sure, they'd crossed paths a couple of times during the last few seasons, but neither had yet try to breach the divide. They were just two professionals at work, the friendship no longer relevant.

It made about as much sense as going a year without talking to Samantha, meaning none.

"I'm sorry," Terry said aloud.

He wasn't sure why he was apologizing or to whom. It just seemed like the right thing to do.

Arcadia eyed the slow moving car through the front window from a seat on the sofa. Elliot was asleep on the floor behind, atop a makeshift bed of throw-pillows. As it was with the food, Arcadia wouldn't permit him to use any of the beds upstairs. Every so often a mumble would escape the little man's mouth, but for now his snoring was the only sound.

When the car moved out of sight, Arcadia relaxed again and stared up at the ceiling, contemplating his next move. The earlier phone calls, first to the stadium for Connors and then to Sanchez's cell phone, would no doubt inspire a response. In the case of Connors, Arcadia was relatively certain it would take some time before the FBI put the pieces together, *if ever*. For Sanchez, well, that call was likely to result in something much sooner, but Arcadia didn't mind.

Sooner or later, Sanchez, like all the others, would pay for what they'd done.

Chapter 31

Philadelphia

My plan to sleep in got busted up by a call from Thomas a few minutes after eight A.M.

"Dude, it *has* to be too early for something bad," I said.

"Good things may come to those who wait, but bad things don't care."

Despite the fact they usually fit, his use of odd and obscure quotes and sayings could be as annoying as his flat tone and lack of facial expressions outside of the eyebrow thing. I wasn't in the mood for it.

"Very fucking funny," I said; then after a pause to sit up in bed. "So what happened now?"

"Agent Hastings and I would like you to accompany us on an errand. A stop for breakfast is included to entice you."

I shook some of the sleep out of my head and looked around the room. It was too big and too empty. And there wasn't any food. And there wasn't going to be any further sleep either.

"Fine," I said. "Breakfast I like, but what kind of errand are we talking about? I can't be out all day."

"Nothing overly taxing," Thomas said. "I'll have you back in plenty of time."

I stood and headed for the bathroom.

"How much time do I have to get ready?" I said.

"We're waiting in the lobby."

"Of course you are," I said with a sigh. "Hang on. I'll be down as soon as I get dressed."

After the dream-inspired discovery, Sandy had worked into the wee hours before eventually quitting and stealing a couple of hours of sleep. Part of her would have liked to stay nestled in bed longer, but she knew Alex would be annoyed if she was late. After a quick shower, she grabbed a granola bar from the kitchen and headed out. Ten minutes later, she was in her cube firing up her office computer.

"You ready?" a voice said from over her shoulder.

She looked up to find Alex standing there.

"Hey, five minutes."

He walked away with a nod as the computer finished booting. Sandy inserted the CD she'd burned at home and four minutes later a report was printing on a machine down the hall. With notes in hand, she jogged over to pick up the printout and hustled to Alex's office, ready to tell him all about Andrew Singer.

Upper Darby, Pennsylvania

Twenty-five minutes after leaving the hotel, Agent Hastings pulled his FBI Crown Victoria into a parking spot in front of the Llanerch Diner on Township Line Road. The restaurant had been an institution in the Philly suburbs seemingly forever. There was nothing overly unique about the place, but the lack of specialness was what made it special.

Thomas and I first discovered it by accident one night after a college party, but it had been too long since my last meal there. Still, the lingering smell of grease and smoke from no-longer-permitted cigarettes that hit my nose as soon as we stepped inside brought back a flood of memories. I decided to forgive Thomas for the way-too-early wake-up call.

"So why are we visiting Samantha O'Hara?" I said with a mouthful of pancake a few minutes later. "Couldn't you guys handle it without me?"

Hastings looked up from his waffle.

"She wasn't at the game last night and isn't returning phone calls," he said.

He seemed a little tense. I hoped it wasn't because of the food.

"Maybe she's not home," I said with a shrug.

"Possibly," Thomas said. "We felt it prudent to check."

I almost asked why, but I let it go. I got that I was the buffer and that she'd probably be more receptive to me. I hadn't been to the O'Hara house in a long time, but it seemed like a good idea. Then again, most of Thomas' ideas were good. I took another slab of pancake.

"Well, if nothing else, at least the food here still rocks," I said.

Thomas nodded.

"Indeed."

Philadelphia

Alex scanned the printout in front of him. After several seconds, he looked up.

"OK," he said. "What am I looking at?"

Sandy could see the stress on his face. She dove in to make it go away.

"Remember I told you Singer's name sounded familiar?"

Alex nodded.

"It was on the results of the search you had me run on the O'Hara clan. Singer was a teammate with Terry O'Hara at USC."

"I know," Alex said. "Connors confirmed that last night."

"Oh, OK," Sandy said.

She double-checked something in her notes.

"His full name is Andrew James, but he uses AJ," she said. "He grew up in Cupertino, California, a suburb west of Santa Clara. He had a normal childhood... well, normal for a seriously rich kid.

Daddy is Dr. James Singer, a PhD in computer science who patented an extensive collection of software programs now used in Silicon Valley. Mommy is Kathleen Abel, holder of two Masters and president of a consulting business specializing in systems security. Both have sizeable incomes. The money afforded AJ plenty of time to pursue things other than a job. One such thing was baseball."

"Go figure," Alex said.

"Yeah, exactly," Sandy said before pausing to flip a page in her notes. "Young AJ played Little League and PONY League and was quite the superstar. In high school he was a standout center fielder. At six-three and 200 pounds he was a scout's and recruiter's dream, what they called a five-tool player. He was offered several scholarships and picked USC. He started there and met Terry in '93. The decision to attend college surprised some, but it was because Mommy and Daddy attached a few strings to future funding streams. The biggest was getting a degree or getting cut off *forever*."

She stopped for a pull of water from a bottle she'd carried in.

"How did you get all of this in one night?" Alex said.

"Mommy was very happy to share," Sandy said. "There was a falling out of some sort. She wouldn't get into it and I didn't press, but she was more than happy to help. She now possesses AJ's old computer and she emailed me a zip file that included a copy of his diary."

"Nice," Alex said. "Continue."

Sandy nodded.

"OK, as we know, Singer was a teammate of Terry. That relationship led to the affair with Samantha, although it was counter to AJ's normal modus operandi. He was a womanizer."

She flipped another page.

"According to his own words, his relationship with her was 'nirvana' and when they broke up he lost it big time. The diary digressed into incoherent ramblings for a couple months. The timing matches what Loeb told you last night about AJ harassing her. From what I've read I'm surprised Terry didn't notice what was going on."

"Maybe he chose to ignore it," Alex said.

"True, but in any case, there was someone else involved."

Alex's eyes narrowed.

"Tell me."

"Nik Sanchez. The trio was very close and known around campus as 'The Three Amigos.' From what I could gather, Nik knew what was going on."

Sandy stopped to finish off the last of her water. Alex picked up a cup, possibly containing coffee, but didn't drink.

"Does that mean Marquez was onto something?" he said.

"I can't see it," Sandy said. "O'Hara isn't the type, not after what he went through to get back into the game."

"Keep it in mind anyway," Alex said. "You never know."

Sandy nodded.

"Anyway, after Terry and Sanchez got an off-campus apartment everything seemed to return to normal. The diary made it seem like Singer was a regular visitor and he went back to his old habits. I lost track of how many women he mentioned. But then it all just stopped."

Alex sat forward.

"What just stopped?" he said with a renewed look of concern.

"All of it," Sandy said. "The diary, the Amigos, everything, it all just stopped. Mommy doesn't know why, although I got the feeling she didn't really care, like maybe she was happy."

Alex sat back again and began to rock in his chair. A second later his head began to shake.

"I find that hard to believe."

"Me, too," Sandy said. "That's why I'm still digging."

"Then don't let me stop you."

Chapter 32

Springfield

Inspired by the mistreatment the day before, including the resulting lousy night of sleep, Elliot finally decided to push his agenda forward. He'd played along with whatever the hell Arcadia was doing long enough, now it would be his turn to control things. The two were in the kitchen of the borrowed house, at a small table there. Elliot had taken the chair closest to the back door as a precaution. Just in case a need to run arose.

Of everything he was plotting, that might have been the best idea.

"I know who you are," he said with as much confidence as he could find.

Arcadia looked up and his eyes slowly narrowed.

"Is that so?"

The tone, the look, or maybe both, caused Elliot to shiver and he lost most of his courage. He also lost his place in the script he'd worked up in his head. The confusion stayed until Arcadia snapped his fingers a few times. Elliot jumped at the noise.

"Focus, Elliot, who am I?"

Elliot swallowed. It produced an odd squishing noise.

"I uh, I know your real name isn't Peter Arcadia," he said. "And I know you're doing this because of what happened to you in college."

Arcadia laughed. Elliot's shivers increased and he began to fidget. Mario had definitely been right. This was a bad idea, the greed inspired recklessness now simply reckless.

"Care to explain?" Arcadia said after the laughter faded.

"Uh… maybe now's not the time," Elliot said in a tentative voice, his head slowly shaking.

"Oh, it's too late for that. You opened the can, Elliot. *Now tell me what's inside.*"

As Samantha came out of the fog caused by whatever the little man had used on her she realized she was naked. Thoughts of rape flashed through her mind and she started to panic, but her attempts to catch her breath were stunted by a gag. With great effort, she managed to find enough composure to use her nose instead and after a long moment filled with deep nasal breathing, she regained enough control to refocus.

OK, Samantha, nice and easy, she thought, where are you?

Her eyes were open, but she couldn't see. She tried to raise a hand to her face, but found both bound behind her body. OK, I'm naked, gagged, blindfolded, and tied up, but what else? There were no sensations between her legs so she dismissed the notion of having been sexually assaulted. She was on a bed, or maybe just a mattress, and there were sheets, cheaper than ones she bought, but passable, and a single pillow under her head. She tried to gauge the width of the mattress, but her legs were bound as well. The conclusion was obvious.

I've been kidnapped, she thought, before searching for a reason. One came quickly.

Andrew Singer was back.

Philadelphia

Buck was in his hotel room when the end came. He had long expected it and done his best to prepare, but it was worse than anything he could have imagined. The pain knocked him back into a chair and he groaned loudly as he buckled over, grabbing at his mid-section. After several seconds, he managed to raise his head, but couldn't see through the tears caused by the pain. His phone was on the nightstand next to the bed, but there was ten feet of space between there and the chair, ten feet farther than Buck could possibly hope to travel.

One of his last thoughts was that he had to try, for Marshall.

The young man needed to know why.

Michael wasn't sure he was awake. His head was throbbing and his vision was blurred. It felt like someone was pushing his eyes back into his brain. He began squinting hard to suppress the feeling as he tried to focus.

"You OK, baby?" a sultry voice said from somewhere nearby.

As the tumblers clicked into place he rolled over in the direction of the voice.

"Michelle, right?" he said. "I met you at the food table, at the game."

"Gee, nice of you to remember," she said; then after a pause. "Just get out."

Sultry had changed to icy.

"Whoa, hang on," Michael said.

He tried to stand, but the hangover was too powerful and he stumbled back onto the bed.

"Nice," Michelle said. "Please just get out."

Michael rubbed at his eyes and looked around the room.

"Yeah, sure, OK," he said. "But could you help me find my clothes first?"

Gabi and Mark were about to eat breakfast in the lobby lounge when an explosion of frantic voices and noises erupted from near the front desk. A second later, two EMTs rushed around the corner from the elevators, a stretcher in tow. Mark recognized the rider almost immediately.

"Ah, shit," he said.

He raced across the tiles and out the door, reaching the fast moving emergency crew just as they pushed the stretcher into a waiting ambulance.

"Hang on," he said in a shout. "I'm coming with you."

Springfield

Hastings pulled the cruiser onto Thornridge and stopped in front of Samantha's house. The perfect grass and beautiful shrubs and flowers were all elegant without being pretentious, just as I'd remembered, but I knew we weren't there to admire the landscaping.

"So, what, you want me to go knock?" I said from the backseat.

"Go ahead," Hastings said. "We'll go check out the perimeter. If she's there, wait for us."

"Cool," I said. "Let's split up. We can do more damage that way."

Hastings shot me a half-grin. He must have been a *Ghostbusters* fan, too. I had to admit I was starting to like the agent. Despite an undertone in his expression that said "sad" he had a good sense of humor. I imagined it drove Thomas a little nuts, like mine, but I pushed it out of my head as we headed off in different directions.

It wasn't long before we were all back on the front porch.

"No reply to my knocks," I said. "Is her car in the garage?"

"No, the garage is empty," Thomas said.

"Back door is locked up tight as well," Hastings said. "I didn't catch any movements inside."

I looked around and started to remember how tired I was. I had a brief urge to go crash at my parents' house, but I got over it. They weren't home and Mom didn't like such visits.

"So, what now, spy men?" I said as I refocused on the original task. "Are we giving up?"

Before they could answer, my cell chimed. Mark's number came up on the display. I stepped away from the others to answer.

"Hey, Mark."

A minute later I closed the phone and the whole world closed in around me. Everything felt like nothing and my brain started to shut down.

"Marshall?" Thomas said from somewhere in my confusion.

I looked up. I think I may have been crying.

"It's Buck," I said. "The son-of-a-bitch just died."

Philadelphia

The brisk air gave Michael a much needed slap in the face as he hit the sidewalk. The cab he'd called for from inside pulled up and he quickly settled into the back seat.

"Where to?" the chubby driver said in a thick Philly accent.

"Know any good places to eat around here?" Michael said.

"You want regular or premium?" the cabbie said.

Michael thought for a couple of seconds.

"Premium," he said. "I need a serious kick start."

"I know just the place. Sit back and relax. Be there in ten."

Michael turned and watched as the cityscape zipped by. His eyes were too tired to focus and his thoughts too scattered to care. He couldn't remember how he'd ended up with Michelle, but that wasn't the female he was worried about. He pulled out his phone and dialed Samantha. The call went immediately to voicemail and he disconnected.

"Shit," he said aloud.

After a few seconds he punched redial and cycled back to where he'd just been.

"Sam, it's me," he said after the beep. "I'm sorry about all the other shit, but I wanted to call about Terry. Was last night not the greatest thing you've ever seen? He's done well despite us. Anyway, that's all. See ya."

He closed the phone and the weight of everything came crashing down like an anvil. Through the new pain he leaned forward and spoke to the driver.

"Hey, bud, I changed my mind. Just take me home."

Chapter 33

Philadelphia

A doctor explained what happened to Buck, but most of the words went right past Mark, drowned out by the regret of having agreed to keep the illness a secret. A lot of people would have wanted to share some time with the man.

"You stubborn son-of-a-gun," Mark said aloud, interrupting the doctor mid-sentence.

"I'm sorry?" the young intern said.

"Oh, sorry," Mark said. "You were saying?"

"Yes, Mr. Walters' body was no longer a match for the cancer. Most of his vital organs crashed this morning. It's actually quite astounding he was able to get to the phone and call for help, but there was nothing anyone could have done."

Astounding, Mark thought, that was Buck all right. The man never gave up without a fight. Mark could have used some of that strength now. When the physician walked away, all of his energy seemed to go with the man. Luckily, he spotted a chair against the wall and managed to sidle over to it.

After sitting, he lowered his head into his hands began to cry.

~*~*~*~*~*~*~*~

Rudy Marquez and his partner, an agent named John King, were on a bench in Logan Square. A scattering of pigeons picked at scraps on the ground near their feet while two homeless men did the same at a trash can across the path. King kicked at the birds and they fluttered away. The vagrants looked up at the noise, but seemed to shrink when the agent made a menacing face.

"Beat it, dirtbags," King said in a growl.

The men slithered away, cursing under their breath as they went.

"Get a goddamned job," King said after them.

"Yo, John, lighten up, will ya?" Marquez said.

"What? They're fuckin' losers," King said as he continued to eye the men's slow departure.

"That may be, but one bad day is all that stands between them and you, so give 'em a break already. Besides, we got bigger things to worry about."

Marquez finished off the last of an apple Danish and tossed the empty wrapper toward the can. It missed and fluttered under a nearby bench.

"I don't care what the director says," he said with a tinge of anger. "Connors is behind the whole damn thing. We need to find the key and nail this sucker."

King was working on the second of three hotdogs, having opted for lunch fare instead of breakfast, and a few crumbs had fallen from one of the buns. He kicked at one of the pigeons that had returned to claim them and laughed as the bird scrambled away.

"C'mon, John, focus," Marquez said.

"Maybe the key is right in front of us," King said as he looked back at his partner.

Marquez eyed the man and slowly nodded as the meaning of the words became clear.

"Like maybe we need to go look, huh?" he said.

"Exactly," King said.

As both stood, King shouted in the direction of the bums.

"Hey, assholes," he said. "Here's some fucking lunch."

He fired his last hotdog down the path and laughed again as the two men scrambled after it.

~*~*~*~*~*~*~

I think it was a bit after noon when we got back to the hotel after the call about Buck. The rest of the crew was waiting for me inside the lobby. They all knew what the man had meant to me. It was good to see them.

"I am so sorry," Bart said after a massive hug. "Buck was a great man."

"Thanks, big man," I said in a low voice. "Yes he was."

The rest of the group added similar sentiments, but I didn't catch who said what. I was just glad they were there. After a few minutes, we made our way to the lounge and settled in around a couple of tables. Jimmy Banks was first to speak.

"Suze Keebler stopped by earlier," he said. "They're putting an emblem on our uniforms, a small patch with 'Buck' on it."

"They sure move fast when they want to, huh?" Pike said.

He must have realized he sounded like an ass because he quickly amended the comment.

"I mean, it was good of them to do something so fast. Buck deserves it."

We let his insensitivity slide. In the scheme of things, it wasn't important.

"I bet Buck was happy with you last night, Marshall," Kirk said.

"I hope so," I said.

A few Buck stories followed. I mostly just listened. It was both sad and happy. I found that fitting given the confusion I'd been dealing with all week. I'm not sure how long we sat there, but eventually it was just me and Bart.

"Is there anything I can do?" he said as he put a hand on my knee.

"Don't worry about me," I said. "I'll be fine."

He offered up a tender smile and gave me another hug before stepping away. I switched to auto-pilot after that. More people came and offered condolences, but everything was a blur. Thank goodness I wasn't working the plate again because I wouldn't have been able to handle it. As it was, just standing out in right field was going to be hard enough. Thomas found me still in the lobby around four in the afternoon and sat next to me without a word. I wasn't sure what he'd been up to since dropping me off, but I didn't really care. I was just happy for his company.

"Don't you need to be going soon?" he said.

I nodded.

"Come on, I'll walk you upstairs."

I couldn't remember if I'd ever heard his voice more sincere. It was a nice change.

"Thanks," I said.

About five minutes later we stepped off the elevator on the fourth floor and headed toward my room. I was about to slide my cardkey into the slot when Thomas reached out and stopped me. His gentle expression from moments earlier was gone.

"Someone has been here," he said.

"I would imagine the cleaning crew," I said with a frown. "Come on, I'm not in the mood."

I started again for the knob, but again he stopped me.

"I understand," he said. "It was not them."

The flat tone was back, but the expression on his face was the opposite of flat as he nudged me away from the door. I forgot I was supposed to be in mourning.

"Dude, how could you possibly know that?" I said.

"I'll let you know in a minute."

Gabi was sitting in the lobby when Agent King came around the corner from the elevators and hurried past. Something in his movements inspired Gabi to stand and follow. King went out the lobby doors and headed away from the hotel, walking fast in the direction of Logan Square. After reaching Race Street, he crossed against a light and moments later joined another man on a bench near the fountain in the center of the Square. It was Marquez.

Gabi stopped a couple hundred feet away and a thought escaped his lips as he watched.

"What the hell are you clowns up to now?"

Chapter 34

Philadelphia

Sandy joined Alex and Damien in the director's office a few minutes after five P.M. Alex could tell by the look on her face she had good news. With no disrespect to Damien, Alex found himself wishing he had a few more agents like Sandy around. Crime wouldn't have a chance.

"Singer has no police record," she said. "I did find a bunch of medical hits. They started when he was in college and continued for a few years. Then he kind of fell off the map."

"Do we know why?" Alex said.

"Remember I told you his parents made future funding conditional on graduating college? Well, Singer never did. He was at USC with Terry and Sanchez, but dropped out around the same time Terry suffered his arm injury. I also found out that Sanchez left school around then as well. That didn't smell right so I dug further."

"O'Hara fell down some steps or something, right?" Damien said.

"Not exactly," Sandy said.

She paused to take a drink from a bottle of water she'd carried into the office.

"I made a couple calls and it took a little urging, but I finally got someone to talk to me, to tell me what really happened…"

Mid-July 1995
Los Angeles, California

The party was crowded, with more in attendance than had been invited. That should have been the first hint something was wrong, at least for AJ. His next hint came when a Latino punk cornered a young lady near a table of snacks. The man was wearing oversized blue jeans, black shit-kicker boots, a white wife-beater t-shirt, and a XXXL red and black plaid shirt, buttoned once at the neck. A dark red scarf on his bald head finished the look, but AJ wasn't intimidated by the gang colors.

"Hey, motherfucker, greasy fucking paws off the lady," he said as he interceded.

"Back off, Puto," the gangbanger said. "I saw the bitch first."

"I don't think so," AJ said in a growl.

His hand shot out and grabbed the banger by the neck. In the ensuing struggle the smaller man managed to spin away from the pressure and trail the sharp edge of a knife across AJ's left leg, cutting all the way through to the bone. He instantly knew he was in trouble, but managed to deliver a thrust kick before collapsing. Without thinking, he ripped the belt loose from his pants and made a tourniquet to stem the spurts of blood shooting from the deep wound.

Seconds later, two more gang members appeared, as did Nik and Terry. The sides paired off and the battles spilled into adjoining rooms. In the minutes that followed, Nik and his foe ended up in Nik's bedroom. Terry and his opponent engaged each other in the hallway near the kitchen. AJ, badly hobbled, managed to hold his own against the original gangbanger in the living room.

Things were mostly even until the man facing Nik pulled a small gun from somewhere under his shirt. At the same time, Terry's opponent also gained an advantage when he grabbed an aluminum baseball bat from a bag on the floor near the kitchen. He took Terry down with a hard jab to the gut and then began delivering blow after blow to Terry's right arm. The sound of the bones shattering was sickening.

AJ was able to use the fresh shot of adrenaline from the fear for his friend and ended his bout with a knee lift to his foe's nose. As he hobbled across to Terry, a few bystanders finally found some nerve as well. The bat-wielding man was quickly subdued by the swarm of bodies, but a shout from the living room stopped everyone in their tracks. The man who'd been fighting Nik was standing there with the gun, yelling for everyone to get off his buddy.

For a second, everything stopped. And then the man's chest exploded from the inside. As he fell, his gun skittered across the floor and an eerie silence descended. Nik emerged from the darkness of the hallway behind the man and stepped over the body, all eyes on the different gun in his hand.

"Enough," he said. "It's over."

The other two bangers hesitated before hustling past him to their fallen mate. On the other side of the room, people were beginning to help AJ and Terry, but both had serious injuries and would need more than ice from the kitchen. A call was made from a phone hanging on the wall near the kitchen. The call did not go to 9-1-1.

Sandy took another drink of water.

"The EMT report that finally got filed was bullshit," she said after swallowing. "Somehow Terry was the only one written up. There was nothing for Singer. That wouldn't necessarily be a problem except for the fact Singer's medical records show he was admitted to the same hospital on the same night. The police report wasn't exactly complete either."

"I thought you said the call didn't go to 9-1-1?" Damien said.

"It didn't, not at first anyway," Sandy said. "LAPD didn't give a shit about the death. To them it was one less thug to deal with, two if you count Sanchez. But the school couldn't afford the negative publicity for three of its prized athletes and played along with the bogus reports. A lot of USC alumni work on the force, but it also took a little money to help with the decision."

"Follow the money," Damien said with a nod.

"And where did that lead you?" Alex said.

"Several places," Sandy said. "I found out the LAPD Police Benevolent Fund got a $250K donation and so did the USC baseball scholarship fund, all within days of the fight. I also found an account in Singer's name with $250K in it, also opened around that time. That's seven-hundred-fifty large in total."

"That's a lot of cash," Damien said. "Someone went to a lot of trouble and expense to make sure this thing went away."

"I know," Sandy said. "But here's the kicker. There has never been any activity on the Singer account. He has never touched it, odd considering he got nada from Mommy and Daddy. As far as banking records go, ignoring that two-fifty payment, he's broke. I mean the Andrew Singer part of him is broke."

"Arcadia?" Alex said.

"Yep, very much *not* broke," Sandy said. "He does well working for Dukabi it seems."

Alex sat back and let the implications come together.

"So, are you confirming these two are one and the same?" he said.

"Yes, but there's more," Sandy said.

She leaned forward and placed a piece of paper on his desk and handed another to Damien.

"Is this right?" Alex said after taking a few seconds to peruse the information.

"Yes, sir," Sandy said. "The money came from Michael and Samantha O'Hara. I think Michael is who Nik called after the fight."

Chapter 35

Thursday, October 23, 2008
The day of Game 2 of the World Series
Philadelphia

"Status, Mr. Arcadia?" Dukabi's deep voice said into Arcadia's ear.

Arcadia adjusted himself on the sofa. He'd expected this call.

"Mr. Stevens has made himself scarce," he said with confidence as he looked at Elliot. "He may be aware of our intentions, but I expect to have him soon."

At first confused by the words, the little man's face quickly filled with fear.

"What—"

A movement from Arcadia's free hand stopped Elliot from continuing.

"Very well," Dukabi said from his end. "Take whatever time necessary."

The line went dead. Arcadia shrugged at the phone before setting it on the table. Elliot's eyes were wide as he watched and waited for an explanation. When it didn't come, he began to fidget.

"What the fuck was that about?" he said in a shaky voice. "Whataya mean I'm 'scarce'?"

A wicked smile filled Arcadia's face. Elliot farted.

"You seem to know everything," Arcadia said. "Figure it out."

I probably looked stupid standing in the hallway outside my room, but all things considered, I'd rather be thought an idiot in exchange for having Thomas inside instead of me. He was trained for this kind of thing. That it took almost ten minutes before he re-emerged didn't bother me in the least. I was more worried about what he might have found.

"All clear," he said.

"That's it?" I said as my brow knitted into a deep frown.

He nodded.

"I can go in?" I said.

Again he nodded and I tentatively stepped past him into the foyer. My head was on a swivel as I moved to the living room, looking for whatever demons he might have found. Seeing none, I turned back to face him.

"OK, what the hell is going on?" I said.

"You had a visitor," he said as he held out his hand. "He left us these."

There were four tiny metal objects in his palm.

"And *these* would be?" I said as I flicked at one with my finger.

"Listening devices, standard Government-issue set of four."

My head started to shake out of instinct.

"Yeah, maybe for you," I said. "None of this shit is anywhere near standard for me."

I turned and headed to the kitchenette. I almost grabbed one of the tiny alcohol bottles on the counter there, but settled for a bottle of water from the fridge instead. I didn't ask Thomas if he wanted one. I didn't care. Buck had died hours earlier and now someone had bugged my room. Add in the threats and it was all a big pile of shit I was seriously tired of. I chugged the entire bottle and tossed the empty into the sink before looking at Thomas again.

"I gotta get down to the shuttle," I said before moving toward the bedroom. "Go do whatever it is you do. I've had enough."

I grabbed my gear and walked out of the suite without another word.

Mark had gone straight to his room after returning from the hospital, speaking to no one until Gabi called to remind him it was time to go to the ballpark. It was ten minutes into their shared cab ride before either spoke again.

"The PR team asked me to give you this," Gabi said as he handed Mark a single sheet of paper. "It's the announcement for Buck."

Mark quickly read the statement and handed it back.

"It'll do," he said into the cab's side window. "Make sure it gets out before the game starts. I don't want it used as filler during a pitching change."

Gabi pulled out his phone and made a call, speaking in hushed tones. After a minute, he turned back to his boss.

"Done," he said.

Mark nodded but said nothing. Another five minutes passed and the ballpark came into view.

"What else?" he said in a tired voice.

"It can wait," Gabi said.

Mark's head began to shake.

"Nope, tell me now," he said. "I'm fine. People die all the time, even our friends."

Gabi hesitated. He could see the pain on Mark's face, but there was something else there, too, determination perhaps. He knew the feeling.

"I think those FBI agents are up to something," he said. "I gotta find out what it is. I don't trust them."

Mark's face twitched a little.

"You and me both," he said.

Thomas called Alex from Marshall's suite.

"You're sure?" Alex said. "Forget I said that, of course you're sure. What do you want to do about it?"

Thomas eyed the bugs and contemplated a suitable reply. If left to his own, he would handle things a lot differently than Alex. His best friend was in danger and didn't need crap from the supposed good guys, whether they worked for Alex or not. He had seen what happened when renegade agents chased ghosts during his days in the CIA. He wasn't about to let anyone go down that path with Marshall.

"It's your mess now," he said. "I think you should make that call. I'm somewhat biased."

A loud sigh came through the phone.

"OK," Alex said. "I imagine so. All right, hang tight. I'll be there in fifteen minutes."

Chapter 36

Philadelphia

As he did after every start, Terry had spent a good portion of the day taking electrotherapy treatments on his right arm. Such had started during the rehab from the fractures. The pain never completely disappeared, but the stimulation helped the arm relax and heal. In truth, at this point it was as much for his head as it was for the arm. It was part of his routine and ballplayers didn't like to mess with their routines.

Such superstitions were behind the phone call he was making to his mother. In his mind, he'd done it before Game 1 and his team won, so there was no point not doing it again. Most of his disappointment from Samantha's no-show had faded. She had always been overly nervous for his games, so how could he have expected a change now, World Series or no?

"Hey, Mom," he said when Samantha's voicemail picked up.

He took that as a good sign as well; the same had happened yesterday.

"I left tickets again tonight. If you don't want them, tell Dad. At least that way he can stay out of trouble. See you soon."

~*~*~*~*~*~*~

Springfield

It took several moments for the right neurons to fire to tell Samantha she was awake. As her senses came on line, she found her right arm was asleep. She started to adjust herself to get some blood flowing again, but stopped when a noise hit her ears. She went rigid to listen. There was a series of muffled footfalls followed by the sound of a folding door. After a second passed, more footfalls came. Samantha bit down on the gag to hold back an overwhelming urge to scream.

"I know you're awake," a man's voice said. "I'm not going to hurt you, but you need to do *exactly* as I say. Here's how this works. I lift you out of bed and take you to the bathroom. I untie your feet, but everything else stays."

Samantha bit harder when a pair of surprisingly warm hands went around her body and lifted her from the bed. She tried to count the paces as she floated along. She got to six when she was lowered and her bottom landed on something cold. The man's hands untied hers, but quickly rebound them again in front of her still-naked body. He then unbound her feet.

"The paper is directly in front of you, a couple inches above your knees." the voice said. "There's nothing else on the wall so don't bother roaming. Do whatever you have to do, but remember I'll be right here."

Samantha had no problem using the toilet in front of a man, naked or otherwise, so the thought of being watched didn't bother her. She was more concerned with filling in more of her mental map of the layout and made the pee last as long as she could. In a twisted sort of way, it felt really good to relax for a few minutes.

"OK, good girl," the voice said after she finished up. "I'm going to tie your legs again."

She felt the binding return to her ankles before she was lifted off the toilet. The movements were choppy. The bathroom was small. Samantha added it to the mental picture as she started counting steps again. After another six, she stopped.

"Meal time," the voice said. "I'm putting you at a table. The gag comes out, but if you make one sound other than chewing, no more food and I stop being nice. Nod if you understand."

Samantha moved her head vigorously, but had no idea if the man could see it. A second later she landed on cold vinyl and a violent shiver raked her body.

"It is a little chilly, isn't it?" the voice said from somewhere above her.

As she drew more lines on her map, she heard more footsteps and then something soft and plush brushed against her body. The man pulled Samantha's arms up and over his head. She got the message and hung on to his neck as he lifted her off the vinyl. The soft material was worked around her body. Samantha guessed it was a robe or maybe a blanket. The coldness began to subside fairly quickly. She was thankful for the small gesture.

"A paper plate is directly in front of you," the voice said. "At the plate's twelve o'clock is a bottle of water. Eat the food, drink the water, but do anything else and you lose all privileges."

The warm hands came to her face and the gag was removed.

"Enjoy," the voice said after something was placed on the table.

Samantha worked her jaw rapidly from side-to-side before reaching for the water. The lid turned easily, but she ignored the chance it might be laced and downed a few gulps. A second later, the aroma of the food hit her nostrils. Her stomach did flips as she felt for it. Recognition came quickly. The chicken strips and fries were lukewarm and more carbs than she would ever consciously eat, but she didn't care about that at the moment. She ate quickly and when her fingers found nothing left, she finished off the rest of the water to wash it all down.

"What—"

"*No talking*," the voice said sharply, cutting her off. "We're just gonna sit here for a few minutes and then you get another potty break. After that it's lights out again."

Samantha still had a tremendous urge to talk, but the gag came back to her mouth before she could give in to it. Things got quiet after that and she used the time to fine-tune her map. She wasn't sure how long it was before she was lifted and taken back to the bathroom. If nothing else, moving around had done her good. Some of the stress had faded, but when she was returned to the bed, the robe was removed and she instantly felt very cold again.

"Sleep tight and we'll do it all again tomorrow," the voice said.

A second later she felt a prick and her body started to shut down. As she faded off, one last thought took hold. In her mind, she spoke it aloud, but as it was, it never left her lips.

"Andrew, why are you doing this?"

Philadelphia

"*Still nothing?*" Marquez said. "What the fuck, John?"

At a console in front of them, King was frantically working buttons and knobs.

"I don't get it," he said. "We should have heard every breath."

The cramped space inside the surveillance van added to the anxiety caused by the blank recording. Marquez had commandeered the vehicle under false pretenses. If that hadn't been risky enough, the malfunctioning bugs were making sure of it. The situation was deteriorating rapidly. The agents were sinking fast and neither had a life preserver.

"Jesus, man, this was *your* idea," Marquez said. "You better take care of it or both our asses are in deep shit."

"I'm aware of that," King said. "I'll fix it."

Chapter 37

Game 1 had been about precision and elegance, two dominating pitchers locked in a taut battle of wills. Game 2 was more like a circus under the direction of a three-year-old with ADD. It fit with how I was feeling. The third man up for the Rays hit what should have been a routine inning-ending ground ball, but the Phillies second-baseman sailed the throw into the dugout. Things unraveled after that and seven more Rays batted. By the time the half inning was over, the home team was looking at a 5-0 deficit.

The Phillies struck back with two runs in the bottom of the frame, two more in the second, and had the bases loaded with no outs in the third when I got involved. The home run-hitting hero from Game 1 was at the plate and lofted a high fly ball toward the right field corner. I had a perfect view as the ball began its descent and might have been the only one to see the ball nip the outside edge of the foul pole.

The stadium erupted seconds later as I signaled home run. A collection of Rays responded by chasing me down and cornering me near the foul line. As a general rule, players and coaches weren't supposed to argue fair and foul calls—or balls and strikes; not that they still didn't do that—but in this case, I couldn't blame them. It had been close. I was pretty sure of what I'd seen, but I agreed to ask for help from the rest of the crew.

"Anyone care to differ?" I said after joining them in shallow right field. "I saw it hit the pole, but I'm open for discussion."

Kirk responded.

"Let's check the replay," he said. "That's what it's for, right?"

Instant replay was new to baseball. Of the six of us, only Bart had used it to that point.

"You can't always tell," he said. "Sometimes the cameras lie."

"A lot of things lie," I said.

No one asked what I meant by that, thankfully, and after another minute, we agreed to go check. Kirk stayed out on the field, by rule one of us had to. The rest of us headed to a small room down the walkway from the Rays dugout. I had to admit, the technology was cool and we were able to see exactly what happened in full-HD quality. Part of the pre-Series preparation had been to spruce up the foul poles. Apparently, the cold weather had kept the yellow latex from completely drying. The replay cleared showed a sliver of it come off as the ball grazed the pole.

"Son-of-a-bitch," Art said after we ran the video. "You were right."

"Nice eyes," Bart said.

"Hey, I try," I said.

We trotted back out to the field and I signaled home run again. The Rays manager wanted to protest some more, but I reminded him about the new rules. If we checked replay, you weren't allowed to still question it. He finally gave up and headed back to the dugout and the game resumed. Like Art had said, we'd gotten it right. I felt good about the latest small victory.

It was the least Karma could do for taking Buck from me.

Thomas was watching the hotel entrance from a seat at the bar in the hotel lounge when a sudden increase in the noise level stole his attention for a second. He glanced at one of the TVs there just in time to catch sight of Marshall jogging across the field. It appeared there was a dispute of some sort. Thomas shook his head. In trouble again, he thought, before turning away.

Just over two minutes later, Agent King pushed through the entrance and made a beeline across the lobby toward the elevators. Thomas moved to follow, but when King stepped into a waiting car, he went into the adjacent stairwell instead.

Taking the steps three at a time, he reached the fourth floor just as the elevator arrived. His instincts had been correct. King stepped off the elevator and resumed a fast stride toward Marshall's suite. Any comfort Thomas felt was lost when King reached the door and unexpectedly removed his weapon before going into the room.

Thomas raced down the hall, but was still two steps away when he heard the gunshot.

The grand slam put the Phillies up by three, but it was far from the last scoring of the game. I managed to stay out of further trouble, but the same couldn't be said for the pitchers on either team. The Rays came back and scored twice each in the fourth and fifth to go up 9-8. The Phillies answered that with an outburst in the bottom of the fifth to regain the lead, 11-9. The Rays responded in the top of the seventh and tied the game at 11.

That set the stage for another dramatic finish. This time it was a two-run home run in the bottom of the ninth. Four hours and twenty-five minutes after the game started it was finally over. Final score: Phillies 13, Rays 11, and the Phillies were headed to sunny Florida for the next three games with a 2-0 series lead. As I left the field I couldn't help but wonder what kind of fun I might find there.

If it was anything like the past week, I wasn't sure I could take it.

Alex was in a chair near the window. He was holding a blood-soaked towel against his left shoulder, but his face reflected anger more than pain. Damien and Thomas were on stools near the kitchenette. King was on a sofa across from his boss. He had his head in his hands and his weapon was on the coffee table in front of him, along with his badge and the bugs.

"So, John, care to explain?" Alex said through a grimace.

King did not respond. Alex grabbed a bottle of Tylenol from the table and poured the remaining tablets directly into his mouth. After he finished, he fired the empty container at King. The small bottle bounced off the agent's head and came to rest at his feet. King slowly lifted his head and gazed at his ex-boss.

"Answer me, you stupid son-of-a-bitch," Alex said through a tight jaw.

"Fuck you," King said in a seething tone.

The words triggered something in Thomas, something tucked away for many years. Before anyone else could react, he was at the sofa and had King in a choke hold.

"Fuck *you*," he said in a hiss into King's ear. "You're a disgrace to that badge. And you tried to screw with my friend."

Damien started to move to intercede, but Alex held up a hand and shook his head.

"Let it go," he said.

Damien nodded and backed off as King's face slowly turned red and unconsciousness crept in. After another few seconds, Thomas jerked him up and over the back of the sofa. His hands were a blur as he released the agent's neck and delivered a two-handed thrust to the chest. King went sprawling toward the kitchenette and came to rest near Damien's feet. Damien smiled at the heap before looking up at Thomas.

"Impressive. Can you teach me that move?"

Chapter 38

Friday, October 24, 2008
The day before Game 3 of the World Series
Philadelphia

Michael was asleep by the time the game ended and didn't see the dramatic finish. Before then he had tried several times to reach out to Samantha again, but each attempt failed and he spent the evening pouting and using a bottle of Jack Daniel's to drown his sorrows. Just before passing out around one A.M. he left her one last message.

"Sam, it's me," he said with a slur. "I'm sorry. I really screwed up. Call me, please."

After ending the call, he tossed the phone toward a chair across from the sofa, but missed badly. It slid along the floor and came to rest under a pile of clothes in the corner. It was still there two hours later when it received a text reply from Samantha's phone. It would be two days before Michael would find the phone and message and realize it had not been she who'd sent it.

~*~*~*~*~*~*~*~

Mark stopped by the umpires' room after the game. He told me he was impressed with how I handled the home run call. I'm not sure it had been all that impressive, but I thanked him anyway. Mostly I just wanted to get out of there. The game had been a nice diversion, but all the bad thoughts of the day had returned by that point.

On the shuttle back to the hotel, Bart sensed my funk and tried to help again.

"Pretty crazy game," he said.

"It sure was," I said. "We did OK, huh?"

"We got it right, Amigo."

That started fifteen minutes of Bart talking and me listening. He was a great storyteller and it admittedly pushed most of the bad stuff away. I was glad, but it didn't last, thanks to the large collection of police-looking vehicles that greeted us when we got back to the hotel.

"What now?" Bart said to me as we stepped off the van.

I shrugged.

"I'm not sure I want to know."

An hour later I was laughing. I didn't know why. What Thomas had told me wasn't funny, but I guessed sometimes you just laughed when you didn't know what else to do.

"A perfect ending to a perfect day," I said after the chuckles ran their course. "The FBI plants bugs in my room and then shoot each other. What else could go wrong?"

Thomas didn't respond, but I could see there was something on his mind. It was just the two of us in my suite. Director Harris and Agent Hastings had left an hour earlier after offering up their version of the story. Harris had a nasty wound, but was all-business, despite his obvious discomfort. Between apologies he insisted he'd be fine. As for me, I wasn't so sure. Thomas' expression was one I'm not sure I'd seen before.

"So what happens now?" I said. "With the FBI, I mean."

"Director Harris will publicly regret but personally enjoy accepting Agent King's resignation. Mr. King will go become a security consultant or something similar. Agent Marquez will get knocked back a few grades into a desk job and will quit within a year from the boredom."

I waited for the rest. Nothing came.

"That's it?" I said. "A fucking slap on the wrist... what is *that* shit?"

Thomas' eyes narrowed for a split-second before relaxing.

"I'm afraid that's how these things work," he said. "They make it go away."

When my eyes narrowed, they stayed that way.

"And how does it go away for *me*?"

It was a few minutes after three A.M., but Alex didn't seem to notice the time or the discomfort from the gunshot. It was not in his nature to show weakness or defeat, and giving in to the pain would have amounted to both in his mind. Besides, Damien and Sandy were with him and he wasn't in the habit of being anything less than a rock in front of his troops. The topic was the continued absence of Mr. and ex-Mrs. O'Hara.

"So we haven't been able to reach *either*?" Alex said.

"Nope," Damien said. "Mr. isn't picking up. I sent someone by his place. He's there. We can go in and get him if you want. As for Mrs., we haven't tried since this afternoon, after we left when we heard about Walters. I can head back and check again."

The mention of Buck reminded Alex of another problem. As far as the legal system was concerned the confrontation with Elliot Stevens in Florida had never happened. Buck died before providing an official statement. Sandy interrupted before he could dwell on it.

"I've been thinking this stuff might have something to do with Amy," she said.

Both men gave her an odd look. In Damien's case, Sandy's relentless pursuit of her sister's whereabouts had bothered him for a long time, more so since the two had become more than working partners. He thought it a waste of time, not that he ever said such to her, something preventing their relationship from being anything more than stress-relief. He had his own demons, of course, but felt they were the opposite. Most notable was a burning desire to get out of the Bureau before it sucked the life out of him, something that had grown tenfold since he'd become intimate with her.

When he spoke, some of his frustration came out.

"Uh, Sandy, what are you talking about?" he said. "What's Singer got to do with Amy?"

Sandy took a deep breath and blew it out.

"I found some matches," she said.

Alex perked up.

"You might want to explain that one," he said.

It took Sandy two minutes to do so. Her program had come up with a new list of possible links to Amy, the first in a long time, and she'd been at her desk in the office since before the game ended, checking the information. The first hit was a report from Bluefield, West Virginia. Earlier in the week police there had found the body of a young woman named Tammy Rogers. She had been missing for more than ten years.

"Her physical description was similar to Amy's," Sandy said. "So were the others."

"OK, now you *really* need to explain," Alex said.

"I think there's more to this thing than we thought. The dream, the stuff about Singer, the World Series, I don't know, all of it made me step back and look at baseball again. Before now I wasn't really sure that had anything to do with Amy's death, but I should have been smarter."

Damien could see the familiar emotions building on her face. He hated when she beat herself up like this. Alex did as well, but was too tired to offer up any comfort, he'd leave that to Damien. He'd learned about the relationship long before anyone else in the office, but because they worked so well together he had decided to let it alone. Now was another time to do so.

"I don't know," he said. "This is all… I mean I get what you're saying, but it is extremely sketchy stuff you're talking about. Maybe I'm just tired."

He trailed off into a sigh. Sandy's expression took on a touch of disappointment.

"You're right," she said. "By itself, the hits don't mean anything. That's why I need to make some calls. I was going to start with the cops on Rogers then move to the others… assuming, of course, I have your permission?"

Alex peeked at his wristwatch before one of his fingers started tapping on his desk. He seemed to be staring at something, but neither Sandy nor Damien could tell. After about a minute, Alex looked up.

"All right, tell you what," he said. "You guys get out of here for a couple hours. Go home, sleep on it, and if you still feel the same way in the morning, go for it. I think we've all had enough for today."

Springfield

After a quick check on his guest, Arcadia made his way back to the Connors' living room and sat in the darkness. Time to move things along, he thought, as he pulled out Samantha's cell phone and navigated to the message center. The soft blue light from the screen gave his face an eerie quality as his fingers went to work on the tiny keypad.

> I have your wife. You pay me lots and lots of money and you get her back. You'll be the hero and she might even thank you. Now here's the catch, so pay attention. Go to the police, she dies, go to the FBI, she dies, go to anyone, she dies, it's that simple. I'll be in touch with further instructions.

He re-read the note and tapped *Send*. He tossed the phone to the cushion and pulled out another device. Within seconds his fingers were at work again.

> I thought your team was better than that. Did you forget how to play? Or is something else bothering you? Maybe I can help. I have O'Hara's mother. I'm sure if you tell him he'll be more hittable next time. You can thank me later.

He pushed *Send* and seconds later was back at another blank message. He sat in silence and contemplated for several moments before typing.

Shame about Walters, I'll bet you're really torn up. If not, maybe this will get you there. I'm going to kill Samantha O'Hara and when the dust settles, her death will be on your hands.

He pushed *Send* one last time and laid the phone on the sofa next to Samantha's. His head fell back against the top of the seat cushion and he closed his eyes. He knew no sleep would come because the cravings were strong and he needed all his strength not to act on them.

Not yet, he told himself, but soon.

Philadelphia

The Rays headed for their charter immediately after the game, more than happy to get out of town after the two tough losses, but mechanical problems delayed the flight for several hours. Most of the traveling party boarded anyway and took advantage of the time to get some sleep. Nik was not one of them; he had more pressing matters with which to deal.

He had expected something from AJ, but the text message told him things were a lot worse than originally thought. Kidnapping Samantha was more than anything he could have imagined, even from AJ. He needed to find a solution, but going to the police was out of the question, just as it had been years ago. No, this was a personal problem that needed a personal touch.

All Nik needed now was to figure out how to apply it.

Chapter 39

Philadelphia

I managed to get out of my room in time to catch the seven-forty-five A.M. airport shuttle. I looked pretty ratty in a grey t-shirt, warm-up suit, running shoes, hat-covered-bed-head hair, and stubbled face, but I didn't care. I just wanted to get on the bus, close my eyes, and forget about everything for a few hours. I should have known that was too much to ask.

Gabi intercepted me just as the shuttle pulled up to the door.

"Hey," he said without much oomph. "We added some extra bodies for Florida. I realize you have some special eyes looking out for you already, but I thought you'd like to know."

"Did something else happen?" I said.

"Nah, at least no one told me," he said. "We're, uh, just being careful."

Being careful hadn't done me much good, but I let it go. Gabi was right about the special eyes—Thomas'—but it did help a little knowing there were going to be more. Like the home run call had told me, you could never have too much help.

~*~*~*~*~*~*~*~

A dull ache lingered along Alex's left side. He was in his kitchen at a small round table, his phone and an untouched cup of coffee in front of him, the coffee courtesy of his wife who had since returned to bed. He had balked at staying overnight at the hospital, but was more than happy to accept the bottle of Percocet. The pills were helpful, but the sling he needed to wear to keep the arm still was annoying. Or maybe it was the situation around the World Series that was causing the discomfort. Either way, he was not a happy camper.

There were at least fifty people he wanted or needed to talk to, but at the moment he couldn't think of one name. After a deep sigh, he gave the phone a spin. When it stopped the small antenna nub was pointed in his direction and he chuckled at a memory of the first time he'd played spin the bottle as a kid. He'd never kissed a girl, but he managed to fake his way through and deliver a half-decent one to a girl named Missy Summers. Missy gave Alex a few more firsts before she disappeared from his life.

A sudden buzz chased the memory away. Alex scooped the phone off the table.

"Hey, thanks for the break," Damien said into his ear. "Sandy still wants to go after her leads. If you ask me, I'd agree. After talking through it, she might be on to something."

Alex didn't hesitate.

"Fine, tell her to do it," he said. "What else?"

"I just got a call from an old friend. I think we might have something on Stevens."

Damien left Sandy's apartment just before eight. Her living room was a mess from their intense love-making session. They'd never made it to the bedroom. Sandy laughed at the memory as she cleaned up. The sex had been great, but nothing compared to the brain-storming after. Damien had helped her focus by asking lots of questions, questions she would now use in the phone calls to the list of contacts from the case files.

She was confident of success. No, make that *hopeful*. A lot of time had passed and Sandy had no idea if there would still be anyone out there who could help. She knew firsthand from Amy's case that people had a tendency to forget when things went badly or when they failed.

At exactly eight-thirty she took a deep breath and made the first call.

"I'm trying to reach Detective Eduard Garcia," she said in a firm tone. "This is Agent Hood from the FBI."

A female voice responded defensively.

"*Captain* Garcia just arrived," the voice said. "Please hold."

Not a good start, Sandy thought. She had to wait almost five minutes before a man's voice came on the line. His tone was more pleasant than the operator's had been.

"This is Captain Garcia, but call me Eddie," he said. "How can I help you, Agent Hood?"

"Captain, sorry, *Eddie*," she said. "What can you tell me about Tammy Rogers?"

Springfield

When Damien slipped into the Acura's passenger seat, he was still in the same clothes as yesterday.

"Good night?" Thomas said.

"Yep," Damien said.

They glanced at each other and left it at that.

Not quite fifteen minutes later they were cruising north on I-476. The trees along either side of the road were dropping their multi-colored leaves and Damien noticed a lot of bare branches in the morning breeze. It was another change of season and he wondered if he would make it through the winter.

The job was taking a toll on him and last night's soiree with Sandy had heightened his desire to move on to something else, something less dramatic in a place less cold. For a few seconds, he debated talking about it with Thomas, but decided not to burden the man. The case was enough to deal with. The FBI wasn't paying

Thomas to be a shrink, too. As the car slowed at the Springfield exit Damien pushed the thoughts away.

"That was fast," he said without a hint of sarcasm.

"I try," Thomas said.

Philadelphia

With all my distractions I didn't realize my phone had died until I dropped it into the plastic container at the airport security line. Damn it, I thought, as I pushed the basket into the X-ray machine, I need to get focused. After a grumpy TSA agent cleared me through I quickly headed for the concourse between terminals B and C. I still had time before my flight to plug in and check for messages. I got lucky and found an open chair near a power outlet.

After I saw what was waiting for me, I didn't feel so lucky any longer.

Michael felt like shit, but managed to shower, shave, get dressed, and make it to the brokerage office as it opened at nine-thirty. His plan to use his money to cover the Dukabi debt and Samantha's for the casino markers had failed and he was staring at a tough decision: Pick one and hope for the best. A thought to try Samantha one last time died when he couldn't find his cell phone. That little annoyance added to his sour mood as he sat in front of his broker, a rotund, pompous ass named Charles Faldowski.

"As I mentioned, there is a rather substantial transaction fee," Faldowski said again.

"I got that the first few times you told me, Chuck, I'm not stupid," Michael said. "Can we please just fucking get this done?"

"Very well," Faldowski said.

His tone was like that normally used on a child and Michael's face twitched through an urge to reach across and punch the fat bastard in the nose. He suppressed it as Faldowski pushed one last key then left the office. Alone, Michael uttered a few expletives under his breath before standing and moving to the windows of the office. Across the Delaware River, the flatness of New Jersey stretched out for miles.

As Michael stared, he made his decision.

Springfield

Springfield Mall sat at the intersection of Baltimore Pike and Route 320, about a mile east of I-476. It was relatively small by today's standards, especially when one of the big box spaces was unoccupied. That was the current situation and Thomas had no trouble spotting the police cruiser parked near the empty shell's lower-level entrance. After parking, he and Damien stepped out into the chilly morning air as the other driver did the same.

"Officer Woods," Damien said. "You're looking fit."

"Agent Hastings," Woods said as they shook hands. "You look like shit. Who's your friend?"

"This is Thomas Hillsborough," Damien said, ignoring the insult. "He has skills you and I could only dream of."

"Is that so?" Woods said as he reached for Thomas' hand. "Then the pleasure is mine, Mr. Hillsborough."

"Call me Thomas."

"OK, Thomas, call me Dean," Woods said. "And now that we're all best buds, let's take a walk. I think we found what you boys have been looking for."

Chapter 40

Philadelphia

Sandy listened intently as Captain Garcia told the story of Tammy Rogers.

She'd lived by herself. Outside a woman named Emma Sampson, Tammy's aunt and landlady, she had no family in Bluefield. Because of that, she'd made a lot of noise over the years about leaving town. At first, most everyone, including Eddie and Emma, thought that's what she'd done. It was two weeks before Emma finally called police, inspired by an overflowing mail slot and past due rent.

Emma confirmed she'd last seen Tammy on the day of the Orioles' first game. She also confirmed it was the last time she'd seen Tammy's car outside the building. A search of the mail revealed the first clue, a paycheck from the truck-stop where Tammy worked. Her boss there corroborated the timing of the disappearance, telling Eddie she had worked a half-day the day of the game and never came back. Interviews with co-workers came up empty. It wasn't until Tammy's purse was found a week later that police began to think foul play was involved.

The purse was discovered by a security guard on his regular visit to an abandoned warehouse on the outskirts of town, a known hangout for teenagers. Inside the purse was a $150 ATM receipt, a half-full container of Tic Tacs, and a waitress nameplate with "Tammy" printed on it. The receipt was the first real break. The date matched Emma's story and the withdrawal came from a machine at a bar with which Eddie was familiar.

"You have to understand, Agent Hood, we didn't have a lot to go on," he said to Sandy. "Everything up to that point had come up empty. There were a lot of prints on the purse besides Tammy's, but we couldn't get a match. Best guess was they belonged to the kids that left it there. I can send copies if you'd like."

"That would be helpful," Sandy said. "What did you find at the bar?"

"I had a discussion with the owner," Eddie said. "The man was more than happy to answer my questions, but got nervous when I told him Tammy was missing. My first instinct was he did something or knew something, but turns out he was more worried about Tammy's unpaid tab."

After a few seconds to process, Sandy found new questions to ask.

"Did he remember anything unusual? Was she with someone?"

"He told me Tammy spent most of the night talking with a man, but he had no idea who he was and couldn't really give me a description."

"Do you think a picture might help?" Sandy said.

"The guy still runs the bar, it couldn't hurt to try."

Michael left the brokerage house with four cashier's checks totaling $650K, the grand total owed to the casinos. Even though the paper weighed no more than a few ounces, it felt like a boulder in his pocket, pressing down on him with a vengeance. The transactions with Faldowski had pretty much depleted his entire net worth. Without Samantha's contribution he might not ever be able to rebuild it.

He was doing his best not to think about that fact, but his pace as he walked west on Market Street, toward 30th Street Station, reflected the added burden. As he crossed 22nd Street, the marquee for the Forum Theater caught his eye. He peeked at the posters of the current airings as he passed. He had visited the Forum more than a few times back in his playing days. The box office was already open and he had a fleeting temptation to go catch a show, but managed to kill it and continue toward the train station.

When he reached 30th Street he crossed the intersection and stepped up to the first vendor truck parked along Market in front of the Post Office. In short order he had a carry-out plate of eggs, bacon, homefries, and toast, along with a large black coffee. The breakfast cost $6, but Michael handed the vendor a $20 bill and didn't ask for change.

He carried the bag into the station where he added a morning newspaper. The greasy breakfast was just what his body needed and he ate slowly as he flipped through the news. Fifteen minutes passed before he finished, but the next New Jersey Transit train to Atlantic City wasn't until eleven-forty. He sat in silence and killed the time watching the passing faces. None paid him any attention and the longer he sat, the more his mind gravitated toward Dukabi.

Maybe picking the casinos wasn't such a good idea, he thought.

"Goddamn it, Samantha," he said aloud. "Thanks for nothing."

Springfield

Officer Woods led Thomas and Damien under a height-limit railing at the far end of the mall parking lot.

"It's mostly mall workers and carpoolers down here," Woods said. "There are a few cars left every night, you know, people hook up after work, one leaves their car, nothing out of the ordinary. Mall security does a few drive-bys and our guys might do a pass or two, depending on what else is going on, but if you're going to leave a car for a couple days, it's not a bad spot. None of the security cameras reach this far down."

"Who found it?" Damien said when he saw the car.

"Our night shift guy," Woods said. "It's not exactly a minimum-wage grunt kinda car. He noted the plate in his log and it matched the hit list you guys circulated."

The black Cadillac STS was facing forward in a spot, a position designed to hide the license plate from view. Pennsylvania only required one plate, in the rear. Backing in was a simple tactic to make discovery difficult. Obviously, this driver knew the trick.

"That's our boy," Damien said as Thomas joined him at the rear bumper.

"Indeed."

"So who is this guy?" Woods said.

"He may or may not be involved with a crime that may or may not have taken place," Damien said.

"Lucky you," Woods said.

"Something like that," Damien said.

Fifteen minutes later, a flatbed hauler arrived and pulled the car out of the spot. At least that was one benefit of being parked face-out, it made the tow job easier. Five minutes after that, Damien signed the driver's form and the truck pulled away. He watched for a few seconds before rejoining Woods and Thomas.

"Thanks for finding it," he said.

"Wasn't too hard," Woods said; then after a pause. "Don't be such a stranger, especially if you find more bad stuff in my township."

He slid into his cruiser and pulled away as Damien and Thomas moved toward the Acura.

"What are you thinking?" Damien said.

"We have his car, so how is he getting around? I don't see Mr. Stevens as the walking type."

"Good point," Damien said. "So what would you do?"

"Borrow someone else's," Thomas said.

Damien studied Thomas' face and began to nod after a few seconds.

"Works for me," he said. "Let's go find out."

Chapter 41

Early-September, 2001
Columbus, Ohio

A man was watching the game from a seat along the first-base side, no more than ten rows from the field. Most of the seats in Cooper Stadium, home of the Columbus Clippers, were like that, close to the field. The cozy confines made fans feel like they were part of the game, the way it was supposed to be. For the man watching, "the way it was supposed to be" meant something else. He should have been out on the field instead of in the stands.

Baseball had always been a source of great joy for the man, but it was now a source of great pain. It wasn't always that way. There was a time not long ago when America's pastime was his dream, a dream in which baseball was his soul mate and each day was filled with the happiness derived from the game's simplicity and grace. It was perfection personified and nothing else came close. And then it was all ripped away.

He'd since found other ways to fill the gaping hole.

Three young women were sitting in the row behind the man, watching him almost as much as the game and whispering to each other between giggles. None were as young as the laughter indicated, but something about the handsome man left each feeling very much like a school girl. Their crushes had been instant and strong, and after much debate, one finally acted on the impulses. Her name was Becky Tate.

"Excuse me," Becky said as she leaned forward and tapped the man on the shoulder. "Would you like some peanuts? I can't eat all of these by myself and you look hungry."

Becky held out the bag with an inviting smile.

"Sure, thanks," the man said as he reached into the bag. "I *am* hungry."

He took a handful of shells and turned away.

"Thanks," he said over his shoulder.

"You're welcome," Becky said.

Another series of whispers and giggles followed, but Becky had seen and heard enough to know she wanted more. She tapped the man's shoulder again.

"Hey, why don't you sit back here so you don't have to keep twisting around?"

"Maybe I like to twist around," the man said.

Seconds later he was in a seat next to her. Becky pushed a few loose strands of long blonde hair back behind her ear and held out her hand.

"I'm Becky," she said. "What's your name?"

"Peter," he said as the urges came rushing back. "Peter Arcadia."

Chapter 42

Sandy read the list of cases again.

> Tammy Rogers—Bluefield, WV, June 20, 1997
> Maureen Sullivan—Charleston, SC, July 12, 1999
> Elizabeth Jennings—Greensboro, NC, May 31, 2000
> Becky Tate—Columbus, OH, September 8, 2001
> Amy Hood—Reading, PA, July 9, 2002
> Lauren Bishop—Reading, PA, July 9, 2002

She reached to the floor and picked up the Sullivan file. Inside she found the name and number she needed.

"I'm trying to reach Detective Martell, please. My name is Sandy Hood. I'm with the FBI."

"Honey, Vincent is no longer with the force," a woman said in a soft southern accent. "He retired last year."

"Is there a way I can reach him?" Sandy said in a pleading tone. "It's important. He may have information that can help us with a current case."

She held her breath as the phone went silent. A few seconds later the sweet voice returned and so did Sandy's heartbeat.

"Lieutenant says it's OK to give you Vincent's number. Hold on and I'll fetch it for ya."

Springfield

Timing, like luck, can be good or bad. For Elliot, it had been very good. He had pulled Samantha's car into her garage exactly eight minutes prior to Terry's drive-by after Game 1, thus allowing the player to see the reflection through the windows. The following morning, he had backed the car out of the garage and driven away exactly nine minutes before Damien, Thomas, and Marshall arrived.

And now, a mere fourteen minutes after he once again drove away from the house, Thomas was pulling into Samantha's driveway. After parking the Acura in front of the garage, he and Damien got out. Moments earlier they had informed Alex of their idea. The director had given the OK to search the house. In his opinion, they had probable cause. The U.S. District Attorney might not agree, but Alex was willing to take the risk. He was running out of other ideas.

Thomas confirmed the garage was empty before heading around the far side of the house. Damien went for the front steps and knocked hard at the door. Despite several added shouts, there was no response. He quickly worked the lock and stepped into the foyer. A quick sweep of the front rooms revealed nothing. As he stepped back into the hallway, Thomas appeared at the far end, just inside the kitchen. He motioned with his hand to Damien.

"You find something?" Damien said as he reached the threshold of the room.

Thomas had moved to near the sink.

"Several things," he said.

Philadelphia

"I'm gonna have to give that gal a talkin' to," a deep Southern-accented voice said in a playful tone through the phone. "Just givin' out a man's number, now that ain't right."

"Thanks for taking my call, Mr. Martell," Sandy said.

"Call me Vincent," the ex-policeman said. "My 'Mister' days got retired when I did. Now, how can I help you? You said something about an old case of mine?"

"Yes, sir, Maureen Sullivan," Sandy said. "I was hoping you could shed some light on what happened, or at least what you think happened."

When Vincent replied his tone was no longer playful.

"I hope you got some time, young lady," he said. "That might take a while."

In his fragile state, Elliot completely forgot Arcadia's very specific instructions: "Leave *her* car at the mall and take *yours* to the airport." The mistake was both fortunate and unfortunate. Fortunate for Elliot because he avoided running into the police at the mall, but unfortunate for Arcadia because knowing about the police would have been important.

As it was, he was barely able to drive and almost got into three accidents along the way to the airport. The confused and distracted state-of-mind was brought on by another Arcadia beat-down. Elliot had no desire to go to Florida, but Arcadia had made it clear he had no choice. Elliot's jaw still hurt like hell from the message.

After parking at Philly International, he sat for a minute and surveyed his reflection in the car's rearview mirror, wondering how someone learned to inflict such pain without leaving a mark. Mario's original warning once again returned and a thought escaped Elliot.

"Maybe I should stay in Florida."

Vincent Martell's story about the old case was as detailed as Eddie's had been. Water had added a bit of a challenge, but the coroner's office eventually gave a time of death of between one and four A.M. Vincent and his team interviewed fifteen witnesses in the next couple of weeks, starting with Maureen's two friends, and the time of death fit into every story, but little else did. A few remembered seeing her, but none recalled whether she'd been with anyone other than the two girlfriends. Toxicology reports revealed her blood-alcohol level to be three times the legal limit. Vincent had a bad feeling from the beginning, but was never able to find the Holy Grail of evidence, or any grail for that matter, to alter the conclusion.

"Best I could ever come up with was the girl was stone drunk and fell into the damn harbor and drowned," he said to Sandy. "I didn't want to sign off on it, but I had nothin' else. What could I do? My budget wasn't big enough to chase it forever."

"I understand," Sandy said. "Did any of the witnesses mention anything happening at the baseball game?"

"Hmm, I'd have to look in the files," Vincent said. "Why, does that have something to do with what happened to the poor girl?"

"It just might."

Springfield

The blood spot in front of the sink was barely the size of a dime and the shard of glass was virtually the same tint as the white porcelain of the sink. Damien was sure he'd have missed both, but left that out when he called Alex.

"The rest of the house is clear," he said through the phone. "What's next?"

"OK, wait for the cavalry," Alex said. "We'll make a show of it. Maybe one of the neighbors saw something."

"We'll be here," Damien said before disconnecting.

He rejoined Thomas in the front foyer.

"OK, partner, reinforcements are on the way. Let's get outta here before we fuck up any more of the crime scene. The techies tend to get pissy when that happens."

"As do I," Thomas said.

The sharpness caught Damien's attention.

"What are you thinking?" he said with concern.

"From what I can tell, someone has already corrupted the scene."

~*~*~*~*~*~*~*~

Tampa

Terry dialed Samantha's home number not two minutes after Thomas and Damien stepped out of her house. He was calling from the team bus, headed for their hotel in Tampa. When the answering machine picked up, he frowned through the instructions.

"Hey, Mom, it's me... *again*," he said after the beep. "Where the heck are you? I've been trying your cell, but I keep getting busy signals. Did you forget to charge it? You might want to check that. Anyway, I'm pitching again on Sunday. I'm gonna leave tickets for you for all the games in case you decide to come down. I'd love it if you did, but I'll understand if not. Anyway, call me back already. I'm starting to worry about you."

The frown stayed in place after he closed the phone. It wasn't like Samantha to be *this* quiet. Sure, they'd had a fight and she got nervous whenever he pitched, but this was getting to be a little much. For a few minutes he pondered asking Michael to go check on her but squashed the idea, thinking it would just cause more problems.

With a sigh, he stowed his phone and looked out the window next to him. The sun outside the bus was bright. Some of the warmth was getting through the glass. It felt good and he let his head fall against the pane. Along with the vibrations of the engine it helped him relax and his thoughts slowly left his parents. They were adults. They'd figure it out.

It's not my problem, he concluded, as he closed his eyes.

Chapter 43

Tampa

Having been unable to reach Thomas before my flight left Philly, I was dialing as soon as the wheels hit the ground in Tampa.

"Hey," I said after he answered. "Where have you been? I just forwarded you a text."

"I'm reading it now."

His tone was more serious than usual. Mine was probably still about the same as the last day or so, meaning seriously frazzled.

"What do you think?" I said.

"It certainly explains the first two notes," he said. "Agent Hastings agrees."

"Hastings is with you?" I said. "What are you guys doing? Where are you?"

"At the moment we are standing near Samantha O'Hara's porch awaiting permission to re-enter the house."

I stopped reaching for my carry-on from the overhead and dropped back into my seat.

"Do I want to know why?" I said.

"Unlikely, but it would be better if you did."

Springfield

Using Marshall's parents' house had added a nice touch of irony to Arcadia's plans. He doubted anyone else would ever see the connection, but it put a nice bow on top of everything. Coupled with Elliot being out of the house and the fact he'd never see the little shit again, it left Arcadia in a great mood as he settled onto the living room sofa.

The calm was shattered by a sudden parade of vehicles out on Rolling Road. Arcadia stood and watched through the front window as the cars continued past the house and turned onto Thornridge. Within seconds he realized what was happening and raced up the stairs to Marshall's old bedroom. From his vantage point there, he counted ten vehicles and fourteen bodies around Samantha's house. Most wore blue jackets with "FBI" emblazoned in bright yellow across the back, but two standing near the back door did not.

Arcadia squinted through the glare of the sun at the window and focused on those two.

"Shit," he said aloud as the recognition set in.

He watched as a jacketed agent emerged from the house and approached the two men. There was a brief conversation and all three went back inside. Arcadia stepped away from the window and tried to find an explanation for what he was seeing. He knew nothing had been found yesterday when Connors and the two men had visited. This circus would have happened then if so. He was also fairly confident Michael O'Hara was not the culprit. He was stupid, but not *that* stupid; he wasn't going to call anyone.

No, this was something else.

Arcadia moved back to the window. It took about twenty seconds for the answer to come.

"You stupid little fuck," he said aloud when it hit him.

An agent interrupted Alex in the middle of a call to Damien.

"Excuse me, sir, Elliot Stevens just showed up on the grid," the man said. "He was on a flight out of Philly that landed in Tampa about an hour ago."

"Did you hear that?" Alex said into the phone.

"Yes, sir," Damien replied. "What are you thinking?"

"I'm thinking I want you on the next flight to Tampa," Alex said. "I'll make some calls and get some reinforcements, but I'd rather have you guys go get him, it'll make for less paperwork in bringing him back."

"Understood," Damien said before disconnecting.

He stowed the phone and turned to Thomas.

"Tell me again what you think."

Both were leaning against the side of Thomas' car watching the movements of the agents and technicians around Samantha's house. In addition to the blood and glass, a large collection of prints had been discovered, at least five different sets. Someone *had* cleaned, but not very well. Damien expected three sets to be accounted for, Samantha's, Michael's, and Gabi's. He knew the other two would be the keys to learning Samantha's fate.

"She was abducted from the kitchen," Thomas said. "I'd say Arcadia or Stevens or both."

"That's good, because the latter just showed up in Florida," Damien said as he pushed away from the car. "Alex would like us to go escort him back."

Steven White had been an FBI field agent for all of three weeks. At first he was both excited and nervous about being on the call to Samantha's house, but both emotions had faded significantly during the past hour. So far his interviews had been a bust. No one had seen or heard anything unusual, and he was fairly certain that wasn't going to change as he and an older agent named Joe Khori walked toward the last house on their side of Rolling Road.

"You ever use one of those things?" White said as he eyed an old RV near the garage.

"Can't say that I have," Khori said.

"Me, either," White said.

"You got a point, rookie?"

White nodded.

"Yeah, I'm starting to think it would be fun to tour around in one, a lot more fun than this."

Khori shook his head.

"I don't recall seeing where it said this job was supposed to be fun," he said; then after a few more steps. "Tell ya what. Take this one on your own. That's as much *fun* as I can make it."

He stayed at the bottom of the steps as White proceeded to the door. A minute later a man greeted him there.

"Can I help you?" the man said.

"Um, yes, sir, you can," White said. "I'm—*we're*—with the FBI."

He turned slightly and motioned to Khori.

"We need to ask you a few questions."

The man at the door appeared shocked.

"The FBI?" he said. "What's this all about? Have I done something wrong?"

"No, not at all, sir," White said in a reassuring tone. "We're just conducting interviews regarding a case in the neighborhood. It shouldn't take long."

The man at the door hesitated, before beginning to nod.

"Oh, I see," he said. "Wow, the FBI, in *this* neighborhood? Nothing exciting ever happens around here."

Chapter 44

Philadelphia

Sandy was wearing blue jeans and Damien's Widener University sweatshirt and it generated more than a few odd looks as she made her way to the break room. She didn't care. Given the long hours recently and quick turnaround this morning, she knew Alex wouldn't mind, and frankly, he was the only one that mattered.

At the machines she bought two bags of Doritos and a Diet Coke. Back at her desk, she opened the soda and one of the bags and sampled some of each before focusing her eyes on a spiral notebook resting atop her keyboard. The number of used pages in the book had increased significantly during her earlier phone calls and she needed to regroup and take it all in again.

After a deep breath, she flipped back to the first page.

OK, there's a pattern here, she thought, as she looked at the list of cases again, but what is it? Elizabeth Jennings, Becky Tate, and now Tammy Rogers were all officially murders; the autopsy report for Rogers concluded she'd been suffocated and the body moved after death. Maureen Sullivan was still classified as an accidental death, but Vincent Martell had agreed it was worth another look and volunteered to ask a few questions of the coroner.

There was nothing new for Amy and Lauren, but Sandy left them in the mix anyway. It was a gut feeling based on a few things, but mostly the fact that all six women had the same basic physical appearance: mid-late 20's, blonde hair, 5'8" to 5'10" in height, and 110-120 pounds. They all had something else in common, too: Baseball.

Each location where they'd last been seen was home to a minor league team. All except Tammy Rogers had attended a game as well. Sandy knew that wasn't enough though. Everything could be attributed to nothing more than a convenient set of coincidences, one that ended more than six years ago. That last point taunted her as she chomped at another handful of chips.

"What the hell am I missing?" she said aloud as she chewed. "What ties it together?"

She washed the chips down with a shot of Coke.

"Cities with baseball teams, a progression of years, think, think, think," she said. "Is it the cities, the years, or the women? Nah, it can't be the women, that's got to be the end, but what then, what ties baseball and a progression of years across different cities?"

She finished off the first bag of Doritos and wiped her hands on her jeans. After another drink of soda, she started to rock in her chair. After a few seconds she reached up and ran her hands through her hair. On the sixth stroke she held fast and tied the locks into a pigtail and sat forward again. Another long gulp of Coke was followed by a loud burp seconds later.

An idea came along with the exhale of gas.

"Oh wow, a player or coach could do that," she said aloud. "And maybe it stopped because they quit. Shit, that's gotta be a long list."

She sat back again and pondered her next move.

"Of course," she said aloud. "He'll know."

She picked up her phone and scrolled through the contacts until the right name appeared.

"Hey, you busy?" she said as soon as the call was answered. "I got something you're gonna love. And don't say no because I really need your help."

Philadelphia

None of the FBI air assets were available, so one-way tickets to Tampa were waiting at the USAirways counter when Damien and Thomas arrived at the airport. They'd come directly from Samantha's and neither had a bag, but both had weapons, and the guns caused some tension at the security gate. Damien's active FBI ID granted him safe passage, but a phone call was required to clear Thomas through.

"Friends in high places, huh?" Damien said after they moved away from the screening area.

"They come in handy, yes," Thomas said.

Five minutes later they took seats in front of the window at their departure gate.

"We should have a fix on a location by the time we land in Tampa," Damien said. "He shouldn't be too hard to find. Of course, that assumes his phone is still on."

"I'd be shocked if it were not," Thomas said. "He's there for a reason. He'll need to stay connected and available."

"Yeah, 'connected and available' so we can nab his sorry ass."

Springfield

"Good luck with the job search, Mr. Arcadia," Agent White said after stepping to the porch. "Thanks again for your time. Don't hesitate to call if you remember anything else."

"I won't. And good luck to you with finding the bad guys."

White jogged across the front yard and rejoined Khori along the sidewalk. When the two disappeared around the corner, Arcadia went back inside. The young agent had made a lot of mistakes and shared entirely too many details. Arcadia now had confirmation his earlier guess about the FBI's appearance had been correct.

On his way to the kitchen, he made a call on Samantha's phone.

"Yeah, I know what I said, but I want it done *now*. I've had enough of that stupid fuck."

Chapter 45

St. Petersburg

The baseball home of the Tampa Bay Rays was located in St. Petersburg, Florida, just off I-175, on a patch of land between 10th and 16th Streets South and 1st and 4th Avenues South. The structure was originally named "Florida Suncoast Dome" and later "ThunderDome" before eventually becoming "Tropicana Field"—as in the orange juice of the same name.

The 1.1 million-square-foot stadium and its cable-supported translucent Teflon-coated fiberglass roof were not designed for baseball. The lid was great at keeping the Florida sun at bay, but with its system of catwalks and a max height of 225 feet, wasn't so good for the game. A lot of baseballs hit stuff and it made for some nuanced ground rules. We were in the process of reviewing said rules, but with the weight of the text message hanging off of me, I wasn't really paying as much attention as I should have been. Bart noticed.

"Hey, are you OK?" he said in Spanish in a low voice.

"Not so much, big man," I said. "But I'm a good faker."

"Excuse me, gentlemen," someone said. "Do you have a question?"

I looked up. It was the head groundskeeper. I think he'd just explained something and he was looking at me like I had smacked his mother.

"Um, no, *yeah*," I said. "Say that last part again."

"*As I was saying*," he said with obvious contempt for my existence. "If a batted ball hits any of the four catwalks, lights, or suspended objects in foul territory it is automatically ruled a dead ball and called a strike."

That was pretty much a quote from the rules, a copy of which was in my hand.

"Right, exactly, once foul, always foul," I said.

"*Anyway*, moving on," the man said after a sigh.

He led the group forward into the outfield. Bart nudged me with his elbow and smiled.

"Nice save, Amigo," he said.

"Fake it 'til you make it, baby," I said.

That approach had gotten me through the past few days so why stop now?

The Phillies team bus made two stops. First was the Grand Hyatt on Bayport Drive in Tampa. The second was at Tropicana Field. Terry stayed in his seat until that second stop. He was on a fixed schedule and a session with Ernie Goff was on tap. After he stepped off the bus, the warmth of the sunshine felt more refreshing than it had through the window. He turned his face skyward and closed his eyes to soak in a few rays.

"Feels good, huh?" a familiar voice said.

He opened his eyes to find Clarence Riggs walking toward him.

"Yo, Cee, what are you doing here?" Terry said.

"A favor for Gabi Loeb," Riggs said. "He wanted a few more bodies around. Didn't say why and I didn't ask. I'm getting paid and that's all that matters."

"Well, you alone are a few bodies," Terry said. "I hope he's paying you double."

"Yeah, he should be," Riggs said with a nod. "Remind me to tell him."

Both men chuckled as they started toward the entrance.

"Oh, and I'm *your* shadow. Loeb said he'd tell you why when he gets here."

Terry stopped and looked up at the taller man. After a second, he shrugged.

"Cool."

At the same time, Nik was at his locker in the Rays clubhouse, listening to AJ's latest message for the umpteenth time. He still wasn't sure if it was true, but he knew it had to be discussed. He and Terry needed to deal with the ghosts of the past once and for all. They'd avoided it for too long, waited too many years.

It was time to tell the truth.

After the walk-thru I ventured up to the press level and found an empty seat in one of the suites there. The rest of the crew had headed back to the hotel. We were staying at the Westin Harbour Island in Tampa, but I wasn't up for any company. I needed some alone time to work through the text message. Samantha O'Hara might be in trouble and somehow it was connected to me. Even with knowing Thomas was working on it, it was bothersome to say the least.

Below me on the field, a scattering of Phillies were taking advantage of the off day and were working out. I spotted Terry in the outfield. He was near the left field bullpen, doing long-tosses, easily covering the width of the field with each throw. If anyone had told him about his mother, he wasn't showing it. My guess was he didn't know. I wasn't going to be the one to tell him. I just sat there and watched.

It didn't take long before I started to zone out, hypnotized by the long, high arcs of each throw. Before I got totally lost, another familiar figure emerging from the Rays dugout caught my eye. Nik Sanchez was walking with a purpose and I started to get a bad feeling—no, sorry, *another one*. When he stopped near the spot where Terry was standing, it got worse and I stood. The two started talking, but Terry continued to throw at first. After a minute or so, Nik's animations increased and Terry stopped and turned.

When they stepped to within inches of each other, I turned and ran for the elevator to field level, hoping to get out there in time.

"I still have the fucking welt on my back," Nik said. "So, yeah, I got that you didn't believe me, but you better fucking believe me now."

Terry closed further until their noses almost touched.

"Why should I?" he said in a low growl. "How is AJ my problem?"

"He has your mother."

I reached the field and broke into a jog toward the bullpen. Nik was already gone, but I found Terry on a bench there. He was talking on a cell phone, but as I neared, a large man in a painted-on black shirt intercepted me. Luckily, for me, we both quickly recognized each other.

"What happened, Clarence?" I said. "Where's Nik?"

"I don't know," he said in a heavy tone. "It's bad, whatever it is."

Terry looked up when he heard our voices. From the pain in his eyes, I got my answer, but he confirmed it anyway.

"Jesus Christ, Marshall, *he's got my mom.*"

~*~*~*~*~*~*~

An hour or so later, I was in a conference room in the Rays office area. The mood at the impromptu meeting was understandably strained. With me were Terry, Nik, Gabi, and Mark. Via speakerphone, Director Harris, Agent Hastings, and Thomas had joined us. Mark's face had the same darkness he'd displayed to me back in Philly, but I'm sure the same could have been said for all of us at that point.

Mark was first to speak.

"OK, let's get to it," he said in a serious tone; then after focusing on Terry and Nik. "I just got finished speaking to the general managers and managers of each team. They were made aware of the situation in *very* general terms only."

The two ballplayers nodded.

"Whether you two play in the rest of the series is your choice," Mark said. "If you decide not to, we'll provide an appropriate media release. The, uh, true nature of things will remain confined to those in this room, however. Did I get that right, Alex?"

All eyes turned to the phone.

"You did," Director Harris' voice said. "Thank you, Mark. Obviously, until we know more, any leaks could further endanger Mrs. O'Hara."

Terry's face twitched and he leaned in toward the phone.

"What *are* you guys doing about this?" he said sharply.

"This is what we know so far," Harris' firm voice said through the speakers. "Mr. Connors received two threats earlier this week, but neither was specific. Last night, he received a third. Mr. Sanchez received a similar message and we now suspect your mother may have been abducted. We have several suspects, a Peter Arcadia and an Andrew Sing—"

"*What?*" Terry said, interrupting. "Jesus Christ, man, Peter Arcadia *is* AJ Singer. Arcadia is the fake name he used when he took chicks to hotels so no one would recognize him. Tell me you fucking people knew that."

"We suspected as much," Harris said. "Bear in mind, and I have to emphasize this, as of now there is no direct evidence to suggest your mother has been harmed. She is missing, but we have no demands outside of the cryptic messages. We are pursuing several leads. Agent Hastings and Mr. Hillsborough are in Florida doing that as we speak, but I can't divulge any more than that."

"When the fuck was someone going to tell me?" Terry said. "How long have you known?"

He was starting to lose it. I wanted to do something, but had no idea what.

"What about my dad?" he said after a pause. "Does he know anything?"

"I will inform him of the situation as soon as we reach him," Harris said.

"*Michael's missing, too?*" Terry said as he leaned back in his chair. "Could someone please tell me what the fuck is going on?"

Chapter 46

Atlantic City

When Michael stepped off the elevator, the noise overwhelmed him. Caesar's poker room beckoned from his left and he stopped to look in at the tables. Most were in use, but it wasn't overly crowded. He stared for a few seconds, fighting hard against the urges to step past the half-wall separating the room from the rest of the casino floor. Minutes earlier he had delivered the fourth and final cashier's check. His intent had been to get off the elevator, get outside and get the hell out of town as soon as possible, but the cascade of sound was triggering myriad sensations. The sudden grip of a large hand was the strongest.

"*Not today,* Mr. O'Hara," a voice said as the hand squeezed. "We'd hate to have to void that check you just gave us."

Michael flinched and looked up at the man holding him. He was wearing a black suit that strained to maintain its weave over massive muscles. Another similar looking fellow was just behind, but where the first was muscled, the second was just plain massive. Michael somehow managed a small smile despite the increasing pain in his shoulder.

"I, um, I thought I saw an old friend," he said. "I was just going in to say hello."

"Not today."

St. Petersburg

Collin George caught the tail-end of the argument on the field from a seat in the press box. Thinking it was related to the beaning from Game 1, he'd headed down to intercept one or both players for some follow-up comments before they left the park for the night. On his way, he'd spotted Mark and Gabi rushing into the Rays executive offices, and a glance in revealed Terry and Nik already inside.

It was now forty-five minutes later and Collin was still loitering outside the offices. No one had yet to re-emerge and he was beginning to worry. He'd tossed out a tease to his editor about the pending new angle on the Series, but was almost out of time to still hit the deadline. He was about to give up and call it off when Mark and Gabi came through the doors in front of him.

"Hey guys," he said. "Can I ask a couple questions?"

Mark glanced back, but didn't stop. Gabi did, but his expression was not friendly.

"What's up, Gabi?" Collin said. "Is there a problem with O'Hara and Sanchez? Does it have something to do with the hit-by-pitch?"

Gabi's eyes narrowed and then relaxed.

"There are no problems," he said.

The reporter ignored the dismissal.

"C'mon, Gabi," he said. "I know there's something up. I'm just trying to do my job here."

"I know exactly what you're trying to do," Gabi said.

With that, he turned and walked away without another word.

"Don't be like that," Collin said to his back. "C'mon... *shit.*"

Gabi didn't stop and Collin turned to look into the offices. There was no sign of anyone else and he decided to give it up for now. He'd get another chance later. Whatever was happening, he was determined to get some answers.

~*~*~*~*~*~*~

After the meeting broke up, I called Thomas.

"I didn't know you were coming to Florida," I said.

"Nor did I," he said. "It appears to have been a good choice."

I shifted in the uncomfortable chair. OK, maybe it wasn't the chair, maybe it was me.

"Yeah, tell me about it," I said. "This thing is getting worse by the minute."

"Yes, it appears Mrs. O'Hara is in serious trouble."

Terry was still nearby, standing outside the open door to the conference room with Clarence Riggs and Nik. I turned so my voice wouldn't carry out to them.

"And that's why you guys are here, right?" I said into the phone to Thomas.

"As Director Harris noted, we are in pursuit of a lead, yes."

"And after you find the lead, then what?"

"We find Mrs. O'Hara."

He sounded confident, as usual.

That made one of us.

~*~*~*~*~*~*~

Atlantic City

Mario Pastelli was in his office reviewing his latest batch of gaming data. The amounts he had to pay various moles inside the casinos' offices to get it were steep, but almost always worth the cost. This day was turning out to be no different. He'd found several juicy morsels he could turn into nice profits, but it was another familiar name and set of transactions that had his attention at the moment, on the list of repayments.

He leaned forward and pointed the cursor to each occurrence, clicking through to the details one at a time. As he read, he began to get more annoyed. That emotion came out when he spoke into his cell phone after reviewing the final transaction.

"Looks like you got yourself a problem," he said.

"What problem?" Arcadia said into his ear.

"Michael O'Hara is a fuckin' liar."

~*~*~*~*~*~*~

St. Petersburg

Elliot didn't understand why Arcadia needed him to track Connors and the two ballplayers, but he didn't question it. He was just happy to be away from the man, something he more and more wanted to make permanent. The task had been relatively easy. He had simply stationed himself near the ballpark and waited for each to arrive. After all were inside, he paid an attendant at the entrance $500 to call when any came out.

In the meantime, he made his way to a bar across the street and commandeered a small table facing the door. Afternoon had faded into evening as he waited and pondered his future. His company was a glass of whiskey, but no matter how many times he emptied and refilled it, it didn't seem to help. His plan to use the information he had on Arcadia was a bust. He'd lost control of the situation and had no way to get it back.

Arcadia was too strong, in every way possible. Elliot was nothing more than a pussy with a gun, and the faux-toughness had always been a house of cards destined to collapse. Mario had known it for years, so had Arcadia. Elliot was the only one who didn't.

He was about to find out.

"This is it, Central Avenue at 13th Street South," Damien said to Thomas.

Both looked out of the car windows at the four options at the intersection and reached the same conclusion.

"Bar," Thomas said.

"Bar," Damien said in agreement.

The light on Central turned green, but as Thomas guided the car forward he was interrupted by a combination of familiar sounds. He pulled to the right as two police cruisers roared past and screeched to a halt in front of the bar. Four officers emerged and rushed inside.

"That can't be good for business," Damien said.

A minute later they were inside. Elliot was face down on the dirty floor, his head surrounded by a pool of blood that looked like a sadistic reverse halo. On the wall behind the table was a sickening abstract portrait of blood and brain matter. The four other drinkers in the bar would later swear they heard nothing more than the badly-dressed fat man hitting the floor and that no one came or left immediately before or after it happened.

Neither Damien nor Thomas was surprised.

Fear of being next to end up dead had a way of doing that to people.

The St. Pete cops had been initially astounded by the sudden appearance of a Federal officer, but quickly came to understand the situation.

"Looks like someone beat you guys to it," one said after Damien told them of the pursuit.

Damien nodded as he looked down at Elliot's body.

"It happens," he said. "Try to make sure no one touches him until I say so, OK?"

He pulled out his phone and joined Thomas at the bar.

"None of these people saw anything," Thomas said as the call went through.

"Indeed," Damien said with a nod.

Thomas looked at the agent. Damien shrugged.

"When in Rome—"

He cut himself off when Alex came on the line.

"We have a little problem," he said.

"I take it you mean Stevens," Alex said.

"Yes, sir, he's a dead end, literally."

On his end of the line, Alex grimaced and let out a small groan. Damien tried not to make it worse and gave his boss the short version of what happened. A sigh from Alex followed about a minute later.

"I'll send someone to deal with the locals and the paperwork," he said. "See if you can get Stevens' cell and get back here. Maybe we'll find something good on it."

"See you soon," Damien said.

He pocketed the phone and nudged Thomas.

"We need to get his—"

He stopped when Thomas produced Elliot's Motorola.

"Thanks," Damien said.

He took the phone over to one of the cops.

"We're takin' this," he said. "Write it down."

The cop did so, recording the time and date on an evidence bag before Damien dropped the phone in. After signing the log sheet, he took the bag and rejoined Thomas. They watched in silence as the police continued to pollute the crime scene, not that it mattered. Everyone who needed to already knew about Elliot's demise.

No one else would give a shit.

Chapter 47

Springfield

Samantha offered no resistance when Arcadia raised her out of bed and deposited her on the toilet. Yesterday's meal wanted out in a bad way and she spent a few extra minutes in the bathroom. She wasn't embarrassed by the noise or the smell because there were far more important issues at hand.

"Why are you doing this, Andrew?" she said after the gag was removed at the table.

The sound of her voice momentarily startled him, but he recovered quickly.

"Because you deserve it, Samantha, that's why."

"How could I possibly deserve *this*?" she said.

Peter Arcadia, nee Andrew James "AJ" Singer, studied her through the dim light in the small cabin. After a few seconds, he reached across and tore the blindfold from her face.

"You humiliated me," he said. "And now I am returning the favor."

Samantha saw the rage on his face and heard the same in his voice, but fought past it and found the strength to continue.

"Andrew, please, you don't have to do this," she said. "I'm sure there's something else I could do for you. *Please.*"

AJ laughed.

"I always liked it when you begged," he said. "*Fuck me, AJ. Please, fuck me harder.* Remember? You couldn't get enough. Is that what you want now? You want me to fuck you some more?"

The ferocity crashed through Samantha's walls and she began to sob uncontrollably. Her breaths came in spurts and she started coughing loudly from the strain. It was too much noise and AJ reached across and clamped a hand over her mouth as the other went to her throat. The noises stopped as he applied pressure and put his face next to hers.

"I can't stand it when you cry," he said. "It's so hollow and insincere, something you do just to get your way. Well, guess what? It isn't going to work this time. I'm calling the shots now."

He squeezed again before pulling his hands away. The crying and coughing were gone, but so was something else, all hope.

Philadelphia

"How soon can you get back?" Alex said into his phone.

"We're already at the airport," Damien said. "We should be there around midnight."

"Good, I'll see you then."

Alex pushed a button to end the call and walked to the window facing the common space outside his office. There was a beehive of activity, but the scene was surreal because of the quiet on his side of the glass. It reminded him of a television on mute. Too bad he couldn't simply change the channel or turn it off.

With a sigh, he went back to his desk and tried to organize his thoughts. Elliot Stevens was dead, no doubt because of the mess he'd left at Samantha's house and the mistake with his car, but the idiot was the only current link Alex had that could lead to Singer. Being dead wasn't going to be much help. There had been no ransom demands. There had been no communications at all outside of the messages to Sanchez and Marshall.

"Shit," Alex said aloud as his frustration grew. "What the hell is going on?

Damien closed Elliot's phone and looked at Thomas. They were in the first row of first class on a Delta flight. The airline had been told they were security advisers to the White House and the gate attendant was more than happy to accommodate them. Thomas had already made a mental note to send flowers to his lady friend at Langley, the one who'd made the call.

"Stevens never bothered to erase his call logs," Damien said. "There's a lot of activity with Samantha O'Hara's phone and I think from the one that sent the text messages."

"We won't be able to trace the latter," Thomas said.

"Yeah, you're probably right. Stevens was the stupid one."

"True, I don't suspect Mr. Singer to follow in his partner's footsteps," Thomas said.

Damien nodded and slipped the phone back into the evidence bag. The "Closed" printed on the side of the bag caught his eye as he slid the plastic zipper across. Yeah, like people can't figure that out, he thought, as he stared at the word. After a few seconds he turned to Thomas.

"Who knows, maybe Singer *is* that stupid. A lot of other people sure are."

Michael made quick work of getting out of 30th Street Station. The train ride back from Atlantic City had been slow and tortuous. He just wanted this day to be over. He was almost broke, but still owed Dukabi a shitload of money, had suffered the humiliation of delivering the checks to the casinos, and had gotten kicked out of Caesars—*again*.

Outside the station, a group of Middle-Eastern-looking men were standing behind a line of cabs. Michael headed to the first in line, not caring which driver claimed it.

"18th and JFK," he said in a bark as he climbed in.

One of men jogged up and got behind the wheel. Within seconds after the car pulled from the curb, a nasty odor hit Michael's nose. It was the final straw. He sat forward and snarled at the driver.

"Stop the fucking car, I need to get out. Your fucking cab smells like shit."

Larry Crane was an old school-mate of Sandy's who now worked at the Elias Sports Bureau, the gurus of all MLB statistics. He was a maniac with numbers and minutiae and a total baseball nut. It was why Sandy had called him in the first place.

"Sorry it took so long," he said. "You know you could have found most of this online?"

"I know," Sandy said. "But I would have ended up asking you to confirm anyway. You know how I get."

"I do," Crane said. "Anyway, I just sent you an email with a zipped file. It includes rosters for each team playing on the dates you gave me, plus any from the day before and after if the teams changed. Give a shout if you have any problems or questions. And good luck, I think."

"Thanks, Larry, I owe you for this."

"Feel free to send over some Series tickets."

"Done," she said before disconnecting.

She made a quick note to do that before she turned her attention to the monitor on her desk. Sure enough, a message with an attachment was waiting and she flew through the necessary commands to download, decompress, and save the file to her hard drive.

"OK," she said aloud to the screen. "Let's find our missing link."

Chapter 48

A hiccup in the airspace of the FAA's Eastern Region Air Traffic Division caused the flight to be delayed and Thomas and Damien didn't make it back to the FBI office until almost two A.M. Their special status had allowed Damien to make a call from the air and Alex was aware of the situation, not that it made him any happier. As soon as they both sat in front of him he punched at a button on his desk phone.

"Santiago," he said in a shout. "Come get this cell phone and get me a list of calls yesterday."

He didn't wait before punching another number, but his voice was softer this time.

"Sandy, the boys are here, you're on," he said.

"Be right there," she said before Alex disconnected.

He sat back, folded his hands across his stomach, and began to rock the chair. Damien studied him for a few seconds.

"Boss?" he said.

for it," he said. "You're gonna love it."

Tampa

Collin George had a severely bruised ego after failing to get any dope on the blow-up between O'Hara and Sanchez. He was nursing said bruise from a stool at the bar in Gabriella's, the lounge in the Renaissance International Plaza Hotel in Tampa. A single shot of whiskey to take the edge off hours earlier had turned into a parade of Heineken drafts. He knew he would pay for it later in the day, but for now, he didn't care.

"Hey, Collin George," a voice said in a shout. "Don't sit there all alone, come on over."

Collin turned. All the faces were fuzzy from the beer. He shook his head and stared out through the haze, eventually finding the source of the call-out, Tim Fray, on-air reporter and all-around pain-in-the-ass, seated at the head of a table full of other TV types.

Fray was a man who had a knack for asking all the wrong questions at all the wrong times to go with a complete lack of self-awareness. He was genuinely despised by the writing corps, but Collin's defenses were long since shot to shit from the alcohol. He simply shrugged and carried his beer to the table. Fray pointed to a chair and Collin managed to sit without spilling anything.

"You're almost empty," Fray said, pointing at Collin's glass. "What are you drinking?"

"Heinee," Collin said.

"Barkeep, fill up this man's Heinee," Fray said in a shout toward the bar.

A few of the others at the table started laughing. It took Collin a few seconds to catch up.

"Oh, ha, nice one," he said. "You guys are a bunch of dicks."

The laughter increased.

"Oh, wow, you want a dick up your Heinee?" Fray said. "Sorry, man, I'll pass."

"Fuck you," Collin said.

He started to stand, but Fray put a hand on his shoulder.

"Whoa, ease up. I was kidding," he said. "Geez, you have a bad day at the office?"

"You might say that," Collin said in an unsteady voice.

A bar maid came by with a fresh draught and Fray told the girl to add it to his tab.

"Thanks," Collin said before emptying half of the amber liquid.

"OK, now that we're drinking buddies," Fray said. "Why don't you tell me about your troubles and maybe old Timmy can help you fix 'em."

Philadelphia

"The program only provides theoretical connections," Sandy said. "I had to do some leg work before I could say anything. Otherwise, it was circumstantial and coincidental."

"*Was?*" Damien said. "What changed?"

"A few things," Sandy said. "I had a good day with the interviews, but when Alex gave me the scoop on what happened in Florida I got a nagging feeling I was missing something. We knew Singer and Stevens were working together, so I got hold of the EMTs in Tennessee, the ones that took care of Wil Clemmons. I sent them a photo of Singer from his days at USC. They were both sure he was the guy they saw when they arrived."

"The hospital is rechecking to see if there was anything in Clemmons' system," Alex said. "We should know by morning."

Sandy looked at her boss. He nodded at her and she continued.

"Assuming they confirm, that puts Singer as the catalyst to everything," she said. "My best guess is he has a serious grudge against the O'Haras and Sanchez. It was because of them he got injured, in the fight, and had to give up the game. Terry and Sanchez both made it to the big leagues and the big bucks and all Singer got was a broken heart and messed up leg. He wants payback. I'm not entirely sure about Connors, but it makes for a sick little trifecta."

She took a second to adjust herself in her chair before continuing.

"I'm pretty sure Michael O'Hara hired Sanchez to rough up Singer because of the affair with Samantha. Sanchez farmed it out to his homeys and it went seriously bad. Michael tried to cover it up when he paid Singer's hospital bills and made the two donations, but I think the final payment from Samantha was the ultimate insult. It might explain why he's never touched it."

Thomas shifted in his chair and the other three looked at him.

"I know that face," Alex said. "You have something to add?"

"I don't think Singer *just now* lost it," Thomas said. "Agent Hill, I take it you believe he is involved with the cases you mentioned, possibly or probably the killer?"

"Yes," Sandy said.

"But you don't yet definitively have him at any of the past murder scenes?"

"Correct, *not yet*," Sandy said in a determined tone. "But I do have someone else at each of the sites on the night of the murders. Terry O'Hara was at the first and last two, Nik Sanchez was at the two in the middle, and Connors was at the third. For that last one I did some more digging and found out that Singer once attended Buck Walters' umpire school and the date fits the timeline. It was the first season after Singer had been rejected."

"Thus removing any coincidences," Thomas said.

"I'm sorry?" Sandy said.

"As you've mentioned, the physical characteristics of each female victim are similar to a younger version of Mrs. O'Hara," Thomas said. "The proximity of the others you've just mentioned confirms that Mr. Singer has been stalking these people for a long time, and the six dead women are, sadly, an unfortunate by-product of the man's instability."

"But why now?" Alex said. "Going after the others, I mean. What sparked that?"

"I think Terry and Sanchez making it to the Series finally pushed him over the edge."

It was Sandy. Thomas nodded.

"OK," Alex said. "We need to find this guy before he takes anyone else with him."

"Indeed."

Chapter 49

Philadelphia

Several hours later, Damien and Thomas were back at the FBI building in a small conference room two doors down from Alex's office. Damien had stolen a nap, but looked beat. Thomas looked totally refreshed. How so, Damien didn't bother asking. He'd gotten used to the fact nothing seemed to faze Thomas. In front of each on the table was a copy of the list of calls to and from Elliot's cell, covering more than two months. The most common number was the source of the text messages. A quick trace revealed it to be a prepaid phone sold for cash in Denver, Colorado. Damien knew that was a dead-end, but the call times did help tie some things together, as did another frequent number.

"Check out the fifth one down, on the second page," Damien said.

Thomas did so.

"Interesting," he said. "Shall we pay him a visit?"

~*~*~*~*~*~*~*~

Michael finally found his iPhone, but it was dead. It took another hour to locate the charger and by the time he plugged it in and turned it on it was close to ten-thirty A.M. Still beaten from the bad day in Atlantic City and the prospects of facing Dukabi empty-handed, the sight of "FBI" filling the "From" column barely registered. It was only when another name appeared that Michael perked up. The call, a text, had come early Friday morning from Samantha's number.

Chills raced up and down his spine. Had she had a change of heart? Was she going to give him the money he needed? He wanted to know, but he didn't, and he hesitated before selecting the item from the queue and opening it.

Seconds later the temperature in the room seemed to drop fifty degrees.

"Oh my god, what have I done?"

Atlantic City

Damien and Thomas were heading east on the Atlantic City Expressway in Damien's black Ford Crown Victoria. Traffic wasn't bad, but the flashing red lights in the car's front grill made sure their path was completely clear. Two A.C. agents were already in place monitoring Mario's office on Atlantic Avenue, near North Chelsea. Their instructions were to watch and report if anything changed, but otherwise do nothing until Thomas and Damien arrived. At their current speed, that would be in less than ten minutes.

"You think Pastelli knows where Singer is?" Damien said as the Garden State Parkway interchange came into view.

"If so, I suspect convincing him to share might be our challenge," Thomas said.

Damien flashed on the episode with John King in Marshall's suite.

"Yeah, well, you're pretty good at convincing people," he said.

An odd sound interrupted as Thomas was about to respond.

"Nice ringtone," Damien said.

Thomas shrugged as he pulled out his phone.

"Speaking of a challenge," he said as he held the phone so Damien could see the ID display.

"Michael O'Hara? Lucky us," the agent said. "Ask him where he's been."

Thomas nodded before bringing the phone to his ear.

"Hello, Mr. O'Hara, you're a hard man to find."

Two minutes went by before Thomas spoke again.

"You did the correct thing," he said in a firm voice. "Stay there and we will meet you as soon as we can. Call me if anything changes. We'll find her. You have my word."

Thomas ended the call and turned to Damien.

"Mr. O'Hara just received confirmation his wife has, in fact, been kidnapped."

"Shit," Damien said as he looked away. "Well, at least we know for sure now."

Thomas didn't bother to reply.

Philadelphia

Michael paced his living room in a helter-skelter manner, his mind racing from thought to thought. He was sure AJ had sent the message about Samantha. He was also sure now about what it was he'd seen in Arcadia. He *was* AJ. Michael hated himself for having missed that for so long, but despite the warnings in the message, was convinced calling Thomas had been the right thing to do. The missed calls from the FBI had momentarily led him to consider that option, but based on their initial meeting, Michael figured Thomas would be better-equipped to handle whatever AJ was up to.

On his thirty-eighth lap around the room, a Van Halen song blared into the silence. Michael froze for several seconds as he processed the noise. *Jump* was not Samantha's ringtone—*Evil Woman* by E.L.O. was—and his brain finally guided his feet to the coffee table in the middle of the room.

"This is Michael" he said after snatching up the phone.

"Yo, O-man," a familiar voice said into his ear.

It was his bookie slash ticket broker buddy. Again Michael's mind took extra time to process.

"You OK, dude?" the voice said.

"Huh?" Michael stammered. "Oh, yeah, sure, I'm OK. Wha-what's up?"

"I hooked up primo seats for Sunday in Tampa. They're yours if you want 'em."

A third bout of delayed reactions came and went before Michael replied.

"Yeah, yeah, sure, that's when Terry pitches," he said. "Leave 'em with the guy downstairs. I'll pick 'em up later."

Michael disconnected before hearing the reply and fell back into the sofa. His heart was racing and he was short of breath as he closed his eyes.

"I need to calm down."

Chapter 50

Atlantic City

"Roger that," Damien said into the cruiser's radio. "We're thirty seconds out."

The Crown Victoria sped northwest to Fairmount Avenue where a left was followed by another onto Chelsea. Damien ignored the red light at the intersection with Atlantic and hugged the curb with a sharp right and pulled to a stop in front of Mario's office. A similar-looking beige Crown Victoria was parked on the other side of the road, facing the opposite direction. Two men in standard FBI windbreakers exited and jogged across.

"Is our boy still inside?" Damien said.

"He is," an agent named Watson said. "He arrived an hour ago with two other men."

"That would be his muscle," Damien said. "Is there a back entrance?"

"In the alley," Watson said. "Pastelli's car is there."

"OK, you cover it," Damien said.

"Yes, sir," Watson said before disappearing around the corner.

Damien turned to the second agent.

"OK, Chet, cover the front," he said. "Mr. Hillsborough and I are heading in."

Mario's office occupied the entire second floor of the two-story building. A staircase filled the center of an open-aired lobby and the metal stairs were framed with sheets of glass affixed to thin iron railings. The same held true for a balcony above the first floor. Below and to the right of the stairs was an unattended semi-circle counter. A narrow hallway behind the desk ran the length of the building and in the far right corner was an elevator door. There was a directory on top of the counter. Of the eight offices on the ground floor, five were occupied by sundry medical professionals. "Italian Importing, Inc." was the only tenant listed for the second floor.

"That would be it," Damien said.

He and Thomas moved past the desk to the stairs and headed up. As soon as they hit the landing between flights, the doors to Mario's office opened.

"The welcoming committee," Damien said with a glance at Thomas.

"Inevitable," Thomas said.

The two gorillas wore matching dark suits, white shirts, and black ties. Both had the same build, big, and looked like twins. They moved to the top of the stairs where a fat-fingered hand on the ape on the left came up into an imitation of a stop sign.

"No unannounced visitors," the man said in an Italian accent.

"Is that so?" Damien said as he pulled out his badge.

The badge made something click in the goon's tiny brain and he backed off a few steps. The other did likewise.

"Thank you, gentlemen," Damien said without emotion. "Now go announce us."

Philadelphia

Alex was fidgety. He had used the small apartment-like area on the third floor to get a couple of hours of sleep, but his arm was still throbbing from the wound, despite the Advil and Percocet he'd taken. Sandy was with him and had noticed the obvious discomfort as he repeatedly adjusted himself in his chair.

"Are you OK?" she said. "You really should go home. You can coordinate from there."

"I'm fine," Alex said. "Don't worry about me."

Alex knew Sandy was right, but he had no intentions of phoning this one in. He had four teams on stand-by, waiting to begin the hunt for Samantha. When they began depended on what Damien and Thomas uncovered in Atlantic City. Alex very much wanted to avoid involving the locals, at least for now, because that would take things public and there was nothing like bad publicity to fuck up a case.

Unfortunately, that's exactly what Alex was about to get.

St. Petersburg

Tim Fray prodded and probed all morning to get to the bottom of the story Collin George dropped into his lap at the bar. Access to O'Hara and Sanchez had been denied, but Fray didn't care. Unlike Collin, the lack of facts never stopped him. He had enough innuendo and hearsay with which to run, but needed one last piece of fodder to blow it open.

He hoped to get it as he stepped into Mark Rosenbaum's suite at Tropicana Field.

I had a quiet day. A morning workout was followed by a breakfast of Belgian waffles. I wouldn't say it was leisurely, but there were no threats, confrontations, or shootings, at least that I knew of. From there, I spent a few hours by the pool reading every word on every page of the newspaper. OK, I might have missed a few words because of the distraction of several bikini-clad lovelies, but I got to relax a bit.

Around one P.M. I had lunch with Bart. He was good company, but I kept the conversation light and focused on Game 3 plans. The umpire rotation set up like this: Kirk Unger had the plate, Bart had first, Art Mahaffey had second, Pike had third, Jimmy Banks had the right field line, and I had left. I was hoping we'd get nothing more than a well-played game, but in the back of my mind I had my doubts. It would have been nice if the catwalk and other stuff hanging from the ceiling at the ballpark were behind that, but in reality it was because of the stuff hanging off me. I kept that to myself at lunch. Alex had made things perfectly clear on that point. The situation wasn't to be made public.

So far, it had worked and I was determined to do my part and keep it that way. Still, I was prepared for the worst. That I had come to be like that, expecting it, was sad.

Baseball was supposed to be fun.

Atlantic City

The apes led Thomas and Damien into a small reception area and told them to wait as they went through a door behind an empty desk.

"What do you think?" Damien said.

"This is your show. I'm just the hired help."

"Yeah, right," Damien said.

A few seconds later a loud click sounded from the door.

"Guess that means we've been announced," Damien said.

He led Thomas through the door. The space on the other side was typical modern day office, with a series of work stations set up in groups of four with common partitions connecting each. The dividers were standard fare, four feet high and business-grey, about as neutral as you could get, but the color worked well against a blue-grey carpet and eggshell walls.

"I don't think I like this," Damien said as he surveyed things.

Thomas nodded in agreement as they moved forward. A flat-screen monitor and keyboard was at each work station, but there were no visible wires or PC units. Along the far side of the room, a glass-enclosed space ran the length, but it was empty. As Damien passed one of the workstations, he reached for the monitor.

"Fake," he said with a glance at Thomas. "This is for display purposes only."

They continued toward the far left corner where another glass wall with one frosted panel abutted an expensive-looking wood door.

"Boss's office," Damien said.

"Agreed," Thomas said. "There are eight cameras. Mr. Pastelli doesn't like surprises."

Damien had only picked out five mechanical eyes, but accepted Thomas' count. Another issue had his attention.

"Kinda landlocked back here," he said. "You see any backdoor?"

"Not yet," Thomas said.

"Shit," Damien said. "That would put it in Pastelli's office."

Thomas nodded for the third time as they reached the wood door. Damien grasped the knob and slowly turned it.

"Well, here goes nothing."

Chapter 51

St. Petersburg

Mark listened politely as Fray prattled on for ten minutes. He didn't give the reporter, a generous description in his mind, any indications that what he was spewing was correct. He simply sat and listened until Fray finally stopped.

"I'm sorry, Tim," Mark said. "Was there a question in there? I think I missed it."

"I'm getting to that," Fray said. "I just wanted you to know all the facts first."

"I didn't hear any facts," Mark said.

"What do you think the last ten minutes was?" Fray said. "Which part didn't you follow?"

"Tim, I'll be honest with you, I missed most of it," Mark said. "Nothing sounded remotely like a fact and I don't have time for this crap. If you have a question, ask it, otherwise, you need to get out."

Fray's face knitted into a serious frown. Maybe he was trying to act tough or he had to go to the men's room, Mark couldn't tell. Whatever the case, he hesitated before he started flipping pages on a small notepad he'd been holding. When he found what he needed he looked up again.

"Is there a problem between Sanchez and O'Hara?" he said with a lot of attitude.

"Not that I'm aware of," Mark said.

"Why did O'Hara throw at him in Game 1?"

"I believe that was a wild pitch. I have no umpire reports to suggest otherwise."

"Speaking of umpires, why is Connors chief?"

Gabi perked up at the familiar question. That it was coming up again seemed odd. Apparently, Mark thought so as well. Gabi picked up something in his expression, but Fray hadn't noticed, at least not yet.

"That assignment was performance-based," Mark said in a tone with a little more edge.

"I heard it was because Buck Walters demanded it," Fray said with a sneer. "Why would Walters do that?"

"I wasn't aware Mr. Walters demanded anything," Mark said, the edge getting sharper. "And I'd prefer it if you did not speak ill will toward a dead man. That's low, even from you."

Again Gabi watched for a sign that Fray was noticing the change in Mark, but it appeared not. This guy is an idiot, Gabi thought, as the questions continued.

"There have been some rumors about something else," Fray said. "Where's Samantha O'Hara and why didn't she attend the most important game of her son's life? That seems odd."

Mark's eyes narrowed to slits.

"Again, I wasn't aware of that," he said. "You'd have to ask her."

"OK, Fray, that's it," Gabi said, jumping in. "Time for you to go."

A big smile filled Fray's face as he stood.

"That's OK, I have what I need," he said. "Too bad you guys don't."

Atlantic City

Mario was in a black leather executive chair behind a large oak desk. The desk was positioned in such a way as to create a triangle with the windows on either side. Thomas' best guess put about fifteen feet from the front edge of the desk to the corner of the wall. Mario seemed relaxed as Damien and Thomas approached. The reason revealed itself an instant later when the two gorillas stepped out of the shadows behind them.

"At least we know where they got to," Damien said out of the side of his mouth.

They were ten feet in front of Mario's desk, the apes an equal distance on their flanks. Despite the apparent surliness of each, Damien was comfortable with the stand-off and imagined Thomas felt the same. Unless a few other goons materialized or the idiots started shooting, Damien knew he and his partner had things well in hand.

"Mr. Pastelli, I'm Special Agent Hastings, FBI," Damien said. "We need to ask you a few questions. I'm sure you won't mind."

Mario looked back and forth between his guests as he leaned forward in the chair until his elbows landed on the desk.

"Maybe," he said. "What do you want?"

"Like I said, we need to ask a few questions," Damien said. "It shouldn't take long, but that's entirely up to you."

Mario remained still.

"OK," he said. "Five."

"Five?" Damien said.

"Yeah, numbnuts, as in you got five minutes, so start asking," Mario said.

"OK, where's Andrew Singer?" Damien said. "And it better not take more than five seconds for you to answer."

St. Petersburg

"Hey, Alex," Mark said into his cell phone.

"Mr. Commissioner, are you calling to say hello or is there another problem?"

Mark was alone in the suite, looking out at the field. A few bodies meandered around, but he barely noticed.

"The latter, I'm afraid," he said. "A TV reporter was just here asking all the wrong questions and I have a very bad feeling about it."

"Give me a name," Alex said. "I'll see what I can do."

Atlantic City

Mario didn't answer in five seconds. In fact, he didn't answer at all. Instead, he snapped his fingers and the gorillas closed ranks. As expected, they were sadly outmatched and on the floor in severe distress within seconds, but the diversion allowed Mario to make a dash for a door hidden in the wall. The exit wasn't original equipment, but something Mario had installed for just such an occasion. He was down the first flight of stairs before Damien moved to follow.

He raced down two at a time, but Mario was already gone by the time he reached the bottom. He removed his gun and pushed through a grey door into the alley. He found Mario there, hands in the air and staring down the barrel of Agent Watson's service piece. Damien quickly closed in from behind and wrenched Mario's arms backwards.

"You never answered my question," he said as he applied the cuffs.

Chapter 52

St. Petersburg

Prior to 2008, the Tampa Bay Rays were a laughingstock. The franchise began play in 1998, as the "Devil Rays," and finished last in all but one season. Attendance most nights was maybe ten thousand and there was little interest outside of those few diehards. At some point, someone made a stink that the team's name had too many negative connotations. With all the losses, maybe the guy had a point. It was probably just a coincidence, but after the owners exorcised the "Devil" before the '08 season, things suddenly turned around.

A first place finish in the American League East was followed by two playoff series wins and a berth in the World Series. As Game 3 started, Tropicana Field was packed with more than 45,000 fans, all making a lot of noise. These people were more than ready for the baseball team to add to Tampa's short list of champions.

With all the noise, I had a hard time hearing from my position in left field. Fortunately for me and the rest of the crew, the Phillies quieted things a little when they scored twice in the top of the first, but the peace was short-lived. The Rays responded with a run in the bottom of the frame and I started to think we were headed for another slugfest. Thankfully, the pitching settled in and the next three innings went quietly.

Things got even quieter in the top of the fifth. The first two Phillies singled and after a strike-out, a two-run double made the score 4-1. Tampa's bullpen stirred to life while the Rays pitching coach made a visit to the mound. The pep talk didn't help. The next two batters singled to bump the score to 5-1 and the warm-ups picked up urgency. Another strikeout momentarily slowed things down, but when the next batter launched a ball deep into the right field bleachers for a three-run homer, all the air seemed to get sucked out of the building.

The Phillies had an 8-1 lead and looked to be on their way to a stranglehold on the series.

My adventure, as if I could get through a game without one, came in the bottom of the seventh. Nik Sanchez came up with a runner on second and two outs. He hit what looked like a routine pop-up toward left, but as the left-fielder moved in to catch the ball, it disappeared. The runner from second and Nik never stopped and by the time the catcher crossed home plate, the crowd was going bananas thinking he had just hit an inside-the-park home run.

As I searched for the ball, I began to think maybe the engineers that built this place had a warped sense of humor. I'd heard that about engineers. Whatever the reason, I knew we had a problem and joined Art and Chris behind shortstop as Jimmy, Kirk, and Bart wandered out to meet us.

"Does this happen often?" I said to no one in particular.

"Unfortunately, yes," Pike said.

Bart chuckled.

"It is funny," he said. "I think the catwalk ate the ball."

Kirk began to chuckle and we were all close to losing it. I'm not sure that would have looked too good on TV.

"OK," I said. "We should fix it before we make it worse. It's a double, right? We gotta put Sanchez back on second."

"Yep," Kirk said. "Not that anyone will like it. But that's why you're the boss."

"Thanks for reminding me."

He winked at me and headed back toward the plate. I joined him and we explained things to the two managers. They knew the rules, but the four of us agreed this was a dumb place for baseball. After a minute or so, Nik headed back to second to the expected chorus of boos. The fans were definitely a little more into it, but the Rays were unable to generate any further offense and the rally died.

Little else happened and the game ended with the Phillies on top 9-2, good for a 3-0 series lead. Only once before in major league history had a team come back from that big of a deficit, the 2004 Boston Red Sox. It was beginning to look like we were going to have a nice short series. I was OK with that and the thought had me smiling as we left the field.

And then I found Gabi waiting for me outside the umpires' room again and it all vanished.

"Yogi Berra was right," I said. "It is déjà vu all over again with you. *What now?*"

"There's something you need to see," he said in a somber tone. "Come on."

I didn't bother changing before we made our way to Mark's suite.

"Over there," he said as he pointed with his chin toward the windows.

Mark was in a seat facing the field on the other side of the sliding door. When I stepped through he offered up a weak smile as I sat next to him. The stands in front of us were empty. A lot of the crowd had bolted when the score got out of hand and maintenance crews were already working on the mess left behind. The whine of leaf-blowers filled the air while out on the field the grounds crew repaired the mound and batters boxes. In a way it was very soothing and we both sat quietly for a long moment.

"Goddamn catwalks" Mark said. "That was a weird one, huh?"

"It was," I said. "The Rays skipper told me there's a nice collection of balls up there."

"Good to know I guess," Mark said.

After another few seconds, I turned to look at him.

"I enjoy this, too," I said. "But it can't be why you wanted to see me."

"Nope, it's not," he said as he stood. "C'mon."

Inside, Gabi was waiting near a television hanging from the wall. When Mark nodded he pushed a button and a blue screen appeared with the words *Video-1*. I turned to Mark.

"You'll want to sit," he said; then to Gabi. "Fire it up."

I took one of the chairs facing the screen, but when neither of them joined me I got worried. Before I could say anything, the screen came to life with a segment from the game. I immediately recognized it as the end of the fifth inning. I glanced at Mark with a shrug.

"Keep watching," he said.

After the third out the shot changed to the far end of the Phillies dugout and a man moved into position along the railing. As the camera zoomed and focused I realized the face belonged to Tim Fray. The sound came back and the booth announcer teed up the segment.

"Tim Fray has a report."

"Thanks, Joe. It looks like the Phillies have a situation with pitcher Terry O'Hara. Officials from both the team and Commissioner's office deny any knowledge, but sources tell me O'Hara's mother, Samantha, is missing. I hope to confirm before we leave the air..."

Gabi turned the TV off before I heard any more. So much for not going public, I thought, as I looked at Mark again.

"Director Harris tried to stop it," he said. "Obviously, he failed."

"Only if he was trying to keep it a secret," I said.

Mark frowned at the bad joke.

"Sorry, so what happens now?" I said. "Is the FBI going to do or say something official?"

"No, well, nothing public," Gabi said from behind my shoulder. "They're cranking up the search and may have something, but Harris couldn't tell us what it was."

"Maybe I can find out," I said as I stood. "I'll let you know."

I hustled out of the suite and made my way back to the umpires' room. The other guys were already gone and I had the room to myself. I plopped down in front of my locker and thought about Samantha. Maybe if I'd have done something sooner this wouldn't have happened, I thought, as I picked up my cell and dialed. Thomas answered before the second ring.

"Hey, I guess you saw, huh?" I said.

"Yes, I am aware of the disclosure," he said. "It was unfortunate, but we did find someone who might help with the underlying problem. I'll know more soon."

He was gone before I could reply. I hated when he did that, but it was the least of my problems. After getting out of my uniform, I stood in the shower for a long time, trying to let the warm water wash everything away. It wasn't working and when my skin started to wrinkle, I gave up. Back at my locker, I found a small note stuck to the side of the stall.

Meet me at the lounge. Bart

You must have read my mind big man, I thought. I definitely needed a drink. I tucked the note into my pocket and finished getting dressed. I was almost out the door when my phone began to beep. I'd missed a call while I was in the shower. It wasn't Thomas, but was almost as bad.

"Hey, sweetie, it's your mother..."

As if I wouldn't have known from her voice.

"...Your father and I got to see the game today, I mean tonight. Oh, I still don't follow the whole time difference thing. It's Sunday here, but your father tells me it's only Saturday there. Anyway, we saw you on TV. You looked nice in your uniform. The trip is going great. You should find a nice girl and visit here, it's spectacular..."

Gee, thanks, Mom, way to rub it in.

"...Any who, your father wants me to ask you something. What, Sean? Yes I heard you. He wants to know if you've been to the house. That nosey-body Mr. Hand said he saw someone. I said it had to be you, because who else would it be? Anyway, there's our bus, time to go. Love you, sweetheart, have fun with the rest of the games."

I stared at the phone for a few seconds. I'd been *near* the house, but I didn't remember seeing Hand. The guy was a sneaky fucker, but still, what the hell was he talking about? I hadn't actually gone *in* the house. I shook my head and tried to shake it off. Bart's offer was looking better every second.

I *seriously* needed a drink.

Chapter 53

Sunday, October 26, 2008
The day of Game 4 of the World Series
Philadelphia

Alex's sleep-to-wake ratio was as negatively lopsided as Thomas' and Damien's, but he was a lot crankier than either as he watched the interrogation of Mario from behind the two-way glass wall. The hood's abject lack of cooperation over the past three hours had served only to increase the director's shitty mood and there was little left of his normally abundant patience.

"This is going nowhere," he said with disgust.

"Let me take a shot," Thomas said. "Of course, you might not be able to use anything he might say, given I don't actually work for you."

Alex turned back to the brightly-lit room on the other side of the glass and considered Thomas' words. Against the harsh lighting and bleached walls Mario's dark clothes made him look like an ink splotch or something a baby might leave in a diaper.

"Fuck it. Go," Alex said. "If I end up losing this piece of shit, I don't care, but we need to find Singer and Samantha."

"I'll be subtle," Thomas said.

"Not too much, I hope."

Tampa

I stayed with Bart at the bar until well after closing time, but never mentioned the video or the call from my parents. Instead, we spent the time telling stories to a few MLB staffers, including Suze Keebler. She was dressed in jeans and a form-fitting pale blue sweater and I spent way too much time watching her body instead of her eyes. It couldn't be helped. I was miserable, she looked good, and I needed the distraction. I had the hots for her and she knew it and fed my thoughts with a large dose of flirtation.

"Marshall Connors," she said with a slight slur. "Can I ask you a question?"

It was close to three-fifteen A.M. and she and I were the last two standing.

"Suze Keebler, you just did," I said. "But I'll let you ask another."

She giggled. It was really cute. So was the light slap she gave the back of my hand.

"The question... I mean the *next* question... how come you're not married?"

I expressed mock horror at her Margarita-inspired boldness.

"Ms. Keebler, that's a little forward of you," I said. "Are you offering?"

"Stop it," she said with another slap. "Seriously, why aren't you? You're attractive. You have the best sense of humor. Do you even have a girlfriend?"

My mother sure wished I did, I thought, but kept that to myself as I returned Suze's gaze. She was giving me the most gorgeous smile I'd ever seen.

"Not yet," I said in a low voice as I lowered my face to hers.

We locked lips in a long, wet kiss. I wasn't sure how long it was before we disengaged. I also wasn't sure about her, but I was ready for the next step. A second later I got my answer.

"Come on," she said in a whisper into my ear. "Let's go upstairs."

Springfield

After Samantha refused to eat, AJ angrily returned her to bed with a fresh dose of sedative and left the RV in a rush. Edward Hand watched the escape from behind a row of Arborvitaes near the back of the vehicle. Hand thought himself the neighborhood guardian, albeit without the stability such a position required, and this new sighting only increased his paranoia. As soon as AJ was out of sight, Hand hurried home and snatched the phone from the wall of his kitchen. His pulse raced as he waited for Sean Connors to pick up.

"Sean, I told you someone was in your house," he said in a shout when Sean's voicemail kicked in instead. "And they're using your son's RV, too."

Philadelphia

There was a knock and Damien was surprised to see Thomas through the peephole. He turned to the mirror, as if for confirmation, then shrugged and opened the door. Thomas gave a slight nod and moved past the agent into the room. Damien watched for a second then left. Mario mostly ignored the exchange. When Thomas sat, he looked up with a dead face.

"What the fuck you lookin' at, G-man?" he said.

Thomas did not correct the mistake.

"Mr. Pastelli, my name is Thomas Hillsborough. I'm here to help with your problem."

"I got no problem," Mario said. "You guys are the ones with the fuckin' problem."

On the other side of the mirror, Damien turned to Alex.

"Where's he going?" he said.

"I have no idea," Alex said.

Back on the bright side, Mario crossed his arms in front of his chest and leaned back in the chair. It was a display of toughness, but Thomas was unfazed.

"Mr. Pastelli, I noticed you didn't bother asking for a lawyer," Thomas said. "Why is that?"

After several seconds Mario shrugged.

"I ain't under arrest. Why bother paying the fee," he said. "I ain't what you guys are after."

"And therein lies your problem, Mr. Pastelli," Thomas said. "You are correct, the FBI is not interested in you, but there are several others who *are*, very much so in fact."

Mario squirmed and several beads of sweat popped up along his forehead.

"I don't know what you're talking about," he said as he looked away.

On the dark side of the glass, Damien looked at Alex again. There was a question on his face, but Alex replied with a shrug. Back on the other side, Thomas leaned forward.

"No?" he said. "Well, I suppose I could ask Elliot Stevens. Oh wait, no I can't. He's dead."

The sweat increased. Mario wiped it away.

"Stevens is dead, huh?" he said in a dismissive tone. "Guess you're outta luck then, huh?"

"Not at all," Thomas said.

He pulled out his phone and set it on the desk. After a few seconds, he glanced at his watch. Mario eyed the movements closely but said nothing.

"In five minutes I am going to make a phone call, Mr. Pastelli," Thomas said. "During this phone call I am going to say one of two things. Either I will tell the group on the other end of the line that I know nothing about you, or I will tell them you have systematically misused the information they've entrusted to you. I'm sure you can understand the difference in the options as well as what would happen if I choose the latter."

Mario rocked back for a second before leaning in again. His eyes became slits.

"What kinda fuckin' shit is this, G-man? You can't threaten me like that, I got rights."

"You do indeed have rights, Mr. Pastelli," Thomas said. "I'm sure the FBI will be happy to discuss that with you. As soon as you and I are finished with our business I'll go ask them."

Mario sat back abruptly and the slits were replaced by wide-eyed confusion.

"*Them?*" he said in a shaky voice. "Isn't *them* you?"

Two hours later, Damien was with Thomas in the same conference room as yesterday. Both were tired, but only Damien showed it. Both were also pleased with the results of their efforts. After Mario realized what was happening he gave up everything he had on AJ. Unfortunately, that did not include a current location. That part of the equation was going to take more work.

"There really is no honor among thieves," Damien said as he leaned back with his eyes closed. "I mean, seriously, these guys will give up their own mother to save their ass."

"Proper motivation comes in many forms," Thomas said.

Damien opened his eyes and saw something in Thomas' eyes.

"You weren't really gonna give him up to someone, were you?" he said before throwing up his hands. "You know what, never mind, I don't want to know."

"Some things truly are best left unsaid," Thomas said.

There was a knock on the door and Alex entered. He looked a little better than earlier, but was clearly tired and fighting discomfort in his arm.

"OK, boys," he said with a sigh. "Here's what's what. Singer first contacted Pastelli close to five weeks ago. Thomas, I think what you said yesterday is correct. Singer was stalking the O'Haras and knew Michael was in trouble. He used his association with Dukabi to make that trouble deeper. Mario was more than happy to play along for a cut."

He stopped to take a drink from a bottle of water he'd carried in. After a long pull, he used the back of the hand on his uninjured arm to wipe his mouth.

"Singer hooked up with Dukabi about the same time the string of deaths stopped," he said. "Maybe the new job took his mind off it, who the fuck knows, but the timing fits. As for Stevens, that little shit got used by Singer in a bad way and then got dead. I really don't care, but if I had to guess, my gut says Pastelli used his connections to do it as part of his deal with Singer. Pastelli won't give me that, but I think it's there, especially with the way he reacted to Thomas."

"You think he was telling the truth about not knowing where Singer is?" Damien said.

Alex took another drink of water.

"I don't know," he said. "Stevens might have been the only one who knew Singer's whereabouts. Pastelli swears the last time he saw Singer was before Samantha O'Hara was taken. Says he had no idea Singer was going to do that. His phone records show the last time they talked was Tuesday before the Series started, so maybe he's being honest."

"Or maybe he used a different phone," Thomas said.

"Yeah, I already thought of that."

Alex leaned back and a grimace filled his face as he rubbed at his injured arm. Damien jumped into the pause.

"We got Stevens' car in Springfield and we know he got dead in Florida, so he had to get to the airport somehow. My guess is Mrs. O'Hara's car."

Alex nodded as he sat forward again.

"I already sent two teams to the airport. If her car is there, we'll know shortly. Now all we need is Ms. Sandy to find something more on Singer to flush him out."

"We have that," Thomas said in his usual even tone. "Michael O'Hara."

"Right," Damien said. "Singer's already acknowledged the kidnapping, so if money is part of the equation, he has to call again sooner or later. Either that or he really is just a sick fuck with a few too many screws missing."

"A growing possibility," Thomas said.

Alex and Damien processed that unpleasant thought for a long moment.

"OK, you boys go visit Mr. O'Hara, see if he can shed some light on anything," Alex said. "Six murders are enough. I'd rather not see Samantha O'Hara become Singer's own version of a game seven, no pun intended."

Neither Thomas nor Damien took it that way.

Chapter 54

Tampa

Suze was up and gone by seven A.M. She wasn't running away. She just had a lot of work to do. I did, too, but I was milking the lingering sensations from the night before. I'd forgotten how awesome it was to be next to a warm body, a *curvy* warm body at that. Alcoholically induced or not I was glad it happened. Of course, I'd have been happier had it lasted a little longer, but I was relatively sure it would be occurring again soon.

I finally rolled out of bed, but didn't get too far before my cell rang. It was Thomas.

"Michael O'Hara received a message confirming his wife's kidnapping."

And that killed anything lingering from the night with Suze.

"Shit," I said before blowing out some air. "At least we know now, huh?"

"Indeed," Thomas said. "There is more, however."

I closed my eyes to wait for it.

"Mr. Singer may have killed others in the past."

"Whoa."

I opened my eyes and searched for someplace to land. The corner of the bed won. This was bad, really bad. My head started to spin and I forgot I was still on the line.

"Marshall?" Thomas said into my ear, bringing me back.

"Yeah, I'm here. I, um, I was just trying to process."

"Understandable," he said. "I'll get back to you when I have something new."

He was gone before I said anything else. That was OK; I didn't know what to say anyway. I just sat there for I don't know how long. My thoughts were jumping all over the place. The calls from Samantha I'd ignored, the incident between Terry and Nik, that night with Nik years ago and the killing by the lake, the stories I'd heard about AJ, Michael's problems, Buck's and Mark's odd behavior—all of it meshed together into a confused blur.

"What a goddamned mess," I said aloud as I fell back on the bed.

Redington Beach

Nik slept in his own bed for the first time in a month, but it was not a restful night. His team was down three games to none in the World Series, but that was secondary to his bigger problem of what to do about AJ. The man was orchestrating something seriously bad. Nik had shared the text message with the FBI but not the earlier phone calls and those weighed heavily on his mind. He could have maybe stopped the kidnapping, or at least tried to. Now, he wasn't sure what he could do, if anything.

The sound of his intercom jarred him from the fog.

"Hey Mr. Sanchez, Louie here," a voice said. "The UPS guy just dropped off a package for you. You want me to bring it up?"

"What kinda package?" Nik said, his defenses coming online.

"Little box, it ain't very heavy," Louie said.

Nik hesitated before responding.

"No, no, Louie, I'll uh… I'm comin' down. I'll grab it on the way out."

He released the button and stepped back to his bedroom. As he regrouped and pulled on some clothes, his mind drifted back to the

Series. If nothing else, at least he could go to the ballpark and bury himself in the game for a while, like when he was a kid. There, on the field, he could *do* something instead of waiting. Waiting just made things worse.

Ten minutes later he was at the counter in the lobby, Louie on the other side, a small box between them.

"Just sign right here and you're all set," Louie said as he pointed to a clipboard; then as Nik applied his autograph. "You guys gonna win one tonight?"

Nik's reply was a slight shrug and forced smile as he grabbed the box.

"We'll see, I guess," he said as he turned and moved away.

"Good luck anyway," Louie said to his back.

Nik's eyes went to the box as he walked. It was a six-inch cube with little weight. He gave it a shake and heard a slight rattle from inside. Something about the noise was familiar and a tingling sensation arose in his body. A minute or so later he was in his car in the parking lot. He used the small army knife on his keychain to slice through the packing tape. As he pulled apart the flaps the tingling became a full-on assault on his nerves.

Inside the box were three bullet fragments and several photographs. Nik saw what looked like blood on each of the fragments before moving them aside to lift out the photos. The first was a shot of The Three Amigos at a party. Nik knew exactly when it had been taken. The second was a dead body. Again, Nik knew the moment and face well. The third photo was not familiar, but was the most disturbing. A blindfolded woman was lying naked on a bed, hands and feet bound. Nik stared, not out of arousal, but out of fear, and it was a long moment before he turned his eyes away.

They landed on a slip of paper in the box. Like the first two photos, the handwriting was familiar. Nik took a deep breath and he pulled it out and read.

Let's play pretend. Pretend instead of getting your buddies involved, you did the deed yourself. You always said you could kick my ass, so why didn't you try? Oh, that's right, you're a fucking coward. I thought you might want a souvenir to remind you. It cost a lot of money to get the slugs from your friend's body, but it's a nice touch, wouldn't you say?

Did you think I wouldn't find out what you and Michael and everyone else did? Is that what you thought? Well guess what, motherfucker? I did find out. I found out about all of it and now it's my turn. Revenge is a bitch, Nik, and so is she. You have to admit, she still looks pretty good, though. Yeah, I know you wish you had hit that. You can tell me, I won't tell Terry. Better yet, maybe we should, I bet he'd love it.

Philadelphia

"This is solid?" Alex said.

Sandy was on the other side of his desk. She was a bundle of energy and Alex noticed the sparkle in her eyes. If I could just bottle you up and make everyone else drink, he thought.

"Totally," Sandy said. "The bartender from the Rogers case recognized Singer as the guy she was with. And Martell, the retired detective from the Sullivan case, found two people who identified Singer from that night. He also got the coroner to recheck the file. The man agreed she might have been strangled before drowning."

"Goddamn, girl," Alex said. "You do good work."

Redington Beach

"Agent Hastings, are you still in Florida?" Nik said into his phone.

He was still in his car, still in the garage, holding the picture of Samantha O'Hara in his hand as he waited for Damien's reply. The agent heard the raw emotion in the player's voice, but couldn't decide if it was anger or fear or both. He was on the balcony of Michael's apartment, looking down at the streets of Philadelphia. The mid-morning sun was warm on his face and compensated for a chill in the air, but did little else to offset Nik's tone.

"No, I'm in Philadelphia," Damien said. "Is there a problem?"

"I have something you need to see."

Chapter 55

St. Petersburg

Terry arrived at the ballpark early and jumped right into his game-day routine. An electro-stimulation treatment was followed by a two-mile walk on a treadmill, the pace set low to provide a warm-up, not exhaustion. He was now with Ernie Goff in his stretching session. When they finished, Terry would go eat and take a nap before pregame warm-ups.

Despite his mother's situation, or because of it in his mind, Terry was as determined as ever to pitch in the game and had assured everyone he was ready to go. It was a lie. He was nowhere close to OK. The determination was nothing more than a mask. In truth, it felt like there was an elephant stepping on his chest, crushing his soul, and despite the magnitude of the game, a chance to pitch the Phillies to their first championship in almost thirty years, he was finding it hard to focus on anything but his mother.

"Flip," Ernie said.

As Terry did, he spotted Nik in the doorway. Ernie looked at Terry with a frown.

"It's OK," Terry said. "Give us a minute, will ya?"

Ernie shrugged and walked away. Terry sat up and looked hard at Nik.

"What do you want?" he said as he hopped to the floor.

"AJ sent me a package. This was in it."

Nik handed Terry the photograph.

"Jesus fucking Christ," Terry said aloud.

Terry had seen enough of his mother's body over the years to instantly recognize her. After a few seconds, he looked again at Nik. His mouth began to move, but no words came.

"I'm sorry, man," Nik said, his voice low but steady. "You need to know I did what I thought I had to do that night, what I thought was best. I never knew your mother was involved in the scheme, not then and not now. I'm sorry."

Philadelphia

"Alex sent a team to fetch the package from Sanchez," Damien said. "They'll question the desk clerk about the delivery, but I'm sure it'll be a dead-end. Singer's too smart for that."

He was on the balcony again, this time with Thomas, both at the railing looking out at the city, but not really seeing any of the details. After a silent moment, Thomas turned to him.

"If I had to guess—"

"Please do," Damien said, interrupting. "You make good guesses."

Thomas ignored the compliment.

"There is a definite method to Mr. Singer's madness," Thomas said. "The package to Sanchez was clearly intended to impact young Mr. O'Hara."

"How could it not?" Damien said. "He has to be seriously hurting right about now."

"Indeed," Thomas said. "My guess would be the next step will involve the elder Mr. O'Hara. Singer appears to be playing both. He is very shrewd."

Damien pushed away from the railing.

"More like very disturbed," he said.

St. Petersburg

As I dressed for the game I did my best not to show any anxiety. I was working third base and found myself hoping it wouldn't be too taxing. The way things were going, I was probably being overly optimistic, but it beat the alternative of panicking. Bart was helping in that regard. He had the plate assignment and had been humming a tune of some sort for the better part of the past fifteen minutes as he got ready. It was a nice distraction.

"Yo, big man," I said. "You get lucky last night or something?"

"No, Amigo," he said as he leaned toward me. "That would be *you*, eh?"

I acted surprised, partly fake, but mostly real. I hadn't said a word to anyone about Suze.

"Me?" I said, feigning ignorance. "I'm not the one acting like a teenage boy who got lucky after prom."

He stayed close.

"Good try, Amigo, but I know these things."

I could feel my cheeks getting warm as he stood straight and slowly nodded.

"What *things*?" I said, eyeing him closely.

"Ah, yes, *many* things."

He winked at me and started doing a little dance. I laughed and turned away. A second later, his humming returned. His charm had worked. I felt a little better about things. I would take it.

A little beat nothing.

Collin George spotted Tim Fray near the beverage counter in the press room. There was fire in his eyes and he took hold of Fray's arm with a tight grip.

"I need a second," he said through clenched teeth.

Fray was stunned by the brutality and hesitated to respond. Collin squeezed a little more.

"*Now,*" he said with a lot of force.

"Excuse us," Fray said to the small group he'd been standing with.

Collin released the grip and the two walked to an open area. As soon as they were clear of the others, Fray turned on Collin.

"What is this shit?" he said. "Who do you think you are?"

"Fuck you, Tim," Collin said. "I gave you that info as a friend, not for you to steal it."

The men stared at each other, but neither flinched.

"I don't remember you saying that," Fray said. "Besides, you weren't taking it anywhere."

"No wonder no one likes you, Tim. You're an asshole. Why would you bring that shit out during the middle of the game, hell, during the series at all?"

"Like you weren't going to do the same," Fray said with a sneer. "Don't get all high and mighty with me. You're no damn better. Now fuck off."

Fray shoved Collin and walked away. Collin contemplated pursuing, but decided against it and watched in seething silence until Fray was gone from sight.

"Fucking TV hack," he said aloud.

Philadelphia

"We found it, sir," a man's voice said into Alex's ear. "Garage C, level 2."

"Good work," Alex said. "Get it back here ASAP. And don't let the Philly cops give you any shit. Tell them to call me if they try."

Alex hung up without waiting for a reply and sat back in his chair. He looked up at the ceiling, a pose he realized he'd been repeating far too often lately, and took several deep breaths. He held the last one as he sat forward and reached for his phone. He released the air after dialing.

"We have Samantha O'Hara's car," he said after Damien answered.

"Maybe we'll get lucky," the agent said. "God knows Stevens was an idiot."

"That may be true, but right now it would be better if he wasn't dead."

"Dead men tell no lies," Damien said.

"Yeah, well, I'll trade that for something that tells us where Samantha O'Hara is."

Springfield

AJ sat in silence and rehearsed his words. When he was ready, he picked up Samantha's phone and dialed. As the connection went through, he heard the telltale extra click. After three rings, Michael answered with a tentative hello.

"You are either very stubborn or very stupid. I haven't decided yet," AJ said. "Did you think I was joking when I told you not to involve anyone else? My god, no wonder you lost so much money. Oh well, no matter. Your new friends need to hear this anyway. With your incompetence, I'm better off giving it to them firsthand."

"What are you talking a—"

"Shut the fuck up, Michael," AJ said, cutting him off. "When I want you to say something I'll tell you. Now listen up, all of you. The timing is simple. When the World Series ends, Samantha ends. If I don't get what I want by then, game over. So you all better pray the Rays win tonight because that's the only way she survives more than another day."

"Don't you want any money?" Michael said.

"Gee, Michael, haven't you and the Misses given me enough already?"

Chapter 56

St. Petersburg

I knew Terry was tough, but there was no way he should have taken the mound. He was off from the first pitch and got hit early and often, *and hard*. It was as if the batters knew what pitches were coming because they jumped at virtually every one. I'm sure more than a few people watching thought it was a by-product of Terry pitching with three days rest—something he hadn't done all season—but I knew it was because of Samantha's situation.

When the manager mercifully came to get him in the bottom of the fourth inning, Terry had given up eight runs and ten hits, and only by the saving grace of several double-plays had the carnage not been worse. I found myself wondering if this had been part of AJ's plan: kidnap the guy's mother and if he pitches, he'll be a wreck and get hammered; if he doesn't pitch, the Phillies have to completely change their rotation. If you wanted to influence the games, it was a pretty good way to go about it. I'm no expert, but it smelled pretty bad, and you know what they say, if it stinks like a pig, it ain't a duck. The Rays won 12-2 and had some life, especially with one more home game on tap. They were still down three games to one, long odds to be sure, but stranger things had happened. The Series was most definitely not over.

I had no idea how very fortunate that really was.

Terry did not appear for any post-game interviews, nor was he in the clubhouse when the doors were opened to the press. Rumors were abundant and augmented by word of Tim Fray's sudden removal from the TV crew. That came courtesy of a meeting held twenty minutes before the game during which Mark Rosenbaum banned Fray for the duration of the Series. It was an unusual and potentially controversial move, but none of the TV execs protested. Alex Harris had made sure of that with several phone calls.

Still, there was a buzz among the literati. Reporters were worse than teenaged girls when it came to gossip, and the story about Samantha's absence was growing wings. Collin George stayed away from it and stuck to the game. He simply did his usual professional job and interviewed a few players and the managers, all of whom delivered the appropriate clichés. In truth, the reporter's heart wasn't into it. The confrontation between O'Hara and Sanchez had been interesting, but Collin had never intended to report anything that could alter the outcome of the games. Having seen the damage done to Terry out on the field, the fact Fray had done so left Collin feeling like shit.

He wasn't the only one.

There was another hastily arranged meeting taking place in Mark's suite at the ballpark at the same time. With Mark were the team's general managers, Gabi, an MLB attorney, and two local FBI agents. Alex was linked in via speakerphone.

"I don't want to make a joke of the Series and I sure as shit don't want to cancel it, but the man's mother is in danger," Mark said in a heavy tone. "It clearly messed with his performance. I mean, she could die, right?"

Heads dipped under his gaze. After a sigh, he focused on the speakerphone.

"Alex? Right?" he said. "What do you think I should do here?"

All eyes turned to the three-pronged black device and its tiny blinking green lights. There were a couple of muffled coughs in the room as the group waited for a reply. After what seemed like an eternity, Alex finally spoke. His tone was strong and reassuring.

"You are correct, Mark, Mrs. O'Hara *is* in danger, but experience with such matters tells us that going public could do more harm than good. I know the rumor mill is cranking out a lot of crap right now, but we have to stay above it. More people knowing the truth is *not* a good thing. All that does is create a rash of false claims, especially for something this high-profile, and we end up wasting effort sorting through that, which in turn reduces our effectiveness. Rest assured we have the full resources of the FBI on this case. *We will find her.*"

Mark's head began to shake.

"But will you find her in time?"

"You helped me before, why not now?" a voice said into Nik's ear.

He was in front of his locker, mostly alone in the clubhouse.

"I should have never helped you the first time, Michael," he said in a hushed voice. "Look where that got us."

"But he's gonna kill my wife," Michael said. "*Don't you care?*"

"That's just it. I don't care, Michael, not about *you* anyway."

Philadelphia

"Goddamn son-of-a-bitch—"

The shout from Michael's bedroom ended with a loud bang. Agent Santiago looked up, but when no one else moved, he simply shrugged and returned his attention to analyzing the recording of AJ's call. At the opposite end of the table, another agent was examining the contents of the package Nik received in Florida. It was amazing how fast something could get moved from one place to another when a life was on the line. Out on the balcony, Damien and Thomas were discussing the latest information.

"We know she was taken from her home," Damien said. "We know Stevens was there. We know Stevens left his car at the mall and used hers to get to the airport. We have confirmation a suspected murderer and all-around whack job is holding her, but his ransom demand, if that's what it was, doesn't make sense. We have threats to Connors, but I don't even know what those are about. And it all seems to boil down to jealousy and revenge. Did I miss anything?"

Thomas didn't reply, but Damien noticed something in the usually staid eyes.

"You OK, man?" he said.

"I'm not sure," Thomas said.

Before either could say another word, there was a knock on the sliding glass door behind them as Agent Santiago came through.

"What's up, Carlos?" Damien said.

"I think I found something."

Springfield

AJ carried Samantha through their regular routine. She took her time on the toilet, then ate and drank slowly. Her body was reacting badly to the time spent under sedation. She had cramps, from dehydration she guessed, and a constant headache. As bad as her deteriorating physical condition, her mental state was worse. She just wanted it all to be over and didn't much care how that happened. Death was starting to look better than continuing to suffer.

It wasn't until AJ was putting her back in bed that things changed.

"We're almost done," he said to her as the latest dose of sedative took hold. "All we need now is for your boy to come through. I'm guessing he will. Unlike Michael, *he* loves you."

Chapter 57

Monday, October 27, 2008
The day of Game 5 of the World Series
Tampa

Traffic around the stadium was brutal after the game and the twenty-minute trip took more than an hour. The shuttle didn't get back to the hotel until after one A.M., and as soon as we got inside, the guys quickly dispersed and headed to their rooms. I was about to do the same when Suze intercepted me near the elevators.

"Hey, you," she said. "Got a minute?"

Her adorably cute smile from the last couple of days was missing. I began to worry a little.

"Sure," I said. "I could use something to drink."

We went and sat in the lounge. A waitress came by and took our order, an apple juice for me and a bottle of water for Suze. If nothing else, the choice of beverages meant alcohol wouldn't be the inspiration for any extra-curricular activities that might come up. Chances of that were slim anyway, given how I was feeling. I tried my best not to let her see it.

"So, what's up?" I said.

"I don't know, but I think it's bad. Mark had a big meeting after the game."

That explained the absence of the smile. I took hold of her hand. She squeezed back and I felt a pang despite the mutual stress. I pushed past it as best I could.

"Did Mark tell you what this meeting was about?"

"No. Well, not directly. He said we have to issue a press release in the morning, but he wouldn't say about what and he was acting weird. I don't think I've ever seen him so upset."

I almost said "I have" but held back when she made an unhappy face and looked away. I gave her hand another squeeze. When she looked back the smile had returned and I forgot about all the bad things for a few seconds. Upset or not, she looked awesome, and I found myself wanting this to lead somewhere. Not necessarily at this moment because of the possible implications of Mark's meeting, but eventually.

"Listen, I'll give Mark a call," I said in a reassuring tone. "No need for you to fret."

"Thanks," she said. "I hate to bother you with this stuff, but I needed someone to talk to."

"Hey, no sweat," I said with a shrug. "You can talk to me anytime."

More of her *really good* smile came back.

"OK," she said in a soft voice. "Then after you call Mark, come talk to me some more."

As she stood she handed me a small envelope. It was a cardkey for her room. I got hit with another pang.

"I'll do that."

Philadelphia

"Right *there*," Agent Santiago said.

Thomas and Damien shook their heads in unison.

"What are we trying to hear, Carlos?" Damien said.

"Hold on," the technician said. "I'll put it on the speakers."

Thomas and Damien removed their headsets and watched as the young man connected a series of wires between the console and two Bose speakers on the table.

"I was able to split out the background noise," he said. "Let me play everything again and then we'll listen to each track separately. Try to focus on the moment right after Singer tells Mr. O'Hara to shut up."

He pushed a button and the complete playback started. AJ's voice came up and caused tiny vibrations in the speakers, but the sounds were crystal clear. Damien was impressed with the quality as he and Thomas waited for the critical moment.

"... Shut the fuck up..."

Santiago stopped the tape and worked a couple of buttons.

"Now, here it is again, background track only. Listen carefully."

He touched a button on the console. At first there was nothing but a faint hiss, like the sound of air leaving a tire. Santiago pointed to the speakers just as another sound emerged.

"There," he said.

Damien heard it and sat back. After a second, he turned to Santiago.

"Fuck me," he said. "That sounds like a train horn. Shit, nice job, Carlos."

Tampa

Terry listened to the message on his phone one last time. When it was done, he slipped the phone into his jacket pocket and headed out of his hotel room. He had a small travel bag and walked fast through the deserted hallway to the elevators. On the ground floor, he stepped into the lobby and saw a man dressed in a plain black suit waiting near the front desk.

"Let's go," he said as he reached the man.

The man tried to take Terry's bag, but a raised hand stopped him. He shrugged at the rebuke and led the way out of the lobby, to a black Lincoln Town Car parked near the doors. Eighteen quiet minutes later, the car pulled to the curb at Tampa International Jet Center, a corporate jet terminal near the main ones.

Terry got out without waiting for the driver to open the door. Inside the building, he was met by a pleasant-looking woman wearing a powder blue long-sleeved Oxford tucked into a navy blue pencil skirt. At her collar was a colorful scarf covering her neck. "Madison Aviation" was embossed on a small patch on her shoulder and a name tag on her chest read "Sheila."

"Mr. O'Hara," Sheila said. "The plane is waiting. Follow me, please. Per your instructions the crew knows not to disturb you. If you need anything, however, just ring for them."

She led Terry onto the tarmac where several jets were in view. A shiny white Gulfstream V had its steps deployed. Two smiling crew members were waiting patiently in front. Sheila wished Terry a good flight and passed him to the crew with a small hand gesture.

"Mr. O'Hara, welcome aboard," the male crewperson said, taking his bag. "Ms. Graham here will be in the cabin with you and see to your needs once we're airborne. Climb up and we'll get you to Philadelphia before you know it."

Terry nodded but said nothing as he ascended the steps into the cabin. The crewpersons followed and the stairs collapsed behind them. One hour and forty-three minutes later, the jet landed at Philadelphia International Airport and taxied to the Atlantic Aviation Executive Terminal. As soon as the aircraft came to a stop, a black Cadillac Escalade pulled forward and parked near the nose. The Gulfstream's steps unfurled and Terry stepped out and walked to the car. Seconds later, the sleek vehicle drove out of the airport.

Philadelphia

Alex's cell phone vibrated from his nightstand.

"Harris here," he said.

"Sir, Terry O'Hara has left Florida. The team arranged for a private jet to take him home."

"Damn it," Alex said as he sat up in bed.

His wife rolled over next to him. He reached down and stroked her hair.

"Very well, thanks," he said into the phone.

He returned it to the nightstand and resumed his work on his wife's auburn hair. He loved the sensation on his fingertips and managed a smile at her through the dark. The pain in his arm momentarily disappeared as he readjusted his body next to hers.

"Why do I put up with this shit?" he whispered into her ear.

"It's who you are."

Chapter 58

Tampa

I woke up next to a warm body for the second straight day, and for the second straight day it wasn't going to last long enough. I glanced at the alarm clock on the nightstand: *6:57*. I hadn't set the alarm—I never did—but I had the feeling Suze might have, so I waited patiently for the pending disturbance. Sure enough, three minutes later her cell phone blared to life.

She stretched and arched her back as she raised her arms toward the headboard. Little noises escaped her mouth in the process. What also escaped was her upper body from under the covers, but I didn't mind. I was totally amazed by her breasts, my favorite part on a woman, and my entire being tingled at the sight.

"Oh, shit, I gotta go," she said after seeing the time on the clock.

Any thoughts I had of morning sex evaporated as she sprang from the bed. Her phone sounded again and she moved to a small table next to the bed. Her back was to me, but the sun through the windows gave her body an aural hi-light. It was impressive and I silently thanked various sources for giving me the nerve to finally get with her. My privates got happy again, too, and I had to shift my position on the bed so she wouldn't see.

It didn't quite work.

"Ooh, ooh, ooh, now that looks tempting," she said in a sexy voice after turning back from the table. "But I have to get going. Save it for me, huh?"

Oh, yeah, and she wasn't bashful in bed, either.

"Sure, I'll keep my hands to myself," I said. "Oh, wait. I mean I won't do that. Sorry."

She giggled and hopped on the bed, landing on her knees next to me. Her breasts bounced a little and the tingles increased, especially in my fingers. I tried to pull her in to satisfy the need for a touch, but she was too quick and bolted from my reach after giving me a peck on the cheek.

"Are you flying back tomorrow on the charter or commercial?" she said while pulling on her panties.

"Whichever you want," I said. "I'm all yours."

She stood straight at those words and locked her eyes on mine. Uh oh, I thought, did I just fuck this up?

"That's nice to know, Marshall," she said through a large smile.

I watched in silence as she resumed getting dressed. It was almost as erotic as watching her get undressed and my body reacted as expected. I was close to making her late, but she moved a little too far from my reach after pulling on the last of her clothes.

"Keep that key," she said. "You can bring your stuff down and stay here again tonight."

"Yes, ma'am," I said; then as she started to move away. "Oh, hey, you didn't answer my question. Which flight am I on?"

"*Mine,*" she said over her shoulder.

Chris Pike was the only person in the fitness room when I got there at seven-thirty. I nodded in his direction as I stepped up on one of the treadmills, but he mostly ignored me and continued pumping on an elliptical machine to my right. We'd been reasonably cordial to each other the past few days, no doubt because of Buck, but there was still a chill.

"You see this?" he said over his shoulder after a few minutes.

He was eyeing a TV in the far corner of the room. I stopped running and leaned over to get a closer look. *SportsCenter* was airing.

"See what?" I said.

"Something about O'Hara," Pike said. "He left the team. No one knows why."

I pushed the stop button on the treadmill and stepped over to the TV. Someone was reporting in on the phone and I picked it up mid-sentence.

"...sources told me O'Hara left the clubhouse before the game ended. I tried to follow up a short time ago, but no one from the team is willing to discuss it. As far as I can tell, O'Hara is no longer in Florida. I don't know if this has anything to do with the earlier report regarding his mother, but considering the Phillies can clinch tonight, it's odd he would leave..."

I bolted out without waiting for the rest of the report and hustled back to Suze's suite. My cell phone was on the nightstand and I dialed quickly.

"So, on a scale of one to ten, how bad is it?" I said as soon as Thomas answered.

"Your scale isn't sufficient enough for a reply."

Suze read the statement back and Mark made a couple of final edits. It was a generic denial of the reports about Terry and an assurance all was well with the Series. When she left, Mark picked up his cell and dialed Gabi.

"Send Clarence back to Philadelphia. If he can find Terry, great, if not, tell him not to worry about it. And tell him thanks."

"I'll take care of it," Gabi said. "Need anything else?"

"Yeah, I'm hungry, is there any food left?"

"Sure, plenty," Gabi said. "I'll wait for you, come on down."

Springfield

AJ moved through the darkness to the RV, the overcast working as a shade against the coming dawn. There was a syringe in his hand as he reached for the door, but another sound caught his ear and he stopped. After a second, he walked toward the row of evergreens near the back of the vehicle and looked around. Seeing nothing, he headed back to the door and stepped up into the Rockwood. As soon as he disappeared, Edward Hand came out of hiding and raced back to his kitchen. He bounced in place as he waited for the latest call to Sean Connors to connect, looking very much like he needed to pee. After six rings, Sean's voicemail clicked on.

"Damn it, Sean," Hand said aloud, as he waited for the instructions to finish; then after the beep. "Sean, I'm telling you, there's someone in your house and the RV. I'm calling the police."

Philadelphia

Alex managed a couple of hours of sleep after the phone call about Terry, but as he got out of bed, his left side was aching again and a low-level headache persisted. Still, he felt better than yesterday and managed to shower and shave without too much trouble. His wife had to help him get dressed, not that he would tell anyone that part. He'd opted for a dark grey Armani suit with razor thin pinstripes, white dress shirt, and red tie. Other than the sling holding his arm in place, he looked normal as he made his way to the office.

Once there, the latest information didn't do anything to improve his condition. The horn on Singer's call was very faint and the audio department couldn't promise a source before tomorrow. Alex hadn't heard from Sandy yet, and Damien and Thomas were still at Michael's condo. Outside of the call last night there had been no further word from Singer.

Alex was about to change that when Damien beat him to it.

"Thomas wants to head back to Mrs. O'Hara's house," he said through the phone. "I'm not sure why."

Alex mulled over the words, but decided not to fight it.

"Hey, if he thinks that will help, go. Santiago and Jelps can babysit Michael."

Springfield

Dean Woods was on duty for all of seventeen minutes when his radio squawked. It wasn't the first time Edward Hand had called to report foul play and Woods knew it wouldn't be the last. The man was nosey and had an extremely overactive imagination, but Woods also knew he wasn't completely off his rocker because every so often he actually did help. He told dispatch he'd check it out, but a traffic accident diverted his attention for several hours. By the time he got to Rolling Road, it was close to eleven A.M. Just as he was parking, a knock on his window made him jump. He pushed open the door and knocked Hand back a few steps.

"*Christ, Ed,*" he said. "Are you trying to get shot?"

Hand backed off a few steps as Woods got out of the car. He was wearing a blue velvet sweat suit with a thin white stripe down the side. On his feet were blue Puma Clydes that must have been thirty-years old. His head was a wispy collection of white strands that gave him a frantic look—think "Doc Brown" in *Back to the Future*—and Woods had to work hard not to laugh.

"OK, Ed," he said. "What's this all about?"

"Nothing now," Hand said. "You took so dang long, you missed it. The man is gone."

"What man?" Woods said with a little more concern.

"The man in Connors' house, that's what man. Geez, why won't anyone listen to me?"

"Calm down, Ed," Woods said in a reassuring tone. "Let's go inside. You can make me a sandwich and tell me all about it."

Chapter 59

Springfield

Woods decided to give Hand the benefit of the doubt, and after a ham and Swiss on rye with mustard, he headed to the Connors property. Despite the old man's general goofiness, there was something in the story that tweaked the officer's interest. Maybe it had something to do with the recent encounter with Damien, but Woods figured it wouldn't hurt to take a look.

Hand was most fixated on the RV so that was Woods' first stop. He tried the door, but found it locked. Strike one, he thought, as he began moving to his left, toward the back of the vehicle. He was walking slowly, stretching up to look through windows, but finding every curtain drawn. After a complete pass, he came back to the door and tried again. There was no change.

He shrugged as he turned for the house, starting at the back. The storm door there was unlocked, but the main door was not. Strike two, he told himself, as he left the small porch and did a slow walk around the perimeter, again looking into windows where possible and trying the front door along the way. As with the RV, everything was locked up tight and he saw or found nothing unusual.

The circuit ended in the driveway. He stood there for a few minutes and looked around at the rest of the property. Again, nothing caught his eye and his head began to shake. Whatever Hand had thought he'd seen Woods could not. Strike three, he thought, punctuating the strikeout with a big sigh.

"Shit, Ed," he said aloud. "There's nothing going on here."

Philadelphia

Terry's appearance shocked the night guard at the stadium parking lot. The man thought there was another game in Florida, but as the pitcher stepped out of the Escalade, he said nothing to explain. He simply walked to his Porsche, got in, and drove out of the lot. Now, two hours later, the guard was retelling the story to Clarence Riggs.

"Don't sweat it," the big man said with a nod. "You didn't do anything wrong."

Clarence moved away and pulled out his phone. Gabi picked up after the first ring.

"He's been and gone. This is where I give up the chase."

"Thanks, Clarence," Gabi said. "Maybe I'll see you Wednesday."

"I hope not."

The walls were closing in and Michael needed to get out of the apartment in a bad way. The FBI agents posed a slight problem, but after a long internal debate, he decided to chance it.

"I need some air," he said as he stepped out of his bedroom.

He was wearing dark green corduroys, an ecru-colored sweater, and brown hiking shoes, clothes appropriate for the weather, and as he neared the front door he reached up and grabbed a black peacoat from a hook on the wall there. It was then that Agent Santiago stood.

"Uh, Mr. O'Hara," he said. "I'm afraid you can't leave."

Michael stopped and turned toward the agent.

"Am I under arrest?" he said.

Santiago hesitated.

"Um, no, sir," he said. "But you need to be here in case the kidnapper calls."

Michael eyed the collection of gadgets on the table where Santiago was standing.

"You don't need me. You guys got it covered."

"Mr. O'Hara, *please*," Santiago said. "This is *your wife* we're talking about."

Michael shrugged.

"*Ex*-wife," he said. "And she doesn't need me either."

He turned and went out the door. Santiago looked at his partner on the sofa, but the man offered nothing more than a shrug.

"Shit, dude, thanks for helping," he said. "Go follow him already, will ya?"

Springfield

Damien was so used to the abused Bureau vehicles that being in Thomas' Acura was a genuine pleasure. Life in the FBI was the complete opposite and he added "nice car" to his mental list of reasons to find a new job. Yes, he liked that he was doing something good for society, but nothing was his, it all seemed borrowed, a feeling the recent time with Sandy had heightened. The stolen moments never lasted long enough.

"So what exactly are you hoping for?" he said to Thomas after pushing away the thought.

"We're starting over," Thomas said. "I need to see things again."

"What things?" Damien said.

"All of them."

Chapter 60

Tampa

I ate lunch on the patio of a sandwich shop two blocks from the hotel. The air was pleasantly warm and out across the bay the sun was dancing in and out of the clouds, creating a lot of sparkles on the water. It reminded me of the day spent with Buck two weeks earlier. It was hard to believe so much had happened since then, including his death.

Before I started dwelling on that last point, a beep sounded from my phone. It meant I'd missed another call, something I'd been doing a lot lately. I fished the cell out of my pocket and quickly navigated to the recording. It was from my father.

"Hey, I know you're heading home tomorrow, I need a favor. Old-man Hand keeps calling about the damn RV. Can you go by the house and check it out? I'm sure it's fine, but your mother is driving me nuts about it. Thanks. Love you. Oh, and don't fuck up any calls tonight."

Great, Hand again, I thought, as a seagull landed on a railing in front of me. As I closed the phone, he began to eye the last remnants of my sandwich. When I didn't give him any, he let out a loud shriek.

"Is that so?" I said aloud in response.

He shit on the railing before flying away. I found it completely appropriate.

My dad's message, whatever the hell Hand was doing, was more shit I didn't need.

Philadelphia

The mid-afternoon traffic was light and Terry arrived at the intersection of 15th and Market twenty minutes early. He guided the Porsche south along 15th and made a right onto Ranstead Avenue and then another onto 16th in front of Liberty Place. A block and a half later he turned into the parking garage beneath JFK Plaza and found an open spot near one of the stairwells on the lowest level. He backed in, shifted the car into park, and took a deep breath as he pulled out his cell to listen to the message again.

"You get paid too much to suck that bad. Guess maybe the picture of your mother didn't help, huh? Tell you what, let's do this. You give me some money, think of it as a refund for that shitty performance. In return, I give you back your mother. I'll be in touch to set up the drop. And for her sake, let's keep this between the two of us. Your father has the FBI busy enough. No need to add to their workload."

Terry pushed the air out through his lips as he navigated to his text box. He read the drop instructions again and slipped the phone back into his pocket. He closed his eyes and didn't move for the next ten minutes, until the slam of a nearby car door made him jump.

"OK, let's do this," he said aloud as he stepped out of his car.

A trip up through a urine-smelling stairwell deposited him on the sidewalk along 16th Street near the Visitors Center, directly across from Suburban Station. He looked around. Pedestrian traffic wasn't too heavy and within seconds he spotted the vendor cart he needed, twenty feet away next to the curb.

He got in line behind a woman there and waited as a man inside the cart handed a bag through the opening. The woman paid for the lunch, or late breakfast, before hurrying off toward Arch Street. After she was gone, Terry hesitated a few seconds. The vendor was supposed to recognize him, but he hoped no one else did. The last thing he wanted was to draw attention because it would undoubtedly cause a scene.

No one seemed to notice and he stepped forward.

"What'll it be?" the vendor said.

Terry reached up and placed a $50 bill on the ledge in front of the man.

"I think you already have my order," he said without making eye contact.

The small man studied Terry for what seemed like hours, but was actually only seconds, before exchanging a yellowish-orange business-sized envelope for the cash.

"Thanks," Terry said as he took the package.

The man did not reply and as soon as Terry turned, the door on the opening slammed shut. Terry ignored it and kept moving forward toward a decorative concrete wall along the sidewalk. He sat, and with a finger on his left hand, tore open the envelope. A single sheet of paper and smaller envelope were inside. Terry pulled out and read what was on the paper.

> That you are reading this means you listen better than your father does, but I'm sure you already knew that. Here's what's next. You're going to make two cash payments. Payment #1 = $500,000. We'll call this a good faith deposit, your guarantee that you haven't told anyone of our business together. Payment #2 = $2.5 million. That one gets your mother back. As soon as I get it, you get her, simple as that.
>
> Payment #1 is due by 6 PM TODAY. Put the cash in the new envelope and go into Suburban Station. There's a newsstand on the first level near the door. Tell the blind man working there you are dropping off and picking up. Give him the envelope and he will give you a New York Times. After the exchange, walk away.
>
> Remember, if you go to the police, she dies. If you fail to deliver, she dies. Don't do either of those things. Just pay me.

~*~*~*~*~*~*~

Samantha's senses were both dulled and heightened from the daily dose of sedative, causing reality and fantasy to come together in a horrible collision in her head. She was asleep but awake, conscious yet unconscious, and had no idea if the voice she'd heard was real or imaginary, her mind's way of coping by giving her something to cling to instead of fear.

Out of reflex, she screamed into the confusion, but the sound was muffled by her fatigue and the gag and came out as nothing more than the hint of a whisper. Before she could scream again, the medicine took hold and she went under.

There would be no salvation this day.

Chapter 61

St. Petersburg

The Rays played Game 5 as if their pants were on fire. It was obvious from the first pitch they had the greater desire to win. As for me, for once my pants were *not* on fire and I enjoyed an easy night. There were a few close plays at second base, a couple of steals and the front end of some double-plays, but nothing overly difficult or controversial. For the most part, the game presented nothing more than standard fare: ball, strike, fair, foul, safe, out.

Exactly the way it's supposed to be.

The same couldn't be said for the Phillies. One of hardest things in professional sports was to win the final game of a series, the clincher. A lot of teams stumbled in that situation, when the taste of a championship got lodged in throats like a piece of leftover chicken. Gag, choke, whatever you wanted to call it, after the 9-4 Rays victory made the series 3-2, headlines in Philadelphia were going to be full of doom and gloom. For a team with a history of failure and epic collapses—1964 being the most infamous, when they blew a six-and-a-half game lead with twelve to play—expecting the worst was a community-wide feeling. The lone championship in 1980 wasn't enough. The faithful were going to be very skittish for Game 6.

I didn't know it as I left the field in Tampa, but so would I.

Philadelphia

As soon as the game ended, Michael left the bar and covered the two hundred or so yards back to his building. He did not appear upset, but maybe the extension on his wife's life was behind that. In theory, the Rays win meant there were two more days to find her, assuming AJ was true to his word, but still, something about Michael's demeanor seemed odd. Agent Jelps tried not to judge as he followed, thinking, hey, maybe the man's just trying to be brave.

Up in Michael's apartment, Agent Santiago was trying to find some bravery of his own.

"Christ, Carlos, where is he now?" Alex said through the phone at a volume north of shout.

"He's coming up now, sir," Santiago said. "Jelps is on him."

There was a hesitation before Alex responded.

"Fine," he said sharply. "Has there been any activity on his phone?"

"No, sir, it's been quiet all night."

"OK," Alex said after a loud sigh. "Please make sure he doesn't leave again."

Tampa

After showering and getting dressed, I checked my messages. At some point during the game Thomas left a very short one.

"Call me."

It was his normal flat tone, but I waited until I got back to the hotel to return the call.

"Hey, you called?" I said as I took a seat in the lobby.

"Good game?" he said.

I found it odd he would ask. He wasn't much for sports.

"Uh, well, yeah, I guess, for me anyway," I said. "For the Phillies, not so much, they lost. We have another game for sure. I'll be back in Philly tomorrow."

"I'm aware," he said.

I was not surprised to hear that. I took it to mean there was something more coming.

"When do your parents return from their vacation?" he said.

And there it was. I flashed on my father's message.

"Not for another week or so," I said very slowly. "Why?"

I stretched the 'why' for about four seconds.

"Agent Hastings and I need to look around their house."

A sharp pain hit me between the eyes. I squeezed them shut, but it didn't much help.

"Why do *you* need to look around their house?" I said.

"Excuse me?" he said.

"Nothing," I said. "Just pick me up at the airport and I'll let you in."

After he disconnected I suddenly felt really tired. Check that, it was an intense exhaustion the likes of which I'd never experienced. The headache wasn't helping. I guessed it was all a natural reaction to everything going on. I didn't know. I just knew I needed to lie down.

I stowed the phone and slogged to the elevators. The wall next to the doors did a nice job holding me up as I waited for a car to arrive. I had just closed my eyes when an arm slipped around my waist and a familiar body snuggled in next to mine.

"Uh oh, I hope it's not that bad," Suze said. "Anything I can do to help?"

I pushed out a small smile.

"You can try."

Philadelphia

The road trip to Springfield produced nothing, at least that was Damien's take on it, but afterward Thomas asked if Alex could arrange for some eyeballs to monitor Samantha's house. He had no specific reason, but Alex knew enough about Thomas' gut feels to consent. Damien made a call to Officer Woods. Inspired by the Ed Hand sightings and a feeling the two things couldn't be a coincidence, he agreed to provide assistance. After the arrangements were in place, Damien and Thomas headed back to Michael's apartment.

Once there, their night got progressively worse.

"Fuck you guys," Michael said. "I don't have to explain anything."

He was on the sofa in his living room. Thomas, Damien, Santiago, and Jelps were all standing nearby. Alex was connected via speakerphone. Michael's outburst had come after the tenth time someone asked a variation of the same question: What were you thinking? The only change with each pass was Michael becoming more and more defensive.

"What is this, Harris?" he said, directing his voice toward the speaker. "I thought you guys were on my side."

A loud sigh escaped from the phone.

"We *are*, Mr. O'Hara," Alex said. "But that still requires your cooperation."

Michael was about to reply when a loud tone interrupted, signifying an incoming call to his cell phone. The Rays victory had extended the Series and presumably Samantha's life, but an acknowledgement would have been nice. Everyone in the room had that exact same thought as Santiago prepped the equipment.

After another three tones, he signaled Michael to pick up.

"Hello?"

"Today must be your lucky day, Michael," AJ's amplified voice said. "Your lovely ex-wife gets to live a little longer."

After a couple of seconds to regroup, Michael sat forward on the sofa.

"What do you want?" he said with disgust. "You're such a tough guy, why don't we settle this one on one?"

There was a hearty laugh in response, a sound made more frightening by the speakers.

"What's so fucking funny?" Michael said in a shout.

The laughter faded and AJ's voice returned.

"Michael, you had that chance years ago, but decided to let someone else get their hands dirty," he said in a dismissive tone.

"Maybe I'll give you another shot, but not today. Today we talk about what's next. I assume the FBI is listening?"

Damien nodded and Michael translated.

"They're listening," he said.

"Good. Here's what I want. Before Wednesday's game you tell the world Samantha is fine. Say she was too nervous and decided to hole up in a hotel. She didn't want to be around anyone. Tell them she gets that way when Terry plays."

Michael knew that was mostly true, but didn't see how it mattered.

"And then what, you let her go?" he said.

There was a pause.

"No, Michael, I do not," AJ said. "When I hear the announcement I'll know you're serious about this and I'll call with final instructions. Have your checkbook ready."

There was a loud click and the room filled with white noise. Santiago flipped a switch to kill it, leaving the room in silence. After a few seconds, he leaned toward the speakerphone.

"Sir, should I play it again?" he said.

"No, that's fine," Alex said. "Get started on your analysis. See if you can find anything that might give a location. Damien, you and Thomas call me back. Mr. O'Hara, Agent Hastings will advise you what's next."

A dial tone took the place of Alex's voice until Damien walked over and touched a button to silence it. Michael simply stood and walked hurriedly to his bedroom. The sound of a slammed door followed as Damien turned toward Thomas.

"Come on, let's call the boss."

Thomas held his ground, a look of concern etched into his face.

"What?" Damien said.

"Things are not as they seem."

Terry had been in a lot of fights in his life, but none had left him as physically and mentally drained as the events of the past few days, the highs of Game 1, the Game 4 disaster, the hastily arranged flight back to Philadelphia, the various demands from AJ, wondering whether his mother was safe. All of it had completely sapped him, and he passed out within seconds of pulling the Porsche into his garage and killing the engine.

Several hours of fitful sleep later, the awkward position of his body or the nightmare he was enduring or both jolted him awake. He sat up and tried to remember where he was, rubbing at the kinks in his neck as his eyes adjusted to the light.

"Shit," he said aloud in a ragged voice when he noticed the time on the car's dashboard: *11:53 P.*

He stepped out of the car and spent the next five minutes stretching to get his blood flowing again. When he was as refreshed as he could hope to be, he reached back into the car and grabbed the newspaper and envelope from the passenger seat, the latest parts of the puzzle. It was time for the next and, hopefully, last round of the fight, one that would end with the safe return of his mother.

Chapter 62

Tuesday, October 28, 2008
The day before Game 6 of the World Series
Philadelphia

Alex tried to sleep, but gave up after two hours of tossing and turning. The call from Damien and Thomas had produced the latest fly in the ointment and if Thomas was right, Alex knew he was going to need a bigger fly-swatter. That thought stayed with him as he made his way to his kitchen at just after three A.M. Once there, he used his cell to call the office voicemail system. He had an idea based on Thomas' ideas and needed help from Sandy, but didn't have the heart to wake her. She'd been busting her ass and deserved a couple of hours of sleep.

"Hey, do me a favor as soon as you get in tomorrow or later today, whatever," he said after the machine beeped at him. "Take a look at the original interviews we did around Samantha O'Hara's house. Maybe your sharp eyes can find something we missed."

~*~*~*~*~*~*~*~

Springfield

The sight of the car parked in front of the Connors house caused AJ to continue past on Rolling Road. He parked three streets away and worked his way back on foot, using backyards and shadows as cover. He came around the house on the side opposite the RV and studied the strange car through the darkness. There were two heads inside, but it was too dark to get a good look at the faces. Definitely local, not Federal, he thought, as he watched intently.

The car stayed for another twenty minutes before slowly moving away. AJ waited another five minutes before heading around the back of the house to the RV.

"OK, Samantha," he said aloud once inside. "Looks like you get some company tonight."

Tampa

Per Suze's wishes, as if I would say no, I gave up my first class upgrade and took the charter flight back to Philly. The trip to my parents' house with Thomas and Damien meant I was going to have to pass on accompanying Suze back to the Four Seasons, so the time on the plane would have to do for a while. She was a little disappointed when I told her, but quickly recovered.

"That's OK," she said. "I have a ton of work anyway. You *are* coming eventually, right?"

"Yep," I said. "But Thomas needs my help on something and I promised my dad I'd check the house. Neither should take too long."

"That's good, because I have something for you."

With that she moved her hand under the blanket covering our legs and squeezed the inner part of my thigh before slowly sliding her hand to my crotch. A crooked smile filled my face.

"I like *your* plan better."

Philadelphia

Alex reclined in his chair and closed his eyes. During a meeting with the audio team he'd learned the horn heard on Singer's call wasn't a train, but a trolley. Research matched it to a make of equipment used by two domestic authorities, one in the Philly area, SEPTA, and one in California. Given it highly unlikely Singer was on the left coast, efforts were concentrated on SEPTA and the Authority's tracking system verified a car had been on the Route 101 line near Rolling Road at the time of the call. That added some punch to Thomas' feeling about setting up the watch at Samantha's house as well as Alex's subsequent request of Sandy.

The latter would see the first returns.

Sandy had been awake when Alex left the message and had arrived at the office a little before six A.M. to start in on the interview reports. She found that they fell into three groups: those with no one home, those with someone home but unwilling to give a statement, and those with a witness statement. Of the eighteen houses covered, only three were in the last category and Sandy's review started there.

The first was a statement from Edward Hand, but it bordered on comical and Sandy set it aside. The second statement came from an elderly woman by the name of Josephine Higgenbotham, but it was obvious the woman had done the interview as nothing more than an attempt to have some company. Sandy felt a slight murmur when she finished reading that one. I hope I don't end up old and alone, she thought, as her mind flashed to Damien. She shook it off as she moved to the third file.

Her epiphany came as she read the first line:

1635 Rolling Road, Connors residence, Peter Arcadia interviewed; Arcadia house-sitting while homeowners traveling

A minute later she was at Alex's door. She looked agitated or excited, he couldn't tell which.

"Tell me," he said.

"Singer was in Connors' parents' house the day we found the blood. We interviewed him, but Agent White had no idea who he was. *We let him walk away.*"

Alex started to look up, but stopped himself.

"Shit," he said as he refocused on Sandy.

"We need to get in there," she said.

"Yes we do. I'll tell the boys. They're heading there right now."

Radnor

Forty minutes after picking me up in front of baggage claim at the airport, Agent Hastings pulled his FBI Crown Victoria into the parking garage of my apartment building. We were there so I could pick up the keys to my parents' house. I didn't carry them with me on the road. I think Hastings was a little annoyed at that, but whatever.

We made our way up to my apartment and a pleasant scent of flowers hit my nose as soon as I stepped through the door. I hadn't been home in almost a month so the aroma meant the cleaner had recently been by. The service was included with the rent, something that came in handy for a less-than-neat and oft-absent person like me.

As we stepped in, Hastings' cell rang.

"Hastings," he said as I closed the door behind him.

I couldn't hear the other side of the conversation, but his face seemed to brighten a little. I wasn't sure if that was good or bad.

"We're at Marshall's place now. Ten minutes if I rush."

His tone told me "bad" was the winner.

"We need to hurry this up, we just got a lead," he said. "It's your parents' place."

I flashed on the calls from my parents and almost said something about it, but stopped.

"I'll get the keys," I said instead as I dropped my bags and hustled into the kitchen.

"Shit," I said aloud seconds later.

"Is there a problem?" Thomas said from the other side of the opening between rooms.

"The keys are gone," I said.

"Tell me you're fucking kidding," Hastings said.

His expression added another layer of concern as I hustled back to the front room and scooped up my backpack, my equivalent of an attaché case, and rummaged through it. No keys. My heart began to race as I reached into my pants pocket and pulled out my keychain. No keys. I closed my eyes and opened them again, then slowly took in everything around me. There was nothing out of place and my pulse quickened even further.

"Shit, shit, shit," I said.

"Marshall?" Thomas said.

"You guys look around in here," I said. "I'll go check the bedroom."

I headed down the short hall and repeated the slow survey in my room, but again found nothing. When I got back to the front room, the other guys' answer was the same.

"Who would have known the keys were for your parents' house?" Thomas said.

I frowned at him.

"Anyone who looked at them, they were labeled," I said. "One set had three keys for the house and the other had two keys for the RV."

"I think we need to go visit Ms. Floyd," Thomas said.

"Ms. Floyd" was Jean Floyd, my cleaning service, a single mom of three school-aged kids who lived in the unit below mine. I doubted she would have taken the keys, but wasn't going to be surprised if she had, not at that point.

"Hey, woman," I said a minute later when she opened her door.

"*Oh my God, Marshall,*" she said excitedly. "How have you been?"

She came through the door and gave me a big hug, but backed off after sensing my tenseness.

"Um, Marshall, what's wrong?" she said. "Is there a problem upstairs? Is this about your friend? Oh god, *did he steal something?*"

I looked at Thomas and Hastings then back at Jean.

"What friend?" I said.

Chapter 63

Philadelphia

Gene McLane was a huge Phillies fan and seeing Terry O'Hara yesterday had been a thrill, so much so that Gene forgot to complete two very important forms: a CTR (Currency Transaction Report) and a SAR (Suspicious Activity Report), both required as part of the Bank Secrecy Act to report high-value cash transactions to the U.S. Treasury Department, generally anything over $10,000. Normally, it would have been an easy enough problem to correct, but after Terry sat in front of him for the second time in as many days, this time with a withdrawal slip fives times as big as yesterday's, Gene knew he was in trouble.

"Cash again?" he said, trying hard not to panic. "Are you sure, Mr. O'Hara?"

"Yep," Terry said. "And hurry, please, it's important."

"OK," Gene said, drawing out the two letters. "Come with me."

Anyone watching would have noticed nothing unusual. Terry was carrying a duffle bag. It appeared to be full. Twenty minutes later, he was still carrying the bag and it was still full, only the contents had changed. The move was designed to provide Terry cover should he be interrupted during the process, which proved beneficial moments later when a group of fans intercepted him on the sidewalk on the way to his car to ask for autographs.

What was not beneficial was taking place at the same time in the bank's executive offices. Gene was being dressed down by the bank president for not filing the forms for yesterday's transaction on a timely basis. The president didn't wait for explanations. He marched Gene back to his desk and stood over his shoulder until the forms were completed and filed.

As Terry slid into his car, the stats of the transactions found their way into the Treasury Department data system. A constantly running search algorithm at the FBI's Philadelphia field office locked onto the information and generated a Critical Action Report (CAR). The CAR was distributed by email to the author of a request submitted weeks earlier. Sandy had made it as part of her work related to World Series background checks. She was not at her desk when the email arrived and the message went unnoticed for almost six hours.

By then it would be too late to matter.

Terry put the bag with $2.5 million on the passenger seat next to him and started the engine. He was sweating heavily, despite the cool temperatures outside, and his heart was pounding inside his chest. Before he put the Porsche into gear, he pulled a sheet of paper from his jacket and read the words again.

> Fill a duffle bag with pages from the newspaper so it looks full. After you get inside, toss the paper and put the cash in the bag. Go to your mother's house and put the bag behind the bale of hay on the porch. There's a candle in the pumpkin on top. Light it and leave.
>
> When I have the bag and get confirmation you're at the ballpark, I'll send a text message on how you find your mother. I'm sure she'll be very happy to see you.
>
> Like yesterday, involve anyone or fail to deliver and she dies.

Terry tossed the note on top of the bag, jammed the car into gear, and roared away from the curb with a squeal of rubber.

"Hang on, Mom," he said aloud. "I'm coming."

Radnor

Jean Floyd was on her sofa with a hand raised to her mouth. The pose reflected myriad emotions, and was accompanied by tears on both cheeks. It had been tough for her to describe what happened, but I tried not to show any anger. I'm not sure I succeeded as well as Thomas and Hastings, both of whom remained stone-faced.

"Hey, it could happen to anyone," I said.

I gave her shoulder a light squeeze. She reached up and took my hand.

"Thanks, Marshall, and I am *so* sorry."

"It's OK. I'll make a huge mess and you can pay me back by cleaning it up, how's that?"

She managed a smile through the tears as I moved to the door with Thomas and Hastings.

"Say 'hi' to the kids," I said to Jean over my shoulder on our way out.

"I will," she said as I closed the door behind me.

Once in the hallway, Thomas looked at me with his all-business face.

"It fits," he said. "Mr. Singer has been watching all of you for a long time. No doubt he figured out the cleaning pattern and easily swayed Ms. Floyd to gain access. I believe he came for the keys. Of course, your labels helped immensely with his search."

"*Wait, what?*" I said ignoring the shot at my anal tendencies. "You think he *wanted* the keys? Why would he—"

I stopped myself as the answer hit with the force of a foul-tip to the mask.

"Oh shit. That's where he has Samantha."

Springfield

Hastings pushed the Crown Victoria south on the Blue Route. None of us had said much since leaving my place, but a burning question finally got the best of me.

"Tell me again why no reinforcements?" I said.

"If Singer's still there, we don't want to spook him," Hastings said. "Thomas and I can handle things well enough. And we'll have another set of hands."

I thought he was talking about me.

"Yeah, well, you guys get paid for this shit," I said. "I don't. I'm just an umpire."

Hastings made a face and I realized he hadn't meant me. I didn't pursue it.

"Anyway, sorry about the keys," I said. "My parents will just have to get over you guys breaking in."

"I'm sure they'll understand," Thomas said.

Terry's black Porsche had exited the Blue Route at Route 1 ten minutes before Hastings' Crown Victoria did and he was now parked at the curb in front of his mother's house. As promised, a bale of hay was on the porch with a carved pumpkin on top. The decorations were similar to those from his youth, but the wicked smile cut into the orange orb seemed to be mocking him. Terry shuddered slightly at the sight before heading up the walk.

Dean Woods watched the ballplayer from the driver's seat of his blue and white police car parked a half-block away on the opposite side of the street. Damien's request for backup had not mentioned young O'Hara being present and Woods' face showed confusion at seeing the man. A bad feeling began to gnaw at him, but after a short internal debate, he decided against radioing Hastings. Stick with what you came for, he told himself, as the pitcher reached the porch.

Terry lowered the duffle bag from his shoulder and dropped it behind the hay. He moved around to the front and picked up the pumpkin. Again, exactly as described, a candle awaited. Terry removed a lighter from his pocket, and after a quick look up and down the street, squatted in front of the bale and reached inside the pumpkin. Seconds later a faint glow flickered to life through the carved openings. Terry started to walk away at the same instant

Woods saw a black Crown Victoria pass through his view out on Rolling Road.

"That's my cue," he said as he cranked the cruiser's engine.

The sound caused Terry to look up. He was a few feet from the Porsche as Woods passed and the two made eye contact. What the officer saw in the young man's eyes made him momentarily forget where he was headed. He pulled his car to the curb instead and hopped out.

"Mr. O'Hara?" the officer said. "Is everything OK?"

Terry's face twisted into a look of confusion as he began to look back and forth between the policeman, the house, and the street around them.

"You need to get out of here," he said. "You're going to fuck up everything."

"Excuse me?" Woods said. "There's no need for that kind of—"

"Fuck that, man, *just leave,*" Terry said, cutting him off.

"Now hold on right there," Woods said as he moved to within three feet of Terry. "Superstar or not, you need to calm down and tell me what's going on."

"I don't need to tell you shit. This is my mom's house. I don't need a reason to be here."

The Crown Victoria backed into view again on Rolling Road. Both men turned to look.

"Shit," Woods said as he held out a hand toward Terry. "Mr. O'Hara, please stay here. Whatever the problem is, I think we can help."

"*What we?* Man, the only way you can help is to leave before it's too late."

The back door of the Crown Victoria opened and a man appeared. It didn't take long for Terry to recognize the familiar movements.

"Marshall?"

AJ was watching the events unfold from a new vantage point, Edward Hand's master bedroom. Hand was bound and gagged on the floor next to him, where he'd been since moments after AJ caught the old man snooping around the RV again. The change of venue was yet another fortunately timed event for AJ in the scheme of things. Hand's house was going to be a whole lot better than the RV or the Connors' home during the next few minutes.

"Oh, now this wasn't part of the deal, Amigo," he said aloud.

Hand squirmed at the sound of AJ's voice. AJ looked down with a blank expression.

"Looks like I have to stay a little longer. You don't mind, do you?"

"Dude, what are you doing here?" I said after reaching Terry and the policeman.

I looked back and forth at both. I now knew the cop was Hastings' extra help, but why he was standing here with Terry was a mystery. So was Terry being there at all.

"Officer Woods, my name is Marshall Connors," I said without offering my hand. "Agent Hastings needs you at my parents' house."

The policeman studied my face for a few seconds before the recognition kicked in.

"You're the Connors boy, the umpire," he said. "OK, this is getting too weird."

"Yeah, well, welcome to my world," I said.

After a second, Woods started for his car.

"Wait, cut through the backyard," Terry and I said at the same time.

We looked at each other.

"Old habits, huh?" I said with a shrug.

Woods added a shrug of his own before heading around the near side of Samantha's house.

"Marshall, we gotta get outta here," Terry said to me as soon as the policeman disappeared.

"What's going on?" I said again.

"I'm getting my mom back, but I hope you guys didn't just fuck it up."

Damien and Thomas were in the driveway, next to the RV, when Woods came through the backyard.

"Y'all didn't tell me young O'Hara was coming along for the ride," Woods said as he reached them.

"Terry's here?" Damien said, looking past the policeman's shoulder. "Where is he now?"

"Over at his mom's place. Young Connors is with him."

Damien nodded and refocused on Woods' face.

"That's probably a good spot," he said before turning to Thomas. "OK, this was your idea. Call the shot."

"I'll take rear, you do front. We'll meet in the middle."

"I'll take watch," Woods said as the other two headed for the house.

In less than a minute, Thomas and Damien were standing in the Connors' dining room.

"Clear on my end," Damien said.

"Same," Thomas said. "Check upstairs. I'll get the keys and head to the RV."

Damien nodded and headed for the stairs while Thomas went back to the kitchen. Within seconds, he was outside again, the extra set of RV keys in his hand.

"All quiet out here," Woods said.

Thomas nodded on his way to the Rockwood. After unlocking the doors, he pushed the inside one forward and stepped up into the darkness of the cabin.

I stared in disbelief after Terry finished explaining.

"AJ was working you the whole time?" I said more than asked. "Makes sense now, but you shoulda told someone."

"You woulda done the same thing," he said with little emotion. "Don't judge me."

"I'm not. I won't," I said. "But we need to tell them what's going on."

We went through the yard in the same direction Woods had moments earlier. The short trip brought back a rush of memories. I could have sworn I saw Terry's equipment, and I stumbled before shaking myself back to the present. No time for reminiscing now, I thought, as we hopped the fence between yards, the same leap I'd made a thousand times in my youth, but before I got hit with another flashback, the door to the RV flew open and my mind went blank.

Thomas came out and began yelling for Woods to call an ambulance as Terry and I reached him. Samantha was in his arms, wrapped in a blanket I recognized as from the RV's bed. She looked ragged beyond description as Thomas set her in the grass just off the driveway.

Terry dropped to his knees next to her and lifted her head to his chest.

"Oh my God, *Mom*," he said through a stream of tears.

"*Marshall, goddamn it, move,*" Thomas said in a shout toward me. "Get some water from the house. *Go.*"

I took off as he gently wrested Samantha from Terry's arms.

"Terry, please, let me help her."

Within seconds, I was back with four bottles from the fridge. I dropped them on the ground next to Thomas. Terry was still kneeling there, but didn't interfere as Thomas opened one and tried to get some of the liquid into Samantha's mouth. I flashed back to the fire in college and realized how seriously overmatched I'd been that day, completely opposite of Thomas right now.

"Ambulance is seconds out," Officer Woods said as he came and stood beside me.

I looked at him, but didn't respond. His next words more than compensated.

"Jesus Christ, this is some bad shit."

AJ made a quick decision as the chaos unfolded in front of him.

"Time to go," he said as he stepped over Ed Hand's quivering body. "Sit tight, old man, someone will find you soon enough. And next time, don't be so nosey."

He smacked Hand on the top of the head before turning and heading out. He bounded down the steps and made his way through Hand's kitchen. He could already hear the first sirens of the coming cavalry as he escaped the house. He ran hard through Hand's backyard. He was exposed there, but didn't hesitate as he tore across the open space toward the O'Hara yard.

Once there, he went around the far side of the house, away from any eyes at the Connors' place, and made his way to the front porch. There was a smile on his face as he ascended the steps. He had bided his time, and the money elicited from Terry would serve as a nice side-dish to complement the entree of revenge.

"Hey, I still win," he said aloud as he stepped around the hay. "You can have the bitch, I'll take—"

He stopped. The smile evaporated. The bag was gone.

"Fuck, fuck, fuck," he said. "Where's my money?"

He stared wide-eyed for several seconds until something inside him snapped. Had there been anyone close they would have heard the sound.

"*Connors,*" he said.

The growing crescendo of sirens caused him to look up from his rage, just as the first rescue vehicles roared past out on Rolling Road. He looked back down at the bale, at the empty spot behind.

"*Fucking umpire,*" he said. "You just couldn't stay out of it."

He turned and leaped down the steps, breaking into a full out sprint away from Samantha's house. A minute later, he was at his car. Another chorus of sirens hit his ears. He ignored it as he slipped into the driver's seat. The image of Marshall was the only thing he could see, and he slammed his fist on the dashboard. The concussion caused several pieces to fly off and come to rest near his feet.

"OK, motherfucker, let's see how you like it when I take something from you."

Chapter 64

Springfield

I was leaning against the hood of Agent Hastings' car, watching the FBI and Springfield Police swarm around my parents' house. The outside was lit up like a gaudy Christmas display, with bright spotlights illuminating the façade. The Rockwood was getting just as much attention, if not more.

It sucked to think Samantha had been there the entire time. I mean, we'd been right around the corner, just days ago. It was all—I cut myself off from over-thinking it. "What If" wasn't going to help. We had her back. That was all that mattered.

She'd been whisked away by the first ambulance to arrive. Terry went with her, but not before asking me and Thomas to take care of his car. It was a subtle exchange in the chaos, but we knew what it meant. There was a lot of cash in the trunk. I'd want that taken care of, too, injured mother or not.

My mind drifted in that direction. I couldn't imagine what AJ thought when he didn't find the bag, but I had a strong feeling we'd all find out soon enough. The sight of Thomas and Hastings walking toward me and a vibration against my leg kept me from getting too worried about it. I pulled out my cell. The call was from Suze. For a split-second, I thought about making something up, but quickly dismissed it. I didn't want to start our relationship with a lie, and we were definitely starting a relationship.

"Hey, you," I said, but without much oomph.

"Uh oh," she said. "What's wrong?"

"I, uh, I have a little problem here. I'm not sure when I'll make it back."

"Marshall, you're scaring me," she said. "What kind of problem? Are you OK?"

In my mind I was screaming NO, but I kept that inside.

"Yeah, yeah, I'll be fine," I said; then after a pause. "We found Terry's mom."

It was Suze's turn to pause.

"Oh, God, *is she OK?*"

"I don't know yet," I said. "They took her to the hospital."

Thomas and Hastings reached me at that moment. I held up a finger to them.

"Listen, Suze, I gotta go. I'll call you as soon as I can."

I disconnected without waiting for a reply. Thomas was eyeing me closely. He had his usual game face on. Hastings' expression was more empathetic as he put a hand on my shoulder.

"You don't have to stay," he said. "It's gonna take a few hours to get through everything here."

I shook my head.

"I'm OK, but thanks," I said. "Any word on Samantha yet?"

Hastings nodded.

"She's stable, but severely dehydrated. It'll be a while before they know anything more."

Thomas made a motion with his head. I picked up the signal.

"A few hours, huh," I said to Hastings. "I am kinda beat. Maybe I will take off."

Hastings nodded again.

"We'll call if something comes up," he said. "Go rest, and sorry about *all this*."

He accentuated the last words by pointing toward the house.

"Hey man, not your fault," I said. "Shit happens."

I shook his hand and began to step away.

"I'll walk with you," Thomas said as he joined me.

"Whatever they're paying you isn't enough," I said when we were clear of Hastings. "I can't imagine how you figured out she was here. Speaking of, do you think Hastings is gonna ask about the money?"

"He'll figure it out soon enough."

"But we're not going to tell him," I said.

Thomas nodded. I got the feeling there was more. I was right.

"We are not," he said. "This is not over."

"Yeah, I kinda figured that out already."

Philadelphia

"Hola, pretty lady," Bartola said in a jolly voice.

He had just joined Suze at the hotel lounge. His face was beaming. She managed a smile in return and motioned for him to sit.

"Mr. Casaba," she said as he did. "I'm glad you made it in OK."

"Yes, thanks to your help."

Bart had stayed behind in Tampa, to visit with some old friends. He was temporarily stranded there when his commercial flight had gotten cancelled, but Suze was able to work some magic and get him back to Philadelphia.

"You are very welcome, Mr. Casaba," she said.

"Please, call me Bart," he said.

"OK, *Bart* it is," she said.

Bart caught something in her words. After ordering a drink, he looked at her, his expression more fatherly.

"Is everything OK?" he said. "You look sad. Where is Mr. Marshall?"

Suze told him what happened. The big Dominican listened intently, and when she finished, he put a hand on her shoulder.

"It will be OK," he said. "This Mrs. O'Hara is in good hands, I am sure. And so is Mr. Marshall."

Suze managed another smile before both began quietly working on their drinks. Two stools to their right, another patron was quietly working his as well, seemingly minding his own business. His clothes were mostly nondescript, blue jeans, red hooded sweatshirt, and a Phillies cap, pulled low on his forehead, with Wayfarers covering his eyes. He looked like any other fan.

After a few minutes, he stood and fished a couple of bills from his pocket. He dropped them on the bar next to his empty glass as he turned to face Bart and Suze. When she noticed, her expression turned dark again. Bart turned to follow her sightline, but the man was already moving away.

"Who was that?" he said, turning back to Suze.

"I don't know," she said. "I'm sure it was nothing."

Springfield

"You gonna share or do I have to guess?" Damien said.

He was with Thomas. They were on the back steps of the Connors' home, their faces washed out by the harsh spotlights. Marshall had left in Terry's Porsche. That tidbit had not been shared.

"Marshall asked that you not destroy the house," Thomas said. "His mother would be most upset."

Damien's eyes narrowed.

"Nice sidestep," he said with a frown; then after a pause. "I guess you've earned a marker or two."

He looked back to the activity around them. After another silent moment, he turned toward Thomas again.

"So why *was* O'Hara here? And no bullshit, your heroism only scores so many points."

Thomas ignored the agent's question by asking one of his own.

"When can we speak with Mr. Pastelli? That might help clear up a few things."

Damien sighed and shook his head.

"C'mon, let's go."

Radnor

I parked the Porsche next to my Honda Civic and slid out. The stark contrast made me wince. The customized 911 was immaculate.

My baby carried the dust of several weeks, which was good, because it hid all the scratches.

"Shit," I said aloud as a realization hit me.

I wasn't wincing because of *my* car. I'd just driven away from a crime scene, in a pro athlete's hundred-thousand dollar custom vehicle, with $2.5 million in cash inside, and was about to leave it in a not-so-secure garage.

"I gotta be nuts," I said as I pressed a button on the key.

The *beep-boop* echoed around the cement walls as the locks engaged. The sound was a small consolation. I did *not* feel very good about the situation. I was seriously off-balance from everything I'd seen at my parents' place, but as the sound faded, I shrugged and turned, hoping Thomas knew what he was doing.

Otherwise, this was going to be a very expensive mistake.

Cherry Hill, New Jersey

Mario Pastelli wasn't surprised when Damien and Thomas walked into the kitchen of the safe house.

"Gentlemen," he said, a big smile filling his face. "I was expecting you sooner, what took so long?"

"Shut up, Mario," Damien said. "I'm not in the mood. Just get over here and sit."

Mario was standing next to a refrigerator.

"Now, now, Agent-man, be nice," he said, opening the door. "You guys want a Coke? They got diet in here."

"Mario, *sit down*," Damien said. "We don't have time for this."

Mario grabbed a can of regular Coke and closed the door.

"There's lots of time," he said.

He popped the top as he slowly made his way to the table where Damien and Thomas had settled.

"So, what do you guys want? I'm guessing you have some more questions for me, huh?"

"Mr. Pastelli, when did Andrew Singer first contact you?"

It was Thomas. Mario slowly nodded in response.

"Very good, mystery man," he said. "You finally pieced it together."

"Just answer the question," Damien said.

"Hey, G-man," Mario said. "How's about a little respect, I'm helping you guys out here."

He slurped a few ounces of dark liquid, loudly. Damien's eyes narrowed, but he held off from commenting.

"Ahh, much better," Mario said after wiping his mouth with his fingers. "Now, what was your question again? Oh, yeah, he called me about a month ago. Said Dukabi needed some new blood."

"How did Singer know to ask you?" Damien said.

Mario laughed before taking another swig of caffeine.

"*Everyone* knows to ask me," he said. "Singer, if that's what you guys want to call him, he told me him and Dukabi were working on a big plan. Said it would work best if O'Hara was the victim. Told me they'd cut me in if I helped make it happen. I'm a businessman, I listened. It was a good plan. I'm guessing it got fucked up, huh?"

"When did you realize Dukabi wasn't involved?" Thomas said.

"Didn't take long," Mario said. "Me and the big man, we go way back. He doesn't play like Singer was playin'."

He took another sip of soda. Damien leaned in toward him.

"What's that mean?" he said.

Mario wiped at his mouth as he considered the agent's question.

"Dukabi is in it for the money," he said. "This Singer, he was in it for somethin' else."

"Were there others involved?" Thomas said.

"Shit, man, guys like Singer work alone, just like me."

Damien seemed to be catching on. He sat back.

"Did Dukabi know what Singer was trying to do to the O'Haras?" he said.

"Mystery man knows," Mario said with a tilt of his head toward Thomas. "Ask him."

After Mario was escorted back to his room, Damien walked to the fridge and checked the contents. The fucker was right, he thought, when he noticed the cans of Diet Coke. He pulled one out and moved back to the table. After sitting he took a long drink.

"So, how long have you known?" he said after a small burp.

"Which part?"

"All of it, but start with Dukabi."

The agent took another hit of soda as he waited for a reply.

"I told you he and I had a conversation," Thomas said. "He agreed to step aside. He was quite cordial about it."

"I'll bet he was. What'd you do?"

"I mentioned that you, the FBI you, would let him stay in business if he cooperated in an investigation. He was very amenable to that."

Damien took another drink.

"And what did you promise—scratch that, I don't want to know," he said; then after a pause. "So he had no idea Singer was working something on his own. Does that help us?"

"It does," Thomas said. "He should be willing to assist. As Mr. Pastelli just said, Mr. Dukabi is in it for the money."

Damien nodded as he finished off the soda. After playing with the can for a few seconds, he crushed it and tossed it into the sink.

"What's our play?" he said.

"We know Mr. Singer put together the plan and set up the diversions with the fake demands on O'Hara senior and Marshall. As far as he knows, however, Mr. Dukabi is still in the dark."

"Sort of like us, huh?" Damien said through a frown. "We were chasing our tails while Singer did the real deed with Terry."

"Hiding in plain sight," Thomas said. "But adding Marshall was risky because it upped the number of 'what ifs' he couldn't control."

"As in what if Walters couldn't convince Rosenbaum, and what if Rosenbaum went to the cops, and what if someone saw him in the RV or at the house, and what if *you* got involved?"

"Exactly," Thomas said.

Damien nodded and let out what might have been a sigh.

"It looks like whatever happened at USC seriously fucked him up," he said.

"That was probably the last straw, yes," Thomas said. "The other women support that theory. Unfortunately, he's still out there."

"And seriously pissed off," Damien said.

"Indeed."

Chapter 65

Samantha ended up in ICU, in the room closest to the nurse's station. The room was quiet, save for subtle pings and beeps coming from the equipment near her bed. Terry sat in a chair along one side, staring at his mother, undistracted by anything around him. His face looked calm in the dull light of the fixture above her bed, but it was an illusion.

His anger had returned.

Michael, standing at the nurse's station, felt the same anger. Through the glass wall of the room, he could see Samantha's form under the covers on the bed, and Terry on the chair, but his son's expression prevented him from moving any closer. All of this is my fault, he thought, as he watched in silence and fought back the tears.

He wanted to go in and ask for forgiveness, but knew it was too late for that. AJ had gone too far. Now, the only thing left was to try and fix it, just like years ago.

Philadelphia

I took a cab back to the hotel, but had no idea what time it was when I arrived. A clerk I hadn't seen before was working the desk when I stopped to get the key for my room. He or she—I didn't really notice—may have said there weren't any messages, but my brain was fried and I didn't notice. At that point, there weren't too many things I would have noticed, but fortunately, one found me.

"Hey you," a familiar voice said from behind me.

I turned and found Suze's smile. It made me forget about everything. I dropped my bag and picked her up into a strong hug. I buried my face in the crook of her neck and breathed in her scent, letting it and her hair tickle my eyes and nose. It was just what the doctor ordered, whichever doctor ordered such things, and I held her for what seemed like minutes.

"So much for no-PDA, huh?" she said after I lowered her to the floor. "Better?"

"Way," I said. "Thanks."

"Come on, let's go upstairs," she said.

"Lead the way. I'm all yours."

A handful of people had lasted at the bar with Bartola into the wee hours, inspired by his baseball stories to hang around. The audience had listened to each with rapt attention until the tales were interrupted by the sight of Marshall and Suze near the front desk.

"You were right, she is taken," a man said to Bart. "Damn, too bad for me."

"It's OK, Amigo," Bart said. "Hay un montón de pescados en el mar, eh?"

AJ laughed. Yes, there were plenty of fish in the sea, but at the moment, Suze Keebler was the only one he wanted to hook.

Mark and Gabi were in the lobby when Marshall dragged himself through the doors and engulfed Suze.

"Good for him," Gabi said. "Tough week, he deserves it."

"We all deserve that," Mark said. "I think I'll go upstairs and hug my wife."

He reached across and slapped Gabi's knee before standing.

"I'll catch you tomorrow," Mark said.

He walked away. Gabi was about to head upstairs as well when he spotted Bart in the lounge. Man sure knows how to have fun, Gabi thought, as he watched. After a few seconds, a man Bart was with stood and headed in Gabi's direction.

There was a slight limp in his stride, but something else sparked a sudden desire for a closer look. Gabi stood and timed his steps so he would pass the man near the front desk. After the man went by and out the door, Gabi jogged to the bar.

"Oh, Gabi," Bart said. "I just closed my tab."

"That's OK, Mr. Casaba, I'm good," Gabi said. "Hey, that guy you were just talking to, did you get his name by any chance?"

"Si," Bart said. "I think he said his name is Peter."

~*~*~*~*~*~*~*~

Sandy apologized to Alex about twenty times for not seeing the email on Terry's withdrawals until it was too late. Alex assured her there was nothing to be sorry about, she'd discovered the connection to the Connors' house and that was enough.

Still, she was upset because it brought back the memories of the pain caused when Amy disappeared. She knew Samantha was far from OK, and suspected the same could be said of Terry. It had left her shaken, no doubt the reason she jumped when her phone rang.

"Agent Hood," she said after recovering.

"Tag, you're it," Damien said into her ear.

A sudden surge of energy raced through her body.

"Where are you?"

"Downstairs. Come join me."

Two minutes later she rushed out of the building and jumped into his arms. After the obligatory kiss, she looked up at him.

"How did you know I was still here?" she said.

"I'm a spy, remember?"

"How could I forget?" she said.

He smiled as they headed for his car.

"Tell me everything that happened today," she said.

"Whew, not sure we have time for that," he said. "You might have to call in sick tomorrow."

"Worse things could happen," she said.

"I don't know, I think most already have."

Chapter 66

Philadelphia

It was raining when I woke up, not hard enough to threaten the game, but that didn't stop Suze from worrying. She had hustled off to tend to whatever needs Mark might have, and I was alone when my cell chirped. The caller ID informed me it was my father.

"How bad is it?" he said.

I spent the next thirty minutes explaining, leaving nothing out of the conversation. Well, nothing except the part about Terry's money.

"I think I'll give your mother a condensed version," he said after I finished. "They will clean up, right? I'll never hear the end of it if not."

He wasn't ever going to hear the end of it unless he left my mom in Europe, but I didn't say that. Actually, Jean Floyd was going to do the job. She still felt shitty about letting AJ into my apartment and was more than happy to help when I asked.

"I took care of it," I said.

After another few minutes we said good-bye, and I headed downstairs. I got lucky and caught the tail-end of the breakfast buffet, eating while I flipped through the newspaper. It was filled with gloom and doom about the Phillies, as expected. Collin George had a piece about Terry and whether he'd be available for Game 7, if it became necessary. It was a good question, but before I could ponder it, Gabi appeared at my table.

He had an odd expression on his face.

"I think Andrew Singer was here last night," he said.

It was my turn to make an odd face.

"*What?*" I said as I stood. "Jesus, Gabi, did you tell the FBI?"

"I just did," he said. "At first I wasn't sure it *was* him. Bartolo was with a guy at the bar. There was something—"

He stopped.

"Gabi, what happened?" I said.

"He said the man's name was Peter. It was late. I was tired, distracted, whatever. The name didn't click until after I went to bed. I'm a damned idiot."

I could see he'd been wrestling with his emotions. I'm sure my look was just as bad, but before either of us could say anything else, Mark appeared behind my shoulder.

"Hey, you guys know where Suze is? I can't seem to find her."

Before I could answer, my cell phone beeped. I had a new text message. After reading it, I almost gave back my breakfast.

"Marshall, are you OK?" Gabi said.

I handed him the phone. He read the message.

> You need to do a better job keeping an eye on your girlfriend.

"Holy shit," he said.

Even if I wasn't numb, I couldn't have said it any better.

In addition to being good at her job, Suze was a kind and considerate person and always willing to help, even strangers. Her friends told her she was naïve, but she dismissed their concerns, telling them if everyone was more pleasant the world would be a better place. It's not like she went overboard with goodie-goodie stuff. She just felt that if you could help someone, you should, and the man frantically pacing near the front desk looked like he needed help.

"*Are you serious?*" he said in a shout into a cell phone. "What am I supposed to do now?"

"Excuse me, are you OK?" Suze said in a kind voice.

"No, I'm not," the man said in a harsh tone. "My plans are screwed and now I'm stuck here."

Suze eyed him for a second or two. He was about the same size as Marshall, maybe slightly taller and more muscular, but it was hard to tell because of the bulky red sweatshirt he was wearing. She thought maybe she saw something familiar in him, but quickly dismissed it.

"Are you here for the World Series?" she said, taking a guess at his issue.

"Not any more, unless you know somebody who is seriously connected."

He squatted and began to root through the contents of a shoulder bag he'd dropped on the floor. Suze bent down and helped him gather up the papers, a big smile on her face.

"Today must be your lucky day," she said. "*I'm* that somebody."

They both stood, but as the man lifted the case over his shoulder, he closed the gap on Suze and took a firm hold of her elbow. Before she could react, he pulled her closer and jammed something hard into her ribs.

"*Don't. Make. A. Sound,*" he said in a hiss through clinched teeth. "Move, to the doors."

When Suze looked down and saw the gun she froze. The man pushed it deeper into her side as he pressed a thumb into the soft underside of her elbow. She let out a small yelp.

"I said *move*," he said again. "Or I'll make this hurt a lot more."

He squeezed again. Suze gave in and let him guide her out through the doors, to the sidewalk along 18th Street.

"Keep moving," the man said in a low voice. "I'll tell you when to stop."

"Who are you?" Suze said in a shaky voice. "Why are you doing this?"

"Ask your fucking boyfriend," AJ said. "He seems to know everything."

Chapter 67

Philadelphia

After leaving the hotel, AJ led Suze eight blocks south to Walnut Street. Once there, he pushed her across the intersection into Rittenhouse Square Park. Other than a few runners, the park seemed dead, and they moved quickly along a path that split the park down the middle. Just as they passed the center point, a man appeared at the far end of the path.

Suze tensed up at the sight.

"He can't help you," AJ said, anticipating her thoughts.

She didn't understand at first, but when they drew near, her confusion was replaced by fear. AJ laughed as he guided her to a stop.

"Well, Michael, I didn't think you had the balls to show up," he said.

"Let her go," Michael said in a shaky voice. "This is between us."

He tried his best to project strength, but when Suze yelped from another poke of the gun, he seemed to lose most of his nerve.

"Not anymore," AJ said with a sneer. "Your wife can't help me so I found the next best thing. Now move, before I shoot both of you right here."

Suze was unable to process anything. Why was Michael O'Hara here? Who was this other man? How did he know Marshall? Why had he taken me? None of it made sense and the confusion stayed with her until the three of them stopped next to a car two blocks later.

"Wha—"

A sharp prick cut off her words, confusion, and everything else, and her world went black.

The FBI's reaction to Suze's disappearance was swift. They quickly closed off every exit and ushered everyone into the hotel's main ballroom for questioning. Two agents went with Yong Lee to view security tapes as other teams began room-to-room sweeps of each floor.

Alex Harris showed up after about ten minutes and took charge. I ended up in a small meeting room with him and several agents I didn't know. Gabi and Mark were with me, and Hastings and Hood showed up a half-hour later.

Somewhere in the chaos my phone disappeared, absconded by someone to analyze the message. The room was noisy, and I was barraged by a torrent of questions. On and on it seemed to go, but just before I lost my mind, a familiar voice restored some order.

"Hey, give the man a break. Jesus, Alex, come on."

It was Thomas, using words and a tone I'd never heard. My tired eyes found him on the far side of the room. He nodded at me, and seconds later Harris' voice sounded.

"All right, you heard the man, everyone out," he said. "Damien, Sandy, you stay."

The room emptied quickly, except for my new best friends. Thomas was first to speak.

"We'll find her," he said.

I knew he meant it with every fiber in his being, but I was too scared and too tired to respond with anything more than a nod.

"Yes we will, Marshall," Harris said.

I nodded at the director, and we spent the next half-hour reviewing everything. I don't remember much of what happened, but Agent Hood seemed to have the most intensity of everyone, even Thomas. It was personal for him, but there was something even deeper in Hood.

At some point, I think around four P.M., they finally let me go. Mark volunteered to walk me back to my room.

"How ya doing?" he said along the way.

"I've been better," I said in a weary voice.

He nodded an understanding.

"I'm sorry for this, all of it. I should have gone to the police as soon as Buck came to me. I let pride and arrogance dictate my actions and I messed up. It was stupid and people got hurt."

His face seemed to be getting darker, or maybe that was just my eyes.

"I'm sure you did what you thought best," I said. "The only thing I care about is Suze. She didn't do a goddamn thing except get close to me."

I really cared about her. The last few days had been awesome, but I couldn't help thinking it was all lost now, just like the way it had happened with me and Terry.

"Listen, you don't have to work the game tonight," Mark said. "I'll get a replacement."

"Fuck that," I said, turning toward him. "Sitting around here won't do me any good."

"Are you sure?"

"More than I've ever been."

"Ideas, please," Alex said from his seat at the head of a conference table.

Thomas and Damien were to his left, Sandy and Gabi to his right. A few other agents had returned to the room and taken up station at the far end of the table, but Alex was ignoring them. Damien was first to reply.

"He wants the money," he said.

"Keep going," Alex said.

"Samantha was revenge against Michael, but this is about the money now. It's the only thing that makes sense. He was set to pick it up when we interrupted."

"About that," Alex said. "Where *is* the money? I thought O'Hara made the drop."

"He did," Thomas said. "And then he un-dropped it."

Alex's expression changed to one Thomas hadn't seen before, and the director stared at him for a long moment. After a deep sigh, he rubbed at his injured arm and looked away.

"Where is O'Hara?" he said into the room.

"Which one?" Damien said.

Everyone waited as Alex processed something in his mind.

"Sir?" the agent said.

"Both."

Chapter 68

Springfield

Samantha was dreaming again, but it was not like the nightmares she'd endured in the RV. No, this was something soft and sweet. She was wearing a white sundress and walking barefoot on a beach. The sky and ocean were perfectly blue and it was hard to tell where one stopped and the other began. The sun was bright and its warmth coursed through her body. Walking next to her was a young version of her son, probably no more than ten or eleven years old. Samantha smiled down at the boy and took hold of his hand. Young Terry squeezed back. The warmth grew and left her more content than she'd ever been.

In the chair next to the bed, Terry sensed the sudden pressure on his hand and looked up. Samantha's eyes were flickering under the lids and he realized it was more than a reflex. He returned the squeeze as he stood and moved his face to hers.

"Mom?" he said softly into her ear. "Mom, it's me, Terry."

In her dream, young Terry was trying harder and harder to squeeze her hand. Samantha marveled at his strength. Such strong hands for a small boy, she thought, as she smiled at him.

"Mom?" the little boy said. "I'm here, Mom."

More of her senses flickered to life, but as they did, the beach and ocean began to fade. Panic set in as young Terry continued to call out.

"Mom, open your eyes. I'm right here."

My eyes are open, Samantha thought, but the beach continued to slowly disappear. Then the sky and water followed, until only the sun remained, bright in her eyes. She tried to blink away the shine, but it would not leave. Then the scents in the air changed from salty to industrial, and confinement replaced airiness. As her mind fought hard to comprehend the sensations, young Terry vanished, and dread filled her body. I'm still in bed, still tied down. But no, that's not right, she thought, I can still feel his hand.

"No," she said aloud in a shout.

The monitors next to the bed began to ping and beep as her vitals ratcheted up. Out in the hallway, an alarm sounded at the nurses' station. Through the sounds, Samantha slowly opened her eyes. Terry squeezed her hand harder.

"Mom, it's OK. You're OK. I'm here," he said.

"Terry," she said in a raspy voice.

His eyes filled with tears and he kissed her delicately on the head.

"Mom, it's over. You're safe."

As her focus returned, she looked hard at her son. A tiny smile blossomed on her face.

"You look tired," she said.

Terry forced his face into a smile. Seconds later, a nurse appeared in the doorway.

"Is everything OK in here?" she said as she hurried to the equipment.

"Everything's great," Terry said without looking up.

The nurse's expression brightened when she saw Samantha's face.

"Welcome back, Mrs. O'Hara," she said. "You gave us quite a scare."

Samantha's smile grew a little, but she said nothing as the nurse adjusted a few knobs before moving away.

"I'll be right out here if you need me," she said as she left.

Terry was still looking at his mother's face. She had his hand in a solid grip. Her features were more alert. Terry gave her a wink.

"A scare is right," he said.

"Bring the bed up so I can see you better."

He pushed a button on the controller and added another pillow under her head.

"Better?" he said.

Samantha nodded and began to look around the room. Terry reached back between his legs and scooted the chair all the way to the side of the bed and sat.

"How long have I been here?"

"Just a day," he said.

Samantha looked away, seemingly calculating something in her head. After a few seconds, she looked back at her son.

"Did you win?"

Philadelphia

Nik Sanchez stared at the phone like it was some kind of alien technology far beyond his comprehension. AJ's words echoed around his mind and punched hard at his senses.

"You will help me or you will die. You, the O'Haras, Connors, everyone, you took my life away and now I want it back."

The anger was more than any Nik had ever felt, even greater than his own years ago. He knew this was about the party, the goddamned place where it all started. He should have told Michael to handle his own problems, but now it was too late.

"Goddamn it," he said aloud.

He was still lost in the regrets when he stepped off the team bus in front of Citizens Bank Park an hour later. He had said little on the flight from Tampa and even less since getting the call from AJ. His teammates brushed off the silence as Nik being Nik and finding his game face. The sight of the ballpark actually let some of that happen.

I'll use the game, he thought, just like always, and then I'll deal with AJ.

No more deaths, not because of me.

~*~*~*~*~*~*~

Chris Pike had home plate duty for Game 6. I decided to let him run the show. If something came up, I'd put on my crew chief hat and deal with it, otherwise, I planned on being invisible, just like they told us in the book. The best umpires are the ones nobody noticed: Do your job, make the calls, and go home. I would be more than happy for that to be the case.

"Gonna need the thermals tonight," Bart said after we stepped off the shuttle in front of the ballpark. "It's cold."

At least it wasn't raining.

"So it seems," I said.

"You gonna be OK?" he said.

I knew he wasn't talking about the weather or our choice of underwear.

"I'm good."

He scoffed.

"*I'm good*," I said again.

In truth, I was far from good. Suze was out there, somewhere, and the only thing pushing me through was faith that Thomas would find her in time.

~*~*~*~*~*~*~

"Terry O'Hara is with his mother. We do not have a current location for Michael O'Hara."

The young agent left the conference room. Alex turned from the windows and walked back to the table. After sitting, he looked up at Damien.

"Would you two go ask young Mr. O'Hara if he knows where his father is?" he said. "Maybe we'll get lucky."

Damien signaled Sandy with his eyes and they both headed out.

"Hastings," Alex said before the two agents cleared the door. "Be smart."

Five minutes later, Thomas and Alex were the only two left in the conference room.

"Yeah, yeah, yeah," Alex said. "I know what you're thinking, just keep it to yourself."

Thomas' eyebrow went up and he tilted his head at Alex, but said nothing. Alex stood and paced away from the table. He stopped at a dry bar on the far side of the room and poured a cup of coffee from a large canister. He turned and leaned against the edge of the counter. A few seconds went by as he sipped at the hot beverage.

"I know they're seeing each other, and I know she hasn't been a field agent very long, but she's good," he said. "Damien will look out for her."

Thomas didn't question it.

"Now, as for *you*," Alex said.

He pushed away from the counter and tossed his cup into a trash can.

"Can you please go find Singer and end that sorry son-of-a-bitch before anything else bad happens?"

Springfield

Damien pushed the FBI cruiser hard, and he and Sandy reached Springfield Hospital twenty minutes after leaving the hotel. He parked in a restricted spot near the Emergency Room doors and was about to get out when Sandy grabbed his arm.

"His mother was kidnapped," she said. "Don't be too hard on him."

Damien gently removed her hand. A look of concern settled on his face before he spoke.

"He might be our only hope."

"Oh, God, I hope not."

Inside, both were relieved to learn Samantha had regained consciousness, but getting in to see her and Terry proved to be a challenge. The head nurse in the ICU was not impressed by their badges and gave both a long look, the kind a mother gives when she has no intention of letting someone disturb her babies.

"She's awake," the nurse said in a stern voice. "But I don't think you should be bothering them. They both need some time to heal."

"I understand, ma'am," Damien said. "But another life is in the balance and this might be our only chance to help."

The nurse's scowl remained for a few more seconds before finally receding. Her voice, however, remained stern.

"I'll be *right here*," she said. "Make it quick. She needs her rest."

As they moved away, Sandy's face had a look similar to the nurse's.

"What?" Damien said. "I was nice."

Chapter 69

Philadelphia

Suze tried to shake loose the cobwebs, but the motion exaggerated the pounding in her head. A wave of nausea overcame her, but she managed to turn her head before vomiting. After several ejections, she turned away from the mess and wiped her chin on her shoulder, but the smell of the bile hit her seconds later. She hacked through a round of dry heaves before her nose finally adapted. She took long slow breaths through her mouth and tried to regain some composure.

She hated being sick and the pile of goop embarrassed as much as reviled her. After a long moment, she pushed it out of her head and started to wonder where she was. Based on the non-reaction to her sickness, she figured it was somewhere no one could hear a scream, or more frighteningly, where no one cared. She took several more deep breaths to hold back the fear. This was no time for panic, she told herself, as she took an inventory of the surroundings.

The room was reasonably furnished. The colors and designs revealed an African motif. Suze was directly in the center of an intricate but now-soiled area rug. To the right of the door was a fireplace, but she was pretty sure it was fake. Two love seats faced the hearth, each with a long-stemmed floor lamp behind. A large roll-top desk with chair sat in front of a window. The drapes were open, but the shade was dropped, blocking any view out. Suze's best guess was this was some sort of reading room.

"Why would they let me see this?" she wondered aloud.

The fear kicked up again, but she pushed it away by concentrating on what else she could see. From the lack of any light at the edges of the shades over the window she guessed it was evening. That means I've been here a few hours, she thought. Someone must be looking for me by now. The momentary relief from that thought was quickly replaced by confusion as her abductor's words came to mind. She'd replaced Samantha O'Hara. That's what the man had said. As she began to realize what that meant, a chill raked her body and a tear escaped her eye. She was close to sobbing, but suppressed it by focusing on Marshall.

He'll find me, she thought, I just have to hang on.

Springfield

Terry stared at the FBI agent, his intense expression close to one usually saved for the playing field. Samantha did not react from the bed, but the monitors above her registered a slight change in her vitals. Sandy noticed, but Damien did not. His eyes were locked on Terry.

"What do you mean you think my parents tried to cover up my accident?" Terry said in a low voice. "How could you possibly—"

He stopped when Samantha put her hand on his. The touch caused him to move his gaze to her. A subtle shake of the head gave him pause.

"Mom, what are they talking about?" he said. "This isn't *our* problem any longer."

"I'm afraid it is," Damien said. "Singer has taken another hostage. We have reason to believe your father may know where they've gone. So again, have you seen or heard from Michael?"

The muscles in Terry's face began to flex aggressively. Samantha noticed and squeezed his hand. He turned. She gave him a firmer headshake.

"No, Son. He's right," she said. "This *is* our problem and you need to know why."

Philadelphia

The fans may have been dreading another collapse by their boys, but they more than compensated by being extremely loud. Despite the open-air setting, the sound at the start of the game was as loud as anything experienced under the plastic roof in Tampa. Add to that the thousands of white towels waiving en masse and it was admittedly cool. I wasn't supposed to get caught up in that stuff, but it was helping ease my mind, at least a little, and as we waited for the National Anthem, I nudged Bart standing next to me.

"Pretty wild, huh?" I said in a shout.

"Yes it is."

His smile helped me forget about Suze's predicament for a few seconds, but the danger never strayed far and by the time the Anthem finished, the doubts and fear were back. Maybe Mark was right. Maybe I should have sat this one out. I was a mess. When the coaches came out, I managed to fake my way through the lineup exchange. As the meeting broke up, Bart caught the struggle in my eyes. He stayed with me as we headed out to our positions.

"Amigo, you OK?" he said, his voice thick with concern.

I sighed and shook my head.

"No, I'm not, but this is the only thing I can do right now."

"Let her go," Michael said with all the courage he could find. "This isn't about her."

He was facing AJ in a room he was familiar with, but like the last time he'd been here, he did not feel very lucky. That AJ had brought them here, to Dukabi's, had at first made sense, but that feeling was long gone. In the minutes after their arrival, it became clear Dukabi had not been aware of AJ's intentions, with Samantha or this new victim. It also appeared, however, that the big man was not going to intercede.

"You and your opinion are no longer relevant," AJ said to Michael in a calm voice.

His hands began to move, very deliberately, as if to make sure Michael didn't miss anything. A metal tube came out of one pocket as a gun emerged from the other side. He slowly screwed the tube onto the end of the pistol. Michael's eyes went wide as he realized what was happening.

"What are you doing?" he said. "Dukabi, don't just stand—"

"*Enough,*" a booming voice said from behind, interrupting.

The slight diversion was enough to save Michael's life. He was able to move just as a flash appeared at the tip of the silencer. The bullet struck near the top of his right shoulder—instead of between his eyes—and the bones there exploded. The force spun him in a clockwise motion and he went down. AJ casually walked forward and watched in silence as blood escaped the wound and pooled on the wood floor.

A big smile worked onto his face as he took aim at Michael's temple.

"*Enough,*" Dukabi said again in another booming shout.

AJ did not turn.

"He deserves to die," he said.

"That may be so, but not today and not by your hand," Dukabi said. "*Lower the weapon.*"

The words echoed through the room. After several seconds, AJ complied.

"Go tend to your guest," Dukabi said. "You've done enough here."

"Not even close," AJ said as he stepped over Michael and left the room.

Dukabi came forward and knelt next to Michael. After finding a pulse, he pulled out a phone.

"Come quickly, your assistance is needed."

Within seconds a small man entered from a door opposite the one AJ exited.

"Take him to one of the spare bedrooms and treat the wound as best as possible. Alert me immediately if his condition worsens."

I wouldn't know about the drama at Dukabi's until much later, but the drama at the ballpark was every bit as intense. Of course, no one got shot, but for sports, it was pretty serious stuff. It was a clean game from an umpiring standpoint, but not so much for the two teams. Sometimes, though, errors and misplays added to the beauty. Accentuating that was the crowd. As the game ebbed and flowed, so did the noise, and despite my neutrality, there was no way not to notice.

Things started out OK for the home team, but a chance for a big first inning drowned in the swell of a double-play and strike out, and a 1-0 Phillies lead somehow seemed like a bad thing. The Rays stole the momentum at that point and scored a single run in each of the next four innings while the Phillies bats went silent. As loud as the crowd had been at the start, by the bottom of the fifth, it was completely the opposite and the air was thick with anxiety. I began to wonder what it would be like if we had to come back for Game 7 tomorrow.

If so, I had the feeling I wasn't going to be the only one having trouble breathing.

~*~*~*~*~*~*~*~

Sounds at the door caused Suze to hold her breath, but thirty seconds passed before the door finally opened and AJ came through. There was enough light from the hallway for her to make out small movements in his head, as if he was searching for something. When her lungs finally reached their limit she pushed the stale air from her body and gulped in a fresh supply. It was filled with the smell of the puke and she coughed.

AJ stepped toward her, but stopped when his foot found the gunk.

"What the fuck," he said as he looked down at the mess. "I'm afraid I'm going to have to ask you to clean this up."

He moved to the chair and put the blemished shoe into Suze's lap. He pushed against her and the chair toppled over. Her head bounced once off the carpet when she hit the floor. He then began to wipe the shoe along her body, leaving bits of mess on her clothes. She was close to hysterics as she tried to turn her head from the abuse. Tears mixed with sweat and goop, and the smell was worse than before. She closed her eyes and tried to wish it away.

"Open your eyes," AJ said in a sharp tone.

He lowered himself into a crouch. When she did not comply he grabbed a handful of hair and forced her head sideways. As he used the hair to clean away the last bits from his shoe, she finally looked at him. AJ saw the fear on her face and a wicked smile filled his.

"That's better," he said. "Now, you know why you're here, yes?"

She shook her head rapidly. His grip on her hair made the movements painful.

"No?" he said. "I'll give you the short version. Your boyfriend has my money and I want it back. You are going to provide the proper motivation."

He released her hair and stood. Suze's mind raced. What money? What had Marshall done? What did this have to do with me? The more she thought, the less sense everything made.

"I'm sure he'll come through," AJ said. "If not, I'll kill him. And then I'll kill you."

He walked away without another word. As soon as the door closed, the darkness closed in again and uncontrollable sobs shook Suze to the core.

An error by the Rays shortstop gave the Phillies life in the bottom of the fifth. I sensed the crowd thought this was the start of the rally they'd been waiting for. The next batter laced a single into left and the noise got louder. That was followed by two more singles, two runs, and decibel levels back to pregame readings. The score was 4-3 and one more hit could tie it or put the Phillies ahead, but it never happened because of Nik.

A curveball to the next batter bounced and he made an unbelievable block, pounced on the loose ball, and fired a strike to second to pick off the runner there. He followed that by gunning down an attempted steal on the next pitch. Going from two on and none out to two outs and none on seemed to suck the energy out of the Phillies and the rally died. It got more somber when the Rays came out and scored another run in the top of the sixth and held on from there.

Final score: Rays 5, Phillies 3. The Series was now even at three games apiece and every demon, jinx, curse, and bad vibe held by the people of Philadelphia immediately escalated to dangerous levels. The only saving grace, if there was one, was the thought of Terry pitching in Game 7. But even that was a stretch. After what he'd been through, I didn't see any chance he would pitch.

Luckily for everyone, I was wrong.

Chapter 70

Springfield

"You never saw it because you didn't want to see it, Son," Samantha said.

That she was right didn't make Terry feel any differently.

"It doesn't matter now, Mom," he said. "The police will take care of it. It's over for us."

He walked to the windows of the room. Outside it was dark, a perfect reflection of how he felt inside. Myriad thoughts waged battle in his mind and he couldn't focus. After the fight, he'd closed out everything and everyone. It was easier that way. "Just get back to the game, that's all that matters" is what he told himself over and over again. It was what got him through the pain and agony of the operations and rehab on his arm.

That he couldn't—wouldn't—see the truth in what his parents did didn't matter.

Baseball was *his* truth. The rest meant nothing.

As he stared into the darkness a collective groan from the hallway caught his ears. The disturbance triggered something and he moved to the bed and lifted the controller from near Samantha's hip.

She eyed him intently as he turned to a TV hanging in the corner. After a few clicks he found what he was looking for.

"Shit," he said to the screen when the final score of the game appeared.

He pushed a button. The screen went blank as he dropped the controller by her feet.

"Terry—"

"No, Mom, it's over," he said, cutting her off.

He turned and walked out without another word. It was time to get back to the truth.

His team needed him and he needed the game.

Philadelphia

The Rays clubhouse was in a highly agitated state after the game and Nik was at the center of attention. Reporters asked question after question and he quietly answered each, displaying little in the way of excitement. A few thought he was being arrogant, but his attitude grew out of his preoccupation with thoughts far from the game, and when the last of the hoard finally moved away, he pulled out his phone.

"What do you want me to do?" he said as he sat facing his locker.

"See, now that's the spirit," AJ said. "I knew you'd see the light."

"Fuck you, AJ. I'm not doing this for you."

~*~*~*~*~*~*~*~

After leaving the hospital, Damien and Sandy met Thomas and Alex in the conference room near the director's office. It was close to midnight, but no one seemed to have noticed the time.

"What are we looking at here?" Alex said.

Thomas was pacing, but after a minute or so, turned and focused on Alex.

"Mrs. O'Hara and Mr. Singer have an affair. She breaks it off and he reacts badly. She gets frightened and asks Mr. O'Hara for help."

"You think she *asked* Michael?" Alex said.

"I do," Thomas said. "He went to California on her behalf to advise Mr. Singer to cease and desist, but out of fear or something else changed his mind and went to Mr. Sanchez instead."

Damien sat back and began to nod. Sandy glanced at him, but said nothing.

"Another phony tough guy, huh?" Damien said.

Thomas nodded.

"Mr. O'Hara knew about Mr. Sanchez's past and used it. But Mr. Sanchez was too close to Mr. Singer and farmed it out. He probably figured he could control it, but it went very badly and he and Mr. O'Hara found themselves in quite a bind."

He moved to the dry bar and picked up a bottle of water before continuing.

"The O'Haras tried to solve it by writing a few checks, and Mr. Sanchez couldn't deal with the pain of betraying his friends and disappeared."

"Right," Damien said. "But then it all goes away and they live happily ever after."

"Except they forgot about Mr. Singer," Thomas said. "He lost his career and a lot more, the kind of things that *don't* go away. Samantha O'Hara fucked him, literally and figuratively, thus the hatred of her and most every woman that looks like her. The O'Haras further insulted him with the payments. He didn't need it, his family was well-off, which would explain why he never touched the money from Mrs. O'Hara. I believe the final straw was watching his former teammates make it to the World Series, a place he no doubt felt he deserved to be."

"I can see how that would leave someone with a head full of rage," Alex said. "But how does that get us to today?"

"Mr. Singer bided his time until he could exact his revenge," Thomas said after a shot of water. "First he served up Mr. O'Hara to Dukabi, then he kidnapped and humiliated Mrs. O'Hara, and then he topped it off by dropping the whole thing into the laps of Terry and Mr. Sanchez, knowing full well it would impact their performance in the Series, as evidenced by Terry's most recent effort."

"And Connors was included because of the umpire school rejection, right?" Sandy said.

"So it would seem," Thomas said. "He was at the core of Mr. Singer's last chance to stay in the game. It was Marshall who delivered the rejection as part of his duties helping Mr. Walters."

"Oh, wow," Sandy said.

There was a brief pause before Alex spoke again.

"That's a lot of payback and a few too many victims," he said. "We need to end this before Singer adds to it."

Chapter 71

Thursday, October 30, 2008
The day of Game 7 of the World Series
Philadelphia

I wasn't in the mood for company after the game so I took my time changing. As I sat in front of my locker contemplating the prospects of Game 7, I checked my phone. There were no new calls and I guessed that was a good thing. If something had happened to Suze, someone would have told me.

At a few minutes after midnight I left the ballpark and took a cab back to the hotel. It may have been because the Phillies had blown a 3-0 lead in the series, but as the taxi moved along Broad Street the entire cityscape seemed to have a dead feel. Or maybe it was just me. To combat the growing depression, I headed to the hotel bar in hopes a tall glass of something might help. It was there that Mark and Gabi found me around one-thirty.

"You boys are out late," I said. "Please don't tell me we have more problems?"

"Nah," Mark said. "The weather forecast has everyone a little jumpy, but I told them if it rains, we don't play. It isn't rocket science."

The last words reminded me of Buck. Hearing it gave me a little shot of courage.

"Speaking of rocket science," I said. "I want the dish for Game 7."

Mark's face showed no emotion as he studied me.

"Is that supposed to be a surprise?" he said evenly. "You're scheduled for it, why wouldn't you work?"

"I just thought—"

"Don't think too much, Marshall," he said, cutting me off. "It's not good for you."

That comment reminded me of Thomas and I managed a small smile. Mark gave my shoulder a solid squeeze as he smiled back. Maybe things weren't so bad, I thought, as I motioned for them to join me. They obliged and stayed long enough for a beer before heading up to their rooms. After that I took Mark's advice and tried not to think about anything, but the sudden appearance of Thomas twenty minutes later put an end to that.

For some reason I wasn't shocked to see him.

"We need to talk," he said.

"I'm sure we do."

I had been asleep for maybe twenty minutes when my phone rang at three-thirty-three. I didn't have the mental capacity to check caller ID before picking up, but the voice I heard on the line made every nerve in my body explode to attention.

"Marshall?" Suze said in a ragged voice.

My heart skipped a beat as I sat up.

"*Suze*," I said in a shout. "Where are you? Are you OK?"

She started to say something before her voice was replaced by one far less friendly.

"OK, that's enough," AJ said in an icy tone. "It's time to get down to business."

"I don't know what your problem is Singer, but it has nothing to—"

"Shut the fuck up," he said, cutting me off. "My problem has everything to do with this young lady. You interrupted my transaction with Terry. Now I'm going to interrupt her life until you fix that."

"What do you want?" I said after a few seconds.

"You know what I want," AJ said. "Do your job tonight and I'll be in touch."

The line went dead and eight seconds later there was a knock at my door. Two FBI agents, part of the latest Alex Harris team assigned to monitor me and my room at the hotel, were on the other side. In a way, I was glad he'd set it up. It provided a level of comfort. Of course, it meant I lost the next hour of my life answering their questions. That was OK, too, because at no point did I tell them the one thing they needed.

That was still between Thomas and me—and AJ.

After leaving the Four Seasons, Thomas met with Damien outside the FBI office. The two men were sitting in Thomas' Acura.

"Any luck locating Michael O'Hara?" Thomas said.

"One of the nurses saw him last night, but he didn't go in the room," Damien said from the passenger seat. "He hasn't shown up at the apartment either."

"That is unfortunate," Thomas said.

"Thomas, where's the money?" Damien said in a sharp tone, changing the subject.

Thomas studied the agent's face. He was impressed by the man and liked working with him, but was not willing to share that piece of information. Marshall was his responsibility, and he was going to do everything possible to protect him, including keeping Terry's money out of the FBI's hands. By doing so, *he* could control what came next. He was prepared to tell Damien another lie to ensure that control stayed in place, but the agent's phone interrupted.

Damien listened for a minute or so, but ended the call without a word.

"Connors just got a call from Singer," he said. "Alex is sending it to your phone. What's going on?"

"I'm trying to help my friend."

Damien saw the fierce determination in Thomas' eyes.

"I can help with that."

Thomas held the agent's gaze for several seconds.

"I know," he said. "And when the time comes, I will ask."

"You're an interesting man," Damien said with a shake of the head.

"Indeed."

Damien sighed and stepped out of the car. Seconds later Thomas called Alex.

"Is that what you expected?" Alex said.

"It is," Thomas said. "Thanks for keeping it close to the vest."

"Don't thank me. Just don't fuck it up, OK? I like my job and it might be hard to explain this to my bosses."

"Understood," Thomas said. "I'll be in touch."

Alex put his phone down and closed his eyes. He was extraordinarily tired and his arm was throbbing again. After a few seconds he opened his eyes and a quick glance at his watch told him it was close to four-thirty. He took a deep breath and headed for the elevators. As he waited, he rubbed the arm and made one last call.

"I'm going home. I suggest you do the same. I have a feeling we're in for a very long day."

Damien closed his phone and looked at Sandy. They were sitting in Damien's cruiser.

"Alex says we should go home and get some sleep," he said. "You game?"

"Drive and I'll tell you when we get there."

"Sir, he's lost a lot of blood, I don't know what more I can do. We should consider proper medical attention."

The man named Hudson was dwarfed in size by Dukabi, but his tone was firm. Few others, if any, could speak to Dukabi in such a manner. Hudson, however, was the one constant during Dukabi's time in America. Muscle came and went, often at Dukabi's whim, but this man was the only person Dukabi trusted.

"Very well," he said. "See to it, but leave no trail."

Dukabi returned to his office. The leather chair's familiar hiss greeted the movements as he sat behind the big desk. The office was dark and it calmed him as he contemplated the situation. He had often resorted to violence, but never for personal reasons. What AJ had done was personal and it greatly disturbed him. The first agreement with Thomas and latest with the FBI had been for no other reason than to recoup Michael O'Hara's debt, but if O'Hara were to die now, he would get nothing.

That thought was not pleasant. That he'd allowed AJ to manipulate him was less so.

He stood and left the office, walking swiftly toward the study. As he stepped into the room an odd scent hit his nose. He flicked the light switch and saw Suze on the floor, still strapped to the chair. Something resembling a growl escaped his throat as he hurried to her side. She was unconscious, and smelled of fear and something worse. He saw the bits of gunk in her hair and on her clothes. The footprint in mess on the floor told him what happened.

"This is unacceptable," he said as he effortlessly lifted the chair upright.

The sound of his voice was just short of a freight train, but Suze did not hear it. A second later, he pulled out his phone and dialed Hudson again.

"As soon as you finish tending to Mr. O'Hara, come to the study. Necessary actions are obvious. See that she is safe."

He ended the call and looked at Suze's ragged form in front of him.

"You have my sincerest apologies," he said before leaving the room.

Agent Santiago wanted to make up for the earlier screw-up and got the chance when Alex assigned him to stakeout Dukabi's building. The instructions, however, had been cryptic: watch for anything unusual and call if you see it. Santiago had spent most of the past three hours pondering an appropriate answer as to what would constitute *unusual*, but when an ambulance pulled to a stop at the curb, he was pretty sure it qualified.

A small man came out of the building and met one of the attendants. They moved as if to shake hands, but an envelope passed between them instead. The attendant went back to the ambulance and spoke to his partner through the driver's side window. After a brief exchange, the first man stepped back and the second exited. The EMTs walked to the back of the van, pulled out a stretcher, and followed the small man inside.

Fourteen minutes later they reappeared, but the stretcher was no longer empty.

"Holy shit," Santiago said before quickly dialing Alex.

Damien and Sandy tried to sleep, but neither could make his or her head stop working, so they tried sex instead. After an unfulfilling romp neither could get into, they talked quietly in the dark, Sandy's head resting on Damien's chest.

"How do you know he's right about all this?" she said.

"I just do. The guy is good," he said.

His words were comforting, but the prospect of reaching the end of her search for Amy's killer bothered her. It had been her driving force and she wondered what would happen when it was gone. She also realized that problem could wait.

"I believe you, but why are we just laying here?" she said. "We can't let Singer kill again."

"Thomas won't let that happen, and neither will I."

Chapter 72

Philadelphia

After receiving the call from Santiago, Alex had to make two more calls to get the rest of the details. Within an hour after that, he and Thomas were standing in the hallway outside Thomas Jefferson Hospital's ICU with one of the attending physicians, the latter explaining what had happened.

"The clavicle on Mr. O'Hara's right side was shattered by the bullet. The scapula and acromion were also broken, but not as severely. There is significant muscle and tissue damage, but we won't be able to tell the extent until we're finished cleaning everything out. I doubt he'll have use of the arm for some time."

"Is he awake?" Alex said.

The doctor seemed offended by the question.

"Of course not," he said. "He suffered massive injuries. We're prepping him for the next surgery. He won't—"

"We need to speak to him before you do that, Doctor," Alex said in a severe tone.

The doctor's face twisted into a nasty scowl.

"*What?* I can't do that," he said with disgust. "It would be torture. It's out—"

Alex put up a hand to stop him.

"*Just wake the man.* We need to know what he knows."

Terry had called his manager as soon as he left his mother's room at the hospital.

"I want the ball tonight," was all he'd said.

There was no argument because he disconnected and turned off the phone before his boss could reply. After the call he got in a couple of hours of sleep before heading out again, to the field, where he was once again the first person to arrive at just after six A.M. If his appearance shocked the guard, the same guy from days earlier, the man didn't let on. He simply opened the gate without a word.

Terry had not thrown since Game 4 in Tampa, but tonight was Game 7 of the World Series and there was no way he was going to stay on the sidelines. Ernie Goff's magic hands and extra electro-treatments would help, but it would be the anger caused by his parents' actions that would provide the main push to get him through, just like it had done most of his adult life. And there was something else as well: Terry's hatred of AJ.

Springfield

Samantha was awakened by the morning duty nurse, a large black woman named Ethel, the same imposing figure who'd confronted Damien and Sandy yesterday.

"Where's your son?" she said with a frown while changing the IV bags above the bed.

"He left to get ready," Samantha said. "He has a game tonight."

Ethel's frown deepened and her head began to shake as she made some notes on the chart hanging at the bottom of the bed.

"He should be here with you," she said in a tone similar to the one she'd used on Damien. "It's just a game."

Samantha's head began to shake.

"It's not just a game to him."

Philadelphia

I slept, or *tried to* anyway, past my normal time for a day with home plate duty, not rolling out of bed until just before nine-thirty. It had been a fitful night, especially after the call from Suze. It sucked not having her next to me. We'd only shared two nights, but it seemed like more, like she'd been with me forever. Maybe that was just the stress of her being taken, but whatever, it left me feeling like shit.

Getting another call from AJ didn't help.

"Mr. Connors," he said after I answered. "You slept well I assume?"

"Fuck you, AJ. What do you want?"

There was a pause and when he came back on the line his voice was a lot darker. I immediately regretted snapping at him, fearing he would take it out on Suze.

"OK, tough guy," he said. "Don't forget what I have. And don't forget what I want for it."

"I want it recorded somewhere that I strongly object to this," the doctor said.

He was next to Michael's bed, syringe in hand. Alex and Thomas were on the opposite side. Of the two, Alex's impatience was more obvious as they waited for the doctor to revive Michael.

"It's noted, Doctor," Alex said. "Please proceed."

"He's going to be groggy," the doctor said turning toward a collection of IV bags over the bed. "I won't be surprised if he passes out fairly quickly."

"Noted," Alex said again.

The doctor curled his upper lip, ala angry Elvis, as he inserted the needle into a connection on one of the bags. The medicine worked quickly and within minutes Michael's head began to roll from side-to-side as a low groan escaped his mouth. The doctor checked his pulse, his head shaking the entire time, before turning and walking away, lab coat flowing behind.

"He's all yours," he said over his shoulder with more disgust than earlier. "I'll be outside."

It was a grand exit, but neither Thomas nor Alex was impressed. Michael had created a plague, one that had infected Thomas's best friend, and any pain was well-deserved and paled in comparison to what Thomas might have done to the man on his own.

As Michael came out of it, Alex moved closer to the bed.

"Michael, can you hear me?" he said in a firm voice.

Michael's eyes slowly opened, but they were filled with tears from the pain. When he noticed Alex, he closed them again and his entire body seemed to sag.

"Michael," Alex said. "I'm sorry for doing this, but I need to know what happened."

Again, Michael's eyes opened, but his face was scrunched up in a big knot. Clearly, he was in a great deal of pain, but Alex pushed on.

"Why were you at Dukabi's, Michael?" he said. "Was Singer with you?"

The knot loosened and Michael's eyes opened a bit wider.

"I tried to stop him," he said in a raspy voice.

Alex leaned in.

"Where is he?" he said.

Michael's head began to shake. Alex wasn't sure if it was from the pain or something else.

"Michael, do you know where he is?" he said.

Michael groaned again and his eyes closed behind a more severe wince. It was several seconds before he reopened them and looked at the director.

"He's at... Dukabi's... with the girl," he said, his voice fading. "He wants the money... and he wants... all of us to die—"

A loud yelp came, cutting him off, before his body sagged again. Several alarms sounded on the monitors above the bed. The doctor rushed back in and pushed Alex out of the way.

"Damn it. Get out," he said in a shout.

Alex backed off as a pang of pain ran through his own injured arm, but he ignored it.

There was no time to waste on that now.

~*~*~*~*~*~*~

When Suze woke up, it took a long moment for her to get her bearings. Her surroundings were dramatically different. She was no longer bound to a chair and the awful smells were gone. As her eyes came online, she realized she was in a bed, a very comfortable bed. Was it all a dream? No, wait, she thought, this was neither her room nor her bed.

"Where am I?" she said aloud.

She reached up and touched her face and a light scent came to her nose, lilac maybe.

"Morning, Miss," a soft voice said, startling her.

She sat up quickly and found a small man standing near the foot of the bed.

"Who are you?" she said, her voice cracking a little.

"I apologize for the intrusion," he said. "I brought you some breakfast and your clothes. I'm sorry I couldn't find more appropriate sleeping garments."

Suze looked at herself. She was wearing a humongous white t-shirt.

"But how—"

"It's ΘK, miss," the man said. "You are safe now."

"Who are you?" Suze said again. "Where—"

"Enough questions," the man said. "You will be comfortable here. This room has everything you'll need. The bathroom is there, to your left."

Suze still had a million questions and a strong desire to run, but ceded to the situation.

"Wait," she said as the man turned for the door. "Am I… am I still a hostage?"

"You were never a hostage, miss. But you must stay here for now."

Radnor

After a quick shower, I headed downstairs and grabbed a cab. The ride to my apartment was lousy. Traffic was a mess and we didn't get to Radnor until after eleven. After telling the driver to wait I hustled inside. Thomas' instructions were very specific, but when I got to my door, Jean Floyd was there. She was not part of the plan.

"Hey," she said as I reached her. "I was just about to clean your place. Good timing, huh?"

"What's to clean?" I said in too-harsh of a tone. "I haven't fucking been here."

She backed off.

"Shit, sorry, not your fault," I said. "I'm running a little late. Just skip me today."

She eyed me closely, but a small nod found its way past the uncertainty.

"OK, you sure?" she said.

I nodded.

"Yeah, it's good."

She started to move away.

"Hey, uh, Jean, listen," I said. "Thanks for taking care of my parent's place. I really appreciate it."

Her face brightened a touch.

"You're welcome, Marshall. I wish I could do more."

"Like I said, it's not your fault," I said. "Anyway, I gotta go. I have a cab waiting."

I gave her a peck on the cheek and she moved away. Good save, I thought, as I stepped through my door. Hopefully, it wouldn't be my last because I was pretty sure I'd need a few more before the day was over.

Chapter 73

Philadelphia

It took an hour for Alex to get Legal to agree to a raid on Dukabi's apartment. Another hour was lost getting a judge to review the paperwork and issue a signature. Finally, at just before eleven-thirty, everything was in place and a full assault team was waiting for the "Go." That would come based on what Damien and Thomas found once they were inside.

"OK, take me through it again," Alex said through the speaker on Damien's phone.

Damien was with Sandy and Thomas at a table in a bar across the street from Dukabi's building. Several agents were outside monitoring the building's front and back doors. The armed-assault crew was two blocks away.

"Thomas and I will go in first," Damien said. "If we get any resistance, send in the cavalry."

Sandy's face tightened. Damien noticed and put his hand atop hers.

"Don't find any resistance," Alex said.

"Works for me," Damien said.

There was a click as Alex disconnected. Damien stowed the phone in the pocket of his overcoat as Sandy looked hard at him. When he noticed, he gave her hand a squeeze.

"It'll be fine," he said in a strong voice. "Just be ready if we call."

He winked at her, and he and Thomas left the bar and jaywalked across Chestnut Street. As soon as they disappeared into Dukabi's building, Sandy spoke into the transmitter near her collar.

"You all heard that, right? We need to be ready to move if they find trouble."

The rest of the team acknowledged and Sandy took a deep breath before uttering a last comment to an image of Damien.

"Please don't find any trouble."

Radnor

I was in and out of my apartment in under a minute and raced down the inside stairwell to the garage, Terry's keys in hand. The Porsche was where I'd left it and I felt a huge sigh of relief. I grabbed the bag from the trunk and jogged to the street exit. The promise of a reward had worked and the cab was still waiting for me in front of the building.

So far, so good, I thought, as I hopped in the back seat.

"Pay?" the driver said in a thick Eastern-European accent as he eyed me closely.

I pushed a crisp $100 bill through the slot in the partition. He smiled.

"Back to hotel?" he said.

"Back to hotel," I said with a nod.

The car pulled from the curb and I realized I was sweating heavily, despite the cool temperature outside. I guessed it was because I was sitting next to a bag full of money, or maybe it was from the down-in-the-pit-of-my-stomach fear I was feeling not knowing if Suze was OK. Either way, I could be excused for some excess perspiration.

"Jesus, I hope you know what you're doing," I said aloud to the window.

The cabbie shot me a questioning glance through the rearview mirror.

"Not you, you're doing fine," I said. "This mess is all me."

Philadelphia

Damien and Thomas stepped to a counter in the lobby. The doorman nodded at the agent's badge and buzzed them through a low gate there. After they moved away, the doorman pushed a red button below the countertop. Seconds later a phone next to the button buzzed. The doorman lifted the receiver and told Dukabi what to expect. Damien caught the sounds as he and Thomas waited for the elevator.

"Yeah, yeah, I know," he said. "He knows we're coming."

Above them, in the penthouse, Dukabi returned the handset of his phone to its resting place on his desk and put his focus back on AJ. There was a lot of fire in AJ's eyes, but the big man was unmoved by it as he gently rocked in his chair.

"Now, you were saying, *Mr. Singer*?" he said.

AJ was momentarily startled at hearing his real name, but quickly regrouped.

"Where is she?" he said. "I'm not fucking around. She wasn't yours to take."

One of Dukabi's eyebrows moved slightly, but the rest of his face remained undisturbed.

"The same is true of you," he said.

AJ reacted by stepping forward, which in turn caused Dukabi to stand. The face-off lasted for a few seconds until Dukabi snickered, as much as a man of his size snickered.

"Yes, I'm afraid it is time for you to go, Mr. Singer," he said. "Hudson will show you out. I suggest you go for your own safety."

AJ's eyes narrowed.

"I'm not going anywhere without the girl," he said with a snarl.

The office door behind him opened. He missed it.

"She is no longer your concern," Dukabi said. "The men on the elevator are, however."

"You son-of-a-bitch," AJ said through clinched teeth. "You set me—"

A loud click stopped him. It was followed by the feel of cold metal pressing against his jaw.

"Hudson will show you out now," Dukabi said again.

Despite the gun at his face, AJ held his ground.

"This ain't over," he said. "You want your money, I need the girl. You do the math."

Hudson pushed the gun further into AJ's cheek.

"I already have, Mr. Singer," Dukabi said. "Now go."

Hudson directed him from the room and away from the office. They stopped in front of a door near the end of the hallway.

"These stairs lead to a tunnel. Go to the end and exit. You will not be seen."

AJ looked hard at Hudson before turning and pushing open the door. It closed tightly behind him. There was no latch on the inside. After a few seconds, he gathered himself and started down the dimly-lit stairwell.

"This ain't fuckin' over," he said again. "Not even close."

Thomas waited near the elevator while Damien moved down the hall to Dukabi's door. After a few seconds, the agent signaled all clear and Thomas joined him there.

"He's being nice," Damien said with a slight motion of his head. "It isn't locked."

Thomas nodded as Damien grabbed hold of the knob.

"This is starting to become a habit with you and me, strange doors, bad guys on the other side, fun stuff, huh?"

"Indeed."

Chapter 74

Philadelphia

Suze showered again. The thought of someone touching her while unconscious had left her feeling dirty, despite the pleasant scent on her skin and hair. When she finished, she left the giant t-shirt on the bathroom floor and pulled on her own clothes. They also had the scent of being freshly washed.

"What the hell is going on?" she said aloud as she returned to the main room.

She was having a hard time reconciling her emotions. She wasn't a hostage, yet couldn't leave, but they were treating her like a guest. It was twisted logic she didn't understand and it continued to nag at her as time passed. She ended up parking in an oversized chair near the bed to wait. How long, she had no idea, there was nothing in the room to tell her, but after what seemed like a few hours the sound of the door opening made her look up.

"I brought some lunch," the small man said as he entered.

Suze watched as he placed a large white bag on the table where her clothes had been.

"How long am I going to be here?" she said in an unsteady voice.

The man looked at her with a slightly tilted head.

"However long it takes, I'm afraid."

AJ counted twenty-five flights on the way down and realized he was several stories below street level. There were no doors on any of the landings, meaning the stairs were clearly designed as a one-way trip. The counting, the quiet, and the semi-darkness all served to calm him slightly, but it also gave him time to reach an important conclusion. Dukabi had saved him. Yes, part of that was because he would never do anything to jeopardize getting his money back. But still, it was shrewd. Controlling Suze had been the perfect play.

AJ was contemplating an appropriate response as he hit the bottom of the stairs. The tunnel was in front of him as promised and he moved forward into the dark corridor. It took several minutes to reach the end and another door. He didn't hesitate before pushing through into a large space filled with cars. It was a parking garage. The door shut behind him with a soft click. Like the one at the top of the stairs, there was no way to reopen it. The only way out was through the garage.

He briefly considered stealing a car, but decided against it. There was no point triggering an alarm now. He was safe, but he put his hand on the gun in his pocket just in case as he hustled to an exit ramp at his left. There was a stairwell next to it and he ducked in. After two flights up he emerged into the chilly October air on Walnut Street.

After a moment to get his bearings, he saw he was two blocks from Dukabi's building, across the street from the Center City campus of Thomas Jefferson University Hospital. He was again impressed. The secret passage meant Dukabi could leave his building unnoticed, have a car waiting, and be gone before anyone realized.

AJ relaxed a touch, but before he got too happy, he caught sight of something disturbing. Two large black vans were parked along 11th Street. Beside the lead vehicle a heavily-armored FBI agent was talking into a radio. It wasn't hard to figure out the destination. AJ began to nod before heading off in the opposite direction.

Maybe the big fucker isn't so bad after all, he thought.

Damien and Thomas were surprised by the sight of a small man appearing in the hallway in front of them. He had a calm look on his face and stood with hands folded together in front of his body. Damien shrugged at Thomas and both lowered their weapons. The action elicited a small nod from the man.

"Mr. Dukabi is expecting you," he said. "Follow me, please."

The man led the way to a door along the right side of the hallway and motioned them in. Damien and Thomas stepped through, but the man did not follow.

"Gentlemen," a booming voice said from across the room. "Come, sit. We have much to discuss."

"You must know why we're here," Damien said in a firm voice. "I'm not sure there's a whole lot of discussion necessary."

"Ah, but there is, Agent Hastings, very much indeed," Dukabi said. "Please, sit."

He watched with a smile as his guests situated themselves in the armchairs in front of the mahogany desk. When he was satisfied they were comfortable, he eased into his leather chair.

"Mr. Hillsborough, so *very* nice to see you again," he said.

"Mr. Dukabi," Thomas said. "I'm afraid I can't say the same."

A slight chuckle escaped Dukabi.

"Understandable," he said before a pause; then to Damien. "As I said, Agent Hastings, we have much to discuss. First, I'd like to hear what it is you want from me."

There was no hesitation from the FBI agent.

"We want Singer and his hostage," Damien said. "We're prepared to do whatever's necessary to achieve that goal."

Dukabi's head moved slightly, an almost imperceptible nod, but enough of one to acknowledge they had his complete attention.

"I have no doubt as to that, Agent Hastings," he said. "The FBI is most thorough in such matters. Unfortunately, neither Mr. Singer nor his guest is here. You may check, of course, but I assure you, you will find nothing on these premises."

Damien glanced at Thomas. There was no response and he refocused on Dukabi, a little off-balance. This was not what he'd expected, not even close, but he was starting to see where it was going. The easy access in, the lack of any noticeable defensive gestures, the free pass to check the penthouse—something they would definitely be doing—were all because Dukabi knew that what the FBI had on him was sketchy at best. Outside of AJ and Elliot being employees, nothing in the events of the past week actually tied to him.

Damien blew out some air and tried a different approach.

"OK. Where might they be?" he said.

"A fair question," Dukabi said. "And what are you willing to offer for an answer?"

OK, Damien thought, as he glanced to his right again. Thomas was still, but the agent thought he saw something brewing and figured Thomas would share when necessary, which was apparently not yet. Damien's eyes went back to Dukabi's.

"Let's say I don't bust you for your poker games."

Dukabi made a sound that was probably meant as a laugh, but it came out more like a tiny explosion.

"Come now, Agent Hastings, surely you can do better than that," he said after recovering. "I'm offering the whereabouts of the man you seek, including where he is at this very moment and where he will be later this evening. Surely that is worth more. Why don't you take a moment and call Director Harris. I'm sure he will find something suitable. By the way, how is Mr. O'Hara? I understand he suffered a rather serious injury."

The last comment sparked a reaction from Thomas and he put his hand on Damien's arm. Damien looked over with a knitted brow, but Thomas' eyes were focused on Dukabi.

"Mr. Dukabi," he said with no emotion. "The FBI has rules to follow, I don't. The deal is you get to keep my earlier promise of repayment of Mr. O'Hara's debt and I let you live to use it."

Whoa, Damien thought, I didn't see that coming either. What he did see was the reason Thomas hadn't revealed his knowledge of the money. He also realized Alex must be involved with whatever Thomas was doing so there'd be no point to interfere. He just sat back and waited for Dukabi's reply, impressed by Thomas' dedication to protect Marshall.

"Ah, now that's more like it," Dukabi said. "See, Agent Hastings? A little imagination goes a long way. Your terms are acceptable, Mr. Hillsborough. Now let us discuss the details."

~*~*~*~*~*~*~*~

By the time the assault team got word and swarmed the parking garage, AJ was long gone. Damien wasn't surprised. The negotiation session was Dukabi's way of providing AJ time to escape. Well, not exactly escape, more like temporarily remain free until Dukabi could deal himself an unbeatable hand. The only fly in the soup was Suze Keebler. Damien knew Dukabi played that card to cover his own ass, but he also knew they needed Suze to flush out AJ. It was a fine line, but for now, he kept that concern to himself. He trusted Thomas' judgment and skills to make sure nothing happened to the girl.

He, Thomas, and Sandy reconvened twenty minutes later in the bar.

"Mr. Singer needs to get near Marshall," Thomas said. "He also wants the money and the ballpark gives him the chance for that as well as proximity to inflict harm on Mr. Sanchez and young Mr. O'Hara should he so desire. We have the advantage because he now no doubt thinks Mr. Dukabi a friend. I suspect he'll do whatever the man suggests."

"Sending the sheep to slaughter," Damien said.

"But what if Singer has a different agenda?" Sandy said. "What's to keep him from changing the plans?"

Thomas did not reply, a trait Damien was beginning to understand entirely too well. He frowned and looked away for a second before responding.

"Yeah, well, that's the million dollar question," he said. "We'll deal with it if it happens."

"So how is the exchange supposed to take place?" Sandy said. "Connors can't just leave the game and it's not like Singer can just walk out on the field. How does he get to him?"

"He needs help," Thomas said. "My guess is Mr. Sanchez."

"Oh, wow," Sandy said; then after a pause. "This could get ugly. Singer is going to try and kill everyone tonight, isn't he?"

"I believe so, yes," Thomas said.

There was a brief lull before Sandy looked at the two men. Her expression was one of sheer determination.

"Then we need to stop him."

I had made it back to the Four Seasons around twelve-thirty and headed straight to my room. My first chore was done and now I had to get my mind around Game 7 and my real job. That's what AJ wanted, that's what Thomas wanted, and most of all, that's what I wanted. Do my job and get Suze back. I spent the rest of the long afternoon waiting to hear from Thomas, but as of five, I still hadn't. My only contact with anyone came as I ran into Mark on the way to the lobby to wait for the shuttle to the field.

"Director Harris just called," he said. "He told me to do whatever I could to make sure you were ready to do your job tonight. He said you would know what that means. *Do you?*"

I nodded, but Mark continued before I could say anything.

"The only thing I can do is tell you Gabi will be close by and ready to help."

"Thanks," I said.

"No, Marshall, thank you," he said. "You don't need to be doing any of this."

"Yes. I do."

I was glad to be getting out of the hotel, especially because of the extra baggage I was carrying, baggage I wanted to get rid of as soon as possible. I knew whatever was going to happen was going to happen at the game, but I also knew that if AJ wanted the money he was going to have to go through me and Thomas to get it.

Neither of us had any intentions of letting that happen.

Chapter 75

Citizens Bank Park, Philadelphia
Game 7 of the World Series

I read the note again. It didn't help.

GIVE ME THE MONEY OR SHE DIES

I had come to the ballpark fully prepared for *something*, but this was more than anything I could have imagined and the last of my courage drained away faster than free beer on college night. I looked up and I think my mouth might have moved, but no words came out. What could I say? I'd been wrong about Nik's involvement—shit, *about everything*.

OK Marshall, I thought, now what the hell are you going to do?

Nik *wasn't* a victim. He was working *with* AJ. It was a little too much to comprehend and I think my head started shaking. After he took the last of the warm-up pitches and made a throw down to second base, he stood and pulled off his catcher's mask and glanced at me. There was a lot of anger on his face, but almost as much strain. I'm sure he saw the same thing in me after I moved into position behind him to start the bottom of the first.

"Not what you expected, huh?" he said, the edge still firmly in place. "Maybe next time you'll mind your own fucking business."

Before I could respond he jogged out to the mound to chat with his pitcher. I don't think I could have said anything anyway. On top of the confusion of the note, the crowd noise was overwhelming. I tried to find some composure as I looked around. The see of red and white was pulsating. I suppose I couldn't blame anyone for that. These people were starving for a championship, and despite the past failures, including blowing a 3-0 series lead, they were beyond hopeful. It was as if they were screaming for someone to remove the veil from in front of their eyes so they could see clearly again.

I knew exactly how they felt.

Brad Shipley was a production assistant for the TV broadcast, his assignment: monitor audio from the home plate umpire's microphone and if something of interest comes up, queue it for broadcast. It wasn't a glamorous role, but Brad did it with gusto in hopes of getting noticed for something better in the future.

He'd been thinking about that when he heard Nik's comment to Marshall. "Not what you expected" and "mind your fucking business"—what the hell could that mean? Confused, he turned to another PA working next to him, a man named Nate.

"Yo, Nate," Brad said. "Listen to this and tell me what you think."

Nate was busy working on other aspects of the broadcast and shook his head.

"Dude, I got my own shit here," he said. "Can it wait?"

Brad pursed and rolled his lips for a few seconds.

"Yeah, yeah, I guess," he said. "It's probably nothin' anyway."

When the TV producer near the dugout signaled we were ready, I took a deep breath and gave the go-ahead to the Rays pitcher. He kicked and delivered. I heard the ball hit Nik's mitt, but I honestly didn't see it get there. I called a strike and the Phillies lead-off batter looked at me sideways, confirming I'd totally missed the call.

"C'mon now, Blue," he said in a low voice after stepping out of the box and kicking at some dirt. "It's a little early for that shit. You gotta be better than that."

He was right. I had to be, but it wasn't going to be easy.

Despite wearing my heavy umpire's sport coat, I was shivering. The temperature at game time had been forty-eight degrees and dropping, but that wasn't the reason. I nodded at the batter and called time-out before pulling off my mask. Pull it together Marshall, I told myself, as I took a couple of seconds to fake clearing something from my eye.

It wasn't going to be the last thing I would need to fake on this night.

Hudson returned to Suze's room. He was wearing an overcoat.

"It's time to go," he said. "You'll want this, it's quite cool this evening."

He was holding a dark colored peacoat and she reluctantly pulled it on. It fit perfectly, but only added to her confusion.

"I don't understand any of this," she said. "What's going on? Where are you taking me?"

Hudson smiled.

"To somewhere safe, but we must hurry," he said. "We have a promise to keep."

Suze hesitated as her face filled with more worry.

"What kind of promise?" she said.

"To deliver you unharmed."

Thomas, Damien, and Sandy arrived at the ballpark during the top of the second inning. Alex and a large team of agents were already there, waiting.

"You're sure about this?" Alex said when Thomas met him in the parking lot.

"I am," Thomas said. "Dukabi did his part and Ms. Keebler is on her way."

"Is she safe?" Alex said.

"She is," Thomas said. "I've been assured Hudson will stay with her the entire time."

Alex's knowledge of Hudson was limited, but he trusted Thomas's assessment. It wasn't as though he had a lot of choices. As much as AJ was controlling things, Dukabi was as well. He took a deep breath and blew it out in a loud hiss. The noise got lost under a louder din, that coming from the 46,000 people inside the stadium, in seats or standing. They were something Alex could not control and represented 46,000 chances for something to go seriously bad.

Alex did not like when things went badly, it tended to put him in a lousy mood.

"OK, so tell me again how this is going to work."

I managed to get through the bottom of the first, the Phillies did not score. I was very happy when Nik got out of my personal space. Being in such close proximity to him had been difficult. I hadn't said anything about the note. I was still working on that. My focus coming in had been on following Thomas' plan, but Nik's involvement changed everything. Thomas told me to expect some kind of contact, but I had no idea it was going to be Nik. As I stood there, I began to wonder if Thomas had expected it. It wouldn't shock me if he had.

Of course, he wasn't around at the moment to ask. I was on my own.

Taking deep breaths to recompose, I took my usual between-innings station along the foul line, this time on the third-base side, and stared out at the field as the Phillies warmed up for the second inning. Most of the movements went unnoticed as I searched for a solution. Come on, Marshall, think, I told myself, what's done is done. Just concentrate on what's next.

The only problem was I had no idea what that was.

The staffer at Will Call had no idea the ticket and small envelope left by Nik Sanchez was for AJ. It was marked "Peter Arcadia" and the young lady simply handed it to him when he presented his fake ID. Among the contents of the envelope was an all-access pass allowing AJ entry through the press entrance, a spot not being monitored by the FBI.

Once inside, he moved quickly to the first level concourse behind home plate and joined the sea of red there. His rudimentary disguise of the red hooded sweatshirt and Phillies cap was more than enough to prevent detection. He was able to move freely through the crowd as he made his way to a spot near the fan entrance gate off of Pattison Avenue, near the McFadden's restaurant.

Out on the field, the Phillies were finishing their warm-ups when AJ's phone vibrated. He quickly navigated to the message screen: *Connors knows*. He smiled and slipped the phone back into his pocket. One down, one to go, he thought, as he turned to wait for what was coming next. A check of his watch told him it was nine-twelve. An earlier text had confirmed that Suze would arrive at exactly nine-thirty. AJ was again impressed by Dukabi's thoroughness.

He still had no intention of giving him any money, but at least the man had kept his word.

That's good business, AJ thought as he waited. I can respect that.

Suze was next to Hudson in the back seat of a car. She had no idea who was driving, but didn't much care. She had not said a word about anything since leaving the room, but when Citizens Bank Park came into view, a small sense of relief, or maybe hope, poked through and she turned to look at him.

"Is this... Are we going to the game?" she said.

As the car turned left onto Pattison Avenue, Hudson handed her a cell phone.

"Dial five," he said. "All will be explained."

He flashed the reassuring smile again. Whoever or whatever this man was, Suze was becoming more and more thankful for his presence. She nodded and took the phone. Seconds after touching the digit, a deep voice came into her ear, one she thought she'd heard before.

"Young lady, I sincerely apologize for the treatment you received earlier. It was most unfortunate and I can assure you will be dealt with accordingly. In the meantime, the gentleman next to you is named Hudson. He will see to your safety inside the stadium, but you must stay with him and do exactly as he says."

The line went dead and Hudson gently pulled the phone from Suze's hand. She looked up, the confusion back on her face.

"Why are you helping me?" she said. "What happened to the man who took me?"

Hudson's smile remained firm.

"That is not your concern," he said.

"But—"

"We must go," Hudson said, cutting her off. "Fear not. There are others inside as well. You will be safe."

Chapter 76

Philadelphia

The game remained scoreless into the last of the third inning. It was looking a lot like Game 1, in that Terry was in complete control. I'm not sure where he was getting the strength, not after what had happened to his mother, but it was impressive. Me, well, "impressive" was not a word I would have used. In fact, I was barely hanging on.

"What happens now?" I said to Nik after he finished taking the last warm-up pitch.

He kept his face forward as he squatted for the start of the inning. I moved behind his left shoulder and waited for a reply as he pushed some dirt around with his hand.

"You tell me where to find the money," he said. "I tell you where to find the girl."

"Just like that, huh?"

"Pretty much," he said. "It ain't rocket science."

His last words reminded me of Buck and Mark. At least when they'd said it, I believed it, but now, not so much. If Nik was telling the truth then AJ and Suze *were in* the ballpark. But how was I supposed to make the exchange without screwing up the game? I got lost trying to figure that out and again allowed the first pitch of the inning to happen on the fringes of my focus. Thankfully, the batter swung at it and I didn't have to miss another call.

What I did miss was something that would have been very helpful to remember.

People were watching me, *and listening.*

"What the heck," Brad said in a mumble after the latest exchange between Marshall and Nik. "What money? What girl? What are these guys talking about?"

"Did you say something?" Nate said.

Brad looked at him, but couldn't focus past the confusion.

"Huh?" he said.

Nate's brow knitted up a little.

"You were mumbling about money," he said. "What's going on?"

Brad looked back at his monitors and watched the next pitch. It was a foul ball. Marshall slammed a new one into Nik's mitt a little too forcefully. Brad looked away for a second to process something in his head.

"What's that guy's name, the MLB security guy?" he said.

It was Nate's turn to show some confusion.

"Why, what's up?" he said. "You got something?"

"I don't know. I'm not sure."

Nate handed him a slip of paper as a director's voice hit their ears.

"Bradley, you got anything good for me?" the director said.

Brad's eyes went to Nate as his head began to shake.

"Um, no, not really," he said. "This guy doesn't say too much."

"How about you, Nate, you got anything for me?"

Brad took a deep breath. With the director moving on, he figured he was safe in the lie for now. He turned back to the screen. Nik and Marshall were no longer talking to each other, but a disturbing thought hit Brad as he watched a few more pitches. Were these guys working together to throw the game? Was *that* it or was there something else going on? Or were they simply just playing some kind of joke on each other? They both seemed a little too pissed for that. The more Brad thought, the more he began to worry.

He looked down and found Gabi's name and number, then turned to Nate.

"Hey, cover me for a second. I gotta go make a call."

The car stopped in front of McFadden's, located at the southeast corner of the ballpark. There was a big crowd inside the bar and outside in its courtyard. Hundreds more were roaming the sidewalk in front of the stadium. Suze looked out and began to wonder which might be the "others" that Hudson had mentioned.

"It's time to go," he said, stepping out of his side of the car.

Within seconds, the door next to Suze opened and he guided her to the sidewalk. The car drove away as they quickly made their way through the crowd, ending up at a turnstile at the far right side of the entrance gate. A large guard was waiting there. Suze couldn't read the name printed on the ID placard hanging around his neck, but she was sure there was something familiar about his face.

"Everything is ready," the guard said to Hudson. "We'll be within a few feet at all times."

Hudson nodded and the guard scanned something across the top of the turnstile. A green *OK* appeared on a small LED readout. The guard motioned with his head for Suze to move forward. She hesitated and looked back at Hudson.

"It's OK," he said into her ear. "He is with us."

She turned back to the guard. Again he motioned and she moved through the gate. He bumped her slightly as she reached the other side, but she didn't notice. She was focused entirely on walking, something that had become increasingly difficult since leaving the car, and something that would have been even more so had she noticed the face watching from twenty feet away on her right.

AJ focused past Suze to Hudson. Dukabi had explained the man's presence as security for his share of the money, but AJ had a doubt that's all there was to it. The episode back in Dukabi's office came to mind. The little man definitely knew how to handle a gun. And now, again, there was something in his movements AJ didn't quite like, but he tucked it away for later and moved off toward the rendezvous point.

At the same time, Clarence Riggs was moving away from the turnstile to get in behind Suze and Hudson. On either side of him, Damien and Sandy came out of the crowd and took up positions ten feet or so ahead, their proximity forming a protective triangle. If anyone made a move toward Suze, they'd be able to easily intercept.

At least that was the plan.

Four minutes later, Hudson guided Suze forward to a spot along the railing behind the section of seats directly behind home plate.

"We'll be safe here," he said to her when they stopped moving.

A small nod came in response from Suze. Behind them, Damien lifted his collar slightly and spoke into a small radio transmitter embedded there.

"We're in position," he said. "All teams stay alert. I want check-ins every two minutes."

Aided by his disguise, AJ had avoided the watchful eyes and worked unseen into a spot behind the section immediately to Hudson's and Suze's right, next to the aisle. To get the desired position, he'd had to not-so-subtly displace two over-beered men in the process. They'd stomped off with a few grumbles, but little other resistance.

Clear of interference, AJ glanced to his left. Hudson was directly behind Suze, protecting her against the railing with his body and an arm on either side. AJ looked back to the field to find a scoreboard. The plan was for him to make contact during the middle innings, something that was just now beginning. He decided not to rush it, his concerns about Hudson the inspiration. The plan required him to remain with Suze until AJ made contact, unless something changed.

After another minute, AJ decided to make something change.

As promised by Mark, Gabi was in the first seat to the left of the Phillies dugout. I thought about telling him about the note, but I couldn't take the chance. If Nik or someone else saw me doing that, it could end up hurting Suze. No, I would need another idea and one came after the Rays batted in the top of the fourth inning.

After moving to my position along the foul line, I took a second to adjust the straps on the back of my chest protector, under the sport coat. During the effort my hand knocked loose the small box attached to my belt, the wireless transmitter for the microphone I was wearing. As I reaffixed it, I suddenly remembered what I'd forgotten in my state of confusion.

As innocently as possibly, I looked down and whispered into the mike.

"Hey, if anyone's listening in the truck, I need some help. Tell Gabi Loeb—"

I stopped when I realized no one was going to be able to answer me. The mike wasn't a two-way devise. Gabi wouldn't be able to talk to me, not without seriously screwing up the game, or again, jeopardizing Suze's safety. Nice going shithead, I thought, as I dejectedly pulled on my mask again and walked back to home plate.

Nik was eyeing me closely as I moved in behind him.

"All right, enough fuckin' around," he said. "Where's the goddamned money?"

I took a deep breath and let it out. With my mask on, it sounded Darth Vader-ish.

"How do I know Suze's safe?" I said.

"You don't."

Two on, two out for the Phillies here in the fourth… They've had a lot of big two-out hits in the playoffs so far and could really use one right now… Here's the pitch. Line drive, fair ball, rolling down into the right field corner, two runs are gonna score…

Despite the outburst of offense, the bottom of the fourth came and went in a blur. The crowd reaction to the Phillies breaking the scoreless tie barely registered. All I could hear were Nik's words about Suze and I found myself doubting everything. Why had I agreed to work the game? Why had I agreed to Thomas' plans? Why had I gotten involved with Suze at all? I should have stayed in the shadows, kept to myself, and just done my job. I wasn't cut out for this hero shit.

Nik reminded me of that as the inning ended.

"Next inning, Connors," he said as he was walking away. "Or say goodbye to the bitch."

I stared at him for a few seconds before heading over to the first-base line. A tug on my sleeve seconds later shook me out of the funk. I looked down to see the Phillies batboy.

"Hey, Austin," I said. "What's up, kid?"

"These are for you," he said as he handed me a couple of new baseballs.

I didn't catch that he'd also left a note in my hand until he'd jogged away. As casually as I could, I deposited the balls into my pockets and moved others around until only the note remained in my fingers. I then took a few steps to my right and began playing with the straps on my mask to hide that I was unfolding the small slip of paper. I wasn't sure if any cameras were on me, but I didn't want to be too obvious.

That got harder as I read the note.

> We heard you. I'm the only one listening now. Director
> Harris is with me. Says you should do whatever you and
> Thomas planned. Said you'd understand—Gabi

As I started back toward the plate I glanced into the seats. Gabi was gone. Wow, whataya know, I thought. My plan worked, go figure.

Score one for me.

In the audio control room, Gabi looked up at Alex after seeing the batboy deliver the note.

"OK, there it is, he knows," he said. "What's next?"

Alex looked at one of the monitors. It was a crowd shot and the reminder of the 46,000 people gave him a slight shiver. He began to wonder again if this was the right move. Get a grip, he told himself as he shook away the thought, it's not like you've never done this before.

"Now we wait for the fun to start."

Gabi's eyes went wider.

"It sounds like it already has."

~*~*~*~*~*~*~

"Roger that," Damien said into his transmitter after getting word from Alex of the events taking place out on the field. "All teams check in again, please."

As they did, a frown filled Damien's face. The news about Nik's involvement wasn't good.

"Roger," Damien said again after the reports hit his ears. "Stay sharp. We may have some deviations to deal with."

To his right, the first one was about to take place when the two drunks reappeared. Damien had no way of knowing that AJ had hoped they would.

"Yo, mo'fuck, that's our spot," one of the men said in a slur. "You need to move."

AJ ignored him at first. That inspired the second lush to reach out and tap a plastic beer bottle against AJ's head. When he spoke, his speech was less impaired than his friend's.

"Are you deaf?" he said. "My buddy said move, fuckhead. *That means you.*"

Others nearby overheard, and sensing the building confrontation, instinctively stepped back, creating some open space in the process. Sandy was first to notice the movements, but was having a hard time seeing over the people around her.

"Uh, hey, Clarence, can you see what's going on over here?" she said into her transmitter. "It looks like we got a little disturbance brewing."

Damien heard, but kept his focus on Suze.

"You guys OK?" he said.

Before either could reply, the first drunk moved at AJ. An instant later he was falling sideways into his friend and both were tumbling backwards into others nearby. Clarence was still trying to get into the fray and began shouting. AJ turned toward the voice and immediately recognized the face from the entrance. As the chaos around him intensified, he scanned the crowd for any other out-of-place faces. He spotted Damien's, staring forward toward Hudson and Suze.

"*Son-of-a-bitch,*" he said under his breath as he started to move.

"What's our status?" Alex said into his agents' ears at about the same time.

"We got a minor fan disturbance going on, but otherwise nothing from Singer," Damien said.

That changed seconds later.

Nik came to the plate in the top of the fifth inning with two outs and a runner on second base. The Rays were trying to cut into the 2-0 Phillies lead. It was a big spot, but on a two-two pitch that every replay would forever show to be about an inch outside, I rang him up with a vengeance. I'm not going to say I missed the call—it wasn't like it was an Eric Gregg-crazy-wide-strike zone situation from the 1997 League Championship Series—but it might have been more of a corner than I'd been giving up to that point in the game. Either way, it got Nik's attention and he stared at me for a long moment before finally heading back to the dugout.

I stepped away from the plate and whispered into my mike.

"Uh, yeah, fellas, that last pitch will probably get some things moving. You might want to be ready for something to happen."

A minute later, Nik came back from the dugout. His face was set in stone and he ignored me as he took his spot behind the plate for the warm-up pitches. After he finished, I moved behind him before the first batter arrived.

"Guess maybe that last pitch was iffy, huh?" I said.

"Fuck you, Connors," he said without looking at me. "Just tell me where the goddamned money is… *now.*"

I had a little bit of extra courage knowing the good guys were watching me and ran with it.

"Nope," I said. "I told you, you get nothing until I know Suze is OK."

He stood suddenly and turned on me, what some call "getting in my grill"—as in his face mask was actually touching mine.

"Are you fucking insane?" he said, his tone bordering on maniacal. "Do you even have the slightest clue as to what is going on here?"

It would have been easy for someone nearby to think the words applied to the game, but that didn't exactly help me. In fact, it made it worse. He'd hit upon what we umpires liked to call a magic word—the f-bombs—and done so in a way that made it personal. On any other day, such would be an instant ejection. This wasn't any other day. If I tossed him, I'd have no idea where he was, meaning Suze would be in even greater danger. I'd also have no way to complete the exchange, meaning Suze would be in even greater danger.

It quickly became clear to me I'd just walked myself into a seriously bad corner.

"Maybe not," I said backing off.

He backed off a step as well.

"Then just do it already, before we *both* run out of time."

Suze felt a change in the pressure being applied to her body by Hudson. At first, she thought maybe he'd been pushed by someone in the tussle, but when his eyes went wide and his mouth fell open, she realized something was horribly wrong. He tried to say something before falling away from her without a sound. As he did, it started a new shoving match. Suze wanted to scream, but the fear left her paralyzed.

"Goddamn it, what the hell is going on?" Damien said in a shout into his radio as people began to move back into him. "Sandy, can you see anything?"

"I got nothing," she said in reply. "I'm getting run over here."

"Shit," Damien said as he tried to push forward.

At his right, a few more security guards had joined Clarence in settling the first problem, but the new one was escalating rapidly. The growing roar was magnified in Damien's ear by the listening device Clarence had dropped into Suze's coat pocket at the entrance. As he tried to decipher the sounds, he heard a scream. Whether or not it was Suze, he couldn't tell.

"Can anyone see the target? Do we have a visual on Keebler?" he said into his radio.

"Negative," he heard someone say in reply.

Suze was being pushed back against the railing. Hudson's body was in front of her, being stepped on as others tried to move out of the way. There was a small stream of blood flowing from his mouth and nose. Again she wanted to scream, but the air was stolen from her lungs when a familiar face appeared in front of her.

"*Move,*" AJ said over the din.

He grabbed her arm and pushed her to his left. Damien got to the spot seconds later, but found only Hudson's fallen form on the ground in a growing pool of blood.

"Code Red," he said into his mike. "Hudson is down. Keebler is gone."

In his ear, he heard Sandy calling for Clarence's help as he turned in search of Suze. After a second or two, he stepped up on the railing for a better view, training his eyes on the area to his right, away from his earlier position. There was a lot of scattered movement, but he finally spotted Suze several hundred feet away, moving quickly toward an exit.

He jumped down from the railing and started the chase.

"Sandy, if you can hear me, I'm going after Keebler. Singer has her and they're moving west along the third-base concourse," he said. "All units move to the exit. *We can't let them leave.*"

Chapter 77

Philadelphia

I'm not sure if it was Nik's eyes or his words or just my imagination, but something hit me as we stared at each other.

"What do you mean, 'both of us'," I said.

"No, no more questions, Connors," he said. "Tell the ballboy you need something from your bag. Tell him to get the attendant to bring it down to the dugout. I'll handle the rest."

OK, so that was his plan, but it only made things worse. Why did he care so much about the money? He made millions playing baseball and I seriously doubted AJ was going to be sharing, at least not enough for Nik to have gotten this far down in the muck. No, whatever was going on was about something more than money.

"Why are you involved in this?" I said. "What does AJ have on you?"

His expression changed again and his shoulders slumped.

"Goddamn it, Marshall, please, just do it."

~*~*~*~*~*~*~*~

Thomas moved fast along the corridor under the stands toward the umpires' room. Alex was waiting there and an attendant had already opened the door. Seconds later, Thomas was back in the hall with a black duffle bag hanging from his shoulder.

"You're sure?" Alex said.

"Yes."

Alex watched along with the confused doorman as Thomas ran off. When he was out of sight, Alex turned to the guard.

"You don't want to know," he said.

AJ pushed Suze out the gate. The implications of leaving the confines of the stadium hit her like a brick wall and her legs stopped working. AJ pulled her close and squeezed her arm hard. The rage in his eyes was more than anything she had ever seen and she screamed in response. Damien heard it through his earpiece and stopped to get a fix on their location, hoping either would say something else to give it away.

"I have killed women a lot stronger than you for a lot less, so don't fuck with me," he said. *"Now move."*

Damien started running again.

"Northwest entrance, all units converge."

The gate was a couple hundred feet to his left. He put his head down and ran with everything he had. Seconds later he was outside the stadium, but there was no sign of AJ or Suze.

"Goddamn it," he said aloud.

It was another two minutes before the rest of the agents reached him. By then, Damien knew the search was going to be extremely difficult. On the left and right were parking lots filled with thousands of cars.

"We need to put a body on every hole out of this place," he said. "Get stadium security and Philly Police, as many as we can. Singer's got a three-minute head start so move fast."

Thomas had made it to the hospitality area, a converted parking lot bordered by Darien and 10th Streets and Phillies Drive, within a minute of leaving the ballpark. The lot was surrounded on three sides by a decorative black aluminum fence and an eight-foot-high brick wall along the fourth, the side facing Phillies Drive. Inside the perimeter were three large party tents and several smaller ones for food preparation.

Thomas made his way inside and listened to Damien's updates from a position in the darkness between two of the larger tents. He would not share his location with the agent unless absolutely necessary. In his head, that meant not at all. Ending this, ending Singer, was *his* responsibility now.

If Dukabi had done his part, Singer would arrive momentarily and it *would* end.

The addition of two more pedestrians along Phillies Drive raised no red flags, despite the awkward gait of both. Suze was moving like the living dead and AJ's head was on a swivel as he watched for any pursuit. After a complete lap around the outside of the tent city to ensure there was none, he stopped within twenty feet of the entrance and pushed Suze against the fence there before putting his face next to hers.

"Don't. Move," he said in a harsh whisper.

He reached into the pocket of his sweatshirt and pulled out two passes to the hospitality area, courtesy of Nik. He put one around Suze's neck and dropped the second over his head as he wrenched her away from the fence. Seconds later they went past the check-in table with no questions asked.

Sandy finally gave up trying to resuscitate the drunk who'd confronted AJ. There was nothing she could do. He'd been stabbed, just below the rib cage along the right side, and had lost a lot of blood. She cursed under her breath as she stood to wait for Damien's latest instructions, but another sound hit her ear first.

She snapped her head around toward Clarence.

"Can you handle this?"

She was gone before he could reply.

I called time and moved around to dust off an already immaculate plate. Nik was still staring at me. He knew I was stalling. The batter was standing in the box with a quizzical expression, probably trying to figure out what the heck he'd walked into. I think he'd missed most of the shouts, but I couldn't tell. I wasn't too worried about that.

"I can help," I said into Nik's ear when I got back behind him. "Let me try."

He hesitated for a few seconds before squatting. I took that as a good sign. Still, he didn't say anything and the batter stepped in and the inning started. Fortunately, it was a short one, just eight pitches in all. After the last out, on a fly ball to left, Nik stood and faced me again.

"The only way you can help is to get me the money."

Two police helicopters were diverted to Damien's command and were now doing low passes above the parking lots. The rest of the agents had teamed up with Philadelphia Police and all access points were covered. If Singer was within the perimeter, Damien would get him. The only problem was he had no way to tell if that was the case. He was about to call Sandy and find out her status when he saw her come running through the stadium gate.

"What are you doing?" she said breathlessly when she reached him. "Didn't you hear?"

"Hear what?" Damien said. "How's Hudson?"

"He's dead," she said. "But that's not what I'm talking about."

"What then?"

"The music... from the bug," Sandy said through a pant. "I think they're at the tents."

Terry was in a zone more intense than for Game 1. He'd gone out to the mound for each half-inning with a singular purpose, to win, and had not deviated since the start of the game. Baseball had saved him before and he was letting it do so again, inspired by the emotions brought on by the recent events he'd endured. Until that point, nothing else had registered. He'd batted twice, but each time, had completely ignored both Marshall and Nik. Whatever was taking place between them wasn't on the periphery of his mind; it no longer existed at all.

That changed when a teammate came and sat next to him on the bench between innings.

"Yo, T, what's up with your boy and Sanchez?" he said.

Terry looked at the man, his face revealing a lack of comprehension.

"Your boy, what's up?" the other man said again as he pointed toward the diamond. "Didn't you catch all that shit last inning? He and Sanchez were really goin' at it."

Terry turned and saw Marshall standing near home plate.

"I, uh… no, man, I missed it," he said.

"Yeah, they were really heated. It sounded nasty."

As Terry eyed Marshall, everything that happened during the past week came rushing back to the front of his mind. His teammate noticed the sudden change and immediately regretted having said anything.

"Aw, dude, sorry. My bad," he said. "That shit ain't your problem."

"Actually, Frankie, it might be."

"Tell me again what you heard," Damien said a bit too harshly.

Sandy ignored the tone; she understood where it came from.

"Music," she said. "It has to be from the tents."

Both turned and looked across 10th Street. The hospitality area was several hundred feet away, but they could clearly hear music. Damien instantly realized his mistake. The area should have been one of the first things covered, but he'd completely missed it.

"Goddamn it, you're right," he said. "Come on."

When Nik returned in the bottom of sixth the strain was back in his eyes. Thomas had said I should delay as long as possible, but I wasn't sure how long was long enough. I had no idea if I'd run out of time. Here I was, Game 7 of the World Series, thousands watching from the stands, millions more on television, and the farthest thing from my mind was the game. I was seriously missing the days when I came to the field, did my job, and then went home.

It took a certain type to handle all this suspense stuff. On most days, that wasn't me, but for Suze's sake, I dug in and tried.

"Nik, if you can't give me your word on Suze's safety, there's no way I'm giving up the cash. I'd have to be an idiot."

"You're already an idiot, Connors," he said. "You have no idea what you've done. Singer is fucked in the head."

He turned and resumed his squat. A batter arrived and I pointed to the mound to give the pitcher the OK to start. It was the first of two messages I gave. The second was a little more cryptic and came when Nik moved away to back up a play.

"All right boys," I said into the mike. "Whatever you're gonna do, now might be a good time for it. I'm outta ideas here."

Hopefully, someone was still listening.

Gabi looked at Alex for guidance.

"Was that for you?" he said.

"I think so," Alex said. "I need to get down there and talk to him."

"We can't stop the game," Mark said from behind Alex's shoulder.

He'd joined Gabi and Alex after getting word of the events taking place.

"So what *can* we do?" Alex said.

"I'll go," Gabi said. "You need to be here to monitor things. I'll go to the dugout and talk to Connors between innings."

Alex considered the suggestion for a second.

"OK," he said. "Here's what you need to tell him."

Chapter 78

Philadelphia

Base hit up the middle, that'll plate the fourth Phillies run and it's now four to nothing... give Jackson another RBI, his fifth of the Series and third tonight...

Terry was already in control, but the extra runs in the bottom of the sixth seemed to give him even more strength. He breezed through the top of the seventh, retiring the Rays in order and striking out two, numbers nine and ten for the game. As I took my place along the first-base foul line after the third out, I noticed him walking straight toward me, moving slower than normal.

"Everything OK?" he said as he reached me.

I hesitated. Had he noticed my chats with Nik?

"It's all good," I said. "Just like your pitching."

"Nope," he said. "I saw what happened and I know you."

He held my gaze. He did know me, more than almost anyone else.

"This shit ain't over, is it?" he said.

"Doesn't matter, it's not your problem. Your mom is safe. You just pitch."

He considered me for a few seconds before walking to the dugout. I followed him with my eyes, wondering what he thought he could do. I didn't get that answer, but what I did find was Gabi's face looking out at me.

Talk about the shit not being over.

After killing time in the first party tent, AJ pushed Suze toward the last tent in the row. Right on time, Thomas thought, as he watched their approach. Dukabi was off the hook, at least for now, but Thomas didn't dwell. As he prepared to step from the shadows, the sight of Damien and Sandy running up 10th Street made him stop. Damn it, Thomas thought, as he watched both agents stop when they spotted AJ and Suze inside the fence.

A split-second later, weapons were drawn.

"Hold it right there, Singer," Damien said in a shout. "You're under arrest."

AJ pulled Suze closer, using her as a shield, as a smile filled his face.

"I don't think so," he said in a calm voice.

Before either agent could react, AJ turned and pulled Suze toward the space between the tents. She screamed again and all heads turned toward the sound. The added sight of the guns was like Raid on a beehive and bodies took off in every direction all at once.

"Call for back-up," Damien said to Sandy as he pushed through the swarm. "Cover this side. I'll flush him out."

Sandy glanced at him then back to the tents, and her brain got stuck for a second as AJ and Suze got propelled backwards out of the darkness. As they went sprawling, Sandy saw that Thomas was entangled with them. Suze took the brunt of the collision and her head smacked hard on the pavement. When AJ hit the ground, Thomas was unable to hang on. He sprang to his feet and took off again.

"He went between the tents," Sandy said in a shout as Damien reached Thomas. "Go, I'll come get the girl."

Damien helped Thomas to his feet and both quickly disappeared between the tents. Sandy ran as fast as she could and reached Suze seconds later. She knelt and found a spot of blood behind the woman's head, but also found a pulse.

"Suze, can you hear me?" she said. "Hang tight. Help is on the way."

She stood and barked into her radio.

"All units converge on the hospitality tents. And send an ambulance to the 10th Street gate."

Within seconds the first agents reached her.

"Stay with her," she said. "And don't let anyone get past."

She turned and ran into the darkness.

I started toward Gabi, but he held up a hand as the batboy popped out of the dugout. The kid handed me two new baseballs and another note. I didn't even bother trying to hide this one and read quickly. A second later I nodded at Gabi. Sure, I'll meet you after the inning, no problem, I thought. All I have to do is deal with Nik again first.

No big deal.

The blow from Thomas broke two of AJ's ribs, but adrenaline prevented any pain from reaching his brain. His leg was also hurting, having taken most of Thomas' weight in the fall, but he limped through it. As he came out of the dark aisle on the far side, he found no security personnel. All had gone to the front of the tents after Suze's scream. After a quick calculation he started running again, heading for the northeast corner of the lot behind the row of food tents.

Damien and Thomas emerged into the aisle seconds later. Seeing nothing, they split up. Damien went left and Thomas right. Damien's path took him around the food tents where he spotted AJ less than fifteen feet from a low gate in the far corner of the lot. Thomas came around the front of the first food tent, but AJ was several hundred feet away.

He was about to pursue when the sound of footsteps on his left made him turn. He watched Sandy's approach and was impressed by her athleticism, but he didn't dwell. He made a motion with his hand for her to follow and raced around the corner. Sandy made the turn and got another twenty feet before two sounds hit her ears.

Both were muffled, but she knew exactly what they were.

She stopped and watched in horror as Damien stumbled a couple of steps before falling face first to the pavement. Sandy screamed and tried to move, but her feet wouldn't work and she watched helplessly as AJ ran up Darien Street away from the lot. Thomas was closing, but changed directions and headed back to where Damien lay. Sandy silently cursed the decision because she knew it didn't matter.

Damien was already dead.

Nik squatted without a word, but I felt the heat of his anger, or maybe it was fear. I couldn't imagine what AJ had over him to elicit such raw emotion, but I didn't want to make it worse. I was just trying to get through the inning without any more trouble, but two things happened to prevent that.

First, a pitch was thrown.

Second, I went down like a dropped sack of potatoes.

Imagine a person standing directly in front of you. Imagine said person swinging a hammer at your head and connecting. That's how I felt after the high fastball slammed into my facemask. Nik hadn't bothered trying to catch it. If ever asked, and he never was, he would say he got crossed-up (that's when the catcher calls one thing, but the pitcher throws something else), but I knew the truth. It was a message.

I didn't miss it.

When I finally opened my eyes, there was a sea of faces over me. I think the entire umpire crew was there, along with the trainers from both teams, but my vision was seriously blurred and I couldn't be sure.

"Holy shit, that was nasty," Bart said. "You OK?"

I tried to focus on his face, but my eyes hurt. Check that, my entire head hurt. It got worse when one of the trainers started talking.

It sounded a lot like Charlie Brown's teacher from the old cartoons and I put up my hand to stop him. Someone thought that meant I wanted to get up and they pulled me into a sitting position. I almost puked and quickly lowered my head back between my knees. All of that movement just made my head hurt even more.

"Whaa whaa-whaa," I heard again.

I ignored it as I pulled off my mask.

"Give me a minute, will ya?" I said.

When I looked up again, one of the trainers tried to get me to follow his finger, but I looked past him toward the mound. Nik was there with the infielders and pitcher. Despite my blurred vision, I easily made out the smile on his face. I nodded, which hurt, and he returned the gesture. Mine meant: *OK, Nik, I get it*. I'm pretty sure his meant: *Fuck you, Marshall, just give me the money*.

The trainer in front of me must have thought the nod was meant for him. He started talking again.

"Whaa whaa-whaa," was all I heard.

I ignored him and raised my arms. Someone hoisted me into a standing position. That hurt more than all the other movements combined and my stomach did another flip, but I managed not to spew. After a series of deep breaths, I found a small modicum of balance.

"OK, boys," I said. "Let's go. I've already wasted enough time."

That was true on every possible front. The trainers began protesting again, but I waved them off. They and everyone else finally gave up and left. Nik returned from the mound a few seconds later. His smile was gone. I guess he could tell he'd won, but I told him anyway.

"I'll send someone to get the bag after the inning."

Thomas recapped the events in the tent area for Alex. The loss of Damien was a serious blow to the director, but at least Suze was safe. She had a cut on the back of her head and a slight concussion, but her return had ended one part of the mess. Alex asked Thomas to go find AJ and do whatever was necessary to end that part. He was confident Thomas would handle it.

Still, that left the garbage on the field, something that smelled a lot worse after Alex saw the replay of the pitch striking Marshall's face. OK, time to end *that* shit, too, he thought, as he left the audio booth.

Two minutes later he found Gabi in the runway off the Phillies dugout and told him what had happened outside. Gabi was shocked, but more so when Alex advised him he would take care of talking to Marshall. He protested for a second, but backed off when he saw something in Alex's eyes.

"OK, you got it," Gabi said before jogging away.

"I got *something* all right," Alex said aloud to his back.

The headaches during the past week from the stress were nothing compared to the one created by the fastball. If nothing else, at least it gave me a good excuse to head into to the Phillies dugout after the inning ending. I'm sure no one thought anything of it. Most were probably wondering how I was still standing after the blow I'd taken. I knew Nik thought I was doing it to get the money bag. Either way, my head was throbbing with each step down from the field. When I saw Alex Harris in the tunnel instead of Gabi, the pain somehow increased.

"What happened?" I said. "Where's Gabi?"

His face was filled with concern and what might have been anger.

"I'm not going to ask if you're OK, because I know you're not, but this should help," he said. "Ms. Keebler is safe. She took a blow to the head. Not as bad as yours, but she'll be fine, *physically*, at least."

I could have done without the last disclaimer, but I held my tongue. She was safe. That was the important thing. If she now hated me, I'd deal with that later.

"That's—"

Alex cut me off.

"Agent Hastings is dead," he said. "Singer is still loose."

The pain in my head went up a few notches and I stumbled a little. Thankfully, the wall was there to keep me from falling.

"Go tell Sanchez it's over, whatever he's doing doesn't matter," Alex said as he put a hand on my shoulder. "If he tries to run, I have two agents in the dugout. He's not going anywhere."

I looked up, but a hundred tiny hammers were rapping against the inside of my head and I couldn't see straight. I took a few seconds to blink away the pain before focusing on Alex's face.

"Where's Thomas?" I said.

"Looking for Singer," he said. "He'll find him."

I nodded before pushing myself from the wall.

"That works for me. Thomas is good at finding things."

Thomas met Sandy at the back of an ambulance out on 10th Street, the black bag he'd taken from Marshall's locker once again over his shoulder. Suze was inside the rescue vehicle, being tended to by EMTs. Sandy was sitting on the bumper, her face a blank slate. The usual bright eyes and smile had been replaced by a stark emptiness. Thomas felt a momentary pang of regret. The unexpected arrival of her and Damien had prevented him from ending things with Singer, but he didn't want to blame a dead man and kept that to himself as he sat next to her.

"What now?" Sandy said without looking at him.

"I end this," Thomas said.

"That's what you were doing before we messed it up, right?"

Her comment caught him by surprise, but not too much. She was smart and hearing her say what he'd been thinking only added to his respect for her.

"There are ways to correct that," he said.

She turned to him. Her empty expression was severe in the exposure to the bright lights.

"Agent Hastings' death was unfortunate," Thomas said. "But Singer still has unfinished business and so do I. Another set of eyes and ears would be most helpful."

Sandy studied Thomas for a long moment and some of the life returned to her face in the process. So did something else.

"And how helpful would another gun be?"

Chapter 79

Philadelphia

Before the bottom of the eighth started I went into the dugout again, this time for some cold water. By the time I slowly made my way back to the field, Nik was at the plate taking the last of the warm-up tosses from a new pitcher. He didn't notice me as he jogged out to the mound. I took that as my chance to take my spot behind the plate. When he returned, I could see through his mask he was still angry, but I no longer cared.

"It's over," I said.

The anger deepened into something more menacing, but I held my ground.

"What the fuck do you mean it's over?" he snarled.

"Singer fucked up and we got Suze back," I said. "It's all over."

He moved to within inches of me and his mask almost touched mine again. I bet that looked great on TV. I could feel the heat of his breath.

"You're bluffing," he said. "Do I need to give you another lesson?"

I moved forward and our masks clanked against each other.

"I don't give a fuck what you do," I said. *"This shit is over."*

Two more things then happened.

First, Nik shoved me hard with both hands, sending me sprawling to the ground.

Second, Terry came from the on-deck circle and tackled Nik even harder.

That caused both benches to empty and a sea of bodies to swarm toward the plate area. Terry had Nik on the ground and was driving a forearm into the catcher's neck. He was screaming, but I couldn't hear over the roar of the crowd. I was on my ass at the back of the dirt circle, hoping not to get stepped on. The chaos lasted for a few minutes, filled with a lot of shouting and swearing, and pushing and shoving. At some point, Bart and Pike managed to pull me out of the mess as others got between Terry and Nik.

"Goddamn, Marshall," Pike said. "You sure know how to have fun. I was wrong about you."

"You are having a helluva week, my friend," Bart said. "Are you OK?"

"I have no idea, Amigo," I said.

After I got my breath back and things settled down, I had a quick confab with the rest of the crew. There was no question I had to eject Nik. You can't shove an umpire and stay around to talk about it. Terry was the bigger issue. I knew he had come to my defense, but no one else did—and I sure couldn't say anything about it. That left him as starting the brawl. As with Nik, there was no way we could let him stay in the game. The other guys agreed.

After we doled out the punishments, Nik was led down the dugout steps by several teammates. Within seconds, the two FBI agents moved in, just like Alex had promised. There was a brief objection by the other players, thankfully *not* captured on TV, but flashed badges quickly changed everyone's mind.

On the Phillies side of the field, I caught sight of Terry just before he ducked into the dugout. He was beaming and pointed and winked at me. I smiled back at him and for a brief moment we were teenagers in high school again, two best friends looking out for each other. It felt good and gave me a shot of energy to get back to the game and, even better, for the game to take center stage again. I was OK with that.

I'd had enough attention, thank you very much.

~*~*~*~*~*~*~

At the far end of Darien Street, AJ ducked into the lobby of the Holiday Inn there. The space was crowded and provided plenty of cover as he searched out the restrooms. Once inside the men's room he found an empty stall and locked himself in. He slowly lifted his shirt and saw a large bruise on the left side of his chest. Every breath was a struggle, similar to after the fight at Nik's apartment years ago, and he quickly realized one of his lungs had collapsed. It would slow him down, but not stop him.

Money or no money, O'Hara, Sanchez, and Connors were going to pay.

"Call him," Alex said to Nik.

Nik was still in his uniform. His hair was a mess and there was sweat dripping from his face, but no one offered a towel. He looked at Alex before moving his eyes around the room to take in the other faces. He held Thomas' gaze the longest before looking away with a sigh.

"You can sit there and do nothing or you can help us," Alex said. "Helping would be better because I'm not in the mood for you doing nothing."

Nik closed his eyes for several seconds. When he opened them again, it was obvious he was a beaten man.

"Michael O'Hara paid me to hurt AJ," he said.

That wasn't news to anyone.

"We already know," Alex said. "Save the confession for later. All I need now is for you to call Singer so we can end this."

Nik looked at the other faces again. He was clearly coming apart and Alex tried to guide him back to what they needed.

"*Call him,* Nik," he said. "Tell him you have the money and to meet you at the players' entrance twenty minutes after last pitch. We'll take it from there."

Nik stared at the bag resting on the table for several seconds before moving his eyes to Alex. There was no expression on the player's face until slowly, almost unnoticeably, his head began to nod and he picked up the phone.

The Phillies failed to score in the bottom of the eighth inning, but I got whacked by another foul ball, this time on the chest, but pushed through it. The Phillies needed three more outs, which meant I needed three more outs. After that, I was going to take the next few months off. That was plenty of motivation to ignore how bad I felt.

I think some of the fans were trying to ignore how they felt as a new pitcher jogged in from the bullpen. My ejection of Terry was unpopular, but in all honesty, he was done anyway. He'd thrown 122 pitches through eight innings, a ton when you consider it was on three days rest. I think he realized the same thing when he decided to save my ass.

Of course, the fact that the Phillies had one of the best closers in the league and were 86-0 when leading after eight innings didn't hurt. All-in-all, the team was in pretty good shape. Me, I was hanging in, too.

It was almost over.

Chapter 80

Philadelphia

The buzzing of his phone momentarily startled AJ, but he recovered quickly.

"Where are you?" he said.

"Clubhouse," Nik said. "I got Connors to toss me. I got the money."

"About fucking time," AJ said. "Meet me in an hour at—"

"No, fuck that," Nik said, cutting him off. "I don't want this shit around me any longer than it has to be. Come get it now, outside the players' entrance."

Thomas and Alex caught the mistake, but were helpless to fix it.

"Fine, whatever," AJ said. "I'm on the way."

He snapped the phone shut and another round of pain raked through his body as he started to move out of the stall. The pain was accentuated by the fact every law enforcement person within earshot of the ballpark was now looking for him. It was a troublesome thought, but he ignored it.

Anticipation of killing again was a strong motivator.

Some might say he was nothing more than insane. They would be wrong. His mind was askew in many ways, but to him, everything he'd done since the fight in the apartment made perfect sense. He'd had a bright future in front of him, one destined to include accolades and rewards commensurate with his talents. But all of that got ripped out of his hands by the O'Haras. Samantha had rejected him. Michael had tried to punish him. Nikolai had helped carry that out. Terry had ignored it all.

They'd driven him to kill.

And now it was their turn to die.

The noise was intense and it added to the throbbing in my head. In a way, I liked it because it gave me a shot of adrenaline, something I desperately needed. Still, I was almost fried. If the game ended up going beyond three more outs I was pretty sure I wouldn't make it. Luckily, that didn't happen.

The first batter stepped into the box. Three fastball strikes later there was one out. The second batter stepped in and his results weren't much different, slider for strike one, fastball for strike two, slider for strike three. That made two outs, one to go. Around me, it sounded like a 747 was taking off inside my head.

I took a deep breath and tried to focus as best I could.

The next Rays batter walked to the plate. The pitcher delivered a nasty slider. A swing and a miss produced strike one. The decibels increased. Another nasty slider followed and there was another swing and miss for strike two. More decibels rocked my head as the batter stepped out of the box to regroup. I wanted to reach over and strangle him.

"Get back in the fucking box," I said as loud as I could manage.

I don't think he heard me over the din, but he did return to his stance.

And then the final two things happened.

First, another slider came and one last swing and miss equaled strike three.

Second, a wave of players rushed out of the Phillies dugout and created a huge dog pile on the mound. The Phillies were the champions of baseball. Good for them, I thought, as I watched the chaos unfold for a few seconds before turning and slowly making my way off the field. My battle, like the one for the teams and their fans, was over.

I had no idea another was just beginning.

AJ came out of the bathroom and found a man wearing a Tampa Bay jersey and cap. Seconds later, AJ was wearing both pieces of apparel and the other man was propped up on a toilet in one of the stalls. He wasn't dead, but was going to have a bad headache for a few days. Anyone who noticed was either a Phillies fan or too drunk or both, and no one interceded.

"Time to end this," AJ said aloud as he headed out of the hotel.

At the players' entrance, Thomas and Sandy took flanking positions fifteen feet to either side of the door. From there, they'd be able to take AJ down as soon as he arrived, but the end of the game brought with it a swarm of people and seriously compromised the plan.

"How bad is it?" Alex said.

He was inside the foyer with Nik, ready to protect the catcher from any confrontation.

"It's bad," Sandy said. "No way to get a clear shot now."

Alex looked at Nik.

"This is no good," he said. "You'll need to get him to come in here to you."

Nik nodded, but said nothing. Outside, Thomas and Sandy understood as well. When AJ showed up they would have to close in and pin him inside the doors. The bodies running in every direction were going to make that difficult, but it was the only option.

AJ was on his way and it was now or never.

Out on Darien Street, AJ was fighting against a flow of bodies. The Rays gear wasn't helping and people were shouting in his face and slapping at him as they ran by. Each blow sent waves of pain through his body, but he pushed through it and finally made it to the area in front of the entrance. There were more bodies running every which way there and AJ knew the mass of humanity would make it hard for the cops to spot him. Inside the brightly lit space, Nik was standing just to the right of the door, a black bag in his hand. AJ smiled.

"Very good," he said aloud. "Now step out here so I can put a bullet in your fuckin' head."

He was ten feet from the entrance, directly in front of it, but had to work hard to hold his ground as another swirl of bodies passed in front of him. When Nik didn't move, a scowl filled AJ's face. He motioned for Nik to come out, but the catcher did not move. After a long few seconds, AJ's anger finally got the best of him and he raced forward and pulled open the door.

"*What the fuck are you doing?*" he said in a shout. "Give me the goddamned bag."

Nik did just that, but not in the manner expected.

A blur of black whipped around and slammed against AJ's left side. The bag exploded and the air filled with bits of paper as the gun flew from his hand. A split-second later the door opened and Thomas and Sandy rushed in. At the same time, Alex stepped around Nik and pushed the catcher back.

AJ regained his balance, but came to a stop directly in line with Thomas' gun. Sandy was kneeling a few feet to his right with her gun trained on him as well. Alex capped off the checkmate from his spot next to Nik. No one said anything for a few seconds as the scraps of paper slowly settled to the ground.

AJ looked down. His gun was resting on what was left of the bag, just to the right of his feet, but it was not the reason he began to laugh. The paper wasn't money, but rather scraps of newspaper. AJ looked up again and his eyes came to rest on Thomas'.

"What the fuck you looking at?" he growled.

"Not much," Thomas said.

Nik came around Alex and looked at his old friend.

"Enough," he said. "It's over, man. You got no chance."

AJ turned to Nik and his expression changed to something several notches worse than evil.

"It's over when you all die," he said.

With that, he moved for his gun, but the sound of three gunshots, blending into a single echoing explosion, stopped him. As the sound faded, several red spots appeared on AJ's stolen jersey. He looked down and his sick smile came back as blood began to fill his mouth. The others watched in silence as he dropped to his knees.

Slowly, he raised his eyes to Nik.

"Fuck you, Amigo," he said with his last breath.

He fell forward into the paper and it splashed up like water. Crinkles filled the air until the last of the slips returned to earth.

The sound, along with AJ's pain, was gone forever.

EPILOGUE

Thomas stepped into Dukabi's office at a few minutes past three A.M. Dukabi was waiting in one of the two armchairs in front of the mahogany desk. He motioned for Thomas to join him. He did so, setting a small black case on the floor between them in the process. Dukabi eyed it for several seconds.

"Such a steep price for the life of a friend," he said in a solemn tone.

Like Damien's death on Alex and Sandy, Hudson's weighed greatly on Dukabi.

"It is," Thomas said. "Good friends are hard to come by."

Dukabi nodded.

"Yes, very much so, but this you knew," he said. "Mr. Connors is most fortunate."

"*I'm* the fortunate one."

Dukabi nodded again as a sigh escaped his mouth. The noise filled the room for a second before fading. Both then sat in silence for a long moment before Dukabi spoke again.

"Yes, well, I believe it is time for me to retire," he said. "There is nothing left here... unless... *you* would care to join me?"

Thomas chuckled, a rare sound from him.

"I let you live," he said. "Don't push your luck."

There was a parade a few hours later, unlike any seen in the history of the city. Police estimated the crowd along Broad Street at somewhere around two million. These people had waited a long time for it and did the city proud. I didn't get to see the parade live, but caught a replay later, including a surprising pronouncement from the Phillies' normally quiet second-basemen. "World Fucking Champions!" he shouted during a ceremony at the ballpark. Despite a few complaints to the FCC—the event had aired live—I don't think anyone really cared about the man's choice of words. It was a raw and honest expression of the same emotion everyone was feeling. God knew the town needed it. It really had been too long.

I got what I needed as well, a day in the hospital. I had suffered a Grade II concussion from the fastball to the face and doctors wanted to make sure I was OK. I didn't mind because Suze came by early and stayed late to help me forget about the pain. Her beautiful smile had returned and she said she didn't blame me for anything. I knew it would take time for her to really believe that, but I was glad she was willing to try—and had we had more alone time the attempts would have started in the hospital. As it was, we did steal a couple of heavy make-out sessions.

Thomas came by during the afternoon and gave us a recap of everything that happened after the game. Nik gave the FBI more details about the women AJ had murdered. Apparently, the man had confessed to Nik after each one as some sort of sick power play. AJ told him that if he ever squawked, he would take him down, too. Nik didn't want to risk his career so he played along. With the new evidence, Thomas told me Sandy and Alex were confident all six cases would get settled, something that would at least give the families closure.

Nik's problem from the night of the fight was forgiven in exchange for his cooperation. I'm not sure if it was closure for him, but it beat going to jail. I also wondered about how Sandy felt about the closure thing. She had filled the hole that had been the fate of her sister, but a new one had opened up when she lost her boyfriend in the process. Even though her bullet had helped end AJ, I wasn't sure if it was enough to compensate for losing another loved one.

As for the baseball end of things, Terry was named MVP of the Series. I was happy for him. He called me later that day and we had a great chat. He told me Michael was pretty messed up, but was expected to recover. He'd have to go through a lot of rehab, just like Terry, but in his case, not all of it was going to be on his arm. Samantha was on her way to a recovery, too, but I'm not sure Terry would be forgiving her anytime soon either. Knowing him, however, I was sure he'd try.

The best part of the talk was that I had the feeling when I hung up that he and I might be able to get back some of our past relationship. I could deal with that. One thing I *didn't* have to wait for or worry about was me and Thomas. I tried to thank him about a hundred times for everything he'd done for me in the past two weeks, but as usual, he waived off the attempt. As far as I was concerned we were even, but I knew he would never agree and I would never win the argument so I quit trying. I was stuck with him keeping me out of trouble.

All things considered, I didn't mind.

His plan had worked. Well, mostly. Agent Hastings was killed, but the other parts all played out nicely. At some point after the post-game confrontation with AJ, he went back to the hotel and got the money from my room. Yep, that's right, it had never left there; with the FBI down the hall, Thomas knew that was the best place for it. He went to Dukabi's and paid off Michael's debt. He also made a stop to Michael's hospital room. I think that had something to do with covering Michael's casino problem, but I didn't ask.

Mark stopped by as well and told me he was going to pay Wil Clemmons a nice bonus for his troubles. Wil was recovering from AJ's attack, but Mark felt bad. He had been an innocent bystander and the bonus was the least Mark could do to make up for it. Of course, he couldn't do anything to make up for Buck, and the thought of him going through the cancer alone was a lot for me to bear. I didn't blame him for anything that happened, but I had no chance to tell him that. I would just have to hope my on-field performances would somehow compensate.

On the home-front, my dad ended up finding old-man Hand two days after they got back from Europe. He was seriously shaken, but I had no doubt he'd soon be back to his spying and nosing around the neighborhood, especially after Springfield Police made him an honorary deputy. I'm not sure how my parents felt about that, but I don't think they spent much time worrying. As expected, my mom was having a lot of trouble dealing with all the things that had happened in the house and RV.

Outside of several YouTube postings and some wild rumors, most of what really happened to AJ stayed out of the news. What was mentioned was slightly altered, especially the part about him being shot at the ballpark minutes after the end of the game. Something like that might have put a downer on the celebrations. I guessed credit for that belonged to Alex, but I was OK not thinking about it. In fact, given how my head felt, I was perfectly happy not thinking about much of anything.

For all I knew I'd end up talking myself into believing it had never happened, that it had been some kind of awful dream, which would have seriously sucked because I was looking forward to waking up next to Suze again.

Besides, you can't make this stuff up.

Visit the author online:

Website: www.allenschatz.com
Facebook: www.facebook.com/AllenSchatzWriting
Twitter: raschatz

28033608R00232

Made in the USA
Lexington, KY
03 December 2013